# ELLA'S WAR

SARAH BOURNE

Copyright © 2021 Sarah Bourne
The right of Sarah Bourne to be identified as the Author of the Work has been
asserted by her in accordance to the Copyright, Designs and Patents Act 1988.
First published in 2021 by Bloodhound Books.
Apart from any use permitted under UK copyright law, this publication may
only be reproduced, stored, or transmitted, in any form, or by any means, with
prior permission in writing of the publisher or, in the case of reprographic
production, in accordance with the terms of licences issued by the Copyright
Licensing Agency.
All characters in this publication are fictitious and any resemblance to real
persons, living or dead, is purely coincidental.
www.bloodhoundbooks.com

Print ISBN 978-1-913942-88-5

## ALSO BY SARAH BOURNE

The Train

*For my family, with love and thanks.*

# 1

The woman in the bed put her hand to her temple. Her right arm was in a cast from palm to elbow, her head swathed in bandages and there was a needle in the back of her left hand attached to tubing that snaked up to a drip stand. Weak sunlight shone through the large window, and she shielded her eyes as she turned to the man standing at her bedside.

'Elkington? What kind of a name is that?'

'A surname. Yours, actually.'

'Mine?'

'Yes. Eleanora Elkington of Bamford House, Lower Worthy, according to a letter we found in your handbag.'

She frowned and looked at the man for an explanation.

'Motor accident. You were rather knocked about, I'm afraid. You were unconscious for several days and then became quite agitated, so we've been keeping you sedated for the last week to keep you calm and allow your injuries to heal.'

'So I've been here over two weeks?'

'Yes.'

The woman, who was attempting to reconcile herself with

the name Eleanora Elkington, turned to the view out the window. Snow covered the lawn. A bird was perching on the windowsill, its feathers puffed up against the cold.

'And you are?' she asked, turning back to the stranger by her bed. She put a hand to her throat; it was dry and sore.

'I'm Dr Myers. You're in my private hospital. And your throat is probably a little uncomfortable because we only took your feeding tube out this morning. Do you have any memory of what happened?'

'None at all.'

'And you don't recognise your name or address. Do you know what year it is? Or the month?'

She looked out the window again. 'December?' she guessed.

'It's February actually. 1947.'

The woman didn't feel shocked. She didn't feel much at all, as if the blanket of snow had stretched inside and lay between her and any feelings she might be experiencing. She looked around the large, bright room with its serviceable dark wooden furniture as if she might find a clue there as to her identity. There was a painting on the wall but otherwise nothing personal, not even a bunch of flowers in a vase.

'Tell me a little bit about yourself,' said the doctor, smiling down at her.

She opened her mouth to respond, but there was nothing there. She had no idea who she was, what she did, how she lived.

'I don't remember anything – nothing at all.' Fear hit her in the chest; she felt as if she'd collapsed in on herself. Then her heart started thudding and she couldn't catch her breath. She tugged at her nightgown trying to loosen it.

'Now, now, don't be alarmed,' said Dr Myers. 'You've been unconscious for a while so it'll take a bit of time for everything to return to normal.' He squeezed her hand reassuringly.

There was a tap on the door and the squealing of rubber on polished linoleum as the door opened and a stout woman in a light-blue uniform and starched cap pushed a trolley into the room.

'Ah, Matron, our patient has awoken. Please give her some soluble aspirin in warm water to soothe her throat and see that a light lunch is ordered for her. And I'd like you to give her a small injection of Quinalbarbitone to calm her. She's a little distressed. I'll write it up.'

Dr Myers turned back to the woman. 'I'll leave you in the very capable hands of Matron for now, but I'll look in later to see how you feel. Try to rest in the meantime, you've been through quite an ordeal.'

She wanted to ask what, exactly, the ordeal was, apart from being knocked out for days on end but the doctor swept out of the room and was gone.

'Now then, my dear, how are you feeling?' Without waiting for a response, she went on, 'I just need to take your temperature.'

Matron stuck a thermometer in her mouth, put a cuff round her upper arm and took her blood pressure and felt her pulse. She wrote something on the chart at the end of the bed and then looked up.

'Well that's all fine. Now I'll go and find you something to eat and draw up that medicine.'

When Matron had gone, the woman chewed a thumbnail, swallowing the scream that rose in her throat, desperately searching her mind for something, any memory at all, however small, however insignificant, that might let her know that she hadn't completely lost her mind.

By the time Matron came back a few minutes later, the woman was forcing herself to take long, slow, deep breaths to quell the panic, but she was bunching the sheets into a tight ball.

'Now, dear, lie back and keep taking those nice deep breaths. I'm going to give you an injection and you'll feel calm.'

The woman closed her eyes and felt a prick in her upper arm.

'All done. Are you comfortable?' Again without waiting for a response, Matron plumped the pillows, smoothed out the sheets and tucked the blanket in more firmly, pinning the woman to the bed. She busied herself tidying the bedside locker, straightening the curtain at the window. When her patient's breath settled, she left.

After Matron had gone, the woman lay trying to probe into the corners of her mind for a memory of the accident, but there was none. No memory of an accident, or of anything else. It was as if she had just been born, all life ahead of her, and yet, there were years behind her. How many, she wondered?

*My name is Eleanora Elkington* she repeated to herself, and sighed. *What a mouthful.*

She felt her face, carefully touching her nose, her cheeks, her lips. There were no wrinkles, the skin was taut over a decent bone structure. She sighed and silently thanked Matron for the lovely injection. Her eyes grew heavy, and she allowed them to close.

Moments, hours, or maybe even days later, she was awoken by a nurse pulling a table across her bed and setting a tray down.

'Matron said you should eat, ma'am. So here you are – some poached fish and vegetables. Do you need some help to sit up?'

Eleanora was suddenly ravenous, struggling to get herself upright enough to attack the meal. The nurse helped her with a hand under her armpit, and stacked two more pillows behind her.

'Don't eat too quickly now, your stomach won't be used to

feeling full.'

But Eleanora was shovelling the food in in great mouthfuls, ignoring her sore throat, barely chewing before cramming the next forkful in.

The flavours and textures were heavenly and she wondered if she'd always enjoyed food, or had she, in the past, taken it for granted, eaten purely because one must, rather than savouring each mouthful. Or had she often gone hungry, eaten whatever she could find? She doubted that. Dr Myers had told her that this was a private hospital, so she must have money, or a family who could pay.

She stopped eating at that thought. Did she have a family?

'How old am I?' she asked the nurse, who reddened at the question.

'I'm sure I don't know, ma'am,' she said.

'Approximately – I promise I won't be angry if you tell me I'm old.'

The nurse swallowed. 'About thirty I should say, ma'am.'

Eleanora looked at her left hand holding the fork. A wedding ring sat loosely on her fourth finger.

'I'm married,' she said.

The nurse didn't respond.

'Has my husband been in?'

'No, ma'am. Dr Myers has allowed no visitors at all.'

'But my husband knows I'm here? He has enquired after me?'

'I'm afraid I can't answer that, ma'am. You'll have to ask Matron.'

'What's your name?'

'Rosie, ma'am. I mean, Nurse Fletcher.'

'Rosie's a pretty name. Do you mind if that's what I call you? Nurse seems so formal.'

'That's fine, ma'am – although perhaps you could call me

Nurse in front of Matron or Dr Myers.'

'Of course. Well, Rosie, thank you for lunch. Could you ask Matron to pop in when she has a moment?'

'Certainly, ma'am.' She rolled the table back into the corner and took the tray away.

Alone once more, Eleanora tried again to remember anything or anyone from her life, curling her good hand into a fist and drawing her forehead beneath its bandages into a frown of concentration. Did she have children? How awful not to remember them if she did. A tear slid down her cheek.

As the shadows of the trees lengthened on the snow, she noticed a bell pull beside the bedside cabinet. Rolling over to reach it, she felt a stabbing pain in her hip and another in her neck. She wondered what other injuries she'd suffered in the accident, and slowly lifted the blankets to look at her body in its plain white hospital gown. Her right leg was bandaged, her left bruised and swollen. She tried wiggling her toes, and was relieved when they moved. Somewhere deep inside she knew that that was a good sign and she smiled.

'How are we feeling now?' asked Matron as she bustled in.

'I have rather a headache, and my neck hurts when I move my head. Otherwise I'm fine.'

'We'll get you something for your headache, and I'll speak to Dr Myers about a neck brace.'

Eleanora put her hand to her neck, imagining it held in a rigid brace. 'Oh, really it's not too bad. I'll be fine. When can I go home?'

'Dr Myers will decide that, dear, but I'd say you'll be here a while.'

Eleanora bit the inside of her cheek. She hated having to ask all the questions that pressed on her, but she had to know.

'Do you know if I have children?'

Matron looked at her and her face softened. 'It's an awful thing, isn't it, not knowing these things? Well, I can tell you that you do not have children.'

Eleanora sighed in relief. One less thing to have to worry about.

'Has my husband been in – does he know what happened?'

The Matron paused with her hand on the blanket she'd been smoothing.

'What is it, what's the matter?'

'I think you need to have a talk with Dr Myers,' said Matron, busying herself with the pillows.

Eleanora gasped. 'Was my husband injured in the accident?'

'No, you were alone in the vehicle as I understand it.'

'Then what? Please tell me.' She tried to pull herself up but she felt so weak.

'Now, dear, don't go getting yourself in a bother. I'm sure the doctor will tell you everything you need to know when the time is right. Try not to think of it now. Get some rest, it's the best thing for you.'

Eleanora wanted to scream in frustration. And then she remembered something. 'The letter in my handbag – where is it? Who was it addressed to?'

'I'm afraid I know nothing of that. Rest now.' Matron swept out of the room and the door swung shut behind her.

She closed her eyes and tried to conjure an image, but no memory appeared of a wedding, or of a husband. She needed the letter. If only they would give it to her, she'd know a little more about herself. Eleanora worried that she would spend the rest of her life knowing nothing about her past. Could one be a complete person with no memory of what had gone before?

And had she imagined it, or had Matron blanched rather

when she asked about the letter, as if she knew more than she was letting on?

Her head throbbed.

～

'It's not at all uncommon to have a bit of memory loss after a head injury, and you received quite a bump.'

Eleanora looked at the doctor in his crisp white coat and neatly trimmed moustache and wondered at his choice of words. A bit of memory loss. She could remember nothing, not even her name and address, the name of her husband, her parents. She had no idea if she had friends, what sort of life she led. She felt panic rise again, her breath caught in her chest.

'Now, now, Mrs Elkington, no need for alarm. The memory usually sorts itself out in time. A few days and it'll be right as rain. When your legs are better we'll get you up and sitting in a chair. In a couple of months' time you'll be quite back to yourself.'

Eleanora grasped his hand and held it tight. 'So this is temporary. You've seen it before?'

'Oh yes, several times, and in all cases the memory has returned fully.'

'Oh, thank God.' Eleanora let go of his hand and relaxed back against her pillows. 'And what about my husband, have you been in touch with him?'

Dr Myers stiffened. 'All in good time, my dear. No use getting ahead of yourself.'

'I don't think it's getting ahead of myself to ask about my husband. He must be terribly worried. I'd like to see him.'

'Mrs Elkington, I understand your concern, but I'm the doctor here, and you must trust that I know what's best for my patients. You just let me do my job. Now, I need to see how those legs of yours are healing. It's quite extraordinary really, that apart from your head injury nothing was broken except your wrist. It's fortunate that you were thrown from the vehicle. I'm afraid the car was damaged beyond repair.'

Eleanora clenched her jaw. This really was too much. What was he keeping from her with all this chatter, and why? Suddenly she knew. The blood drained from her face and she felt as cold as the snow outside.

'He's dead, isn't he – that's why you won't tell me anything.'

Dr Myers tensed again. It told her all she needed to know.

'How did it happen?'

'I really don't want you upsetting yourself.'

'I have a right to know. How would you like it if you woke up remembering nothing and the person who could tell you a few details of your life wouldn't?' She was aware that her voice sounded on the edge of hysteria.

The doctor looked at her with pursed lips, as if assessing her mental competence. 'All right,' he said at last. 'I don't usually tell patients with amnesia anything about their past. I prefer that they remember in their own good time because only in that way each recovered memory can be integrated in the right order, but I'm going to break my own rule in this instance.' He took a deep breath and assumed a sad expression. 'I'm afraid I've been advised that your husband died in the war.'

'The war?' She turned her head away and looked at the picture on the wall – a cottage in a colourful garden. She'd lost a husband she couldn't remember in a war she had no memory of. She knew she should be shocked or sad, but there was that feeling again of being somehow shut off from her emotions, as if it was someone else's life they were talking about.

'Thank you,' she said.

'Are you all right? I can give you something if you need it, to help with the shock.'

'No need. I'm fine.' She looked back at the doctor. 'Do you know what happened – the accident, I mean?' She gestured at herself lying in the bed.

Dr Myers looked relieved that they weren't going to have to talk about her husband anymore. 'Only what the boy who found you told me — that you were lying about ten feet from the car which was in a ditch by the Hambleford Road. He made sure you were breathing and then cycled over to tell me. I sent an ambulance and you were brought here. That was two weeks ago.'

Eleanora thought about what he'd said, willing herself to remember the accident, or driving. Where was she going?

'And the letter?' It seemed terribly important that she have the letter. It might be the key to – to what? To the fact that she had a friend or family member she could write to, that she might ask them something about herself?

'Oh, I'm afraid I know nothing of what happened to that. You'll have to ask Matron.'

'She said she didn't know about it.'

'Well, I'll look into it. Now, let's have a look at these legs.'

Dr Myers pulled the blankets back and unwrapped the bandages. He positioned himself in such a way that Eleanora could see nothing while he touched her legs in various places, asking if she could feel anything.

'Yes, I can feel you poking and prodding.'

'That's very good, no nerve damage.'

'Am I scarred?'

'There were some deep cuts that I had to stitch, but I think you'll be happy with my handiwork. Best not to look yet, though, it'll only upset you at the moment. The wounds will heal, just remember that.' He bandaged her leg again and pulled the blankets up. 'Now, let's see what you remember. Who is the prime minister?'

Ella screwed up her eyes as she tried to think.

'No idea.'

'Not to worry.'

'Well, who is it?'

'Clement Atlee, Labour.'

Eleanora shook her head. The name meant nothing to her.

'How about your childhood? What can you recall of that?' he asked.

A picture popped into her head of a blond boy and a dark-haired girl on a beach, digging a hole in the sand.

'Being beside the sea,' she said and smiled. A memory! Or was it? It could have been any two children, but she had a vague sense that it was herself and a brother. The image vanished.

'Very good,' said Dr Myers. 'What was the weather like?'

'The sun was shining, but there were clouds closing in.'

She surprised herself. Had she really noticed that or had she remembered the day?

'Did it stay sunny?'

'No, it poured later and we had to pack up quickly and run back to the house.' She felt triumphant. It was a memory. She could almost feel the rain on her face and the clamminess of her cotton blouse sticking to her skin.

'How old were you?'

'About six, I think.'

'Very good. You see, you're remembering things already. But that's enough for now, we don't want to tire you out, do we? Rest now, that's what you need most. I'll see you in the morning.'

He was gone before she had a chance to ask him anything else. She'd have to make sure that she had a list of questions ready to ask next time she saw him.

Alone, Eleanora tried to conjure the beach scene again, but it had gone and left nothing in its place.

## 2

Two days after she had woken up in Dr Myers' hospital, Matron announced that Eleanora was to have a visitor.

'Who?' she asked, excited at the idea of talking to someone who knew her, who could tell her something of her past, but nervous at the same time about what she might learn. Would she like the person she was when eventually she remembered herself? Had she had friends who valued her, or acquaintances who merely put up with her?

'Your brother. He's been very worried about you, telephoning every day to enquire after you.'

'I don't suppose you know what his name is, do you?'

'Andrew. Andrew Whittington.'

'Like Dick,' said Eleanora.

Matron smiled at her. 'That's right.'

Eleanora thought for a moment. 'I remember having the story read to me.' She closed her eyes, the better to remember. 'A man's voice. My father, perhaps?'

'I'm sure I don't know, but I suspect so. There, another memory. It's all coming back just like Dr Myers said it would.'

There was a knock at the door.

Eleanora put her hand to her head to smooth her hair, and felt the bulk of the bandages instead. She bit her lips and pinched her cheeks to bring a little colour to her face.

Dr Myers came in followed by a tall man with his hat in one hand and a bunch of flowers in the other. His hair was receding which made his thin face too long to be handsome, but when he smiled his blue eyes twinkled behind dark-rimmed spectacles, and the overall impression was of kindness and good humour.

He put the hat and flowers down and approached the bed and held out his hands.

'Darling, it's so good to see you. You gave us quite a fright, you know.'

Eleanora took one of his hands in her good one and smiled up at him. She so desperately wanted to remember him, but there was nothing. The shocking thought occurred to her that these people may not be who they said they were at all. She removed her hand from his abruptly as her heart gave a flip. She looked from one to the other feeling scared and vulnerable. What if she was someone rich or famous, and these people were taking advantage of her weak state to dupe her? They could do anything to her. She bit the inside of her lip and tried to think clearly. She was powerless; all she could do was play along until her memory returned, and in the meantime, watch carefully and hope that her suspicions were unfounded.

'It's lovely to see you too, Andrew, thank you for coming.'

The smile faded from his face.

'You don't actually remember me, do you? Dr Myers warned me that you mightn't, but I didn't believe him.' He fumbled in his breast pocket.

'Here,' he said, and showed her a photograph. 'I thought I'd bring this in. It usually sits on your sideboard. It's us when we were young, on the beach at Torquay one summer. We used to have a cottage there and went several times a year.'

Eleanora looked at the picture and gasped. It was similar to the image she'd had when Dr Myers had asked if she had any memory of her family — a blond boy and dark-haired girl on the beach, laughing at the camera, beside a large hole in the sand.

'It's you and me. I was seven and you were five. Father had bought an Argus C3 and spent the whole holiday taking photographs of us. I think he rather fancied himself as a photographer, but most of them were blurred. This was the best. Mother refused to be in any of them. Do you remember – she said that cameras were the Devil's invention.' He laughed.

Eleanora scrutinised the picture; the boy in the photograph had similar eyes to this man, and although the young face was rounder and the child had more hair, she could, perhaps, believe that the boy in the picture had grown into the man before her.

'Do you remember what happened after the picture was taken?' she asked.

Andrew laughed. 'It started bucketing down – we got drenched as we ran back to the house. Mother ran a hot bath for us so we didn't catch a chill.'

Eleanora looked at him as he spoke. He remembered the rain, just as she had. But Dr Myers could have told him about her memory of the day. They could still be trying to fool her about who they were. And Andrew seemed pleased, almost too pleased, as if he knew he had passed the test. She looked away, not knowing what to make of it all. Tears of frustration and fear welled up, but she closed her eyes and took a deep breath and stopped them from falling.

'My dear girl, it'll be all right – you'll be all right,' said Andrew hastily. 'I'm sure you'll remember in time.'

She realised that the effort of trying to remember was going to be enormous. She felt exhausted at the very thought.

Dr Myers, who hadn't left the room, cleared his throat.

'I'm afraid that's probably enough for now, Mr Whittington. Why don't you join me for lunch and you can have another short visit this afternoon, but your sister has been through a lot and we don't want to tire her out, do we?'

'Of course not,' said Andrew. He took Eleanora's hand and squeezed it in a reassuring way before following Dr Myers out of the room.

Eleanora closed her eyes to stop the tears that threatened again. There hadn't been a glimmer of recognition when he walked in. He could have been any man off the street. How could she not know her own brother? And yet, she found herself wanting to believe he was who he said he was. She wondered if there was some deep, subconscious need to be connected to other people, to trust another person totally.

When Matron brought a vase for the flowers and some lunch, Eleanor couldn't eat. Her stomach was tying itself up in knots. She closed her eyes and tried to recall Andrew and her parents, but ended up with a headache and tightness in her jaw from clenching it so tight as she tried to pierce the thick fog that shrouded her memories.

Andrew sat with her for half an hour that afternoon.

'What did you and Dr Myers talk about?' she asked. He looked hurt, and Eleanora knew that there was distrust in her voice.

'I know this must be terribly hard for you, to wake up and not know anything. I wish I could prove to you that I am who I say I am, and that you're safe here, but I don't know how. All I can hope is that you soon remember everything and we can get back to normal. Dr Myers is certain you will remember eventually but that it's important the memories come back in their own time.' He smiled. 'The good news is he also said that you will not have forgotten how to do things, only what you've done, and that he believes that once you get home, your memory will return quite quickly. And since the doctor seems dead set against anyone telling you about yourself, I thought I'd tell you a bit about me, if you're at all interested?'

Eleanora didn't know how to respond. If this man wasn't her brother and was playing some trick on her, wouldn't he try harder to convince her of who he was? But if he was her brother, surely he must have some way of proving it to her? She shook her head in frustration. All she could do was go along with it all. 'Of course, I'd love to know all about you,' she said.

After he'd gone, Eleanora thought about the stranger who said he was her brother. She liked him. He was the sort of person she would have warmed to even if they weren't related — kind, funny, intelligent, caring. He was married to a woman he'd met in an air-raid shelter in the Blitz, which he'd had to explain was the bombing of London in 1940, a few months after the war started. They had bonded over a thermos of tea and the fact that they were reading the same book: *Appointment with Death* by Agatha Christie. He had looked at her in a curious way as he said the name of the book, and she suspected he knew that she, too, had read it at some stage, so she'd smiled. Encouraged, he'd continued his story. Andrew had been unable to join up because of his poor eyesight, but was a warden in the ARP, and had stayed in London throughout the war, fighting fires and helping the injured in the evenings after a long day working in a bank. He and Sophie, his wife, had two children, Laura, five, and Billie, three.

Eleanora lay back against her pillows. She was relieved to discover that although she could remember nothing before the accident, at least she could retain things she learned after it.

He came to see her again the following day, and handed her a bag.

'I'm staying at your house – I hope you don't mind – so thought I'd bring you your own night clothes instead of that awful hospital gown,' he said.

Eleanora looked at the yellow cotton nightdress, the hairbrush and comb, and suspected by the way he quickly put another bag into her locker that it held underwear that he was too embarrassed to hand over.

'Thank you, how thoughtful.'

'I'm afraid I can't stay long – Dr Myers is adamant that I shouldn't tire you. How are you feeling today?'

'I'm fine. Tell me just the tiniest bit about our family, would you?'

'Well, I don't suppose that can hurt.' He looked at her. 'We had a happy childhood in a house in Richmond. Our father was a barrister and worked long hours but Mother was always at home. We had a holiday home in Torquay and loved going down there.' He stopped.

'Go on, please.'

Andrew looked down at his hands. 'I'm sorry to tell you that our mother died when we were quite young. Father couldn't bear to visit the house in Torquay without her so he sold it and bought the house that is now yours. We had ponies there and it was closer to London, which meant that Father could get there more easily at weekends.'

Eleanora sighed. None of it sounded familiar.

'We were brought up by German nannies – Father was from there originally.'

Eleanora wished she could remember it. The thought of escaping the city for riding weekends must have been so appealing to a child.

'Mother was a beautiful woman. You get your looks from her.'

Eleanora laughed. The glimpse she'd had of herself in a mirror after begging Rosie Fletcher for one showed a gaunt face and dark circles under her eyes. A face she didn't recognise.

'She was so good at entertaining – there were always dinners, and theatre outings. Not for us, of course. For Father's friends mainly. She took us on picnics and invented games or set treasure hunts for us.'

Eleanora felt the tears well up at that, and Andrew apologised.

'I'm so sorry, dear girl. Dr Myers told me not to say too much, to let you remember in your own time. I won't say anything more. It's difficult to share my childhood memories without you being in them.'

'Please, don't stop. I want to know.'

But Andrew smiled and said he had to go.

After he'd gone Eleanora lay staring out the window. She was worried that having learned that her mother was dead, she wasn't feeling more grief-stricken. Was she some sort of monster who felt no emotion? Or was it more to do with the fact that it had felt like she was hearing stories about someone else's life? *Was* it her life? Was this man who seemed so kind and concerned really her brother, and how would she ever know? Yes, she'd felt teary when he told her his stories, but it was more because she could imagine a mother's love for her children than because she actually remembered the treasure hunts and games and the loss of them when her mother died. And she hadn't even thought about her late husband since she was told he'd died. Perhaps there was something wrong with her. Something more than just amnesia.

The days drifted into each other, with nothing to do but lie in bed. Eleanora felt well enough to be up and about, but until the stitches were out, Dr Myers wouldn't allow it. Rosie Fletcher and Nurse Paine worked alternate shifts but Eleanora was always glad when Rosie was on; she was more talkative and friendly than Nurse Paine, who was older, and efficient, but clearly didn't believe in chatting to the patients. Rosie, on the other hand, was always happy, and if she wasn't talking she was humming a tune.

'Do you live nearby?' Eleanora asked one afternoon.

'Yes, ma'am, just over the hill,' said Rosie, gesturing out the window towards the woods on the rise.

'Have you lived there all your life?'

'Yes, ma'am. Except for when I went to Southampton to do my training. My mother thought it was safer than going to London, but I was so unhappy there, I had to come home. It's such a big place, and so noisy. I suppose I'm a country girl through and through.' She smiled and straightened Eleanora's blanket. 'Funny, isn't it, how some people love the city, and others can't abide it? I thought it was dirty and smelly.'

'So you finished your training and came home?'

'No, but I did two years, and Dr Myers said Matron could teach me everything else I needed to know. I've been here nearly a year now, and learned ever so much.'

Eleanora thought for a moment. 'I think you're a marvellous nurse; so kind and thoughtful and efficient. I don't think I could do a job like yours, I suspect I'm not nearly patient enough, but you're made for it.'

Rosie blushed and busied herself with tidying the already neat bedside locker, and rearranging the flowers Andrew had brought.

'Well, I'd better get on,' she said, and scurried out of the room.

Eleanora was sorry she'd embarrassed the young woman,

but she'd meant what she said. And she was equally sure that she'd been right when she said she wouldn't have the patience for it. Nor the temperament. She had no idea how she knew that, but it was a notion she held with conviction. She didn't know whether she had a qualification of any sort, or if she'd even finished school.

It was so frustrating, almost too much to bear, not knowing anything about oneself. She wanted to get home, wherever that was, and see if she'd kept a diary so that she could discover who she was. 'The Sensational Life and Times of Eleanora Elkington.' She still didn't like that name, but she smiled at the thought of a scandalous journal.

'We're happy today, aren't we?' said Matron as she swept in, all starch and crispness.

'You caught me in a good moment,' said Eleanora. 'Most of the time it's so dull here I think I'll go insane. Can I have some books to read, or a wireless to listen to?'

'Dr Myers doesn't want you listening to the news in case you get upset, but I'm sure it wouldn't hurt to bring you a book or two.'

'Thank you, Matron. Do you think you could find me a copy of *Appointment with Death*? I should like to read that.'

'I'll do what I can. Now, take your tablets for me,' and she produced two white pills and a glass of water from her medicine trolley.

'What are they?'

'Something for the pain.'

'But I'm not in any pain,' said Eleanora.

'That's because Doctor prescribed the tablets. Come along now, there's a good girl.'

'I'm not a girl,' said Eleanora.

'That's as may be, but you still need to take your tablets.' She handed them over and waited while Eleanora swallowed them before bustling out again.

As soon as she'd gone, Eleanora spat the tablets into her hand and looked around for somewhere to get rid of them. There was nowhere she could reach, so she'd have to hide them in her lunch and hope no one went through the leftovers. She didn't like the thought of the doctor making her take tablets she didn't need.

On Friday Dr Myers came to take her stitches out.

'What do you know about me?' she asked. She'd decided she had no alternative but to be blunt.

The doctor raised his eyebrows.

'Come on, you must know something. I mean apart from how I got here.' She had prepared herself for denials; she was ready for a fight.

'I know very little. Your brother filled me in on a few details, of course, but there wasn't time to go into anything in depth.'

'Details like what?'

'I needed to know of any existing conditions that might complicate your treatment.'

'And were there any?'

'No. You're generally very healthy, apparently. Now, shall we take out these stitches?'

Eleanora tightened her jaw and spoke through gritted teeth. 'I have a right to know about my life. I want to remember. I want my memory back!'

The doctor smiled thinly. 'In my experience it provokes a great deal of anxiety to be flooded with memories too quickly. It's important that you remember in your own time.'

'So you've said. A number of times. But I'm sure I'll cope. Tell me.'

Dr Myers shook his head and clamped his mouth shut. Eleanora scowled at him but there was nothing she could do; he wouldn't say a word. She fell back into her pillows and fumed as he gently went to work. Once he'd finished he pronounced the outcome very fine indeed. She saw her legs properly for the first time since the accident, and begrudgingly agreed. He may be keeping secrets from her, but he was a good surgeon. The scars were still red, but there was no puckering or raised tissue which she was glad to see. And then Dr Myers told her that she could sit in the chair for a while, and the excitement of getting out of bed put everything else out of her mind.

She sat in a chair by the window, a pale-pink angora bed jacket around her shoulders and a blanket over her knees, and looked around the room. It looked different from this angle. Eleanora could see scuff marks on the linoleum and dents in the door frame from trolleys bumping into it. But it was marvellous to be up. Her neck felt fine now, although her hip still hurt. Dr Myers said she might need a walking stick for a while, but that he was sure it would improve once she started getting moving again.

'I'll leave you to it then,' he said, and promised to look in later and supervise her first walk.

Looking out the window she noted that all the snow was gone, although there was a heavy frost, and that the first crocuses were raising their bright heads. Snowdrops lined a path around a pond. Beyond the fence was a field of cows, heads bowed as if they were trying to draw them in against the cold, and in the distance, the woods. She wondered if she lived over that way, and what her house was like. Nothing came to her, no sudden visions of domesticity, so she shook her head and turned her attention to the scene outside again.

*Spring has always been my favourite time of year*, she thought, and raised her eyebrows. Where had that come from? She knew it to be true as soon as she thought it. Images of flowers and weak sunshine flashed through her mind, and she sat back to enjoy them.

She was in a good mood when, after lunch taken in the chair, Dr Myers returned with a walking stick and helped her to her feet.

'Now then, slowly does it,' he said as she took her first step, refusing his arm. As she traversed the room she gained confidence, and she reached the other side triumphantly, although she was grateful for the stick.

'That's enough now,' he said when Eleanora had circled the room two or three times. 'Take a seat again.'

Elated, Eleanora wanted to keep going, but Dr Myers insisted on rest, and as she sank into the seat, she realised that even that small amount of exercise had worn her out.

'I'll get Nurse Paine to bring you a cup of tea. Well done, though. It's a good start.' He gave her a brief smile and was gone.

The week was long and difficult. Eleanora had stopped taking the tablets she was given, preferring to stay alert even if she was in some discomfort at times. During the day she could manage, but at night she had a recurring dream of a man who was afraid, who was desperate to evade some sort of danger. The awful thing was, the danger seemed to be her. She'd wake trembling, trying to understand what it meant, but the image always faded as soon as she opened her eyes, leaving only a sense of shock and guilt. After a few nights she started taking the sleeping medication again so that she didn't have to relive the nightmare over and over.

But one good thing had happened, too, and Eleanora was looking forward to Andrew's visit at the weekend. She'd remembered something during the week about her childhood. She hadn't told Dr Myers about it, so if Andrew remembered it too, it would prove that he was who he said he was. If not – well, she'd have to think about that. A shiver went up her spine at the idea.

Andrew smiled at her when he came on Saturday afternoon; she was sitting in her chair, *Appointment with Death* open on her lap.

'How are you finding it?' he asked, nodding towards the book and coming over to give her a kiss on the cheek. She allowed him the intimacy.

'I've read it before, you know,' she said. 'I actually remember little bits of it too. Although not who did it.'

'That's marvellous, Ella. Brilliant.'

'Is that what you call me – Ella? I like that.'

'Yes, always have. As a little girl you didn't like Eleanora.'

'I don't like it now either, so I'm glad you call me Ella, I much prefer it. I shall be Ella from now on.'

Andrew smiled. 'That's the ticket. How have you been? It's good to see you up, I must say.'

'It's good to be up. And I'm allowed to go for a walk along the corridor today. I thought you might accompany me. I haven't been outside this room for what seems like years. But first, let's talk.'

Andrew pulled the bedside chair a little closer and sat down.

'So,' said Ella, 'I have been endeavouring to remember more of my childhood this week, and I have a recollection of something.'

'That's good news. What have you remembered?'

'Mother's funeral. All the flowers in the church and Father wearing a black coat.'

The smile fell from his lips. 'Oh, darling, you must have been thinking of something else. We weren't allowed to go to the funeral. Father thought it would upset us too much. We stayed at home and the neighbour, Mrs Jennings, came and sat with us.'

Ella closed her eyes and in her head she said a quick prayer of thanks. When she opened them again, she smiled at her brother.

'Thank you, Andrew. I'm sorry I didn't know it immediately, but now I know you're my brother. I had a memory of sobbing at the window as our father left for the funeral, and of you being there too, comforting me.'

'It was an awful day,' said Andrew, taking her hand. 'What a shame you remember the saddest things first.'

'But at least now I know who you are,' she said, and smiled.

Andrew pulled a silly face, with eyes wide and bottom lip sticking out. 'How can you have forgotten this face?' he asked.

Ella laughed. 'I'm sorry I had to test you.'

'Of course you did. I can't imagine what it's like not recognising anyone. But you're already getting better. We'll have you out of here in no time.' He smiled at her. 'You've always been determined, and now you're up I don't see them holding you here much longer. Dr Myers has suggested you have a companion at home with you for a while. I was thinking of asking Sheila Marchmont or Maeve Bennett. Do you remember either of them?'

Ella drew her forehead into a frown, desperate to remember Sheila or Maeve, and then broke into a smile as an image came to her.

'If either of them has a big smile and curly brown hair I'll take her,' she said, as if she was shopping for a doll rather than choosing a companion.

'Sheila to a tee,' Andrew said. 'Always smiling about something, and a mop of curls that manage to escape all attempts to tame them.'

'Do you know all my friends? Do I have many?'

'Oh, Ella, you have loads of friends who are all mad about you, and I don't think I even know all of them.'

'Why haven't any of them been in to visit? I've been dying of boredom here.'

Andrew paused and bit his lip.

'Oh, don't tell me, Dr Myers wouldn't let them. That man is impossible.'

'Sorry. Anyway, I'll get on to Sheila and see if she can come and give you a hand when you're discharged from here. It'll be nice to see her again. I had a bit of a thing for her once as a matter of fact, as well as several of the others!'

'So you're a bit of a Casanova are you, breaking girls' hearts right, left and centre?'

'I'm surprised you don't remember my reputation as a womaniser.' He laughed.

'Now you mention it...' Ella grinned up at him and caught his hand. 'I know I can't remember most of our life together, but there *is* a familiarity about you that is so comforting and I can't tell you how good it is. I feel that with your help I may be able to piece myself back together. If you can take time out from your womanising that is. By the way, what does your wife think about it, you gallivanting off with a different girl every night?'

Andrew tapped the side of his nose and winked at her, and then became serious.

'To tell the truth, Ella, although I might have admired some of your friends from afar, I never had the confidence to ask a single one of them out.'

'But whyever not, a good-looking fellow like you?'

'Bit shy, I suppose. And the glasses. Didn't think a girl would like a chap in glasses.'

'Bosh! You're a fine-looking man, and I'm not saying that just because you're my brother. Anyway, now you have Sophie, so you're all right.'

'Absolutely. I'll bring her down to see you when you're back at home. You used to get on very well.'

'I should love that, Andrew. Thank you. Now, I need you to help me up and we'll break out of this room and race up and down the corridor, shall we?'

After ten minutes Ella needed a rest. They'd met another patient in the corridor, which heartened Ella – she'd been wondering if she was the only one there, it was so quiet. The only noises she'd heard in the whole time she'd been there were a loud moaning followed by running footsteps and a door banging a few nights before, and the squealing of rubber trolley wheels on the wooden floors of the corridor.

They went back into her room and Rosie brought them both a cup of tea.

Ella looked at her hands, the wedding ring loose on her finger.

'What was my husband like?'

Andrew gulped. 'Where did that come from?' he asked.

'I don't know. Doctor Myers told me he died, but I don't remember anything about him. Did you know him?'

'Yes. Charles was a fine fellow, and adored you.'

'What happened?'

'I don't know if we should be having this conversation. Dr Myers was adamant that you should–'

'Be allowed to remember things in my own time. I know. It's so frustrating.'

'Indeed, but when you remember him, I'll be very happy to talk to you about him. Until then, I'll just say that you loved each other. Very much.'

'Argh!' said Ella. 'I'll never get my memory back if you won't tell me anything.'

'It's for the best. We must follow Doctor's orders.' He smiled at her apologetically.

She had more questions, but Andrew would say no more. At least she knew her late husband's name. Charles Elkington.

In the end, she had to come to terms with the fact that, annoying as it was, she would learn no more from him. She was disappointed, and wondered if she'd always been more daring than him, more willing to break the rules and sail into the wind. Or did she mean against the wind? Was he the logical, dependable older brother, the follower of rules, and she the scatterbrained, daredevil younger sister?

It suddenly occurred to her that the blow she'd received might have altered her personality. Maybe the person she became would have little relation to the woman she'd been.

'What was I like before?' she asked.

Andrew looked at her as if trying to read the motivation for the question in her face.

Then he smiled. 'Bold, bright, beautiful. You've always had this capacity to see the best in people. No, not only to see it, but to bring it out. Everyone who knows you says that they're a better person when they're with you.'

Ella laughed. 'You make me sound like a saint!'

'Not a saint, no. You're far too irreverent for that, but loving, kind and curious. You make people feel that they're the only one who matters when you're with them. You really attend to people, you know, tune in.'

'So now you're telling me I'm like a wireless set, tuning in.'

Andrew shook his head and rolled his eyes. 'I'll not utter another word if you're going to make fun of everything I say. You're just as maddening as ever,' he said, 'and I love you for it. I was worried that you'd be different, but you're just the same.'

Ella took a deep breath. 'I'm glad. I think!'

'Now, I must go and put in a telephone call to Sheila and see if she's able to come and stay for a while, and you must get some rest.'

'Can I ask you one more thing before you go?'

'Of course.' He took the chair by her bed again.

Ella sucked in her lips, unsure how to ask the question that had been demanding her attention.

'What is it, Ella, what's troubling you?'

She let out a sigh. 'It's just – what did Dr Myers ask when you spoke?'

Andrew raised his eyebrows and looked at her. 'He just wanted some medical information. When he first telephoned to tell me what had happened he asked your date of birth and whether you were married or lived alone, that sort of thing. Why do you ask?'

She shrugged. He would probably think she was mad if she admitted that she didn't trust the doctor. 'Just wondered.'

He looked at his watch. 'Sorry, Ella, I really must go.'

'What is my date of birth, by the way?'

'Seventh of March, 1917.'

'Careful – you just told me something about myself. Dr Myers will have you charged.'

He laughed, then gave her a hug and a kiss and was gone.

Sheila Marchmont. Ella desperately tried to remember anything more about her than a vague image of hair and a big smile, but she couldn't capture any more. And poor Andrew being so shy he couldn't summon up the courage to ask her to a dance or the pictures. Still, if he had he mightn't have met Sophie. She couldn't wait to meet her again. And this Sheila. There'd be more hints and clues as to who she was, more stories that would help her piece the mystery of Ella Elkington together.

Three days later, after so much time walking in the corridor that Ella was surprised not to see a trench being worn in the floorboards, a new visitor was announced.

'Sheila Marchmont is here to see you,' said Matron. 'I've told her not to get you worked up. She seems rather an excitable sort.'

Ella snorted. 'What do you mean by that?' she asked, intrigued.

'You'll see soon enough. She's just having a word with Dr Myers and then she'll be up.'

Ella thought about Matron's assessment of Sheila, and her assumed right to express it. In any other person, it might have been rude, but Ella had come to respect the elderly nurse and her forthrightness. She knew that if Matron thought Sheila excitable, then excitable she was. Not that that was a bad thing. Excitable often also went with spontaneous and carefree, and after being cooped up in hospital for so long, they were attributes Ella craved.

She didn't have to wait long to meet Excitable Sheila.

'Ella, oh, Ella! It's so good to see you,' she said as she hurtled into the room. 'I've passed the interview with Doc Myers, he's a bit strict, isn't he? Anyway, he's going to let me be your companion and general factotum for the next few months. We'll have such fun – it'll be just like old times.'

She was tall and full figured, her hair falling out of a bun. Ella's first impression was of a whirlwind. She thought she might get exhausted living with this woman. But she had a wide smile and a kind face, and if they'd shared together before, she would be able to fill her in on some of her life.

'Thanks for coming.' She didn't have to say anything else for the next twenty minutes until Matron came in and suggested that Ella might need a rest. She'd never been more pleased to see anyone.

Sheila had hardly taken a breath as she told Ella that she wasn't allowed to mention anything from their past until Ella herself remembered and started talking about it. So she'd told her instead that Ella was saving her from living with her elderly parents and occasionally looking after a young disabled boy to give his mother a break. She was excited about all they'd do together once Ella was well: dances, films, walks, picnics, perhaps even a holiday. Ella was tired at the thought of it all but assumed these were things she had once enjoyed. Was she adventurous or timid? What had drawn her and Sheila together – were they similar, or quite opposite in character?

'Well, Ella, I must go,' Sheila had said when Matron came in. 'I'll come in with Andrew next week to take you home. I can hardly wait. Goodbye, dearest.'

'Goodbye, and thank you,' said Ella, and got up from her chair and put herself to bed for a nap.

'You see what I mean,' said Matron, nodding her head towards the door through which Sheila had just left, eyebrows raised.

Ella just sank into the pillows and sighed.

# 4

Before he would let her go, Dr Myers examined Ella's legs and hip, checked the wounds on her temple and the side of her head, and admired the replastering he'd done the day before on her forearm. Then he asked some questions.

'On a scale of one to ten, where one is terrible, and ten is marvellous, how would you say you're feeling?'

'Ten,' said Ella, fearing she wouldn't be allowed to go home unless she made the perfect score.

'That's good, jolly good. No more pain from that hip?'

'Oh, a little niggle every now and then, but nothing to complain about.' She smiled to emphasise her tip-top condition.

'And the memory – a few days ago you told me that you remembered a little more of your childhood, which is good. I don't want you to worry too much about remembering too quickly. You'll find that once you get home there will be a lot of reminders, and it's important that you take it easy and don't get overloaded. Try to get a good rest every day, and if anything upsets you, telephone me, or talk to Miss Marchmont about it.'

'Will do,' said Ella.

'And how would you say you're feeling emotionally?'

She was surprised at his question — at no time in the last four weeks had Dr Myers shown the least interest in her emotional life. Was this a trick – did he want to keep her longer for a rest cure for a nervous disorder?

'I feel absolutely fine, and very excited to be going home. I thank you for your attention, and the care I've received from the nursing staff has been exemplary, but it's time to begin the next part of my journey now, I think.'

'So you're not feeling at all worried or down about anything?'

'Not at all.'

'In that case, I'm happy to discharge you from the hospital, although not from my care. I'll come and visit to check on you from time to time, and you'll have to come back in a month to have that plaster taken off that arm. If you need anything, anything at all in the meantime, please telephone me.'

'Thank you, Doctor. I will,' she said, thinking that the sun would have to sink forever before she contacted him. She'd had enough of hospitals and doctors for a lifetime.


After he'd left and Rosie had been in to say goodbye, Ella gathered her few possessions.

She looked at herself in the mirror over the sink and assessed what she saw. The face that stared back at her was familiar now, at least, even if Ella might have changed one or two things about it if she could — her nose wasn't quite straight, and she remembered a fall from her pony had been the cause. She smiled as she did each time a new memory surfaced. The bandage had been removed from her head and her hair washed. It sat around her face in soft waves. There was a scar on her right temple, and some hair had been shaved to stitch another cut on the side of her head, but her hair was thick enough to more or less hide the patch that was beginning to grow in again. A decent haircut would make all the difference. Her hazel eyes were almond-shaped, the lashes thick, and her cheekbones were high. She wouldn't turn heads, but she was passable, she thought. A dab of lipstick, a deep breath, and she was ready to leave.

Andrew, Sheila and Matron were waiting for her in the hall downstairs.

'Ella, you look lovely,' said Andrew, helping her down the last few stairs and taking her bag.

'Ready?' asked Sheila.

Ella nodded, although now that it was real, that she was actually going to leave the hospital, her heart sped up, both from excitement and anxiety, and she had to take several deep breaths to calm herself.

'Ready,' she said firmly, and stepped towards Matron. 'Thank you for all you've done.' She shook her hand.

Matron smiled. 'Mind you don't go overdoing it. I've given Mr Whittington and Miss Marchmont their instructions, and you know yours. Rest, rest and more rest.'

'I will. I'm sure I won't be allowed to do anything.'

Sheila was fluttering around, impatient to be gone. She took Ella's arm and walked her to the door.

'Goodbye, then,' she said as they descended the steps to the gravel drive.

Andrew's black Austin 16 stood ready, the March sun glinting off the windows.

'I'll sit in the back if I may,' said Ella. 'And could we drive slowly so that I can look around?'

'Of course we can. Anything you want.'

'Quietly then too,' said Ella, wondering if Sheila was capable of it.

'Quiet too.' He smiled, perhaps thinking the same.

Matron waved them off from the front step, Andrew slid the car into gear and they were off, avoiding a man in a wheelchair being pushed along the drive by a nurse, and out of the tall gates onto the road. Ella looked back to see the hospital where she'd spent the last few weeks. It was a large manor house, ivy climbing over one end, the garden immaculate around it. She was glad to be leaving.

They drove between hedges that hid the fields on the other side, but she could imagine the cows grazing there, she'd seen them often enough from her window. And then the hedges thinned and ceased altogether as they entered some woods. She wound the window down and inhaled a lungful of icy air, enjoying the smell of the damp leaf litter. The sun glanced through the trees, creating bright strips between the shade. Ella thought she'd never seen anything so beautiful.

'All right back there?' asked Sheila.

'Perfect.' Ella rested her head against the edge of the window and she let her eyes wander over the scenery outside.

Andrew changed down a gear as they wound up a hill. They passed a row of four neat cottages. In the front garden of the first one, an old man was mowing the tiny bit of lawn that hadn't been given over to growing food. All of them had vegetable patches with rows of cabbages, carrots and onions, and frames ready for runner beans. And then they were past, and driving between fields again, and on into a village.

The houses were built of stone, some with thatched roofs. A village green was surrounded by neat cottages and a pub. On one side was a pond and a bench to sit on. They passed a bakery, a butcher, a greengrocer and a newsagent-cum-sub post office. Ella had a brief memory of talking to a redheaded woman in there, but nothing of what was said, nor when it had occurred. And then they were out the other side of the village and motoring between high hedges again.

'Almost home now,' said Andrew with forced gaiety, and Ella realised that he was worried about her and whether she was ready for what lay ahead.

'Super,' said Ella, but her stomach sank. She'd been so excited to leave the hospital she hadn't actually thought about being home. What if she didn't recognise anything? What if it felt like someone else's house? She bit her lip.

'I'll get the kettle on as soon as we get in,' said Sheila turning to look at her. 'Andrew took me shopping earlier, so we have all the essentials. I'll need your ration book too, though, so we can get whatever's available when it comes in.'

Ella was taking deep breaths and wondering why they needed ration books, when Andrew turned a corner and started slowing down. In front of them was a long, low whitewashed cottage with timber beams. The front door was a slightly deeper green than the foliage of the plants in pots on either side. Ella inhaled the smell of the winter garden – damp soil and wet stone, and sighed.

This is my house, she thought. I like it. It looks like a place where one can be happy. And as she surveyed the outside of the house, she had an impression of where all the rooms were, and of how they were furnished. She couldn't wait to go inside and find out if she was right.

Sheila opened the door, and Ella stepped into the hall that she knew, with its hallstand and coat rack. The rug on the floor was worn, just as she had foreseen. She peered into the dining room on one side, the parlour on the other. A small study was tucked in behind the dining room. Ella went into the sitting room at the back of the house, opposite the kitchen. It was as familiar as if she'd been there yesterday. She swung round to see Andrew and Sheila's anxious faces, and grinned hugely.

'I recognise it, all of it!' She laughed in relief and ran her hand over the mantelpiece before sitting briefly at the piano and then going to the French doors and opening them wide.

'I really am home,' she said. 'And look at the state of the garden!'

There were molehills like small untidy mountains all over the lawn, interspersed with tall, hardy weeds, dancing in the breeze.

Ella stood with her hands on her hips and felt truly happy for the first time since waking up in hospital.

She spent the afternoon wandering through the rooms of the house, reacquainting herself with it. The dining room with its oak table and sideboard, deep-green carpet and large picture window was lacking in character, she thought. The parlour was cold and dark, the furniture overstuffed and formal. She was sure she had hardly ever used it. It was clear that the cosy sitting room with its French doors on two sides, leading out to the rear and side gardens, and the bright kitchen were where she'd lived. It was strange to her that she could remember the house itself so well, but she had no recollection of living in it, nor anything that had happened there. But she was comforted by the fact that she knew it and was confident that it was only a matter of time, now that she was home, before the memories started coming back.

In her bedroom she lifted the lids of the creams and potions on her dressing table and stroked her cheek, remembering the fragrances and the feeling of smoothing them over her skin. She opened her wardrobe and found clothes that were designed for comfort rather than company, and realised that she had led a quiet life there in that house, and yet hadn't Sheila told her that she was a social person who liked parties? Had something happened to make her live a different life in this house? She sat on the bed, frustrated. It was impossible to live a normal life with no memory of what had come before, of the ups and downs and changes, and more than that, how she had responded to them. She had no idea what she had been like, what she'd done, her likes and dislikes, her dreams and ambitions, the events that had made her the person she was, good and bad. She felt a headache coming on, anxiety constricting her chest, and lay down to calm her breathing.

She must have slept because Sheila woke her when she knocked on the door to tell her that supper was ready, and to ask whether she'd come down or would prefer a tray in her room.

'I'll come down, I don't want you to treat me like an invalid.'

Sheila smiled. 'Of course I won't. I've told you – in no time at all we'll be off to dances and going on adventures.' She gave a little jig and Ella felt a jolt of recognition remembering that Sheila loved dancing. She laughed with relief. Her friend danced a few more steps, then bowed and left.

When Sheila had clattered downstairs again, Ella's mind drifted back to what she'd been thinking before she fell asleep, wondering if it was possible to build a future without any knowledge of the past. She felt like a ghost, lingering between two worlds. How could she go forward without at least some inkling of a personal history?

She went to the bathroom and splashed cold water on her face, then looked at herself in the mirror, meeting her anxious gaze. She shook her head, then lifted her chin. 'I will remember, and I will be fine,' she said to her reflection, and almost believed it.

Her stomach grumbled with hunger and she made her way down, deciding not to bother Sheila and Andrew with her thoughts; they were being so good to her, and she didn't want to worry them. She found them in the kitchen, Andrew sitting at the table, his long legs reaching across the room making it appear smaller. Sheila was fussing at the stove, her apron on inside out. Ella had a sudden image of her in another place at another time, pulling at her coat and jamming a hat onto her untidy hair. She smiled to herself as she slipped into the chair next to Andrew.

She was glad of the heat given off by the range. It was dark outside and a light rain had started falling, but they were cosy in the cottage.

'De-da! Spam fritters with boiled potatoes and cabbage,' said Sheila as she put the plates on the table.

'Lovely,' said Andrew, rubbing his hands together.

Sheila laughed. 'You almost sounded convincing then, Andrew.'

He looked embarrassed. 'Well, it looks fine, but I have to admit that I'm so jolly fed up with Spam. It's all we ever seem to eat these days.'

'Spam fritters, Spam hash, Spam and eggs – when we can get the eggs – Spam sandwiches; the possibilities are endless.' Sheila pushed her plate away and lit a cigarette, blowing the smoke out of the side of her mouth.

'Well I like it, thank you,' said Ella, chewing slowly. 'This ration book business,' she went on, 'what's all that about?'

Andrew and Sheila looked at each other, eyebrows raised.

'Dr Myers said that we shouldn't talk to you about the past,' said Andrew.

Ella shrugged. 'How on earth am I meant to remember anything if no one ever talks about the past? I'm not so fragile that you can't say anything, you know.'

Sheila took another drag of her cigarette and exhaled a cloud of smoke.

'Exactly what I said to him,' she said. 'It's not as if we're going to tell you anything awful, we're not that silly, but you need to know some things, don't you agree, Andrew?' She looked at him pointedly.

He sighed and put his knife and fork down. 'I suppose so, but only a little at a time.'

'Well, that's got that cleared up. Now, about rationing?' Ella asked again.

'Well,' started Andrew, 'the War lasted six years, and during that time there were shortages of everything because the Jerries started blowing supply ships out of the water whenever they could. One of that swine Hitler's strategies was to starve us into submission. So we were put on rations for meat, petrol, sugar, butter, sweets, coffee and tea – well, most things actually.'

'And there's still a shortage of most things, so we're still being bloody well rationed,' added Sheila, hooking one arm over the back of her chair.

'Not petrol,' said Andrew.

'True, but we can't bally well eat petrol, can we?' Sheila stubbed her cigarette out angrily. 'I thought this government would have things sorted by now, but it's like we're still living in the war.'

'Was it really ghastly?' Ella couldn't imagine it.

'Yes,' said Andrew and Sheila in unison, and laughed.

'Tell me about it.' Ella put her knife and fork down and looked at them expectantly.

Andrew and Sheila glanced at each other again, and Andrew spoke.

'I can tell you what I did, but I think it would be better if Sheila waited a while before telling you about her war – until you start remembering a bit yourself.'

'That sounds mysterious,' said Ella, and glanced at Sheila, who shrugged and winked, giving Ella the distinct impression that she would be far more forthcoming when Andrew wasn't around. The idea filled her with excitement and trepidation.

'Fire away then, Andrew,' said Sheila. Ella looked back at him waiting to hear more about his life.

'Well, you know I couldn't join up because of my eyesight but the fact is, after Oxford, I went into banking, and that was a reserved occupation. I suppose Chamberlain thought that someone had to keep the economy going.' He gave an apologetic laugh, and Ella smiled.

'I'm sure you did a brilliant job. Tell me about the other thing you did – the Air Raid thing.'

'Yes, the ARP – Air Raid Precaution. Early on, we had to give out gas masks and prefabricated shelters to keep people safe, but most people went to public shelters during the raids, and we had to keep them clean and tidy and manage the flow of people in and out. And then there were the blackout patrols. Not a chink of light could be showing to guide Hitler's bombs.' He looked at Ella. 'Do you really have no memory of the bombing?'

She closed her eyes, trying to conjure an image, but shook her head. 'None at all. Sounds like that might be a good thing though. Were there lots of bombs?'

'Thousands. In 1940 the Jerries wanted to flatten London and several other cities – word is they were paving the way for an invasion. That didn't happen, of course. I was living in a flat in Chelsea at the time, so that was my patch, as it were. We in the ARP had to go round in the evenings making sure that there were no lights showing anywhere, and after the bombs stopped, we had to help the people who had been injured.' He shuddered and a faraway look came into his eyes. 'There were some terrible sights – whole houses gone, bits of furniture broken amongst the rubble, people's lives shattered.'

'How awful.' Ella squeezed his arm. Andrew seemed not to notice.

'Yes. There'd be fires burning everywhere, and people wandering around moaning and crying, or silent and confused.

We had to find the wounded and get them to first-aid stations. One night I pulled a whole family from the wreck of their house. Not one of them survived.' He curled and uncurled his fist. 'The youngest was only a baby. What had he done to deserve that?'

'He hadn't done anything,' said Sheila, her voice brittle. 'No one had. It was war, and nothing about it was fair.'

Andrew looked at her and nodded.

'I don't want you to be upset, Andrew. If you don't want to talk about it anymore, I'll understand,' said Ella.

'No, it's all right. It wasn't all like that.' He sat up straighter and smiled at her. 'There was an immense sense of camaraderie too — people who might never have crossed paths in normal circumstances met and became friends, everyone helped each other out, there was a lot of laughter among the tears.'

'Some might call it gallows humour,' said Sheila.

'Undoubtedly some of it was, but not all. There were moments of pure joy and happiness – like finding a loved one whose husband or wife thought had been killed, or managing to save an adored pet who'd been trapped in a basement.'

'You must have helped so many people,' Ella said. She wasn't sure if she wanted to hear more though. There were images of contorted bodies and dreadful wounds in her mind, and she didn't know if she was imagining what Andrew had seen, or if they were scenes she herself had witnessed. Either way, they unsettled her.

'I think I might retire,' she said, getting up and taking her plate to the sink.

'I'll do the dishes,' said Sheila. 'Just leave it there. It's been a big day – I hope we haven't overtired you.'

'Not at all, it's marvellous to be home. Thank you both so much.'

'Goodnight, Ella darling,' said Andrew, rising from the table to give her a kiss. 'Sleep well.'

As she was climbing the stairs, she heard Andrew say to Sheila, 'I'm afraid I upset her with all that talk of death and destruction. I don't know what got into me. It was exactly what Dr Myers didn't want us doing.'

She stopped to listen to Sheila's response.

'Perhaps, but as her memory returns, she's going to have to deal with an awful lot more of that, and I probably don't know the half of it. I wasn't with her in the end when she volunteered for that last ruddy stint. God knows what sights she saw.'

Ella's heart sank, and she went up the rest of the stairs as fast as she could, shut her bedroom door and leant against it, breathing fast. What had Sheila meant?

What had she done? What had she seen?

# 5

Ella looked about her room. She'd searched earlier in all the obvious places for a diary, and found nothing. Given that she lived on her own, it seemed unlikely that she'd hide it, but she decided to look more thoroughly now anyway.

First, she checked the places she'd already looked; the drawer of her bedside table. She pulled it right out and tipped the contents on to her bed. There was an old lipstick, a brooch which had lost one of its stones, a torch, a small leather-bound Bible with gold lettering. She opened it and saw there was a label pasted into the front cover with *Eleanora Whittington* inscribed under the school crest, and *Scripture Prize, 1928,* written underneath. She had been eleven. She sat on her bed as she saw a glimpse of herself receiving it on a stage in a hall, embarrassed in front of the whole school. The headmistress in a black gown, herself in a grey uniform, hair braided so tightly her scalp prickled at the memory of it.

Yes, she thought, I've always hated being the centre of attention. And she smiled, because it was something else that had come back to her.

Turning back to the contents of the drawer she was

frustrated to have her previous search's outcome confirmed: there was no diary.

She took the torch and shone it under the bed. It highlighted dust and a crumpled handkerchief.

In the wardrobe she took the lids off all the shoeboxes and felt in the pockets of the jackets and coats.

There was nothing in the drawers of the tallboy apart from the sensible underwear, socks and cardigans she seemed to favour. Her dressing table held only trinkets and make-up. She leant against the windowsill and surveyed the room. There was nowhere else a diary could be hidden.

Ella wasn't sure which she felt more: disappointment or relief. She was confused by her own feelings; one moment she wanted to know everything about herself, and the next she was too afraid to think. Sheila's words kept circling in her head: 'She's going to have to deal with an awful lot more of that, and I probably don't know the half of it.' The half of what? Had she seen ghastly sights, or worse, performed terrible deeds? What if she had been the sort of person who took advantage of those in need, or was callous in the face of other people's loss? She had nothing to go on apart from Andrew's few observations of her, and they could be biased, a brother not wanting to admit that his sister was nasty or evil. Or perhaps he didn't actually know her that well. After all, he had told her that she had lots of friends, but there was no evidence of them, not even a card to welcome her home.

Her head ached. She didn't want to think ill of her brother. She wanted to be better, to know everything, to trust the people who were helping her.

She sat on the stool in front of her dressing table. 'Ella Elkington, you are fortunate to have two people giving up their time to help you. Be grateful. Trust them.' She gave herself a stern look, then smiled at her reflection. She noticed the beginnings of laughter lines fanning softly around her eyes and was comforted — she saw a woman who had loved and trusted, and who might have seen awful things, but who had responded with compassion. She didn't have the eyes of a monster.

Andrew was putting his overnight bag in the car when she went down in the morning.

'Sleep well?' he asked when she joined him in the drive.

She slipped her arm through his and leant her head against his shoulder.

'It was heavenly being in my own bed,' she said. She didn't mention the disturbing dreams that had woken her several times, and which now, thankfully, had faded back into the gloom. 'Going so soon?'

'I'm afraid I have to. I promised Sophie and the children that I'd be back in time for lunch. The in-laws are coming.'

'Well, you mustn't miss that.'

'I wish I could, actually. Mr Jameson is rather a character. He was a sergeant major in the Great War, and seems to think we're all troops to be bossed about. Mrs Jameson is a saint to put up with him quite frankly. It probably helps that she's a very quiet woman.'

'Maybe she's quiet because he bosses her about – she's learned not to say anything.'

Andrew looked into the distance as if considering the possibility.

'Maybe,' he said at length. 'All I know is that a little of Mr Jameson goes a long way, and I'd far rather stay here with you. Will you be all right do you think?'

'I'll be fine. Sheila will look after me, and you can telephone for a report whenever you like. Why don't you bring Sophie and the children with you next time you come down too? There's plenty of space and I'd love to see them.'

He smiled and squeezed her arm. 'I shall. We'll make a weekend of it, drive down on Friday evening. But it won't be next week, I'm afraid. We have a wedding to go to – one of the chaps at the bank. We'll be in deepest Shropshire.'

Ella felt her spirits sinking at the thought of not seeing Andrew the following week. Her world was so small already. She didn't want him to see her upset though.

'I'm sure you'll have a super time. Don't worry about me, nothing much will happen in this little neck of the woods.'

Sheila had joined them by the car. 'We might have to stir this quiet corner of the country up a bit, what do you think, Ella?'

Andrew didn't notice her wink and was about to say something when Ella squeezed his arm.

'We'll be fine. Drive carefully.'

Not long after they'd waved Andrew off, the heavens opened.

'I hope Andrew's all right, driving in this,' said Ella.

'I suspect he's pulled over somewhere,' said Sheila. 'He always was a sensible one.'

'How well did you know him?' asked Ella, recalling Andrew's admission when first he'd mentioned her.

'Quite well. He used to come and see you when we had days off at the weekends. He'd take us all out for tea, you, me, Maeve, Ingrid. We were all madly in love with him, of course. He was always so dapper, and such a gent. And feeding us tea and cake went down well. We were always hungry.'

'Lyons Corner House? Was that where we went?'

'Yes, on the Strand. What else do you remember?'

Ella thought for a moment. 'Nothing. It's so frustrating. The name came like a flash, but I don't remember actually being there.' She bit her lip. 'Sheila, do you think I'll ever remember things – properly, I mean?'

'I'm sure you will,' she said, taking her hand. 'But now we're on our own, perhaps we can speed up the process a bit, what do you think?'

Ella's pulse quickened. She instinctively looked towards the door to make sure there was no one else around. 'Off you go then,' she said, smiling tentatively.

Sheila suggested getting the fire lit in the sitting room and making themselves comfortable in there.

Ella sat on the sofa with its deep, soft cushions cocooning her. Sheila sat in the old plush armchair, and Ella had a flash of another woman sitting in it, with a blonde child on her lap, reading a book. Her mother and Andrew. It had been her mother's chair, and her father had brought it here from the Richmond house at some stage. She remembered nothing more.

'Are you ready?' asked Sheila.

Ella nodded.

'Just remember, you can stop me whenever you like, if it all gets too much.'

Ella nodded again, closed her eyes for a moment, and opened them to look at her friend. 'I'm ready.'

'It was raining the day we met. We literally bumped into each other on the steps of the hospital.'

Ella gasped and shifted in her seat. Hospital – had she been visiting someone?

'Ella?' said Sheila softly.

'I'm all right. I've got to know. I know I won't want to hear some of it, but I'm not a complete person until I can fill in my past, the good and the bad. Go on. Please.'

Sheila waited as Ella resettled herself.

'I want what's best for you, Ella, you know that. I'll be with you every step of the way.' She took a deep breath and continued.

'It was our first day of nursing training at St Thomas's. January 1935.'

Ella's eyes opened wide. 'Nursing?' And then she laughed.

Sheila raised her eyebrows in surprise, and Ella experienced another jolt – it was such a familiar expression. Then her thoughts returned to what Sheila had just said.

'I can't believe it.' She giggled. 'I told Rosie Fletcher while I thought she was a marvellous nurse, I felt sure I didn't have the temperament for it, and now here you are telling me that I trained as one. Did I finish?'

Sheila smiled. 'Yes, and you made a darned fine nurse – we both did, once we'd learned not to answer back and to carry out orders. It was touch and go for a while though!'

Ella looked out the window at the rain and the few daffodils that had managed to bloom in the biting cold, and sighed.

'You know, I rather like the idea of being a nurse. Did we fall for all the doctors?'

'Of course, and some of them even fell for us, although not for long. Some of them really were beastly, getting a young girl's hopes up only to ask another one to the next dance.'

'Did that happen to you?' asked Ella, hearing the bitterness in her friend's voice.

Sheila looked at her hands, gripping each other tightly in her lap.

'His name was Edwin Blount, a surgeon. Tall, good-looking in a rakish sort of way. Utterly charming. He had a slight limp, which made him appear vulnerable, and the girls all wanted to look after him. But he didn't need mothering. He was hard as nails and used his limp to hook us in. He seemed to take a liking to me. I was nineteen, never lived away from home before, in a new city, lonely – we nursing students didn't know each other very well then, we were all new, all finding our feet – and I was flattered. He took me to dances and films, I thought I loved him. I thought he loved me. And then I saw him with another girl. They weren't doing anything. Not even touching. But I knew by the way he looked at her, the same way he used to look at me, that I'd been replaced. The swine didn't even have the decency to tell me, he just stopped asking me out.' She wiped a tear and looked at Ella, who reached over to take her hand.

'And you still love him?'

'Oh, heavens, no!' said Sheila, looking startled and sitting up straighter. 'I know it's soppy, but I cry because I was so stupid and naïve. The tears are for me. I was so ashamed I'd been duped that I didn't tell anyone what had happened, and I felt so desperately lonely. If it had happened a few months later when we all knew each other better, I would have been able to talk to you or one of the others, but at the time, I felt there was no one.'

'I'm sorry,' said Ella. 'He sounds like an awful cad.'

'He was. Fortunately, he quickly got a reputation and the pool of available girls dried up. It was what he deserved.'

'Let's not think about him anymore,' said Ella. She felt overloaded already. She had been a nurse, had worked in London. There was so much to know, and yet, every little detail, each fact, needed time to sink in, time to find its place in her mind. She thought of herself as a jigsaw puzzle, each piece needing to find the right fit before the next bit could be slotted in to place.

It rained all day, and for the next three days with hardly a pause. Sheila and Ella were trapped in the house, playing endless games of rummy, talking occasionally of their nursing training. Ella was interested listening to the stories, but that's what most of them remained – stories told about other people in another time. She couldn't see herself doing the things Sheila told her she'd done, couldn't feel the emotions she suspected should be linked with the scenes created from Sheila's words.

On the afternoon of the fourth day, she was close to tears of boredom and frustration.

'It's useless,' she said, dropping her head into her hands. She wove her fingers into her hair and pulled hard. The pain felt good. At least it was real when nothing else seemed so.

Sheila said nothing, and Ella suspected she was also frustrated with their lack of progress.

'Perhaps we should invite some of these countless friends you tell me I have down here to cheer us up,' said Ella.

Sheila looked down at the arm of the chair she was sitting in and picked at a bit of loose thread.

'What is it?' asked Ella.

Sheila looked her in the eye. 'About the only thing I agree with Dr Myers on is that you don't need hordes of people about at the moment. Not until you've remembered a bit more. I'm happy to help with the memories, and then you'll be ready to see everyone again.'

Ella gritted her teeth. 'You don't have to baby me, you know.'

'I'm not trying to, but we all believe that the fewer people you have around the better. Just for now.'

'We – meaning you, Andrew and Dr Myers?'

'Yes.'

'So you're all the experts, and I just have to go along with it all.' Ella crossed her arms and turned away. Now she not only had no memory, but was being denied the access to people who might help. 'I suppose it was you who hid my address book?' She had looked for it when she searched for her diary.

Sheila nodded. 'It's for your own good, Ella, otherwise I wouldn't have done it.'

Ella was about to protest when the telephone rang in the hall and Sheila went to answer it. While she was gone Ella picked up the cards, shuffled them aggressively, then threw them back down and watched them scatter over the table and the floor. Then she swept past Sheila, grabbed her mackintosh from the coatrack in the hall and went out, banging the door behind her. She was soaked through by the time she reached the front gate. The rain was coming down in torrents, batted about by a thrashing wind, so there was no keeping it out. Ella stamped her foot in frustration, swirled round and went back into the house. She threw her coat into the corner, went into kitchen and started drying her hair with the hand towel as she went back into the sitting room and took her seat on the sofa again.

'That was Dr Myers,' said Sheila, coming back in. She handed Ella a bigger towel but made no comment about her outing. 'He sends his apologies for not having been before and asked if he could come this afternoon. I told him that was fine, and to bring something to cheer us up. I'm afraid I might have worried him. He seems terribly concerned that you've become depressed.'

'I am jolly well depressed. I feel like a prisoner here, and not only because of the weather.' She cast a scowl at Sheila.

'I'm sorry,' said Sheila.

Ella frowned. She didn't want to argue with Sheila. And with that realisation she wondered if she always shied away from confrontation. With a sigh, she said, 'It's just that I'm sure I'd remember more if I could get out and about, clear my head as it were – although it's pretty clear already.' Ella made a face.

Sheila laughed. 'Still got your sense of humour, I see. It got us through quite a few difficult times.'

Ella didn't want to hear about difficult times. Not yet. She needed to remember some good times, happy times first, so that she had something to hold on to when she recalled the bad, the painful.

'What time is the doctor coming?' she asked.

'He's on his way now. Should be here in a few minutes. I'll put the kettle on.'

'Don't make any for me, I'm drowning in the stuff,' said Ella. She saluted and crossed her eyes, sliding lower in her seat as if on a sinking ship.

'Get away with you,' said Sheila and went into the kitchen.

While she was gone, Ella gathered up the cards she'd thrown and composed herself for Dr Myers' visit. She wanted him to see how well she was doing now she was home.

## 6

The following day the sun appeared from behind the clouds for long enough to raise Ella's spirits. She suggested a walk.

'Good idea,' said Sheila. 'Let's go and find the pond, shall we?'

'Pond?'

'Yes, there's one on your property, Andrew told me about it. You used to go tadpoling there. Although I expect with all this rain, the tadpoles have been washed away – or packed their little tadpole bags and found themselves somewhere drier for the duration,' said Sheila.

Ella laughed. 'They'd die without water, silly.' There was something familiar about laughing with Sheila — they'd always enjoyed their jokes. And she smiled at another fact slipping into place. She didn't remember a pond but was keen to get out. 'Let's go and investigate then,' she said, tugging on her mackintosh and wellingtons.

They set off, arm in arm under a glowering sky. The sun had already disappeared, but at least the rain was holding off. They slipped and slid, holding each other up, watched by the cows looking forlorn under the trees. As they climbed the stile in the corner, they spotted the pond in the next field, only it was more of a lake, tussocks of grass sticking out of its smooth grey surface here and there. Some trees on the other side, and a semi-submerged bench marked the usual boundary of the pond.

As they sat on the stile taking in the scene, a man appeared on the other side of the field.

Sheila waved and called out a greeting.

'What are you doing?' asked Ella, her hands flying to her throat. Her heart started thudding. Did she know this man? Should she know him? She had no idea how to greet him – as an old friend, or a stranger.

'Getting to know the neighbours,' said Sheila.

He lifted his head and waved back, then started making his way over to them, wading through water that lapped the top of his boots.

'Morning,' he said as he approached.

'Good morning,' said Sheila. 'I'm Sheila Marchmont and this is my friend, Ella Elkington. We live at Bamford House.'

'Mrs Elkington and I know each other. Morning.' He nodded to her and then turned to Sheila, touched his hand to his cap and gave a little bow. 'Arthur Ashton at your service. My farm adjoins Mrs Elkington's land.' He had a wide smile and ruddy cheeks. Ella's voice had deserted her. It was all she could do to stand there while he and Sheila passed the time of day. She had no recollection of ever having met him.

Just then the rain started again, big, heavy drops. Ella had never been happier to be caught in a downpour.

'Better run,' said Sheila, helping Ella down from the stile.

'Careful how you go, ladies,' Arthur called after them.

'Is everything all right? You're very quiet,' said Sheila when they were home and had dried off.

Ella shook her head and sucked in her bottom lip. 'I had no idea who he was, yet he said we'd met. I don't know what he knows about me, or I about him. I was terrified. Do you realise, Sheila, that it's going to be the same every time we go out. People will greet me and I will have no idea how we know each other, if I should be asking after their children or husband, if we were good friends or hardly knew each other. Heavens, I might have enemies in the village and not know it, so I'll smile and start talking and they'll cut me dead.'

'I can't imagine you having enemies, but I do see what you mean about the other stuff.' Sheila took a puff of her cigarette, half closing one eye as she blew the smoke out of the side of her mouth. 'Tell you what,' she said, 'how about I do a recce in the village and see who knows what about you. I can tell them you've had an accident and can't remember much, so if you ask odd questions, they're not to worry. How would that be?'

Ella smiled. 'Thank you. And I believe I owe you an apology – I think you're right about not seeing too many people at the moment.'

～

Later in the day, with the rain once again set in, Sheila went into the kitchen to prepare dinner.

'I'll see if I can work out a new way to cook Spam and potatoes,' she said as she disappeared.

Ella had had enough of reading, playing cards and listening to the wireless. She got up and opened the bureau to put the cards away, and stopped. In a back section of the little desk was a bundle of letters.

She reached for them. They were all addressed to her in

beautiful, precise handwriting. The top ones had an address in Torquay, but the lower ones were addressed to her at Bamford House. She turned one over. They were from Mr H M Whittington, Ferndale House, Richmond Hill, Richmond, Surrey.

Her father.

Her heart stopped.

She studied the postmarks and dates. The first one was from July 1925. She would have been eight.

With trembling hands, she opened it and read.

*My Dear Ella,*

*How good it was to get your letter. I am so very sorry to hear that it rained and spoiled your visit to Berry Head. I do hope Mother can take you another time, as the views from the top are spectacular.*

*I am missing you all very much, but I am in the middle of a very important case. Hopefully it will be over next week and I will come to Torquay to be with you all.*

*In the meantime, give your mother and Andrew a kiss from me, and a big one for yourself.*

*Your loving Father.*

Ella sat down, the letter in her hand. She saw her father in her mind's eye, a tall man with a moustache and dark hair. And she felt a sense of safety.

And then she remembered an older version of him lying in a hospital bed, his face lopsided, one eye drooping, unable to speak. She uttered a small cry, and clutched at her chest. He'd had a stroke. She had been at St Thomas's, still training, and Andrew had telephoned to tell her their father had been taken to Guy's. Ella had asked the ward sister for the afternoon off to go and see him, and had run the whole way, arriving out of breath, fearing the worst. And the worst was what met her.

Andrew was at their father's bedside and she joined him, asking in hushed tones what had happened.

'He was in chambers working on a new case, so his clerk told me, when he just keeled over. That was it.' Andrew looked crumpled in on himself, and out of place in the hospital. He held Ella's hand, as if begging her to do something. But there was nothing to be done. Henry Whittington had another stroke during the night and died.

Ella looked out the window at the rain still lashing down and let the tears flow. She'd remembered her father and lost him again within minutes.

~

'I found the letters,' said Ella at dinner.

Sheila reddened. 'What letters?'

Ella bristled. 'Don't play me for a fool, Sheila. You put them in the bureau knowing I'd find them.'

Sheila eyed her across the table. 'All right. I did put them there. I thought about it after you were so angry about the address book, and realised that, after all, you had a right to these things. Andrew found them before you came home, and gave them to me for safekeeping until such a time as you were ready.'

'And I suppose you've read them?' Ella's voice was icy, her stare glacial.

'Of course not! What do you take me for? I would never read anything private.' Sheila lit a cigarette and snapped her lighter shut. 'I'm hurt that you should even think it.'

'You're hurt! How do you think I feel? You're not my keeper, you know.'

'Not your keeper, no, but your guardian. Andrew and Dr Myers gave me strict instructions.'

'Oh damn Andrew and the bloody doctor! You're all acting like prison guards. You have no right–'

Sheila stood abruptly, sending her cutlery scattering across the table. 'Listen, everything I am doing for you I am doing because we think it's for the best. If you would like me to leave, so be it.'

'I think that would be a good idea,' said Ella, also getting to her feet and glaring at Sheila, eyes narrowed.

Sheila drew back her shoulders, stubbed her cigarette out and marched out of the room. Ella slumped back into her seat and sat staring at her plate. Instead of feeling elated as one might expect at winning an argument she felt depressed. She didn't want Sheila to go, but she did want to be treated like a competent adult. She took some deep breaths and followed Sheila up the stairs.

'May I come in?' she asked as she knocked on the bedroom door.

'I can't stop you, it's your house after all.'

Sheila had her suitcase on the bed and was emptying her underwear drawer into it.

Ella stood by the door, wringing her hands. 'Please don't go,' she said.

Sheila stopped and turned to look at her. 'Is that meant to be an apology?'

'Not exactly. I mean, I am sorry I was angry, and that I didn't trust you not to read my letters, but I'm not sorry about the rest of it. I'm fed up to the back teeth with being treated like a child. I know you're just following orders, but what happened to the Sheila you told me about who ignored curfews and partied till dawn, the Sheila who broke the rules and did what she pleased?'

Sheila sat on her bed, a pair of stockings in her hand. 'She became a nurse in the war and learnt to follow orders,' she said, looking at the floor.

'Well, we're not at war anymore, and you can't be court-martialled by Andrew or Dr Myers, so let's just get on with it, shall we – make our own rules from now on?'

Sheila looked at her. 'I just want you to be well, Ella.'

'I am well, and I need to start remembering. I know you all think I'm some fragile little thing, but I can't be, can I – I nursed in the war. I survived it once, and I'll survive it again. And you were there first time round, and you're here now – if you'll stay, that is – and we can face it together again.'

Sheila got up and put the stockings back into the drawer. 'You're right. If I doubted it before, you've just proved that you're ready.'

'Thank you. Now, have you anything else of mine hidden away?'

Sheila bit her lip and then opened her bedside table. She handed Ella three notebooks, battered and worn. On the top one, in her handwriting, it said *E Whittington, Nurse Training, 1935–1939*. Ella's stomach dropped and her heart thudded. Here was her past. Once she'd read the letters and journals, she'd know all about herself again. She had wanted to be treated like an adult, to be the mistress of her fate, but now was gripped once more by the fear that she mightn't like what she discovered.

Taking a deep breath, she picked up the first journal to look at the one underneath. The second one was titled, *Staff Nurse! 1939–1944*. She didn't even want to look at the last one; she remembered Sheila's words to Andrew on her first night home, about the things she might have seen. She wasn't ready for that.

Ella sank into the chair by the window. She took several deep breaths to calm herself and then turned to Sheila, who was looking at her, concern written all over her face.

'Did we used to have fights like this before?'

Sheila thought for a moment. 'No. But we might have if we hadn't always been so darn busy. We're both rather headstrong, as anyone will tell you. And although we shared a room, we were often on different shifts and weren't cooped up together for days on end like we have been.'

Ella smiled at the idea of being headstrong. She felt more anxious than anything, and hoped that her strength would step in when she needed it.

'Pax?' she said to Sheila, offering a hand.

'Of course,' said Sheila, taking her hand and pulling her onto her feet and into a hug. 'We're a team, and a jolly good one.'

Over the next few days, Ella tucked herself away in her room every afternoon and read. Tempting though it was to start with the diaries, she'd decided to start at the beginning, to build the foundation of a childhood from which to launch herself once more into adult life and memories. She took out the letters from her father. She found memories rushing back, and she'd spend hours remembering details of her life as a child, but, more importantly, her family. She came to realise that although she was younger than Andrew, she felt protective of him. He was shy, and she was outgoing. He loved reading, she loved being active. He followed rules, she stretched them. In company, he would retreat, stay silent, and she would speak for him, defend him when others were unkind, as children could be. She particularly remembered one incident when they were still at the local primary school, before Andrew had to go up alone to the boys' school. John Barton, the biggest bully there had cornered him after class and stolen his glasses. He was taunting him, calling him names and laughing at his weak attempts to defend himself. Ella had found them and without a second thought, had kicked John in the back of the knee, making him buckle, and as he'd fallen, she'd snatched

Andrew's glasses from him, grabbed her brother's hand and they'd run off before John knew what was happening. She smiled at the vision of the event that played itself in her mind, wondering if Andrew remembered it, and what he'd made of his little sister.

She remembered her mother as a quiet, intelligent woman, who made up games and read to her endlessly. Her father, a busy man who nevertheless loved his family and had made Ella feel like a princess. As she read the letters, she could almost smell his pipe tobacco and feel the warmth and comfort of his hand when she held it, the scratchiness of his favourite tweed jacket when she cuddled into him on his lap.

A few days later, after dinner, Sheila banked up the fire and Ella stared into the flames and told her friend some of what she remembered of her father.

'He was a King's Counsel. One day he took Andrew and me to the courts. I was awed by the splendour of the building he worked in. I couldn't imagine anything more grand, and I was so proud of him. Andrew, ever the pragmatist, asked if it got terribly cold in winter with all the stone and marble. I remember Father gazing at him with such a curious look on his face, as if half wanting to laugh, and half terribly impressed.

'Another time, I think we were in the cottage at Torquay, he performed a magic show for us, producing pennies from behind our ears, and guessing cards we picked and so on. We thought he was the cleverest man in the world. Andrew spent hours working out how he did the tricks, but I was happy thinking of my father as a magician.'

'He sounds the most marvellous of fathers,' said Sheila, and took a drag on her cigarette. 'Mine wasn't at all like that. He was hardly ever home, and when he was he was behind a newspaper. My only memories of him are of Sunday dinners, which were spent in silence so that we didn't upset his digestion.'

'How sad. We always chatted at mealtimes. Father taught us how to argue a point and develop an opinion. Mother used to try and stop him; I think she was worried that if I was too clever, I'd never get a husband.'

Sheila stubbed her cigarette out and smiled at Ella. 'I'm glad you're remembering your family. You didn't talk about them much – heaven knows we didn't have the time – but you always spoke of them with such warmth.'

'It's these letters – I must have written every few days while we were away, and busy as he was, Father always replied. And by his comments, I must have complained about things all the time. I must have been an awful brat when I was eight or nine.'

She leaned forward and picked up one of the letters.

'Listen to this;'

*Dearest Ella,*

*What a delight to get your latest letter. I'm so sorry to hear about your sore knees. When I come down at the weekend, I'll repair that dastardly bicycle so it doesn't deposit you on the road again.*

*I had dinner with the Giles's last evening. Bobby asked to be remembered to you. I think you have an admirer!*

*Looking forward to seeing you in two days so that I can give you a kiss and a hug. In the meantime, look after each other,*

*From your loving Father.*

Ella put the letter down and shrugged. 'See what I mean?'

'He sounds like an absolute dear,' said Sheila, pulling another cigarette out, tapping the end on the case before lighting it and continuing, 'How about we dodge the showers and walk into the village tomorrow; do you think you could manage that? It's only about ten minutes on foot, and we could rest once we were there.'

Ella realised that perhaps she'd been insensitive going on about her father so much when Sheila's clearly wasn't much to write home about.

'That sounds like a good idea. I need to stretch my legs. I have a feeling I used to walk a lot, and all this sitting around isn't good for me. I think my hip may be less stiff if it got some exercise.'

'That's settled then. We'll go as soon as the rain allows.'

The weather didn't allow an outing for several more days. The cold gave way to milder temperatures, but the rain was relentless. The front lawn was like a bog and the back garden not much better. Ella began to worry about the roof springing a leak, and checked several times a day to make sure that there were no damp patches on the bedroom ceilings.

The post brought a note from Andrew hoping she was well, and enclosing a drawing that Billie had done for her which was meant to be a self-portrait, and a letter from Laura, written in large, round letters that sloped towards the bottom right-hand side of the page.

*Dear Aunt Ella,*

*I hope you are well. I am well. Love from Laura.*

Ella tried to imagine the little girl, her niece, writing it. She couldn't remember anything about her, but felt a rush of love as she reread the letter. She put the drawing and the letter in the book she was reading so she could look at them whenever she wanted, and found some paper and a pen and wrote back.

*Dear Laura,*

*Thank you for your lovely letter. I am really looking forward to seeing you soon.*

*Lots of love,*

*Aunt Ella xx*

She also drew a picture of herself for Billie and thanked him for his.

Sheila dashed into the village on the third day to post the letter and see what food was available. She returned, soaked to the bone, with some cod, milk, custard powder and a cauliflower.

'I was hoping to get some cheese, but it ran out before I was served. Pity – I would kill for a piece of cheddar and a nice Bath Oliver.'

Ella laughed. 'We might have to butter up the local farmer then.'

Sheila went to change out of her wet clothes and Ella sat thinking about the neighbours. She didn't remember any of them and had no idea how long she'd lived in the house. She wondered about that, about the fact that none of them had made any attempt to visit her. Sheila had offered to find out any information she could in the village, but the weather had been so foul, she hadn't hung around to chat on her quick forays to do the shopping. And then Ella wondered if perhaps she hadn't lived in the house very long as an adult – she had, after all, spent many years in London, and then the war came... She shuddered and hugged herself. She didn't want to think about that.

'Tell me more about our training,' said Ella over dinner of cod, mash and cauliflower in white sauce. A totally white meal. Ella craved bloody meat and mountains of greenery.

'Have you started reading your journals yet?'

'No, I thought you might tell me a little first. I don't know what it is, but I feel a little afraid of what I might find in those notebooks.'

Sheila nodded. 'God, I wish I'd got some cheese, it would have pepped up this cauliflower no end.'

Ella laughed and said nothing about her own cravings. Sheila was being so good to her, she mustn't criticise, and anyway, it wasn't her fault there was no decent food to be had. 'A nurse marches on her stomach,' she said.

'Too right,' said Sheila. 'In which case, I'm surprised we ever got anywhere. Anyway, what do you want to know?'

'What did we do first?'

Sheila thought for a moment, and then said, 'We all met in the foyer of the hospital but were taken immediately to Nightingale House, the nurses' home, and allocated our rooms. We had to share, two, some even three to a room. You and I were in together, Maeve and Ingrid were next door. Edie, Nina and Joan were the other side.' She stopped, glanced at Ella.

'Hold on – I remember vague things about them. Joan had a wicked sense of humour and long legs. Edie had really dark hair, didn't she? And Ingrid was almost white-blonde. We all wanted to know how she did it, but she said it was natural.'

Sheila laughed. 'That's right. And to this day her hair is so light you can almost see through it. She's living up north now.' She looked at Ella. 'I'm so glad you remember them. We had such fun together. We got each other through. All of us had times when we thought we'd drop out, but we talked each other into staying.'

They talked about their friends for a while, Ella asking questions and remembering more as Sheila talked.

After they'd washed up and put away the dishes and were settled in the sitting room, Ella said, 'Tell me how it all started – the training, I mean.'

'The very first thing we had to do – and I almost got chucked out then – was unpack our things and put them all away neatly. The Home Sister came and checked that we hadn't just thrown our belongings into the drawers. I had to redo mine; I've never been very tidy. Then it was off to meet Matron, Miss McDonald, who was in charge of our training. Do you remember her at all? She had bushy eyebrows and a long chin. And she was tall and terribly thin. We all thought she looked like a–'

'Scarecrow,' finished Ella for her.

'That's right. But a strangely neat one!'

Ella was on a roll. 'And she was terrifying. Although everybody was. The surgeons, the Sisters, the staff nurses, the junior doctors. We were the lowest of the low and no one let us forget it. And we were at St Thomas's, the best hospital in Britain, as we kept being told. We had to maintain the highest of standards in our own behaviour, in our care of the patients, and in our communications with other staff – which were minimal, because we weren't meant to talk to anyone. I remember her telling us that every time she saw us.' She smiled. 'It sounds awful. Why did any of us stay?'

'Vocation; it's your calling,' said Sheila in a terrible attempt at a Scottish accent. 'Matron used to drum it into us all the time. "You are here because it is your vocation, your deepest desire to help others. Make sure you do not waste the opportunity that has been awarded you by training at this great institution." It sounded so compelling coming from her. We all felt that we were the crème de la crème, even though we were at the bottom of the heap. There was only one way to go, and that was up, to be the very best nurses we could be. Certainly, when I went to other civilian hospitals, I found the care sorely lacking, and the discipline poor.'

'Gosh, it sounds like we were all brainwashed.'

'Perhaps, but it did the trick. We all made the grade and felt proud to be St Thomas's nurses.'

Ella noticed that they were both sitting up very straight and wondered when that had happened. She also felt an expansiveness in her chest — was it pride, had Sheila's talk of being a St Thomas's nurse touched something in her? There was, she thought, no other explanation.

'Were we really that good at what we did?' she asked.

'We really were. After a slightly difficult start.' Sheila laughed. 'We were all very young and naïve, and found it hard to settle in to the discipline and the routine. Being terrified of the Sisters didn't help either. You and I were sent to the same ward to start with, Male Surgical. We saw things there that no nineteen-year-old girl needed to see! The first time I had to give a patient a bed bath I thought I'd die of embarrassment, and the fact that the chap I had to give it to was only about twenty and rather good-looking didn't help at all. Sister stood over me the whole time, making sure I did a thorough job.'

Sheila accompanied her story with a hand gesture and a look of distaste and Ella started giggling. Soon both of them were doubled over, helpless with laughter.

When eventually Sheila could talk again, she said, 'You weren't any better. You'll see when you get round to reading your journal. You came back to our room one day, I think I'd had a day off, and you swore you'd leave if you had to bathe a patient ever again.'

Ella saw it in her mind's eye. An old man who'd had a bowel operation. She'd also been watched over by Sister, and when it came to washing the man's penis, lying in the wispy, greying pubic hair, she'd thought she might throw up. She'd never seen anything so ugly. It was like a worm lying there; a fat, ugly worm. She'd flicked the washcloth around without looking, and when she had to dry him, she'd patted the towel all around without actually touching the awful thing. Somehow Sister had let it go, even though Ella was certain she'd noticed her disgust. And she remembered telling Sheila all about it, and then the two of them laughing until their sides hurt and Maeve and Ingrid came in to see what was going on.

'Oh, the things we had to do,' she said, and Sheila smiled.

'Yes, and that wasn't the worst of it. But it'll do for today, it's probably best to do this in small doses,' she said.

Ella thought about the memory of Mr Jacobs (the name suddenly came to her), and wondered if the events that made the greatest impression were the first to return. There were still great gaps in her childhood, but enough islands of memory to feel that she had substance, that she had a past. And she realised that nobody remembered everything they had ever done, and nor would she. But she was glad that she'd remembered the things she had, that slowly it was all coming back, and despite Sheila and Andrew's and Dr Myers' caution, she felt ready to know more.

## 7

The rain continued, keeping Ella and Sheila indoors too much of the time, and relying on each other for company. Ella began to worry that she was a burden on Sheila. It was all very well if both people could remember shared times and carry the conversation equally, but too often, Sheila was introducing topics or people of whom Ella had no memory. So she decided it was time to delve into the journals. Thanks to Sheila's patience so far, Ella had a reasonable idea of how their training started, and some of the more hilarious things that had happened, now she would fill in the gaps.

Ella picked up the journal dated 1935–1939 and opened it at random.

June 18th, 1936
*Thank heavens for a day off. Last night I was so tired I couldn't even be bothered to undress. I just kicked my shoes off and crawled under the blankets. There was a cold draft from the window that won't shut properly, and it sent its icy fingers down my neck, but even that couldn't keep me awake.*

Ella shivered at the thought and drew her cardigan more tightly round her shoulders.

*It was the busiest day I can remember. I was on my own – they must have been desperate to let me, still a student, look after the whole ward! Esther, the staff nurse, has sinusitis and will be off for a week at least, and there was no one else who could fill in, they're all dropping like flies. Women's Surgical is full to overflowing too, with appendixes and hernias all threatening to burst at the same time. It's funny how that happens; a few weeks ago it was hysterectomies and haemorrhoids.*

Ella sat back and closed her eyes. An image of the ward shimmered and then firmed. Sister Cooper, she thought. And then, 'She hated me.' She remembered being told off at least half a dozen times for running on the ward, but what was she meant to do when everyone needed a bedpan or an injection, a kind word or a plumping of pillows at the same time?

Sister Cooper, the dragon with the nasal voice. 'It is unseemly for a nurse to be seen rushing about, and it upsets the patients,' she'd say. Ella smiled at the recollection. Oh, how I hated that voice, she thought. But she'd had to do as she was told, in spite of believing that the patients were much more upset by waiting for a bedpan or their pain medication than they were by seeing a nurse running full pelt down the ward.

*In the middle of the day, when I should have had two hours off, I was getting the ward ready for Mr Hudson's ward round, making sure the bedside lockers were tidy, that the beds and the patients in them were spick and span. Poor things.*
*Mr Hudson, the senior surgeon, and a god in this hospital, swept in after lunch with his entourage of registrars, junior doctors, medical*

*students, Sister and the new nurse probationers; pink, well-scrubbed*
*young things with a zealous glint in the eye and a bouncy step.*
*They'll soon lose both.*

Ella remembered the way they all gathered round Mrs
Brookes' bed, Mr Hudson telling his audience about the patient.
When he lifted her gown to illustrate a point and show how neat
the scar was thanks to his stitching, she was so embarrassed she
blushed all the way up her neck. They moved from bed to bed,
and then God and his followers left, the doors swinging on their
hinges behind them. The whole thing lasted twenty minutes, in
which no one but him said a word.

*With his departure, the patients started asking once again for*
*bedpans, trips out onto the veranda for a cigarette, bowls to be sick in,*
*and I was running around like a mad thing for the rest of the*
*afternoon.*

Ella could almost feel her sore feet and tired legs. They were
such busy days — thirty patients to look after, and someone
always needing something. She scanned the entry and her
attention came to rest on Miss Christie. She remembered her on
the ward; a lively old lady who'd come in with ileitis. She was a
tiny woman, never any trouble, but that evening she had a high
fever – the red cheeks and bright glazed eyes were a dead
giveaway. Her abdomen was distended and she was in a lot of
pain. Ella remembered calling for Sister and telling her that she
thought Miss Christie was bleeding internally and needed to go
back to theatre.

And Sister's response came to her as clearly as if it had
happened yesterday. 'It is not your place to have an opinion,
Nurse Whittington. I will telephone Mr Hudson's registrar and

he will decide what needs to be done. In the meantime, give patient a bath to get her temperature down.'

*I felt like screaming, and was beginning to think that I wasn't suited to a profession in which I wasn't allowed to think for myself. Perhaps I should have pursued a career as a concert pianist after all. But then again, while it had been satisfying in some ways, it didn't fulfil my desire to help people. And everyone said there might be another war, and what use would a concert pianist be in a war?*

Ella stopped reading. Concert pianist? She looked at her hands, the long, tapering fingers. Pianist's hands. But she had no memory of playing. She tucked the information away and returned to the diary. As she read she became sad and angry. She'd rushed off to get towels and water for the bed bath, but it was all too late.

*Dish of water, soap and towels in hand, I could see from across the ward that something was wrong. Miss Christie was lying at an odd angle, and her usually darting eyes were unmoving. I galloped over – that really is the only word to describe it – and took her wrist to feel for a pulse, but I knew it was no use. I took a deep breath, thought rather than said a prayer, and placed the screens around the bed before going, once again, to find Sister, wondering as I went if I should proffer the opinion that Miss Christie was dead, or if I'd get into trouble for that too.*

After Sister had been and made her clinical assessment, and one of Mr Hudson's registrars had done the paperwork, the great man himself having no truck with the dead, Ella remembered spending the next hour washing the body and laying her out, and then waiting with her until the orderly came to take her to the morgue. She'd hummed quietly as she worked, knowing that Miss Christie loved music, and so giving her the best send-off she could.

Ella sat, thinking about the day on the ward, and other days like it, when she was too tired to think and longed for a hot bath and bed. She wondered how she'd got through the training – how any of them had. Long hours, terrifying Sisters, demanding patients, little time off – it had been character-building, if nothing else.

*I practically crawled back to my room, grateful for once not to have a date for the evening. Daniel had wanted to take me to a dance, but I declined. He's rather too keen, and I find his attentions at once flattering and annoying. I can only take Dr Daniel Hawthorne in small doses. And anyway, it's Charles Elkington that I really want to dance with; Elegant Elkington as we call him. An orthopaedic surgeon with a quick smile and a ready wit. So unlike Mr Hudson and his tight jaw and enormous sense of importance. I've heard that Elegant Elkington actually speaks to his patients and seems to care how they are. I hope that when I leave Women's Surgical I get Orthopaedics, although I suspect I might have to do a stint on the fever ward instead with the dyptherias and tuberculosises. Or is it tuberculoses?*

Ella stopped. Here was her husband in the pages of her journal. She'd found him, but she was also aware that in the pages of her diary she would lose him again, that this was all that was left of their love affair, their marriage. She felt unspeakably sad, and couldn't go on.

'How do you feel now, Ella?' asked Sheila as she entered the room with the tea tray.

Ella turned to look at her friend. Torn from her journal and Charles, she felt disorientated and couldn't answer immediately.

'You look rather pale.' Sheila put the tray down and took

Ella's wrist, looking at the watch, pinned nurse-like, to her blouse.

Ella didn't want to talk to Sheila about Charles, not yet. It felt too private, too precious. 'I'm fine, just so very tired all the time, I don't understand it. I'm not doing anything, just sitting here all day while you run about after me, and yet I feel like I've ploughed a whole field on my own or wrestled with a bull.'

'You'll feel better soon, I'm sure of it,' said Sheila. 'Dr Myers did say it would take time, and it's only been a few weeks since the accident. You'll just have to be patient, my dear.'

'I don't think it's in my nature,' said Ella, and sighed. 'Oh, I should stop grumbling and put all my energy into trying to remember, but I can't force it.'

'I know, and it must be frustrating for you. Gosh, you've never been good at waiting for anything!'

'No? I was just remembering a time when I was nursing, and how impatient I was then. And how I thought I knew better than everyone!'

'Yes, that's another trait you have. But then again, you often did know more than those around you.'

'Not when I was a student nurse on Sister Cooper's ward, as she often pointed out to me.'

'Is that what you were reading about just now?'

'Yes. It's strange really – I read these specific memories in my journal, but they're tied up with vague notions of other things. I didn't know until I said it to you just now, for instance, that I had thought Sister Cooper so intimidating.'

'Good old Sister Cooper. What a battleaxe she was. You know she died of a heart attack just after the end of the war? She was at work and collapsed in the middle of a ward round, and even with the whole medical team there, they couldn't revive her.'

'How sad. I was terrified of her, but I didn't dislike her,

especially once I'd left her ward; I remember now she gave me a nice report. In fact, I think it was the best I got during my training. She was tough, but she was fair.'

'It seems to me that talking about these things helps you remember more and more. I can't think why Dr Myers doesn't want us to discuss them.'

Ella wasn't sure how to respond. She didn't mind talking about the innocuous things, the day-to-day pleasant memories, but she didn't want anyone poking and prying into her mind. It was important that she kept control so that she wasn't broadsided by whatever it was that lurked at the perimeter of her thoughts.

'What about all the young men we used to dance with?' asked Ella.

'Those were the days – a different partner for every dance. What fun we had! Anyway, here's your tea.' Sheila handed her a cup and placed the plate of bread and butter next to her.

Ella looked at it; it was bright yellow. Not margarine-pale yellow. She lifted a piece to her nose and smelled it, closing her eyes at the memory. 'Butter – real butter – who have you been flirting with?'

Sheila reddened. 'I didn't have to flirt at all. Arthur Ashton gave it to me along with a couple of eggs and a little piece of gammon for dinner.'

'Yum. That'll make a change from vegetables, vegetables, Spam and more vegetables. Not that I'm complaining, but one does like a bit of proper meat every so often. I'm glad you're getting out and about and meeting the neighbours. Have you discovered anything about them that I should know? It's been a while now, and none of them has come knocking to see how I am, and I haven't remembered any of them.'

'Interesting you should ask. I was just talking to Arthur – Mr Ashton – about that very thing. He said that you kept to yourself

SARAH BOURNE

when you came here. In fact, it wasn't until you put an advertisement in the newsagent's window offering piano lessons that anyone knew you were here.'

Ella looked over to the piano. She hadn't played it since she'd been home. She hadn't been sure why; yes, she had a plaster on her arm but she had a feeling that that wouldn't have stopped her before, and anyway, she could move her fingers quite well even with it on. Now that she'd read the journal entry, she knew that it had been a big part of her life – that she must be very good to even consider a career as a concert pianist. She felt unequal to the task. What if she couldn't play anymore? The idea of trying to play and failing at it loomed over her like an enormous thundercloud.

'Did I ever play for you?' she asked, nodding towards the instrument.

'I should say! You played little trills whenever you came across a piano, and you could always be depended on to thump out a tune to sing along to at a social. You've got a nice singing voice too.'

Ella considered that. How did that piece of information fit in with the other facts she'd been told and the fragments of memory she had of herself? Nurse, pianist, singer. She felt so distant from all of it.

The next day, while Sheila was out shopping in the village, Ella limped over to the piano. She wasn't using a stick anymore, but sometimes her hip played up and she had a pronounced limp on those days. She opened the piano stool and took out the top sheet of music. Chopin's Polonaise in A-flat major, Opus 53. She looked at the notes and began to hear the music in her head, reading it as easily as if it were words in a book. And an image flashed into her head of a hall with an intricately moulded ceiling and hundreds of people sitting on red plush seats. She put the music back and shut the stool with an emphatic thud, her heart pounding.

What was she scared of? This fear had come over her a few times in different situations since she'd been home. There didn't seem to be a pattern to it. She'd be doing something and all of a sudden her heart would be racing and she'd feel terrified. But to give in to a 'sense' without any evidence felt cowardly, and she didn't want to be a coward. So using every ounce of willpower she possessed, she sat at the piano and opened the lid. She would not let fear stand between her and something she must have loved. Her hands settled lightly on the keys almost without conscious thought. It was as if they knew what to do with no message from her brain to set them in motion. She took a deep breath and started playing, quietly at first, and then with more confidence and volume, until her hands were rushing up and down the keys, the notes strong and true. Chopin in all his glory, and Ella, tears rolling down her cheeks, transported to the Young Pianists Concert in Brighton, 1928. She was eleven and playing in her first competition. She'd played for the memory of her mother who had died a few months before. It was she who had introduced Ella to the instrument and who had always loved listening to her play, who had encouraged her when she was frustrated and applauded her when she played well. She had died without ever seeing Ella perform, but she would have been so proud.

She played to the end of the piece and sat, breathing hard, stroking the keys, and then she shut the lid and got up. She felt full of light, as if her heart had opened and let in the sun as she played. She pulled the sheet music out of the piano stool and hummed along as she read different pieces. She would have danced had her hip been better. She could still play, and there was nothing to fear from the piano. In fact, quite the opposite; it had evoked memories of her mother that felt warm and loving.

She hugged the music to her, closed her eyes and sank into her armchair. She tried to conjure an image of her mother to go with the feelings, but she couldn't. The sunny feeling left, leaving her instead with an ache of longing. She sighed, a tear slipping down her cheek.

And then a fuzzy image appeared at the edges of her consciousness. A young man cowering against a wall, hands held up in front of his face, whimpering like a wounded animal. Ella, terrified, balled her hands into fists and shook her head, and it was gone. He was gone. She had no idea who or where he was, nor how he related to her. She opened her eyes, took a deep breath and stood, looking at herself in the mirror above the mantelpiece. Or rather, she looked over her own shoulder into the room behind her, with its comfy old furniture and slightly mismatched fabrics, as if expecting to see something there. Was this man the thing she was too frightened to remember? Was there something about him that was too painful to endure? Was he somehow linked with her mother, or with her piano playing? She didn't dare allow herself to think about it anymore. She was convinced that this was something she would rather not remember.

Dr Myers still visited every three or four days to check on her hip and her arm, but more importantly, to see if she had remembered any more. She gave little snippets and knew she disappointed him. Ella was aware he was only trying to be kind and do his job, but his manner was so irritating.

'I was wondering, Ella, if I could write up your case for a journal – I haven't come across a case of amnesia quite like yours before.'

'What do you mean, quite like mine?'

The doctor raised his eyebrows and looked into the distance, pursing his lips. Ella waited. Eventually, he looked at her again and said, 'I haven't known the memory to take so long to come back. I suspect it may be related to – that is to say, you no doubt witnessed a great many unpleasant events in the war.' He passed his hat from hand to hand, turning it in a circle.

It was Ella's turn to pause. She looked at him through narrowed eyes. 'So you're saying you think that apart from the accident, there's some terrible event in the past that is preventing me from remembering?'

'Dr Freud believed that unwanted memories could be suppressed to enable the patient to function in the real world.'

Ella, who had been sitting on the sofa, pushed herself up and stood almost toe to toe with Dr Myers.

'I am not a mental patient!'

He took a step back and held up a hand. 'I am not for one moment implying that you are, only that there may be some mental mechanism going on here that–'

'That's quite enough thank you, Doctor. I think you can see yourself out. Good day.'

Ella turned away, arms crossed, jaw clenched. She was still standing like that when Sheila came in a few minutes later.

'Ella – I saw Dr Myers leave. Whatever's the matter?'

Ella relayed the conversation. Sheila nodded, looking thoughtful, but said nothing.

'God, Sheila – you don't agree with him, do you?' She clenched her fists. 'Say it now, let's get it out in the open.'

Sheila closed her eyes momentarily and then said, 'Calm down, Ella. Of course I don't think you're mad, but–'

'But what? Not mad but insane? Not mad but crazy as a loon?' Ella was shouting.

'If you'd let me finish,' said Sheila, pulling herself up to her full height, 'I was going to say that there are a lot of people who came back from the war wanting to forget what they'd seen, and that maybe, since you had that knock on the head anyway, your mind is letting you remember more slowly, when you can deal with the memories.'

Ella looked at her, the anger draining away. She sank onto the sofa again, looking at her hands clasping each other in her lap. 'I'm sorry, Sheila. It's just that he hit a nerve. I am worried about what I'll remember, but also that I won't remember it all. That doesn't make any sense, I know.' She smiled and shrugged. 'I wonder if I might be hampering my own recovery. I feel so confused.'

Sheila sat next to her and took her hand. 'Ella, you are one of the bravest people I know. You can face up to whatever lies in your past. And you've got me beside you. I'm quite brave too, and I'm also a good listener.'

Ella squeezed her hand. 'Thank you. And now I'm afraid I sent Dr Myers off without asking him for a sleeping draught.'

'Still not sleeping well?'

Ella sighed. 'Not so well, and I want to be knocked out so I don't dream.'

Later, with Sheila out in the village searching for something interesting for dinner, Ella telephoned Andrew to have a chat. He was at work, so couldn't talk for long, but he did tell her that they were all looking forward to their weekend with her and Sheila. Then she turned the wireless on, tuned in to the *Light Programme* and listened for a while to the Grenadier Guards Full Regimental Band, but she found the music irritating — pompous and somehow overdone, as if each instrument vied for supremacy rather than creating a harmonious whole. Switching the radio off, she glanced at the piano, standing by the French doors in pride of place in the large sitting room. There had been a silk cloth and photographs displayed on it when she first came home, she now remembered, but the pictures had since disappeared, no doubt hidden away by Andrew who took Dr Myers' word as law, and put away anything that might remind her of the past too soon or distress her. She limped round the room from chair to piano to fireplace, round and round, letting her fingers glide over silk and polished wood and brocade.

She opened the French doors and stepped into the side garden, taking deep lungfuls of air and stretching her back, looking up at the treetops. The rain had finally ceased, leaving drops sparkling on the leaves in the wan sunlight. Something moved in the periphery of her vision and, lowering her gaze, she spied Sheila making her way back from the village, swinging her string bag in one hand. The lane wound between overgrown hedges and fields of black-and-white cows grazing. She'd been told they were her fields, although not her cows. The pasture was rented to Arthur Ashton, the farmer who was generous with his butter, and who now, Ella saw, had caught up with Sheila and was offering her something. Sheila smiled and tucked a small package into her bag, but Arthur didn't leave, he fell into step with her, calling his dog to heel, hands in his pockets.

Sheila lifted her head and Ella drew back inside, not wanting to be caught witnessing what seemed to be an intimate moment. By the time Sheila reached the front door and let herself in, calling a cheery farewell to Arthur, Ella was mending a pair of stockings with great concentration.

'Liver today,' Sheila announced as she came into the room. 'Not my favourite, but at least it's a change.'

Ella looked up and smiled. 'Lovely,' she said. 'What news from the village?'

'Oh, nothing really. It's such a quiet place. But Mr Ashton gave me some more eggs and – oh, heaven! – a bit of cheese.'

'He's very generous all of a sudden.'

Sheila blushed. 'He's very kind. He was wounded in the war, you know. Took a load of shrapnel in the leg and stomach in '40 and was invalided out. He needn't have gone at all, of course, being a farmer, but he wanted to do his bit.'

Ella noted the attempt to change the topic, but she wasn't having any of it. 'Is he married?'

Sheila looked away and took great care in straightening the silk cloth on the piano.

'His wife died in childbirth, the baby too.'

'How sad. He must be lonely.'

'I don't think he has time to be lonely, running the farm on his own. He's very busy.'

'It doesn't matter how busy one is, one can always be lonely,' Ella said.

'But you're not lonely, are you, dear one? You've got me and Dr Myers, and Andrew is coming this weekend with Sophie and the children.' Sheila took a deep breath. 'I'll have to try and get some decent food for their visit, I'm sure they won't want to eat potatoes and cabbage all weekend.'

'They'll eat what they're given and be grateful, as I am. But if Mr Ashton wanted to give us a nice bit of lamb for Sunday lunch, we wouldn't say no.'

'I don't think he keeps sheep,' said Sheila, and then looked at Ella who was laughing.

'You're making fun of me!'

'No, dear, I'd never do that. But I do think he might be sweet on you, and maybe you are on him too. I'm right, aren't I?'

Sheila's blush reappeared. 'None of your business.' She laughed. 'I'm going to start lunch.'

Ella knew that this was a habit of Sheila's, this changing of the subject when she felt uncomfortable. And the knowing of it gave her a sense of deep satisfaction; there were things she remembered that she didn't have to work at, and that she wasn't afraid of. Sheila was not only a good friend, but a safe place. They could talk about anything, but Sheila would never push. And every day in their general conversation, Ella was remembering more; snippets of a walking holiday they'd taken together in the Lake District, a day here, a day there, a vision, a word. And she was looking forward to talking to Andrew about their childhood now that she remembered some of it. Perhaps he would tell her more when he came at the weekend.

She made her way slowly to the kitchen.

'What are you doing here? You should be resting,' said Sheila, wiping flour off her cheek with the back of her hand. 'I'm making a flan seeing as we've got eggs,' she added, gesturing at the ingredients laid out on the table.

'Fabulous, that'll be a nice change.'

'But really, you should be sitting with your feet up, be off with you.'

'I can't bear it. All I do is sit. I haven't been out of the house for months.'

'You haven't been here for months – you've only been home three weeks, as well you know, so stop exaggerating. At least sit here.' Sheila pulled a kitchen chair out for her, and Ella sank into it and put her elbows on the table.

'I hate being a patient,' she said. 'Now I know what all those poor people were going through when we were nursing them. Days, weeks, months of boredom. Let's make Andrew take us out in his car this weekend.'

Sheila rubbed the butter into the flour. 'That sounds nice, but not too far, we don't want you relapsing.'

'Oh, for goodness' sake! I don't think there's much chance of that. I'll sit in the car, and then sit in a pub and look at their wallpaper instead of ours, and then we'll come home. I'll go mad if I look at these four walls any longer though. I'll start ranting and dribbling and giving you a hard time.'

The whimpering man she'd sensed after she'd been playing the piano crashed into her head again making Ella gasp. Before he screamed he'd ranted, and before he'd ranted he'd cowered, looking terrified, his hands in front of his face as he scrabbled into a corner.

The colour drained from Ella's face and she clutched the edge of the table.

'What's the matter?' asked Sheila, brushing the flour off her hands and taking Ella's in her own.

'A man, so damaged.' She shook her head. 'I don't want to think about him. I don't know who he was, but he won't leave me alone. When I close my eyes, he's there, haunting me, wanting something from me, but I don't know what. I think he was a young soldier, although I don't see his face, just a mouth and an awful sense of fear. He is so afraid.'

Sheila chewed her bottom lip and took a deep breath.

'What is it, come on, out with it.'

'You haven't got very far in your journals, have you? Still reading the first one?' asked Sheila.

'Yes, you know that.'

'Well, you'll know soon enough if you keep reading.'

'Tell me now, please. What do you know?'

Tears welled in Sheila's eyes and she brushed them away, smearing flour. 'We saw some awful sights, Ella. We were in France and Belgium after D-Day. Some of the soldiers were wounded beyond recognition, and lots of them died. But you must remember that we saved many more, that we helped them back to health, or at least got them well enough so they could be evacuated home to England and recuperate here. Try to remind yourself of that when he appears.'

'Yes,' said Ella, 'all right.' But she knew he wouldn't leave easily, that he was there for a reason and wouldn't be going anywhere until she worked it out. She thought of her diaries, sitting in the bureau, waiting until she got them out. Her heart skipped a beat and her fingers curled, recoiling from the thought of the words and memories held within the notebooks.

# 8

Ella lay in bed, the covers pulled up to her chin. There was ice on the windows and she wanted to stay where she was, cosy and warm. It was going to be a busy day — Andrew and the family were arriving later, and there was shopping to be done and beds to be made up. She'd have to get the carpet sweeper out and give the sitting room a going-over, and Sheila was talking about getting the dining room aired and a fire lit in there as there wouldn't be room for them all to eat around the kitchen table.

She'd been to Dr Myers' hospital the day before to have the plaster off her arm. He hadn't said anything about the last time they'd met, when she'd ordered him out of her house, and she was too embarrassed to bring it up. She felt awkward, but he behaved as if nothing had happened. He was satisfied with how her arm had healed, but she was shocked at how her forearm looked as the binding was removed; raw, limpid and damp, as if it had spent the past weeks under water. And it smelled terrible. She looked away as Dr Myers bent the wrist this way and that and asked if she could do it without his help, which she demonstrated for him. Then she pulled the sleeve of her cardigan over it quickly, letting her hand rest in her lap while Dr Myers asked questions about her past. She told him about the scenes from her childhood that she recalled, and a memory of her first days as a student.

'That's wonderful,' he said and wrote a note in her file.

She looked at him. She couldn't bring herself to like him even though he had saved her life. If he hadn't taken her in, she might have died in the ditch, if not from her injuries, then from hypothermia. He was a good man and a caring doctor. But he had all but accused her of being insane.

Sheila knocked and came in with a cup of tea, turning Ella's thoughts from Dr Myers to the day ahead.

'The rain's stopped, so how about we rug up and get into the village before all the best meat has gone and we have to feed Andrew and Sophie tripe all weekend?'

Ella screwed her face up at the thought. Sheila had made boiled tripe the night before, and try as she had to disguise the taste, there was no good way to cook tripe, as far as Ella was concerned.

'I'll be ready before you can say "boil me no tripe",' said Ella, and swung her legs out of the bed, gasping at the cold. As she washed and dressed, she noticed a feeling of apprehension growing in her stomach; who would she meet in the village, what would they know about her? She looked in the mirror and told herself to be brave. Hadn't Arthur Ashton said that she'd kept herself to herself before the accident? Surely she couldn't have annoyed anyone then, or made enemies. Pulling her shoulders back, she nodded encouragement to herself.

Even in her thickest woollen coat, scarf and hat, Ella felt the wind whistling through her as, arm in arm, the two friends battled into the wind, heads down. The clouds were so heavy-looking that Ella wondered if they were in for more snow, and hoped that Andrew didn't have to cancel the visit because of the weather.

'First stop, the butcher,' said Sheila as they reached the village. Ella lifted her head long enough to look at the few shops and small cottages that made up Little Worthy. It was an attractive street, the front gardens tidy although there wasn't much growing in this weather.

'Morning, Miss Marchmont,' said the butcher as they entered his shop.

He stood behind his butcher's block in a clean apron. The shelves were half filled with sausages, tripe, liver, chops and some fatty-looking bits of steak. The floor had just been swept and the smell of the fresh sawdust that had been put down reminded Ella of pine forests, although she had no idea where or when she'd been in one.

'Morning, Mr Dodson. This is Mrs Elkington – I don't know if you know each other?' She looked from the butcher to Ella and back again.

'I can't say as we do,' he said. 'You used to have your food delivered. My apprentice cycled it round to your house. Nice to meet you, Mrs Elkington. I hear you've been under the weather. I trust you're feeling better?'

'Thank you, yes,' said Ella.

'We have guests this weekend. Any chance of a roast?' asked Sheila.

He laughed. 'Oh, you're always one for a joke, aren't you, Miss Marchmont? I'll tell you what I have got, and that's some nice stewing steak. Pop some suet dumplings in and you've got a meal fit for a king, I reckon.'

Sheila didn't look overly impressed. 'Mmm, well if that's the best you can do, we'll take it. And some kidneys.'

Mr Dodson produced the meat from beneath the counter with a flourish and wrapped it and the kidneys in paper. Sheila put it in her bag, paid, had their ration books stamped, and said goodbye.

Out on the street, she turned to Ella. 'I'm glad I brought you with me – he's never given me anything from under the counter before, you must have taken his fancy.'

Ella smiled, but was much more taken up with what he'd said about her having her food delivered. Had she been a hermit, never venturing into the village, was that why she had no memory of the place or the people? Or had she driven over to Hambleford to do most of her shopping, being a bigger town with more available perhaps?

'We'll need as many vegetables as we can carry to go with this or it will never feed us all,' Sheila said, seeming not to notice Ella's lack of response.

On the way home they had the wind at their backs, nudging them along. Their string bags were misshapen with bread, leeks, carrots, parsnips, Brussels sprouts and potatoes. Sheila was happy, talking about the feast she'd be able to cook up with such bounty. Ella was still mulling over her lack of recognition of any of the people they'd encountered. The woman in the greengrocer had been very friendly, and said that she knew Ella from way back, but Ella could recall nothing about her at all.

She did, however, feel a sense of satisfaction at having made her first trip to the village. She had been nervous about it, but she'd survived. If the worst she'd learned was that she had been a bit of a hermit, then maybe that wasn't so bad. She was still discomfited about not knowing more about how she'd lived her life after the war though. Why had she kept herself to herself? Why hadn't she stayed in nursing? Surely there were hospitals nearby that were crying out for experienced staff, but she sensed that she hadn't worked in any of them. And hadn't Dr Myers said something about Mr Attlee bringing in a national health system of some sort soon – surely she would have had an opinion about that?

'What do you know about this health system that's being talked about?' she asked as they were putting the shopping away in the larder.

Sheila paused, wiped her hands on a tea towel, and said, 'It's a marvellous idea. Free health care for all. No more having to collect money from patients who don't want to, or can't pay. I did a bit of district nursing after I was demobbed, and I hated that part of it. Doing a dressing for someone and then asking for a shilling. It was awful. I think a national health scheme is a very good idea.'

'Will you go back into nursing then?'

'I might. Although it's not here yet. Mr Attlee and that Bevan chap are pushing hard, but there are people who say it will be too expensive, or that it won't work. We'll just have to wait and see.'

'I think I might find a job when I can remember what I'm meant to do.' She was serious, but Sheila snorted with laughter.

'What's so funny?'

'I'm sorry, darling. It was just the way you said it. Get a job when you can remember what you have to do. Do you really not recall what we did day to day?'

Ella sighed. 'Not really. Bits and pieces, I suppose, but I couldn't go into an interview and speak with any confidence about what I did as a nurse, or even where.'

'I'm sure it'll all come back when you read your diaries.'

Ella didn't say that was what she was afraid of. That while she might enjoy learning about what she did as a nurse, she was aware that there was also grief and horror waiting for her in their pages.

Andrew, Sophie, Laura and Billie arrived just after six that evening, the children spilling out of the car eager to stretch and run after having to sit still for the drive. Sheila stayed in the kitchen while Ella went out to meet them.

She held her hands out to Sophie who took them and looked into her eyes.

'How are you, Ella?' she asked. 'I must say, you look very well.'

'I am,' Ella agreed, trying desperately to find a memory of her comely sister-in-law and drag it up from the depths. She swept her eyes over the dark hair in its sophisticated chignon, thinking how much more attractive it was than the victory roll that so many women favoured, and which neither she nor Sheila could master. Her eyes were deep-blue, her skin pale. Ella thought she must be Irish. 'How was the drive?'

Andrew came and gave her a peck on the cheek and said, 'Not bad. A bit of a hold-up getting out of town, but otherwise a clear run.'

He called to the children, running around the lawn. 'Billie, Laura, come and say hello to Aunt Ella.'

Billie barrelled up, almost knocking Ella off her feet. 'Auntie Ella, hello,' he said, and paused before putting out a hand for her to shake.

'I expect more than a handshake, young man.' Ella laughed and pulled him into a hug. Then she held him away from her and said, 'You look exactly like you did in that lovely picture you sent me.' Then she hugged him close again.

In reality, Ella hadn't remembered his face, but she

remembered the feel of him in her arms, the solid bulk of him, his energy, the way he squirmed to be let go. She released him, straightened up and watched him run to his mother and bury his face in her skirt.

Then she turned and looked into the solemn eyes of her niece who had been watching them.

'Hello, Auntie Ella,' she said. Ella looked at her and had a flash of recognition; Laura sitting beside her on the piano stool, listening as she played.

'Can I have a hug with you too?' she asked, and Laura stepped in and held her tightly round the waist.

'You always did have a special bond,' said Sophie, smiling. 'She's missed you.'

'And I've missed you all,' said Ella, and although she couldn't have said exactly what it was she missed, she knew it was true.

Sheila joined them in the sitting room when they'd put their cases in their rooms. Andrew poured sherry, and they chatted about what they'd been doing since last he was there. Ella thought it was all so normal, friends getting together to catch up. Except they could all remember their last meeting and she couldn't. Even Sheila had seen them one time recently when she'd been to their house to discuss living with Ella. She decided that she could either worry about not remembering, or she could spend her time getting to know her sister-in-law and nephew and niece all over again, which seemed like a much better use of the weekend.

They ate early so that the children wouldn't be too late to bed. Sheila's dinner was much appreciated, especially when she produced an egg custard for pudding. When Sophie came down from putting the children to bed, Andrew went up to give them a goodnight kiss, and came back with a request — would Auntie Ella read them a story?

Ella was overcome.

'Of course,' she said, and ran up the stairs.

They were on camp beds in the box room, but Sheila had made sure they had plenty of blankets, and all Ella could see of them were the tops of their heads and their excited eyes. Billie nodded towards the book on the floor next to his bed.

'*Mistress Masham's Repose*,' read Ella. 'This looks interesting. Where have you got up to?'

'We've finished it, Mummy reads it to us, but it's our favourite, so we can start again,' said a muffled little voice from under the blankets.

'All right then, here we go,' said Ella, and opened the book.

She read until her hands were freezing and her throat was dry. Billie had fallen asleep within minutes, but every time she suggested stopping, Laura pleaded for one more page. Eventually, she tousled her hair, kissed her goodnight and promised to read again the next night.

All talk ceased as she entered the sitting room and she realised that they'd been talking about her. Well, she thought, it was only to be expected really. She stood in front of the fire warming her hands, her back to everyone.

'Thank you for reading to them,' said Sophie.

Ella turned and smiled. 'They're delightful children, and although I don't remember them fully, there are snippets of memories here and there. Laura's cheeky grin, Billie's energy. There's a familiarity about you, too, Sophie, although no specifics. I'm so glad you all came, but now you can stop talking about me.'

Andrew looked embarrassed, jiggling the coins in his pockets. Sophie smiled apologetically and Sheila fussed with her drink.

After that the weekend went well. In spite of the weather, which remained cold and wet, they managed to go fishing for minnows in the swollen stream, but most of the time they were confined to the house, playing games and talking.

The best bit of the weekend as far as Ella was concerned had been when Laura asked her to play something on the piano.

'Let's play a duet,' she said, suddenly remembering teaching her niece some simple melodies.

Laura beamed with pride as they played 'Chopsticks' and 'Twinkle, Twinkle, Little Star', and everyone had clapped. Then Billie wanted a turn, and they all tried to keep straight faces as the little three-year-old took his seat with gravity and played a few discordant bars of a tune he said he'd made up especially for Auntie Ella.

'You taught them well,' said Sophie, smiling.

Ella looked at her and winked. 'Great talents, both of them,' she said, and hid her laugh behind her hand. No doubt Billie would get better.

By the time they left on Sunday afternoon Ella was exhausted.

She and Sheila waved them off and then went into the sitting room and flopped onto the sofa.

'How do parents do it, having children around all the time?' asked Sheila.

'I have no idea. And it's not even as if they're difficult children. They have lovely manners and don't ask too much, but just having them around seems to suck the energy out of me.'

'Mind you, it might not just have been the children – we have been living a very quiet life here, haven't we?'

Ella was reminded of her thoughts on the way home from the village on Friday; how quiet had her life been after the war? She shook her head and picked up the conversation from Friday.

'Why did you stop nursing – it can't have been just because you had to ask for the money, surely?'

Sheila stared into the fire, as if looking for answers in the flames. She lit a cigarette, blew the smoke towards the ceiling and leant her head against the back of the sofa.

'My heart wasn't in it anymore, I suppose. It was all very well going round and dressing sores and checking on medicines, taking blood pressures and temperatures, and the patients were all lovely and very grateful, but – well, it didn't feel like I was saving lives. Anyone could have done what I was doing really. It felt like a waste of all the training and experience I'd had.'

'It wasn't exciting like nursing in the war, is that what you're saying?'

Sheila sighed. 'Exactly. What we did was so vitally important. We ran on adrenaline, casualties brought in from the front at all times of the day and night. Sometimes we didn't sleep for thirty-six hours straight, but we didn't care. We were saving lives. It just wasn't the same pedalling around Solihull, seeing Mr Smith for his asthma and Mrs Jones for her sore leg, checking on Mrs Brown's pregnancy. I was bored. I think the work we did in the war has spoiled me for civilian nursing.'

Ella thought about that. She still couldn't remember anything about the war or what she did in it, for which she was, at this moment, quite grateful.

# 9

March gave way to April and the rain finally gave way to sun. On the first dry day Ella and Sheila pulled on their wellingtons and took to the fields. As they squelched their way towards the swollen pond, Mr Ashton appeared from the other direction.

'Did you tell him we were coming?' asked Ella under her breath.

'No, of course not,' said Sheila, blushing.

'Aha, so I was right – you do like him.' Ella smiled. 'I'm sure you could do a lot worse.'

Sheila started denying all charges, but Ella ignored her and waved at the farmer.

'Good morning, Mr Ashton. You must be loving the sunny weather.'

'Morning, ladies. Yes, it's a good thing for me and my cows.' He looked over his shoulder at the black-and-white cows in the next field. 'They don't like swimming around in mud, and a couple of them have developed foot rot in all the rain. Hopefully now they'll start to come good.'

'How romantic,' said Ella under her breath so that only

Sheila heard her. Her friend elbowed her in the ribs and told her to shut up.

'How are you feeling, Mrs Elkington – quite recovered?' he asked.

'Yes, thank you. Although I tire easily. In fact, I think I'll make my way back now.' She turned to her friend. 'Sorry, Sheila, I know you wanted a longer walk.' She paused, as if the thought had just occurred to her. 'I say, Mr Ashton, I don't suppose you'd have a few minutes to accompany Miss Marchmont, would you?'

'Of course.' He turned to Sheila. 'We could go up to the old mill. It'll look nice in this light.' And then he looked at Ella again. 'Will you be all right on your own?'

'Perfectly. It isn't far and I'll take it slowly.'

'Well, in that case,' he said, and offered Sheila his arm.

Sheila narrowed her eyes at Ella, but took his arm. Ella smiled and turned to go back to the house.

Halfway across the field she looked back. Sheila and Arthur Ashton were laughing at some shared joke, and Ella congratulated herself.

She didn't go straight back to the house, it was too nice a day, and her hip was feeling good, so she kept walking, and was soon in the village. As she was standing in the street deciding whether to go to the baker or the butcher first, a young man walked towards her leaning heavily on a stick. As he neared he stared straight at her, studying her face. Ella took a step back.

'Nurse? Nurse Elkington, is that you?' He had the raspy voice of a heavy smoker, although he looked quite young.

She stared back at him, confused, and then she remembered her training – here was a man who knew she was a nurse, after all – and smiled.

'Yes, I'm Ella Elkington,' she said, 'but I'm afraid...'

'Oh, I don't expect you to remember me, but I'd recognise you anywhere. February '43. St Thomas's Hospital. You nursed me after I got transferred back from North Africa. You and your bloody cronies have got a lot to answer for if you ask me.'

'I beg your pardon?' Ella was confused.

'So you bloody well should. See this?' He tapped his stick against his leg making a hollow, tinny sound. 'I came back from Africa with a bullet in my leg. Then you lot put me under and took it out and gave me gangrene.' He pointed at her with his stick and Ella recoiled, thinking he was going to hit her. 'I'd still have my leg if it wasn't for you and your doctor friends. I'd have a job and a girl. Now what have I got?'

He paused, and Ella wondered if he was waiting for her to guess, but then he continued.

'Nothing, that's what, and I've had to come to this godforsaken hole to live with my parents.' He spat on the pavement and wiped his mouth with the back of his hand.

'I'm sorry,' said Ella again. 'I really am.'

'Not sorry enough.' He glared at her, unmoving. 'What are you going to do about it?'

Ella had the impression that she was looking at him through thick glass, his face distorting. She felt giddy, and sank onto the low wall outside the bakery to catch her breath.

A woman came out of the shop.

'Are you all right, love?' she asked Ella.

'Oh, that's right, ask if she's all right. Don't worry about me. I fought for this country, and what thanks do I get, what concern do I get, eh?'

'Fred, go home,' said the woman. 'Enough is enough.'

He grunted, and with one more gob of spit at Ella's feet, turned and limped heavily away.

The women watched his slow progress for a few moments.

'His parents moved in next to us a couple of years ago, from Southampton, and now he's there too,' she explained. 'Don't take any notice of him,' said the woman, looking at Ella.

'Right,' was all she could say.

'Do you live around here? Can I help you home?'

'Ella Elkington, Bamford House.' She put a hand out and the woman shook it.

'Maisie Spencer. Pleased to meet you. Didn't you have an accident recently?'

'Yes, but all better now. Thank you for your help, but I really should be getting back.'

'Well, if you're sure you don't need any help...'

'I'll be fine, thank you again. Goodbye.' Ella started walking away on legs that felt weak. That she didn't remember Fred didn't surprise her, but his anger did. What had they done to him?

At the house, Ella went to the bureau and pulled out the second journal. 1939–1944. She sat on the sofa, her hands trembling. She was still afraid of what she might find in these pages. Or who. She took a deep breath and she forced herself to start reading. She learned that she was employed as a staff nurse at St Thomas's after she'd finished her training there, and that soon after the start of the war, the patients were evacuated to hospitals west of London to make way for the war casualties that were expected. The war casualties didn't come. Beds remained empty, staff wandered around chatting, straightening a sheet here and there, looking towards the skies for the planes that would come and drop bombs. They waited for the wounded who would then be rushed to their hospital in ambulances with red crosses on their roofs. There, the surgeons would put them together again and they would be nursed back to health on their wards under their expert care. After some weeks, civilians once again filled the beds. The routine of the hospital returned with the usual howls of pain, sighs of relief, murmurs of death and shrieks of life beginning.

Ella stopped reading and wondered how it had felt to be there. Had she been afraid of falling bombs, tumbling buildings, raging fires, hissing gas leaks? She never mentioned it in her diary, so it appeared not, but surely one couldn't live in the shadow of war and not fear that this might be your last breakfast, your last conversation with a loved one, last kiss?

'Cooee, I'm home,' called Sheila.

Ella closed the journal and hid it behind a cushion as Sheila came in. She didn't want to talk about what she'd been reading.

'Nice walk?' she asked.

'Lovely, thank you. Although I could murder you. You weren't very subtle, you know.'

'Sorry.'

Sheila smiled. 'It's fine, no need to apologise. Arthur's invited us to dinner tomorrow night. His cousin's going to be there too. He's a solicitor with offices all over the place.'

'I don't care if he's got offices in Buckingham Palace as long as his cousin's killing the fatted calf on our behalf.'

Sheila sighed. 'Meat and lots of it. That would be nice. Anyway, what have you been up to?'

Ella told her about her encounter with Fred in the village.

'How awful for you.'

'Yes, but how much more awful for him. Do you remember him?'

Sheila thought for a moment. 'Fred's quite a common name, you know. And bullets in the leg weren't unusual injuries, often with more bullets or shrapnel in several other places too.' She sighed. 'If he was bad enough to be evacuated back here from North Africa, he would have been pretty well shot up. We were forever looking after soldiers, but none of them developed gangrene in our hospital. I should imagine he already had it and no one had told him, so when they took his leg off it was a terrible shock.'

'I'll say. It's ruined his life.'

'Ella, don't blame yourself. It was war that ruined his life, not you. We always did our absolute best for those boys, but we weren't magicians.'

Ella pursed her lips and looked at the carpet, thinking about what her friend had said. Was she right? She wanted to believe her, to believe that her contribution had saved lives, or made some men's final hours bearable. She knew she couldn't make everything better for all those whose lives had been devastated, but she wanted to do something for Fred in spite of his rudeness. The question was, what?

The following evening a car pulled up in front of the house and a tall, well-built man got out and came to the door.

'Good evening,' he said as Sheila opened it. 'David Ashton at your service. Arthur suggested I motor over and pick you up rather than let you walk across the marshy fields.'

'How very thoughtful. I'm Sheila Marchmont, and this,' she gestured to Ella who was coming down the stairs, 'is Ella Elkington.'

David Ashton gave a curt bow and a warm smile.

'Lovely to meet you, and if you're both ready, shall we?' He moved aside and ushered them towards his car sitting in the drive.

It was a cool evening. Arthur greeted them at the door and welcomed them into the parlour with its roaring fire and comfortable sofas. His sister had prepared the meal, he admitted, and left it cooking in the oven.

'She comes in every day. I'm sure she thinks I'd starve if not for her. All I've got to do tonight is throw the Yorkshire pudding in at the last minute. She trusted me to do that, at least,' he said.

And what a dinner it was. Ella was overjoyed to see that he literally had killed the fatted calf, and they had a great joint of beef with all the trimmings.

'How on earth do you hide whole herds of beef cattle from the Food Ministry?' she asked.

Arthur tapped the side of his nose, but then said, 'Every now and then the temptation to keep a bit back gets too much, to be honest. I see what's available in the butchers' shops around here, and it makes me so angry; obviously the best cuts are going to the fancy restaurants or the city folk, leaving the likes of you and me with the worst bits – fatty, tough chops and offal. Well, I don't think that's fair. Call me what you like, I'll keep doing it, just a bit here and there, and only for special occasions, of course.' He had reddened as he spoke, and not looked at his cousin, who was examining his cutlery.

Ella watched him for a moment. 'You don't agree with Arthur's occasional little – what even is it – thievery? Is he stealing from the War Office?'

David put down his fork, turned to her and smiled. 'I can't say I wholeheartedly approve, but then again, I ate it. I'm a bit of a hypocrite when it comes to my stomach. And he really doesn't do it very often. Sometimes a small parcel to his sister and her children for a little treat, but that's it.'

'Well, I can't remember the last time I ate like this,' she said as she finished her last mouthful and sat back, hands folded over her full stomach.

Sheila snorted with laughter and Ella looked at her in alarm. 'Are you all right?' asked Arthur.

Sheila replied, 'Sorry. Very rude of me.'

And then it dawned on Ella why her friend was laughing, and she got a fit of the giggles. The men raised their eyebrows at each other and waited patiently for an explanation. When Ella could talk again, she said, 'In the accident I lost my memory completely, so of course I can't remember eating such a good meal. I can hardly remember my own name!'

David and Arthur laughed, and then David said, 'But we've been chatting all evening and I would never have known.'

'That's kind of you to say so. My memory is coming back, but it's patchy. And I do remember things that have happened since the accident, fortunately.'

They withdrew to the parlour after the meal and played a few hands of bridge, Arthur and Sheila partnering against David and Ella.

'You seem to have a very good memory for cards,' said David as they won the rubber. He smiled at her and held her gaze for an extra heartbeat. Ella felt herself blush.

At the end of the evening David offered them a lift home. As they left, Arthur pressed a package into Sheila's hands, and said, 'Don't tell the ration office.'

Sheila smiled. 'What ration office?'

At Ella's door, David lingered. Sheila left them, claiming overwhelming tiredness.

'I enjoyed tonight,' said David, taking Ella's hand. 'I wonder if you might come to the farmers' dance with me in Hambleford next Saturday?'

Ella felt dismayed at the quickening of her heart. Her head told her that she needed to know more about her relationship with Charles before she agreed to anything with David, but when he looked at her with those kind eyes, and she felt the pressure of his hand on hers, the warmth of his skin, she knew that her heart wasn't listening to her head, that she wanted to spend more time with him, get to know him.

'If you'd rather not—'

'No, it's not that.' She took a breath and looked into his eyes again. 'I should like that, David.'

He smiled. 'Marvellous. I'll pick you up at seven.'

As he drove away, Ella thought that it was about time she learned more about her and Charles. She knew from something that Sheila had let slip that Charles had died fairly early on in the war, but when she realised what she'd said, for once her friend was strangely reticent and would say no more, claiming that Ella needed to remember him in her own time. Now she wondered if she'd had other admirers since, and whether she had loved any of them. She couldn't recall how it felt to love someone, even Charles, and was sad to have forgotten that experience.

She went in, made a cup of tea, and sat on the sofa with her first diary, scanning it for references to Charles. It wasn't long before she found what she was looking for.

*7th March 1938*
*The best birthday present I could have wished for! I am being sent to Orthopaedics at last. Charles Elkington's domain. I must make sure I am the best student nurse he's ever encountered, as well as the prettiest!*
*I'll be sad to leave my lads on Male Chest. Apart from old Humphrey who complains about everything and seems to have been there for months, they're all such cheery souls, and grateful for everything we do for them. And Sister Keenan is the best I've had. She's strict, but not frightening in the way most of the others are.*

Ella put the notebook down and closed her eyes. She had an image of a large, bright ward, fifteen or so beds down each side, a neat, clean man in each one. The Male Chest Ward. Old Humphrey was in a bed near the door, near the nurse's desk, and she could see him there, watching everything that went on with beady, red-rimmed eyes. She couldn't remember exactly what he was there for, only that he was always on the lookout for someone getting more attention than him, or more food, a warmer smile, an extra cigarette (they weren't meant to smoke, it was a chest ward, after all). And then he'd complain about it, long and loud until one of the other patients told him to shut his trap, and then he'd complain about that.

Ella opened her eyes again and looked back at the journal. How shallow she'd been. It wasn't only what she'd written about being the best nurse and the prettiest, although that did make her shudder, it was the patronising way she called the patients 'her lads', when in all likelihood they were all older than her.

She thought back to the entry she'd first read, about how Mr Hudson had treated his patients, and wondered if she'd fallen into the same trap, thinking of the patients as problems or diseases to be sorted into 'nice' and 'troublesome', instead of seeing them as people who were there because they were ill.

She sighed and turned back to the pages of her tiny, neat handwriting. There were mentions of Charles here and there, but for several weeks they only mentioned how caring he was, or how neat his stitching was, how the patients all thought he was the best and kindest doctor they'd ever had, and that she was concerned that he might not have noticed her at all. And then, on 8th June 1938, this;

*Charles Elkington has asked me to a dance! I'm all in a flap. What shall I wear? My last pair of stockings is so darned they look more like something you'd take to catch fish rather than elegant legwear, and all the ones in the shops are that awful American Tan, which looks so fake on 'British White' legs. I wonder if all American girls really are*

*that tanned. I hate them all if they are. Maeve has said that I can*
*borrow her pale-pink dress with the rosebuds on it. When I wore it to*
*the hospital Christmas dinner I received lots of compliments, so I'm*
*glad she doesn't need it the same night. Joan has offered to do my hair*
*– she's so good at a chignon, whereas when I try, it usually drops and*
*flops before I even get out the door.*
*I'm so excited I can hardly write!*
*I'm glad the ward's full and we're busy at the moment, otherwise the*
*next three days would drag interminably. As it is, we're rushed off our*
*feet all day long and hardly have time to breathe, let alone dream*
*about dancing with Elegant Elkington. Sheila says I've been pink-*
*cheeked ever since he asked. If it's true, I'm not surprised.*

Once again Ella put down the diary and let her head rest
against the sofa. She was feeling a tightness in her chest and felt
hot in spite of the fact that moments ago she'd felt chilly. She
realised that she was excited, and closed her eyes, trying to
dredge the scene out of the dim recesses of her memory.

It was the music she remembered first, the dance hall filled
with the enthusiastic strains of jazz trumpet and a big band. The
notes trilled up and down the octaves, making Ella's feet start
tapping even before they'd found a table and Charles had gone
to get the drinks. She'd immersed herself in the music, letting it
fill her body with its rhythm, so that when Charles put her gin
and lime in front of her, she'd jumped to her feet, taken his
hand, and led him onto the dance floor.

And then she remembered the feel of him, the firmness of
his arm around her, the smooth dryness of the hand that held
hers. She'd wanted that moment to last forever, not knowing or
trusting that it could get better, that one day she would know
that she truly belonged in his arms, and he in hers. On that
night of firsts, though, she knew none of that, and didn't want to
take any of it for granted. She felt as if she'd swallowed all the

stars in the sky and they were beating and pulsing inside her, making her shine, and lighting up all around her.

She opened her eyes. She was hugging herself and her cheeks were wet. But she felt happy, the happiness that comes from knowing that you've found love, that within those arms you'll always feel treasured.

She went to bed and dreamed of Charles.

# 10

For the next few days, whenever Sheila wasn't around, Ella delved into her diaries and relived her love affair with Charles. It wasn't that she didn't want Sheila to know what she was doing, just that it felt too intimate to share, even though her friend had lived alongside her while it was unfolding, knew every step of their courtship, and had been a witness at the wedding.

At the dance, Charles had admitted that he'd wanted to ask her out for a while, but that he had a rule about not socialising with the staff on the ward. It wasn't until she was about to be transferred again that he'd made his move.

He was a principled man, there was no doubt about that, but the traits that Ella most loved about him were his quick wit and his compassion. They were evident in everything he did; the jokes he shared with his patients and the hours he spent working to make them better. Nothing was too much trouble, nobody more important than the person he was with.

As she recalled more of their relationship, she began to feel his presence around the house, not in a ghostly way, she didn't believe in all that, but in the picture in the hall that she remembered him choosing and bringing home, although not to this house. It had hung in the bedroom in their flat in Kensington. She traced the outline of the country cottage and the cattle in the field and heard him telling her that one day they'd live in a house like that, far away from the clamour of the city. Her breath caught in her throat when she remembered that and she felt the sadness and injustice that he hadn't lived to share this house with her.

She found some of his books in the bookcase, and remembered him reading to her, poems by Wordsworth and Keats, his voice imbuing their words with such love that she almost believed that he'd written them for her.

By the following Saturday, Ella was totally in love with her husband, caught up in the intensity and ardour of their courtship, and didn't know how she was going to get through an evening with David, nor whether she even should; it felt almost like cheating. Fortunately, Arthur had invited Sheila to the dance too, so she wouldn't have to make polite conversation all night, but she wasn't sure she was really fit for anyone's company. All she wanted was to spend time with Charles, although she knew it probably wasn't healthy hiding away with a dead man. And yet she also knew that David deserved more, better, kinder. So on Saturday, she moved the diary out from under her pillow where she'd kept it all week, and put it away in the bureau. Then she went back to her bedroom and opened her window wide and stood breathing in the spring air, filling herself up with *Now*. The garden, thanks to Sheila's efforts, was looking lovely in the weak April sun. She'd removed the branches that had been blown down in the gusting winds and staked the daffodils which had been flattened but were somehow still flowering. Over by the hedge the azaleas were blooming in their hot pink finery, and in front of them, Sheila had prepared beds and planted vegetables. A cuckoo called in a tree nearby and a couple of starlings darted in and out of the trees, chasing each other in what Ella thought was the sheer exhilaration of spring. In the field beyond, the cows were swishing their tails as they grazed on the luscious grass.

'Are you coming down for breakfast?' called Sheila. 'We've got bacon,' she added, as if that would make Ella appear faster.

Ella dressed and joined her friend in the kitchen.

'So, what are you going to wear tonight?' asked Sheila as she served the food and put the teapot on the table.

'I haven't really given it a thought,' Ella said. She looked at the food, and was suddenly hungry.

'You haven't been yourself this week. I haven't wanted to pry, I know you need time with your memories.'

Ella smiled. 'I've been thinking about Charles.'

'I thought that might be it. Want to talk?'

Ella thought for a moment, and then shook her head. Sheila looked at her and nodded.

'Well then, I'm going to wear my navy dress with the pale-blue bow at the collar. After breakfast we might have to go through your wardrobe and see what you've got.'

Ella allowed herself to get caught up in Sheila's excitement, and found that it was contagious. They laughed like schoolgirls over the plain, make-do dresses in Ella's cupboard, and spent the afternoon at the sewing machine, tucking, draping, adding a bit of lace here and a new collar there. By teatime, Ella had the choice of three new dresses they'd created out of her old ones.

'I think I'll wear the pale pink with the lace collar,' she said, holding it up against herself, and thinking briefly of the pink rosebud dress she'd been wearing for the first dance with Charles before forcing the thought from her mind.

'Perfect,' said Sheila, and went off to run a bath.

At ten to seven, Sheila was sitting calmly drinking a sherry and checking her make-up in her compact mirror and Ella was pacing the sitting room listening for David's car. As the time approached for his arrival, she started towards the stairs.

'Where are you off to?' asked Sheila.

'I can't do this,' said Ella on the threshold, one hand at her throat, the other reaching for the bannister. She didn't want to betray the memory of Charles, and yet she knew that there was nothing to be gained from sitting at home grieving. When she heard the purr of the engine and the tyres on the gravel of the drive she only felt the confusion more. She didn't feel ready for anyone but Charles, didn't want to erase the newly found memory of him by going out with another man. And yet, she couldn't deny that she found David attractive, warmed to him more than she wanted to admit. She stood in the hall weaving her handkerchief in and out of her fingers.

'It'll be all right, you know,' said Sheila. 'It's only a dance, and Charles would be the first to tell you to go out and enjoy yourself. He wouldn't have wanted you to remain a widow all your life.'

Ella wished she knew that, that she didn't have to have other people fill in the blanks in her relationship, but she was also grateful that she had a friend like Sheila who could. It was all so frustrating.

Ella enjoyed the evening. As soon as they got into the car and started chatting, she found herself swept along by the mood and

David's easy friendliness. He was interesting company, a great raconteur, a good listener and a light-footed dancer. He swept Ella round the dance floor to tune after tune until she begged to sit one out and catch her breath.

'A drink?' he asked.

'Lovely,' she said, eyes widening as a bottle of champagne was delivered to their table.

She looked at the other dancers, young and old, the men uncomfortable in their Sunday suits, the women glad of a chance to dress up for a change. Arthur was gliding Sheila around the hall, holding her close.

'They look happy,' she said.

'Yes, they do. I know that he is quite keen on her. And good for him. He hasn't had anyone in his life since his wife died five years ago. It's time he found someone else, and Sheila seems like a good sort.'

Ella's hand started shaking and she spilt some champagne on her dress. She picked up a napkin and dabbed at the damp patch.

David said, 'I'm sorry. That was insensitive. Arthur told me you lost your husband in the war.'

Ella smiled, trying to breathe calmly. She couldn't say anything.

'Ready for another dance?' he asked, standing and holding out his hand.

Sheila and Arthur swirled close to them, Sheila leaning back in his arms, laughing. The look on Arthur's face was one of awe, as if he couldn't believe that such a gorgeous woman would be in his arms, laughing at something he'd said. Ella felt momentarily envious. She wanted someone to look at her like that. She wanted to be loved and admired, treated as a precious treasure. And in the next moment, she realised that she'd had that with Charles, and could have it again, if not with David, with someone else, and that Sheila had been right. Charles would have wanted her to be happy.

~

When they got back to Ella's house, she invited David and Arthur in for a nightcap.

'Better not,' said Arthur. 'I've got to be up at five for the milking.'

'Nonsense,' said Ella, feeling tipsy after all the champagne. 'We'll all get up and help.'

Sheila raised her eyebrows, and David smiled, but Arthur laughed, and said, 'You're on.'

Ella gulped, smiled, and poured the drinks.

'To milking!' she said, and took a sip of her brandy.

'Have you ever milked a cow before?' asked David.

'I don't think so, but then again, maybe I have. I might be an absolute wizard at it. How about you – get out of the office and onto the farm much?'

'Not nearly often enough. You could do with a hand, couldn't you, Arthur?'

Arthur nodded. 'I don't mind the outdoor work — it's doing the accounts that drives me mad, especially with all the information the government wants these days, what with rationing and all.'

Ella put a hand up to stop the conversation.

'I met a man recently who needs a job. Sheila, who was he? I think I've had too much to drink; I seem to be even more forgetful than usual.' She burst into a fit of giggling.

'Fred somebody, wasn't it? In the village.'

'That's right,' said Ella. 'Fred Somebody. Maybe he could do your books, Arthur.'

'Well, I can't pay much, but if he's capable, I'll give him a go. Send him over and we'll have a chat about it.'

'Thank you, Arthur. I will.'

The men rose to leave when they finished their drinks. Ella considered offering another, but she was suddenly tired. The thought of her bed waiting for her upstairs with its clean sheets and soft pillow was all too tempting. She saw them to the front door and waved them off, then went to help Sheila take the glasses into the kitchen.

'What a lovely evening,' said Sheila. 'Did you enjoy yourself?'

Ella leant against the table, the glasses still in her hands. 'Yes, I think I did,' she said.

Ella's alarm went off at four thirty in the morning. She groaned, turned it off and went back to sleep.

When she finally woke after nine, she had a hangover and felt guilty. She padded through to Sheila's room in bare feet and gently shook her awake.

'We missed the milking.'

Sheila stretched and rolled over, and then sat bolt upright.

'Oh, no! We promised. What will Arthur think?'

Ella shrugged. 'Shall I telephone him and apologise?'

'No, better than that. Why don't we find your Fred and take him round to meet Arthur as a sort of peace offering?'

'Good idea.'

Half an hour later, the two women were on their way into the village. Ella was glad the day wasn't too bright, given her headache.

'So, where does he live?' asked Sheila.

Ella thought for a moment. 'No idea,' she said. 'But if we can find out where Maisie Spencer lives, we'll find him.'

It was a mild Sunday morning, and the church bells started pealing.

'That's what we'll do, we'll go to church. We're sure to find someone who knows him there.'

Sheila looked at her and frowned.

'You said you'd never set foot in a church again after what you saw in the war. You said you had evidence that God didn't exist.'

Ella faltered. What could she have seen that made her say that? In spite of the mild day, she shuddered but pushed the thought away, lifted her chin and took a deep breath.

'It's for a good cause,' she said, and started walking towards the church.

It was a pretty stone building with a square Norman tower rather than a steeple. The churchyard was well kept, the yews neatly clipped and the grass around the headstones recently cut. The service was pleasant, the sermon not too long, and Ella remembered the words to the hymns, much to her own amazement.

They shook hands with the vicar on the way out.

'So pleased to see you, Mrs Elkington, Miss Marchmont,' he said, nodding to them in turn. 'I hope you'll join us again.'

'Thank you, vicar, I expect we will,' said Sheila, and they walked on.

'How did he know us?' asked Ella.

'My dear, in a village this size, everyone knows everything, although some are more willing not to trumpet the fact. Now, have you seen your Fred?'

Ella looked around, and there he was, limping down the path ahead of them with an elderly man and woman.

Ella jogged to catch them up.

SARAH BOURNE

'I say, hello! Fred, isn't it? We met in the village a few days ago.'

'I remember,' said Fred, scowling at her.

'And these are your parents?'

'Yes,' he gestured to them, 'Mr and Mrs Miller. This is Nurse Elkington.'

'Ella, please,' she said and shook hands with the Millers, then turned back to their son.

'Fred, I have a proposition for you.'

His scowl gave way to a look of curiosity.

'Do you know Mr Ashton? He's the one who owns Chase Farm, just down the road. He needs someone to do his accounts. I thought you might be able to give him a hand. You said you didn't have a job. Do you think you could help him?'

Mr Miller turned to his son. 'You were always good at arithmetic, son. I reckon you'd be good at accounts and that.'

'Yes,' said Mrs Miller, 'how about you give it a go?'

The scowl returned. Fred clearly didn't want or need his parents' opinion. In fact, Ella was worried that he'd say no to spite them, so it was a relief to hear him say,

'All right. Got nothing to lose.'

The next problem was how to get him there. He couldn't walk that far, and Ella wasn't sure he'd be able to cycle with his false leg. Mr Miller came to the rescue.

'I could drive you over if you like, son.' He turned back to Ella. 'When would suit?'

They arranged that Mr Miller and Fred would pick them up at three that afternoon and take them to the farm.

Ella put her arm through Sheila's as they walked home. She was feeling rather smug. Everything was working out. As long as Arthur forgave them for not turning up to milk the cows, all would be well.

~

And the meeting did go well. Fred seemed cheered by the chance of a job and they didn't see his scowl once. He and Arthur got on well, and when Arthur explained what he wanted and showed him the books, Fred assured him he could do it. Mr Miller seemed relieved, and Ella guessed that having Fred around doing nothing had tried his patience sorely.

The Millers left, and Sheila and Ella stayed for another cup of tea.

'Sorry about the milking this morning,' said Ella.

'Oh, not to worry. David helped. He's gone back to town now, though, so I could do with a hand this afternoon instead.' He grinned.

'We'll go home and change,' said Ella.

'I didn't really mean it – I manage on my own every day,' he said, backtracking swiftly.

'But we made a promise and we mean to keep it.'

They were back in old jackets and wellingtons within the hour and helped Arthur get the cows in from the fields, walking behind them, waving their arms and clapping their hands, although the cows hardly needed it, swaying their way along a well-worn track to the milking barn. Then he patiently taught them how to massage the milk from the udders. Ella found the repetitive nature of the task soothing, and enjoyed the warmth and size of the beasts, their sweet milky smell as she leaned her head against their sides to reach for their udders. She was surprised when Arthur announced that they'd finished and released the cows back into the field.

'You're both naturals,' he said.

Ella doubted that, and had a sore back from crouching on the low stool and leaning in for over an hour, but she felt a sense of achievement nonetheless.

'I'll make farm girls of you yet,' he said, and looked at Sheila who blushed.

'I'm glad I nursed during the war if that's what the land girls had to do,' she said, massaging her lower back and rolling her shoulders. But she had a smile on her face, and Arthur smiled back at her. Ella looked away, taken again by his apparent feeling for her friend, and not wanting to intrude.

# 11

Ella was curled up in the sitting room with her diary and a letter from Andrew telling her all he knew of her husband. She'd telephoned him a few days before and asked him about Charles – what he'd thought of him, how well they knew each other. She'd asked him to write rather than tell her on the telephone, so that she could remember it all. His reply had been swift and detailed, recounting the times they'd met and how much he'd liked Charles. As Ella read it for the tenth time, she felt lucky to have a brother like Andrew who was no longer brushing her off when she asked these questions, and who made time to write a considered response.

She had a hot cup of tea and a sandwich beside her and picked up her diary, planning to stay there a while. Mrs Marchmont had had a fall, and Sheila had gone to see her and make sure it wasn't more serious than her mother was letting on. She wouldn't be back until at least the next day, and Ella was revelling in having the house to herself. Not that she wasn't grateful for all that Sheila was doing for her, but she had a sense that she'd led a quiet life since the war, and wanted some time alone now.

She lingered over Charles's proposal. She'd written about it at length, of course, and her words had triggered memories of the day.

It was a Saturday, early in May, 1939. There was talk of war, but nobody believed it would come to that. Neville Chamberlain would negotiate a peaceful settlement; Hitler would see sense, or so everyone hoped. After the Great War, no one was in the mood for another — too many young men had been killed, women left widows, children fatherless, mothers childless. No, there wouldn't be another war.

Ella's mind drifted back to that Saturday. Charles arrived at the nurses' home with a picnic hamper and drove her to Box Hill. It was a balmy spring day, clouds dotted about against a palette of blue sky. They'd walked, hand in hand, to the summit, Charles spread the blanket on the ground, and they sat, looking out over the Downs, wondering if the line of darker blue they could see in the distance was the sea or the rim of the horizon.

Charles seemed a little unsettled, asking repeatedly if she was comfortable, happy, had enough to eat and drink – the champagne had gone straight to Ella's head – and in the end, she had said, 'Is everything all right, darling?'

'Yes – at least, I think so. It's just that, well…'

He'd got up from the blanket and turned away, pulled something from his pocket, and then knelt in front of her.

'Ella, you know how much I love you. I can't imagine life without you. Will you marry me?'

Ella gasped and her hand flew to her chest. Charles had gone pink like he did when he was worried. Ella smiled and stroked the side of his face.

'Of course I will, silly.'

Charles grinned and thrust a tiny box at her.

'Shouldn't you get the ring out for me? I can't put a box on my finger,' Ella teased.

Charles, so steady and sure in the operating theatre, fumbled opening the box, and dropped the ring on the blanket. His hands were shaking when he picked it up and slid it onto Ella's fourth finger. The solitaire diamond sparkled in the sun as Ella held her hand away from her and moved it to different positions to admire the ring. Then she threw her arms around Charles.

'I love you so much. I know we're going to be so happy.'

Ella sank deeper into the cushions of the sofa and pulled her cardigan more tightly around her. She didn't want to read further for now. She knew that they had been wrong about the war, that it did come, and that it claimed Charles's life. She wasn't ready to let him go.

Her tea had gone cold, and the light was fading. She tried to hold on to the joy she'd felt at the memory of Charles's proposal, but it was already slipping away, leaving emptiness.

The sky was dark when she came to. Her back ached from lying on the soft sofa and when she rubbed her face she felt the texture of the fabric embossed into her cheek. She sat up slowly, switched on the table lamp, reached for her cold tea and drank it, ate her limp sandwich and planted her feet firmly on the floor. She had to find out what had happened next. How much time had they had together? And yet she couldn't make her hand move to pick up the diary that lay on the coffee table in front of her. To her it had become not an innocent receptacle of events, thoughts and memories, but a forbidding presence forcing her towards the loss of her husband and a future she can't have wanted. And yet, that future was already her past. It couldn't be changed however much she might wish it, and avoiding it, living in ignorance and guesswork and what ifs was preventing her from moving forward into new possibilities.

Grief crushed her as she relived her love affair with her husband.

'Oh, Charles.' She sighed, and picked up the book.

She read page after page about dates with Charles. They went to the theatre, to films, dinners and dances, they went out alone and in groups, they went for walks and they went boating on the Serpentine. Charles was a generous and attentive fiancé.

As summer progressed, however, the talk of war intensified and only those who couldn't face up to reality were still talking about a negotiated outcome with Mr Hitler and his Nazi party. So, on 5th August, with war just over the horizon, Charles suggested to Ella that they get married immediately instead of waiting until Christmas as they had planned.

Ella had been thrown into a spin — how to get the dress made, the invitations sent out, the church booked and the dinner organised in so little time?

'Darling,' said Charles, taking her in his arms, 'I mean just you, me and a couple of witnesses at Marylebone Registry Office.'

'But, Charles – what about the wedding we planned?' Ella was torn; she wanted to be married to Charles more than anything, but she'd dreamed of a large wedding with all their friends there, wishing them well as they sailed off into married bliss.

'I just want to be married to you, and with the war coming, who knows what will happen. We can have the whole big white wedding after the war. It won't last long. We'll probably be able to book the church for this time next year.'

'So why the hurry?'

'I just want you to be my wife, I can't wait any longer.'

Ella was swept up in his urgency. They agreed a date a week

away.

The issue then was that married student nurses were not allowed at St Thomas's, and Ella didn't want to give up her work, not until she started having babies. Fortunately, Charles was all for her continuing to work if that was what she wanted. She didn't wear her engagement ring anymore, since the Home Sister had commented on it and started asking questions. Ella had denied the engagement, saying the ring was her mother's and she'd forgotten to take it off after a night out. She wouldn't be able to wear her wedding ring either.

She asked to swap days with one of the other student nurses, claiming a sick relative whom she had to visit, and on Saturday 12th August, wearing a new cream frock and hat, carrying half a dozen red roses, she and Andrew and Sheila had made their way to the Marylebone Registry Office where they met Charles and his friend Dudley Fraser who would be his witness. The ceremony was short and about as unromantic as Ella could have thought possible, and so unlike the wedding she had dreamed of. But she was with Charles who looked so handsome in his charcoal-grey suit with the red rose in his buttonhole, and she was metamorphosed from Miss Ella Whittington to Mrs Charles Elkington. Nothing else mattered. Andrew had brought a camera and snapped a picture of the bride and groom on the steps of the registry office, both caught looking up at a shower of rose petals Sheila had thrown.

They took a taxi to the Ritz for lunch, and Maeve and Nina who had the afternoon off, joined them, as did another friend of Charles's, a short, rather dour-looking man. They drank champagne and there were toasts and pâté and more toasts to the happy couple and beef Wellington and more champagne, brandy, dessert, more brandy.

Afterwards, she and Charles had caught the train to Brighton and stayed at The Grand Hotel on the seafront.

.   .   .

Ella found herself once again snuggling into the sofa. It was where she felt safe enough these days to delve into her past. She lifted her head and glanced out of the window. The night was cloudy and there was only a sliver of a moon. The trees were deeper impressions smudged against the dark night, moving gently in the breeze.

The wedding night had been cloudless with a bright moon and thousands of stars shining their sparkling light on the newlyweds. Ella hugged herself tightly and allowed the memories to drift back. Her sudden anxiety, not over the marriage, but about 'the act'. Charles's gentle encouragement as he kissed her up the neck and along her collarbones, making her forget everything except his lips on her skin, each kiss a point of intensity, like sherbet exploding just beneath her skin. She moved her hands under his shirt and felt the contours of his chest, soft yet firm. And somehow her dress was at her feet and his hands were on her breasts and she shuddered in anticipation as her body responded to his caress. Gone was the anxiety, replaced by need; the need to be closer, one.

She drew her finger through the glistening sweat on his shoulders as they lay together afterwards. He caught her hand and kissed each finger, turned it over and kissed her palm.

Looking into her eyes, he murmured, 'Mrs Elkington.' Just that.

Ella brushed the tears from her cheeks. They'd made love again in the morning before breakfast, and again after a walk on the pebbly beach and along the pier. But then they had to get back to London, and Ella had to go back to the nursing home and lie to the Home Sister about her fictitious elderly aunt's condition.

She had a month before the end of her training, before she could admit to being married and move into Charles's flat. So began weeks of spending the evening with her husband and having to get back in time for curfew. Often she missed it, preferring to stay with Charles as long as possible, and then had to throw stones at the window to get Sheila to let her in without the Home Sister hearing them. Twice they almost got caught as they giggled their way to their room, shutting the door carefully and moments later hearing Sister swish along the corridor, sniffing out rule-breakers.

And on 1st September, when she'd been Mrs Elkington for twenty days, Hitler invaded Poland, and two days later, on Sunday 3rd September, she and Charles sat close to the radio to listen to the news. At quarter past eleven, Alvar Lidell came on and announced that the prime minister, Neville Chamberlain would be addressing the nation. Two minutes later came the broadcast that had England glued to their radios and the news no one wanted to hear.

'This morning the British Ambassador in Berlin handed the German government a final note, saying that unless we heard from them – by eleven o'clock – that they were prepared at once to withdraw their troops from Poland, a state of war would exist between us.'

There was a pause into which all Ella's hopes and dreams swelled.

'I have to tell you now that no such undertaking has been received and that, consequently, this country is at war with Germany.'

Ella didn't hear the rest of the announcement. She buried her head in Charles's chest and sobbed. Charles held her, stroking her hair and rocking her gently.

'It'll be all right, you'll see,' he whispered, but his voice was strained.

Ella lifted her head and looked out the window at the barrage balloons already floating above London, just in case, and thought it looked more as if they were preparing for a party than for war.

When the practice siren sounded, they joined the other residents of the block in the basement. It was cold and smelled of damp and long absence. In one corner was a pile of stored furniture, a tarpaulin thrown over it falling half off and pooling on the floor next to it. Otherwise it was empty. The residents stood around, nodding to each other, as if acknowledging their circumstances, but no one could believe what they'd heard, that Chamberlain had failed to negotiate peace, that Hitler could be so bloody-minded. The older people who remembered the last war, sighed, recounting their losses and saying things like, 'mark my words' and 'no more peace in our times' and 'what was it all for?'

Ella clutched Charles's hand, feeling numb now that the initial shock had worn off. And then she had an awful thought.

'Oh, no! Charles – you're not going to sign up, are you?'

In the gloomy lighting she saw his jaw tense.

'What – what is it?' she asked.

He looked up at the ceiling as if hoping for an answer there.

'Charles–'

Turning back to her, he took her hand and gazed into her eyes. 'Ella, my dearest. I should have told you, I know, but, well, I didn't think it would come to this and I didn't want to alarm you for nothing, but... I joined the reserves. Several months ago, actually. RAMC. I thought I should do my bit – you know...'

'The Royal Army Medical Corps? You'll be called up immediately.' Ella pulled her hand from his and held her head as if trying to stop it from bursting, and then started shaking it. There were words crowding her mind, but she couldn't get them out. In the end, she choked out, 'No.'

When Charles tried to comfort her, she moved to the other side of the shelter and leant against the wall, holding herself, refusing to speak to him until the all-clear sounded and they made their way back to his flat, sat in the chairs they had vacated when the siren sounded. When the war started.

'Talk to me, darling, please,' he said, taking her hand.

'I don't know what to say. I don't know how you could keep something like this from me.' She wouldn't look at him, but she left her hand in his.

'I'm sorry. It seemed like the right thing to do at the time.'

They sat a while longer, Charles trying to convince her that he'd be fine, and then not saying much at all.

Eventually Ella stood. 'I have to go back to the nurses' home.' She pulled Charles to his feet to give him a hug, holding on tight. 'I hate that you're going, and that you didn't tell me, but I'm proud of you too. The wounded will need a good surgeon, and you'll save so many lives,' she said into his chest. Then she rushed out the door.

Out in the streets the mood was subdued. People were talking in whispers as if to say anything out loud would provoke an attack from the Luftwaffe. A woman made eye contact with Ella and then shrugged and shook her head as if to say, 'What now?' Ella looked around her at the city she loved, at the sandbags growing like clumps of fungus around the buildings, and her chest constricted at the idea of bombs landing on the places that she knew so well, turning them to rubble, claiming the lives of those who lived in them. She started to run, desperate to be with people she knew, and was breathless by the time she reached the nurses' home.

Black tape criss-crossed the windows already, and when she found Joan, who was the only person on her floor off duty that day, she was sewing blackout curtains in preparation for a German attack.

'It's too awful,' she said as Ella sat down to help her. 'What are we going to do?'

Ella shook her head. 'I don't know. Charles has signed up – RAMC.' She dabbed at a tear.

'Perhaps we should join up. They'll need nurses,' said Joan.

'They'll need us here too.' Ella couldn't imagine going to war, leaving all that was safe and familiar. She wondered if she was a coward. Was that why she was so against Charles going – because he was being brave and she wasn't? That his courage highlighted her cowardice? No, she thought not. Not wanting Charles to go was all about not wanting to lose him, and even though he'd told her that doctors weren't the ones who got killed in wars, she couldn't believe him.

Despite Ella's fears, the next few weeks continued as if nothing had happened, apart from the black tape appearing on every window, and the ARP wardens tramping the streets at night checking the blackout curtains were all firmly closed. Not the tiniest, faintest sliver of light must guide the German bombs to English targets. But there were no bombs. There was nothing. British troops had left England to fight the Germans, but there was no fighting. The Germans were engaged elsewhere, and the Allies left them to it. It was rumoured that some officers hanging around in France had a pack of hounds and their horses sent over, but were thwarted in their desire to go foxhunting when the French wouldn't allow it in their country. Charles had laughed when he read that. But Ella had thought it ridiculous. What a waste of time and money keeping all those men in Europe with nothing to do.

Talk on the streets and on Ella's ward was that it would all be over by Christmas without loss of English lives.

And then a German U-boat sank the aircraft carrier, *HMS Courageous* off the coast of Ireland. And a month after that, another U-boat infiltrated the British Fleet Base at Scapa Flow in the Orkneys, and sank *HMS Royal Oak*. The war was on their doorstep, and suddenly it was real. Ella remembered going to a shop to stock up on bobby pins and stockings. Other women with different priorities bought sugar, tinned food and toilet paper.

She was relieved, however, that nothing was happening in London, or anywhere in England. After the flurry of Luftwaffe buzzes over Scapa Flow, and the RAF seeing them off, the Germans had once again turned their gaze elsewhere.

And still Charles hadn't been called up.

Ella yawned. It was well past midnight by the clock on the mantelpiece, and she wasn't used to late nights. There was one thing she wanted to do before she went to bed though. She got up, trying to ignore the pins and needles in her feet, and went to the bureau. She looked in every drawer, but didn't find what she was looking for. Hands on hips, she looked around the room wondering where it could be. Her eyes came to rest on the piano stool, but she knew it wasn't in there; she went into the parlour, the cold, damp air giving her a shock. After the parlour, the dining room. And there, tucked away in a box in the sideboard with all the other photographs that had been displayed on the piano, and that Andrew had put away on Dr Myers' orders, she found it.

She pulled the silver frame out of the cupboard and held it up to the light. The picture Andrew had taken at their wedding; she and Charles captured forever laughing as they threw their heads back, waiting for the rose petals to fall.

In her bedroom, ready for sleep, she ran a finger over Charles's face, wanting to feel the dimple in his chin, his skin under her hands. Tears washed her cheeks as she kissed her husband goodnight and placed him next to her pillow.

## 12

E lla slept late the following day, and woke with a headache. She reached for the photograph and said good morning to Charles. She felt less emotional than she had the night before, as if something had slotted into place again.

'Got a bit of a head, darling,' she said, and imagined Charles's response. 'Yes, I know, I'll take some aspirin and have a lovely hot cup of tea.'

She winced at the bright light as she opened the curtains. It was a beautiful day; warm, a light breeze blowing, and not a cloud in the sky.

Over breakfast she read the mail. There was a letter from David saying how much he'd enjoyed the farmers' dance and hoping that they might see each other again soon. How old-fashioned, she thought, to write rather than use the telephone, but then again, how nice to receive a letter.

Ella smiled, finished her toast and went to the bureau to find some paper and her pen. But first she came across the bunches of letters. The thick one from her father, and the other, rather thin, from Charles. Heart racing, she took them to the sofa and started reading.

*28th March 1940*

> *My Dearest Heart, my Ella,*
>
> *I'm not allowed to tell you where I am, but it's not so very far away from you although it feels like a hundred miles. The accommodation isn't too bad, but we only arrived yesterday. Officers get a room to themselves, thank goodness, and the food is very good.*
>
> *Listen to me – I sound like I'm writing a letter to my parents from boarding school instead of the love of my life!*
>
> *Today we were fitted for our uniforms and given the rest of our gear. I'll be living out of a kitbag for the foreseeable future. It's not an inspiring thought.*
>
> *The rest of the chaps seem decent sorts, and there are several nurses here ready for mobilisation. How I wish you were one of them, although I am happy you're staying at St Thomas's – they need you there. We have no idea when or where we'll be sent, but we'll never see anything but the inside of an operating theatre anyway. Such is the life of an army doctor.*
>
> *I love you so much and think of you every minute of the day. When the drill sergeant yelled at us this afternoon, making himself all red in the face, and sending spittle flying yards into the air in front of him, I imagined you getting the giggles the way you do when people do daft things.*
>
> *I miss you,*
>
> *Your ever loving Charles.*

Ella gazed out the window. She'd been sitting in the flat when she first read that letter, she remembered, reading it over and over, the words wrapping themselves round her heart, but instead of comforting her, they just made her feel more alone. Words were a poor substitute for the real thing.

There were more letters about army life, the other officers, and what they ate, which seemed very important to him. Ella smiled, remembering how much he liked his food, and how dismayed he would have been when rationing meant an end to cakes and puddings on a daily basis. He had such a sweet tooth.

And then the last letter. He couldn't tell her where he was going, but given what was happening in France, it was likely to be somewhere over there she'd thought.

*18th May 1940*

*My Darling Girl,*

*We're off. I don't know where, we haven't been told. It all feels rather unreal; we seem to have been sitting around on our backsides for so long, and now all of a sudden everything's a dreadful rush.*

*Think of me doing my bit. I'll be thinking of you every moment that I'm not stitching some poor soldier together again.*

*I don't know how long I'll be away, but I'll write, and you must know that I can't wait to take you into my arms again and tell you how much I love you,*

*Always, your loving Charles.*

He was killed three days later when the hospital ship he was on, *HMHS Maid of Kent*, was bombed and sunk by the Luftwaffe in Dieppe Harbour. They'd gone over to treat the wounded during the fiasco that was the Battle of Dunkirk. He hadn't stitched a single soldier back together. She'd received the black-edged telegram two weeks later, and now held it in her hand, not wanting to read again that he was missing, presumed dead.

Great sobs caught in her throat making her heave and clutch herself, trying to hold in the grief that swept her up and took her to that hour, that day, and all the long, empty days that followed. However much she wanted it, she would never see him again.

Sheila found her in the sitting room a few hours later, still surrounded by the letters and diaries.

'How's your mother?' asked Ella, rousing herself.

'Fine. Better than I expected, and Father's perfectly capable of looking after her. I did a bit of shopping for them, made them dinner last night, and they practically pushed me out the door this morning. Couldn't wait to see the back of me. So here I am.' She swept her gaze around the room. 'I don't need to ask what you've been up to. How's it all going?'

'Fine. I felt bit rocky last night and this morning, but that was my own fault. I read my diary and Charles's letters. I wanted to know more about him, about us. And now I know everything.'

Sheila sat down next to her and took her hand.

'You're sure you're all right?'

Ella nodded. 'If you'd come in a few hours ago, I wouldn't have been, but I got through it. I'll survive.' She didn't really want to talk about it with Sheila, or anyone. Her grief was a private affair. 'David wrote to me,' she said, brightening her tone.

'Oh?' Sheila looked startled by the change of subject.

Ella went on, 'Yes, saying how much he enjoyed the dance and wondering if we might see each other again. I've just written back to him saying yes.'

'Lovely,' said Sheila. 'Perhaps we can do another double date this weekend. Arthur has asked me to the pictures in Hambleford. *Hue and Cry* is showing, I think. I've heard it's very funny.'

'Funny sounds like what I need,' said Ella, starting to gather the letters into a pile and tie the ribbon around them again. She held them briefly to her heart and then put them and the diaries back in the bureau and closed the lid with a satisfying click.

*Hue and Cry* was a very amusing film, and after the pictures they went to The Crown in Hambleford for a drink. Ella enjoyed David's company. He was funny, intelligent and handsome in a solid sort of way. He also made Ella feel special; he was attentive without being overbearing, and guessed what she needed before she knew it herself.

'It comes down to having four sisters and no brothers,' he said. 'And as the youngest, I was always being dressed up and having my hair done by the girls when I was little, and as they got older, I became their confidante when things weren't going right with the young men they were seeing. From being their little doll, I became their expert "man about town"!' David pulled a puppy-dog face, no doubt hoping for sympathy.

Ella laughed and patted his hand. 'You seem to have turned out all right. I don't feel sorry for you at all.'

He caught her hand and held it, stroking it with his thumb.

'You know, Ella–' He stopped, smiled and looked into her eyes.

Ella felt herself blush. She liked David, but she wasn't ready for what she thought was coming. It was too soon. She shifted in her seat.

'Ella, I think...'

Arthur and Sheila came over with the drinks. Ella removed her hand from David's and smiled at Arthur.

'Thank you,' she said as he put a shandy in front of her.

Talk turned to other things, and when David dropped them home, she excused herself for not inviting them in, saying she was tired.

In the sitting room she kicked off her shoes and threw herself onto the sofa.

'Nightcap?' asked Sheila.

'Love one.'

'Are you going to tell me what's troubling you?' Sheila handed Ella a Scotch.

Ella sighed. 'I don't want to lead David on, that's all. I think he's rather keen, and I like him, but I'm not ready to jump into anything. Anyway, you and Arthur seem to be getting on very well.'

Sheila took a sip of her drink. 'I like him. And unlike you, I am ready for marriage. If I don't have children soon, I never will.'

'Gosh,' said Ella, 'I didn't realise it had gone that far.'

'Oh, it hasn't. I mean, we haven't talked about it as such, but there have been hints. He keeps saying how his house needs a woman's touch, and that although his sister would never agree, he is quite well house-trained!'

'Sounds smitten. He's a good man. I'm happy for you.'

'Bit soon for that – like I said, nothing's been said.'

Ella noticed the blush as Sheila turned away to light herself a cigarette.

That night, as she lay with the curtains open and the moon shining into her bedroom, casting its silvery light across the bed, Ella thought about her friend. An image came to her, of Sheila with an RAF man during the war – Keith someone. She'd been devastated when he was killed in a dogfight during the Battle of Britain. She hadn't been able to work for days, and when she did come back to the ward, she kept disappearing into the sluice room. Ella had not long since lost Charles, and wasn't any help or comfort to her friend — she was barely surviving herself.

The turning point for both of them had come not from within, but from Herr Hitler; on 7th September, London had been hit by dozens of bombs, and the Luftwaffe kept it up for fifty-seven consecutive nights before a break, and then on for months more. All patients who could be moved were taken to Park Prewett Hospital near Basingstoke, a mental asylum that was converted to a general hospital. St Thomas's became a clearing station for the wounded, the operating theatres busy day and night, and the wards bulging with the injured. The Phoney War was over, and with it any time to rest, let alone mourn the dead. Ella had volunteered to stay in London, not out of bravery, but because without Charles she didn't care if she was alive or dead. She suspected that Sheila had stayed for a similar reason.

She turned over in her bed and pulled the blanket up. It was warm during the days, but the nights still brought a chill with them. She yawned, wondering how they'd all managed on so little sleep for so long as she felt herself slipping towards it now.

~

The morning post brought a letter from Andrew.

'He wants us to visit,' she told Sheila. 'Next weekend if we're free. What do you think?'

'Lovely. It would be nice to go up to London for a day or two.'

Ella looked thoughtful. 'I haven't been there for ages, have I? I wonder what it's like now. I expect there are a lot of new buildings going up. I should probably go and see the flat too.'

Sheila took a sharp breath, and Ella looked at her, eyebrows raised.

'I'm sorry – the flat – it was bombed. Towards the end of the Blitz. You moved back to the hospital. Well, to be honest, you'd been practically living there anyway.'

Ella became very still, only the index finger of her left hand moving, tapping her teacup rhythmically. She wasn't sure why, but this of all things seemed cruel. She was coming to terms with the loss of Charles all over again, but had thought, somewhere in the low-lit corners of her mind that there was still something of him, something they'd shared. She now realised that she'd assumed the flat would be waiting for her until she was ready to face it. Her next thought was how ridiculous that was; Charles had died over seven years ago, surely if it had still been there she would have done whatever she had to do with the flat before now. It still seemed unfair that it was gone.

'I'm sorry,' said Sheila. 'It was about the middle of March 1941. We'd been working like Trojans for weeks on end and everyone was exhausted. One Saturday night when you had the next day off, you decided to go back to the flat so that you didn't get caught up helping with the patients in the wee small hours. You even joked that maybe Hitler wouldn't bomb us that night so that you could get a decent sleep. The bombing was particularly bad at the time.

'When you came back the next day you had a picture under one arm, and a small suitcase which you said contained all your possessions, everything you'd been able to rescue from the rubble.'

As Sheila spoke, Ella saw it all. She'd been in bed when the siren sounded. She had considered staying where she was, but then she heard the bombers and grabbed her bag and rushed down the street. The Underground station was already full of people with their thermoses and blankets, books and knitting. She realised that she was ill-equipped for a night away from home. An older lady inched along the bench she was sitting on, making room for her to perch on the end.

'Had enough of this, I have. I'd give that Hitler a piece of my mind if ever I saw him. Bloody monster he is.'

Ella agreed. She wished she could lie down. There was a low murmur of chatter, a few snores from the old men who had managed to make themselves comfortable, yawns from the children who couldn't sleep.

The ack-ack of the anti-aircraft guns started. And then the awful sound of explosions and falling masonry as the bombs started dropping. Close. One after another. Even in the shelter they could smell the dust, and then the smoke from dozens of fires. Ella was terrified; it seemed worse to be underground with nothing to do than it was rushing about helping patients. She felt like a sitting duck and looked around for someone to help, but they were all used to it. The Tube station was a home away from home, the bombs just an inconvenience.

'Haven't been that close before,' said the old woman. 'I hope those bloody Jerries haven't destroyed my vegetable garden.'

Ella tried to smile at her, to respond in some way, but she wanted to run, to get out of there and see what was happening. Her pulse was racing, her legs itched to be moving. It was a long night. The wailing rise and fall of the all-clear didn't sound until after six the next morning. Many people, particularly those with children and the elderly, stayed where they were rather than rousing themselves just to go back to bed for an hour. Ella ran up the stairs, desperate to see where the damage was.

The scene in the street was chaotic. What light there was came from the flames the firemen were attempting to put out, dust and ash turning to mud amongst the rubble. The sound of water escaping hoses and burst water mains was offset by the crackle of the fires. A sewerage pipe had obviously been cracked, because there was an acrid smell of human waste underneath the sharper aroma of the flames devouring everything in their orbit. Bits of furniture were strewn all over the place; clothes once contained in cupboards hung in unlikely places – a dress adorning a lamp post which was leaning at a jaunty angle, shoes teetering on the step of a staircase going nowhere, a man's suit lying across a bed looking for all the world like its owner had got it out ready to put on.

Ella covered her nose and mouth with her handkerchief. Her eyes were smarting from the smoke and gritty from the dust and flying ash. She felt something warm against her leg and looked down to see a dog gazing up at her, tail between its legs, terrified.

'It's all right, old thing,' she said, bending down to stroke it.

The dog nuzzled her hand, and wagged its tail.

'Come along then, let's go and see what's what, shall we?' She felt better having something to look after. Braver.

She climbed over the debris, the dog following, making her way slowly towards the corner and home.

'All right, Miss?'

Ella looked round to see an ARP warden approaching.

'I just want to get home.'

'And where's that, Miss?'

'Just round the corner, number twenty. The flats.'

He shook his head and pursed his lips.

'Sorry, Miss. Not a stick standing in your street.'

Ella stared at him, unable to take it in. 'Nothing?'

The sun was beginning to rise, casting its weak light over the hellish scene.

She staggered off over fallen bricks and timber beams, avoiding deep holes in the ground, careful not to dislodge precariously dangling tables and lamps, chairs and sideboards. The dog stayed with her, letting out a cry every now and then.

They got to the corner and stopped. The warden was right. There was nothing recognisable about her street. Tears streaked her grimy cheeks. She sank onto a cupboard that had been thrown from someone's kitchen and landed on its side, spilling its broken contents onto the rubble-strewn street. The dog licked her hand, looking up at her with trusting eyes. She stroked him absent-mindedly, glad for another living being to share this awful moment, the ghastly realisation that everything that she and Charles had owned was gone.

'No!' she heard herself yelling, and then she was scrambling towards the pile of rubble where the flat had been, only recognisable by the fabric of an armchair lying on its side. She found one of her tops hanging out of a broken drawer, but the rest of the chest must have been matchsticks, her clothes, rags.

Her jewellery box lay open amongst the ruins of her wardrobe, most of its contents, including her engagement ring, gone, having slipped between the masonry and shattered beams that had been home. There were a few books and a painting, surprisingly unscathed. Piece by piece she found a few of her possessions, and a battered suitcase that had been Charles's to put them all in. The last thing she found was the picture that Andrew had taken at their wedding. The glass was broken but the photograph was untouched. She held it to her heart and bit her lip to stop the tears. It was the most precious thing she now owned. Then she lifted her chin, took some deep breaths and said, 'What are we going to do with you, old thing?'

The dog sniffled and she felt his wet nose in her palm. She ruffled his ears and sat down next to him on a stove lying on its back.

The dog sat waiting as if he knew she had a decision to make, that his life was in her hands.

'Patch, hey, Patch, boy!' came a call. The dog's ears pricked up and with a last glance up at Ella, he bounded off to be reunited with his owner.

'Thanks for looking after him, Miss,' yelled the youth, while Patch licked his face and wagged his tail in a frenzy.

Ella smiled, glad they'd found each other, but feeling more alone than ever. Finally, she took one more look at the street that had briefly been home, and turned to walk back to the hospital.

Other people were searching the ruins for their possessions. Ella recognised some of them, neighbours she'd never had the time to get to know and now never would.

The week went fast, taken up with preparing for their trip to London, getting the sewing machine out again to revamp old dresses, gardening, and repairing the old swing that hung from the sycamore tree for when the children next came. There was also a visit from Dr Myers, who gave his permission for the trip, even though Ella hadn't asked for it and would have gone whatever he said. He'd been visiting less as time went by, and Ella couldn't help but feel that his attentions were no longer required, but he seemed to think that she still needed his watchful eye cast over her periodically. She decided to tackle that particular issue when they got back from London.

One day when they were in the village doing their shopping, Mr Miller stopped them.

'Good morning, ladies. Trust you're well?'

'Very well, thank you, and you and Mrs Miller?'

'Yes, yes, very good. Just wanted to say thank you for sorting that job for Fred. He's a new man since he started working for Mr Ashton.'

'I'm glad it's working out for him,' said Ella.

'He's got some self-respect back, you see. He's proved to himself that he's still useful. Just thought you should know.'

'Thank you, Mr Miller.'

They parted on the street, and Sheila patted Ella's arm.

'It was a good idea. I know Arthur's finding him invaluable. He's even helping with other things around the farm – mending bits of equipment and such. And apparently has a wicked sense of humour.'

'Who'd have thought,' said Ella, thinking back to their first meeting.

∿

On the train to London, Ella pulled out her diary – 1939–1944 – and started reading from the beginning.

*September, 1939*

*I haven't written for ages because everything has been a whirl. I've finished! My training is over, I've passed my exams, and after rather a worrying wait, I was offered a job at my dear old St Thomas's. I couldn't imagine working anywhere else. I'm a staff nurse on the Female Surgical Ward, the second ward I worked on, under the watchful gaze of the terrifying Sister Cooper!*

She giggled and looked up to find Sheila watching her, one eyebrow raised.

'Oh, it's too funny – I didn't realise I ended up working with the fearsome Sister Cooper again – why didn't you tell me?'

Sheila laughed. 'I didn't want you to have a relapse and end up in hospital again in a state of shock,' she said.

'Oh, listen to this–'

*I'm still terrified of her! But qualified nurses are treated differently to students, we're one rung up the ladder of respect, although it is easy to slide down to the bottom again – an untidy-looking ward, patients up and about when they should all be lined up in their beds, lunch trays not cleared in a timely fashion – these are all terrible lapses, punishable by a stern talking to by Sister. And yet, a patient having to be rushed back into surgery was 'unfortunate', and a death on the ward, while a tragedy for the family, is seen as no more than routine. I find it hard to reconcile myself with these attitudes and have been called in to Sister's office already for a talk.*

Ella shook her head. 'I think I'm glad I don't remember those talks. I'm sure my legs would have been shaking and my mouth would have gone all dry so that I couldn't say anything, even if I'd been allowed to, which I'm sure I wasn't.'

'Go on,' said Sheila.

Ella looked back to her journal and continued.

*I employed you on this ward, Nurse, because you were one of the best students I have ever had, especially given that you were at an early stage of your training when you were here.*

'I really don't remember her ever saying that. Do you think I made it up to make myself feel better?'

'No – I remember you coming back to the nurses' home and telling me – you were so full of it, you couldn't talk about anything else, not even Charles!'

Ella sighed. 'I must have been in shock. Anyway, there's more...'

*Now I find your attitude disappointing, your discipline lacking, and your sentimentality mawkish.*

Ella lifted her head again. 'That's more like it!'

'Yes,' said Sheila, 'you told me that too – she'd peered at you over her half-moon glasses and delivered the slap!'

Ella laughed. 'It hurt, too. And I couldn't answer back, of course, because I needed that job, and anyway, I would never have dared!' She looked back to her diary.

*Over the next few weeks, I worked hard to win Sister's respect. I made sure the ward was tidy at all times, chided the student nurses when routines were not adhered to and hid my feelings when necessary. But I still made time to talk to the patients, to listen to their fears and their hopes, to be kind and gentle and show that I care. I was rewarded for my efforts when I overheard Sister talking to Mr Hudson about the high calibre of her nursing staff.*
*'I believe they are the best nurses in the hospital, and you would do well to remember it,' she said in response to the surgeon making some snide remark. I cheered silently. Only Sister Cooper stood up to Mr Hudson like that and got away with it.*

'Gosh, high praise indeed. She was a dragon, but she was also fair. Although I'm not sure I agree with her about you lot being the best nurses in the hospital – we weren't bad up on the Stroke Ward, you know.'

Ella closed her diary and lay it on her lap. 'I remember always wishing we could do more; sometimes there was precious little we could do for our patients other than keep them clean and comfortable.'

'Don't underestimate the power of cleanliness, Nurse,' said Sheila in a Scottish accent.

'Right you are, Matron,' said Ella, saluting.

They both laughed.

'What did you bring it for, anyway?' asked Sheila, indicating the diary.

'I thought I might go and visit some of the old places. The hospital, the nurses' home, the cinema we used to go to, the tea houses maybe. A trip down memory lane to see what I remember.'

Sheila gazed out the window for a while, the smoke from her cigarette curling around her head and up towards the ceiling. She bit a hang nail and flicked the dead skin onto the floor, then looked back at Ella.

'Do you remember the hospital being hit?'

'No! – wait – I remember working in the basement like a troglodyte.'

'On the second night of the Blitz the nurses' home took a direct hit. Five nurses were killed, but the rest of us escaped with minor cuts and bruises. You and I were stuck under a wardrobe in our room until they dug us out. You suggested playing *I spy with my little eye*, I seem to remember. Which was odd, because we couldn't see anything, and we both got the giggles.'

Ella laughed. 'I expect it was the shock.' Her laughter turned into a shudder. 'Who was killed?'

'No one we knew. Not that time, anyway. Another bomb hit early in October and two surgeons died, Campbell and Spilsbury. Awfully nice chaps, both of them.'

Ella shook her head. The names meant nothing.

'Poor old Tommy's got bombed several times during the Blitz. Most of the patients and staff had already been evacuated, to Basingstoke of all places, but it's funny – those of us who volunteered to stay knew we had a job to do, that it was dangerous, but we didn't care. We were so focused on the patients and getting them into surgery and away to a hospital outside London as soon as possible to recuperate, it didn't really seem to sink in that we could be dead at any minute.'

'Sounds awful,' said Ella.

'It was at first, but I think we stopped noticing the bombs after a while. And we'd sit there in the basement at nights having a cigarette and a drink and talking about the day, and wondering how much longer Hitler could keep it up. But I think in a way, we were all quite happy. Does that sound strange?'

Ella had a sense rather than a memory of what it had been like. Of feeling, on the one hand, invincible, that nothing could harm her while she was doing valuable work, and on the other, not caring if she was killed, having lost Charles. She shook her head.

Sheila carried on. 'It was a good preparation for later. We hadn't seen anything like the injuries before; lacerations and crush wounds from falling masonry, and penetrating wounds from flying glass and metal. Awful, some of them. The surgeons were working all hours. I remember you worrying about them falling asleep in surgery. Well, we were rushed off our feet too, of course. All the fever patients had gone to Park Prewett and all the staff left behind were working in Emergency round the clock.'

'I remember!' said Ella. She had a vision of rushing around

tending to people lined up in a corridor, light slanting in from the stairwell. A little girl clutching her teddy bear, an old man gripping his Bible, a young fellow groaning and flailing about on a stretcher calling out for his mother. Her mind flickered to the whimpering man and with a start she drew her attention back to the present. He didn't fit there, he was somewhere else, somewhere that wasn't that hospital basement.

They were clattering along through suburbs, approaching London. Ella was struck by the drabness. Even though the sun was shining, everything looked somehow shabby. Piles of bricks were stacked at the end of a street next to a church hall that had no roof and only two walls. The houses looked tired, in need of paint or colour. In a number of back gardens, she could see old Anderson air-raid shelters, semi-submerged, battered, being used now as sheds perhaps, as if the owners weren't convinced the war was really over, that they might, at any moment, have to run with their belongings down the garden and take refuge against Hitler's bombs again.

As they got nearer to the centre of the city, the damage was even more apparent. Great gaps in streets where there used to be buildings. Rows of terraces with houses gone like missing teeth. And then they were pulling in to Waterloo, the wheels screeching discordantly, metal on metal, to bring them to a stop.

It was late morning and Ella had told Andrew that they'd make their own way to Richmond as they would probably want to spend the day in London reacquainting themselves with their old haunts. They left their bags at the station and decided to walk the short distance to St Thomas's and see their old hospital, which had also been their home and, as Ella thought of it, the place where they grew from naïve young girls to mature, capable women. At least, she hoped they were that.

As they neared the hospital and saw the space where the nurses' home used to be, Ella gasped. Her stomach sank. It all came back to her, memories crowding her mind one after the other; the bombing, the terror and the grief. Sheila may not have known any of the dead, but Ella did.

'Dolly Jones and Irene Thomas – they were killed in the first bombing, when the nurses' home was hit. They were on our floor.'

'So you remember it. I wasn't aware you knew any of them,' said Sheila.

'I did,' said Ella. 'They were student nurses. Dolly was on the Chest Ward with me for a while, and Irene came from Hambleford. We used to talk about the places we knew. She was so homesick, poor thing.'

Ella shuddered as she remembered more and more of that night. They'd been in their room, fast asleep, when the bomb hit. There had been so little warning, none really, and then chaos. Once she and Sheila had been rescued from under their wardrobe, she'd joined the mass of people running around shouting, calling for missing friends, stumbling around in the dark, falling over masonry and timber beams, furniture and personal possessions. The air was thick with dust, and Ella had wrapped what she thought was a damp handkerchief round her face, only later to discover it was a blood-soaked blouse. As the nurses gathered to assess the damage and identify those missing, they heard male voices approaching. Several doctors who had just finished in theatre rushed in to help. They moved furniture, flashed torches into corners, and helped the wounded out. Ella, her ankle swollen, limped along the corridor, feeling her way, calling names of those she knew had rooms along there. When she got to Dolly and Irene's room she couldn't open the door, there was something behind it. She called their names and got no response, then she yelled for help and two orderlies came through the dark and dust to shove at the door, eventually opening it enough for her to squeeze inside. Ella slid in, sweeping the beam of her torch from side to side, exploring the grisly scene. The two women were still in their beds, a thick beam and half the ceiling on top of them. Irene's eyes were open, surprised, her head turned to one side and hands either side of her chest as if to try and stop the inevitable. Dolly's head and torso were crushed under part of the wall that had caved in. Ella closed Irene's eyes, mumbled a prayer and left to see if there were others trapped. There was nothing more she could do. She leant against the door frame, taking deep breaths and closed her eyes tight to stop the tears.

'Are you all right, Ella? You look like you've seen a ghost.'

Her heart was racing, but as she opened her eyes again and looked at Sheila, she began to calm down, the vision of that night fading back into the past. She watched the people walking round them going about their business without even glancing at the hospital.

'I was thinking of Dolly and Irene. It was ghastly, just ghastly that night, wasn't it? I remember the Home Sister telephoned their families the next day, but I went to see Irene's mother next time I was in Hampshire. She was a thin, anxious woman. Her son was in France, her husband was dead, and she didn't know what to do with herself. She said she'd written to Irene the day before, begging her to come home after the first night of bombing in London, but she wouldn't even have got the letter. And she'd thought nursing was a good career for her daughter, that looking after others was all she'd ever wanted to do.' Ella felt a lump in her throat.

Sheila shook her head sadly. 'I suppose there are no guarantees, are there? It was war, no one was safe. Poor woman. I hope her son survived.'

'Me too.'

'Come on,' said Sheila, 'let's go and have a cup of tea, shall we?'

Sitting in a tea shop a short while later, Sheila and Ella talked a bit more about the bombings, the exhaustion they'd felt, the awful whistling of the bombs and the *crump* as they hit.

'I'm so impressed that you're remembering so much now,' said Sheila, smiling at Ella.

'I almost wish I wasn't. It was all so grim. I can hardly believe we did all that – lived through it all.' She shuddered.

'It wasn't all grim,' said Sheila. 'Do you remember that time we had to accompany the patients to Park Prewett?'

Ella thought for a moment, then shook her head.

'Terrible journey it was – a green bus had been converted to an ambulance, but it hadn't been done very well, and the stretchers slipped about at every corner. Our shins were black and blue and dented like bomb craters. And we'd had to stop twice while bombs dropped around us, and the orderlies had forgotten to put in any sandwiches or a thermos for us, so we had no tea, no dinner and not enough painkillers for the patients.'

Ella grimaced. She did remember it now. How frightened the young men were but how they tried to hide it behind jokes and bravado. She'd wanted to tell them it was normal to be afraid, that they didn't have to pretend for her, but she supposed they weren't actually doing it for her anyway, they were doing it for themselves and each other, keeping their spirits up and not giving in to the pain, the uncertainty. It was what they all did, and perhaps, after all, it was better that way, keeping a stiff upper lip, not letting the Jerries or the war get to you.

'I think I've had enough of London already. Do you mind if we go straight to Andrew's now?' asked Ella.

'Of course, Ella, we'll do whatever you want.'

## 13

The weekend was so busy Ella didn't have time to think about anything other than the present. They enjoyed a family meal on the Friday night — somehow Sophie managed to make a fish pie that actually had plenty of large chunks of fish in it and a thick white sauce. Andrew opened a bottle of claret, and another, and after the children were in bed, the four of them played bridge, although none of them were quite as sharp as usual, and Ella had a bit of a headache on Saturday morning. It wasn't bad enough to cry off taking the children to the British Museum; Laura was fascinated by the Egyptian mummies, but Billie was scared and stayed very close to his mother. He perked up when they got to some Chinese animal statues and even more when Ella bought him and Laura a penny bar of chocolate on the way home.

Andrew and Sophie had organised a babysitter for the evening and they went back into town for dinner and a show. And not just any show — Andrew had managed to get tickets for the premiere of *Annie Get Your Gun* at the Coliseum. Ella had been humming the catchy tunes ever since, especially *Anything*

*You Can Do (I Can Do Better).* She thought it could have been written for her!

On Sunday they took some bread, cheese and homemade pickles, crunchy apples and bottles of ginger beer, and had a picnic in Richmond Park. It was overcast and cool, rain threatening, but Laura counted the deer for a school project while Billie played with his toy aeroplane and the adults sat on the blanket in the shade of an oak tree dreaming of warm fires and hot drinks.

Back in her own home on the Sunday evening, Ella sat on the sofa, her feet tucked under her. She had found the weekend exhausting, but was glad they'd gone. Andrew had been so good to her since her accident, and she loved seeing the children who were growing up so quickly they seemed to change in front of her very eyes.

Storm clouds were gathering, and lightning split the sky. Seconds later, thunder cracked overhead. Ella ducked, as if expecting to be hit. Sheila put a hand on her shoulder.

'It's all right, Ella, we're safe.' She went to the sideboard and poured a sherry for them both, then sat down next to Ella with a sigh as the rain started pelting down.

'It reminds me of France, this weather and the noise of the thunder. Bayeux to be exact. Do you have any memories of it yet?' she asked.

Ella turned to her. Sheila's voice had betrayed nothing, but the question felt loaded with consequence nonetheless. She was about to reply when Sheila continued, looking into the distance past Ella. 'It's three years ago since we started winning the war. The Normandy Landings. D-Day as most people called it.'

Ella shook her head. 'No, I have no memory of that.' She

picked up her book from the coffee table hoping that Sheila would say no more, but her friend was in a talkative mood.

'Operation Overlord they called it. Hundreds of men landed with tanks, cars, machine guns. The RAF bombed the place to pieces too, clearing the path for the infantrymen to move into France and take back Holland and Belgium from the Jerries.'

Ella's heart was racing. She didn't want to hear any more.

'Mobile hospitals followed...'

'No, I don't remember any of that.' Ella stood, knocking her glass which shattered as it hit the edge of the coffee table.

'I'll get the dustpan and brush,' she said, running from the room. In the kitchen, she gripped the sink wondering if she was going to be sick. Her head was full of awful images of young men, faces contorted in pain and terror. No, she didn't want to remember any of that, not yet, perhaps not ever.

Feeling a little calmer after a glass of water and some deep breaths, she went back into the sitting room.

'I'm sorry, Ella. I didn't mean to upset you. It's just that you've been doing so well remembering everything, I thought you might want to talk about...'

'No. I don't. Not now.' She swept the shards of glass into the dustpan, took it out to the kitchen, wrapped it in newspaper and put it outside in the bin. She was angry with Sheila for bringing up the war, for making her try to remember things she wasn't ready for. She needed to be the one who decided when to talk about these things.

'Goodnight,' she called from the hall. 'I'm going to bed now.' She didn't wait to hear Sheila's reply.

In her room, Ella sat on her bed, staring out the window. The dark and rain had obscured the view, and she saw her own reflection instead, her face drawn, hair slightly messy. She put her hand to her cheek and left it there, feeling the warmth, the comfort that it gave her, skin on skin, even if it was her own. Her breathing returned to normal, her heart rate too, as she forced herself to think of Andrew and Sophie, Billie and Laura; the living, not the dead. She wasn't ready for all the dead.

That night, Ella had another nightmare. She woke up sweating, her nightdress tangled round her legs, her pillow wet. She hadn't drawn the curtains, and the rain was making rivulets down the windowpanes. She had a sip of water and tried not to think about the dream, but she knew that the Whimpering Man had been there, worming his way into her consciousness.

She put the light on and stood by the window. The rain had stopped and the moon was bright when the clouds parted. She saw a fox run across the lawn. If only her life was as simple as his, she thought, hunting for food, making a home for oneself, running around without a thought or a care in the world. And then she remembered the hunts she'd been on as a teenager, the hounds baying as they caught the scent, the horses restless, shuffling from one hoof to another until the huntsman blew his horn and the chase was on. The adrenaline surge as they took off, galloping over fields and through woods, jumping hedges and fences, face close to her horse's mane, urging him to go faster, to keep up, to take her safely to the end, to the kill.

She shuddered and reached for her dressing gown, wrapping it round her shoulders, holding herself tightly, swaying as she stood in a pool of moonlight, crying for the fox, for herself, for the people she'd lost and the fear of what was still to come.

In the morning, Sheila apologised again. 'It's just that I've been thinking of it such a lot. I know it's an awful thing to admit, but I miss the war sometimes. Not the bombings and the loss of life, but the thrill of patients being rushed in to theatre, saving lives. And we had some jolly times, too, you know. Shows and films, dances, romances. The Americans were such flirts, and so generous. What they couldn't get hold of wasn't worth having.'

Ella poured the tea, passing a cup to Sheila who stirred it even though there was no sugar to put in it. 'If those Americans were here now we'd have sugar.' She drew her lips into a funny little pout, her eyes wide like a puppy's.

Ella laughed. 'It's good for your waistline not having sugar. And I for one don't miss those brash Americans. They were so full of themselves.'

'So you do remember!'

Ella thought for a moment. 'Not until I opened my mouth. And I really don't feel ready.' She hesitated, then went on. 'I've been having nightmares again. One image recurs in particular, but there's a general sense of horror.' She stopped again, biting her lip. 'I didn't do something terrible, did I?'

Sheila took her hand, a gesture which rather than alleviating her fears, multiplied them. She felt as if Sheila was about to deliver awful news. She sat up straighter.

'Not that I'm aware of. I can't imagine that you did.'

Ella wanted to believe her, but somehow she knew there was more that Sheila wasn't saying. Sheila must have noticed her quizzical look.

'Really, Ella. You were a good nurse in diabolical circumstances. There were probably things that we all could have done better in a proper hospital with better equipment, but you were dedicated and caring – all the patients loved you. Several of them even proposed to you.'

Ella smiled. 'I suppose they asked all the nurses to marry them.'

'Yes, but you more than most.' Sheila sighed. 'Poor things. They were so brave, and so young, and so far from home.'

'Old enough to fight for their country though,' said Ella. 'And die for it.' She shuddered. 'Let's go for a walk and see if your Arthur has any bacon he'd like to give us, or a pat of butter, shall we?'

'He's not *my* Arthur, but yes, let's go out. It looks like it might rain again later.'

With their mackintoshes and boots on, the two women set off with an eye on the sky and the gathering clouds. Ella looped her arm through Sheila's and pulled her close.

'Did you mean it, about missing the war?' she asked.

Sheila looked into the distance as if searching the trees and hedges of England for the correct answer.

'Only in some ways. The friendships, the excitement – yes, Ella, some of it *was* exciting. But what I really miss is feeling like I'm doing something that matters, something important, you know?'

'Why don't you work in a hospital again then, surely that's important?'

Sheila stopped and turned to her. 'I did go back to Thomas's after I was demobbed, but it wasn't the same. My heart wasn't in it, I suppose. I felt bored and became short-tempered with the patients who complained about the smallest things when our boys had endured so much and complained so little. I can't really explain it, but I felt over it all, that nothing would ever be as all-consuming as nursing behind the lines. Thomas's just felt too pedestrian after that. Do you understand? And then the district nursing. Well, you know what I think about that!'

Ella smiled and started walking again, pulling Sheila along towards the stile.

'Do you know what I did after the war?' she asked.

'You were demobbed a lot later than me – you stayed on for a few months at... with the hospital. I didn't see much of you when you got back.'

Ella raised her eyebrows. 'Did we have a falling out?'

'No, nothing like that,' said Sheila quickly. 'I'd had it with St Thomas's by then and moved back to the Midlands to live with my parents and look after my aged aunt. And I did my stint of dragging money out of people for their treatment. You moved down here. It was difficult to get about to see each other, especially with the wretched petrol rationing and everything.'

Ella was about to ask more, but Sheila started walking faster, pulling ahead. It was obvious she didn't want to say any more, and although Ella knew her friend wasn't telling her everything, she decided not to press it. There were definitely ghosts in her past, things she'd done or not done that had consequences she had no idea of yet. But she would remember, and when she did, she would make whatever reparation she could. In the meantime, her friendship with Sheila was too important to risk bringing up old hurts or slights, and Sheila seemed to think the same.

Arthur was in the barn when they arrived, talking to Fred who was fiddling with the tractor's engine. He smiled when he saw the women, and wiped his hands on a rag before shaking their hands. Fred didn't even look up.

'I'm glad you came over, it saved me a trip. David's coming this evening and suggested making up a four for cards. How about it?'

Ella smiled and agreed that it was a lovely idea.

'Why don't you both come to our house and we'll cook for you this time?'

Arthur laughed. 'Thought you'd never ask,' he said. 'But come into the kitchen, there's something there that might help towards dinner.'

Twenty minutes later, after a quick cup of tea, Ella and

Sheila were carrying a skinned rabbit back to Bamford House, as well as some potatoes, carrots and a large yellow pat of butter.

'I think you should marry that man,' said Ella. 'We'll never go hungry if you do.'

Sheila reddened. 'Better hurry – I just felt a drop of rain.'

Ella and Sheila decided to serve dinner in the dining room for a change, and opened the French doors onto the garden in celebration of the fact that the rain had finally stopped. The rabbit stew was tasty and robust, Sheila having added fresh herbs and a good slug of red wine she'd found in the back of the pantry.

'Fantastic meal, thank you,' said David, leaning back in his chair and loosening his tie a little.

'Shall we go through to the sitting room for coffee and cards?' Sheila led the way.

'Actually, rather than cards, would you play something for us, Ella?' asked David.

'I'm very rusty,' said Ella, playing with her necklace. 'I haven't played much at all for ages.'

'I'm sure you'll do fine,' said Arthur. 'Much better than any of the rest of us could.'

'Oh, do play, Ella,' said Sheila. 'I've heard you down here in the past few days, tinkering away. I think you miss it, and we'll be a very appreciative audience.'

Ella gave in and moved to the piano.

'Just one piece then,' she said, and pulled some music out of the piano stool. 'How about this – "Clair de Lune"?'

'Oh, lovely. A bit of Debussy.' David rubbed his hands together, then poured them all a brandy, and sat ready to listen.

Ella sat at the piano, closed her eyes, took a deep breath and started playing. It was one of her favourite pieces of music, the melody carrying her along, transporting her to faraway places; magnificent houses, beautifully dressed women and chivalrous men. Music had always been her escape. When her mother died she'd played all day every day for weeks on end, until her father had insisted that she attend to her other lessons and get out of the house.

She came to the end, her hands lingering on the keys, her eyes still closed. There was silence for a moment and then applause. She opened her eyes to see Sheila and Arthur giving her a standing ovation and David wiping a tear from his eye. Later she wondered if that was the moment she fell in love with him.

## 14

'I'm going for a walk,' Ella called to Sheila as she stepped out of the back door. She had a bit of a hangover from all the cocktails they'd had the night before; David had taken her to a new jazz club in Southampton and they'd danced and drunk the night away. They'd been seeing a lot of each other over the past few weeks, and Ella was enjoying herself immensely. He was being a perfect gentleman. He hadn't even kissed her, except a goodnight peck on the cheek, but she felt she was falling in love, and she liked it — it gave her a spring in her step and a healthy glow in the cheeks. It had been far too long since she'd felt either. She still didn't remember if there'd been anyone since Charles, but somehow it didn't feel like there had been. As she looked at the scenery around her she realised it was also far too long since she'd walked the paths that trailed through the hills, stopping every so often to enjoy the view or peer at a colourful wild flower, and it was just what she needed to clear her head.

It was the first day of July, and already too warm. Ella couldn't remember a heatwave like the one they were having. It had been a nice change from the wet spring at first, but now, two weeks into it, it was still getting hotter every day, and she would have given anything for some cold, wet weather. She smiled. She'd never be satisfied; it was too hot or too cold, too wet or too dry. No wonder the weather was such a topic of conversation. In the village the day before, everyone seemed to be talking about the heat, how it was killing their plants or making the children grumpy, or they had to work when all they wanted to do was go to the seaside or swim in the river. Ella had wanted to sit in the shade with a book and a gin and tonic; the beach had never held much interest for her after her mother died, even on the hottest of days.

She picked her way through the gorse and strode up the path, keen to reach the top and take in the view of the county. She loved the way the countryside was dotted with towns and villages, the houses nestling in the greenery. By the time she was halfway up, she was puffing and had an unladylike sweat dripping down her forehead into her eyes and she was cursing herself for forgetting a hat. She pulled her hanky out and wiped her face and carried on a bit more slowly. Somewhere in the distance, a tractor was chugging along, and above her a hawk rode the thermals searching for a juicy field mouse to swoop on. Ella felt a deep sense of contentment, of everything being all right in the world, and she sighed, stretched her arms above her head, and turned her face up to the sun, eyes squinting in the brightness.

Next minute, she was lying face down in the grass, heart thudding, hands over her head. She waited for the next bomb to fall, forcing herself to take deep breaths to try and stop the shaking. Nothing happened. No more bombs, no planes droning overhead, just birds twittering in the trees, the hot sun beating down on her, the smell of grass and rich loam filling her nostrils. Slowly she raised her head and looked around. There was no bomb crater, no blood, no wounded men groaning nearby. She got up onto her knees, still looking around, still alert, and was relieved to find that all was well. What had happened? Was she going mad? Relief gave way to anxiety. She had thought she was going to die, that the Germans were bombing the hillside. Down in the valley, a car backfired in the distance. She felt a moment of panic again, and then she started laughing — she'd been afraid of a damn car. The tears followed swiftly, thickly. She sat back down in the grass and sobbed, hands covering her face, shoulders heaving. France. The war, the young soldiers being killed all round them, the wounded being brought in trying to be brave, stoical, missing legs, arms, eyes. Or groaning and screaming in agony, and who could blame them? None of them had thought that they'd take a bullet or stop flying shrapnel with their strong young bodies. They'd signed up to kill Germans, not be killed by them, that wasn't part of their plan. Each one was going to be a hero, fight with courage, save the lives of their brothers-in-arms, conquer the Boche, re-establish peace in Europe and come home to their loved ones. Instead, they lay face down in muddy ditches or broken on stretchers fighting for their lives.

Ella took a deep breath and held it. If she could count to ten, she'd be all right. It was a trick she'd learned in the war, and it had always worked then. She fixed her eyes on a church steeple in a village down the hill, and counted, slowly, forcing herself to stop imagining it being blown to bits. When she reached ten, she let the breath out, brushed herself down and stood up. Perhaps it was time to confront what had happened in France. She would have to read the last diary; she couldn't put it off forever.

∼

'Nice walk?' asked Sheila as she entered the kitchen.

'Far too damn hot, even this early,' said Ella, pouring herself a glass of water. She gulped it down and wiped a hand across her forehead. It came away brown, and she realised that she must have dirt all over her face.

'I had a bit of a fall – nothing to worry about, I'm not hurt,' she added quickly when she saw Sheila's expression. 'I slipped on a tree root, that's all. Apart from the heat it was lovely up there – you can see for miles.'

'Hmm.' Sheila didn't look convinced, but carried on, 'Hot for a picnic today, too, but hopefully we can find some shade. I've got some cold tongue, bread, salad and cider. Arthur said he'd bring beer and cheese. Anything else you can think of?'

Ella thought wistfully about champagne and strawberries, Pimms and pâté. 'No, that sounds marvellous. What can I do?'

'It's all ready. You can carry the hamper.'

'Consider it done.'

She went up to wash and change while Sheila pottered about in the kitchen. Ella had never known anyone so adept at pottering. She could spend hours checking on this and that, thinking up new recipes or changing the cupboards around. Ella never had the patience for that sort of thing, but Sheila said she found it soothing.

David arrived in his car at the appointed time, and they went to collect Arthur, who was still in his work clothes, tempting a lame calf into a stall.

'The vet said he can't come until later, but I thought I should bring her in now so she doesn't get worse,' he said. 'It won't take me a minute to change.'

'Take your time,' said David, leaning against the car bonnet, offering Sheila a cigarette and lighting one for himself. 'Have a good wash. We don't need you reeking the car out.'

Arthur smiled. 'The windows will be open, surely? And a bit of Eau de Farmyard never hurt anyone!'

Sheila and Ella walked a little way off and sat on a bale of straw, watching the men.

'He's very caring, isn't he?' said Ella, nodding towards Arthur.

'Very,' agreed Sheila, blushing slightly.

'He'll be good to you.'

Sheila fanned herself with her hanky and looked away.

The day continued to be hot and as they waited for Arthur, David went into the kitchen and came back with cool ginger beer.

'Won't take long to get up onto the Downs. There should be a bit of a breeze up there, and some shade,' he said as he handed them a glass each.

Ella sipped on the drink, hoping that she didn't panic again. She didn't want to make a scene, nor did she want to feel the fear she had earlier. She was afraid she might be going mad, it had all been so real. To distract herself she looked at David — he had a kind face, not classically handsome, but one that invited trust and instilled a sense of safety. And she knew him to be steady, loyal and intelligent. She smiled to herself. She made him sound dull and boring, when in fact, he was anything but. He knew how to entertain and please a woman. She blushed at her thoughts. She didn't know if he would please her in that way, but she was beginning to wonder. Charles and she had enjoyed their intimacies. She sighed, and David turned to her.

'Are you quite all right, Ella? You look a little flushed.'

'Yes, I'm fine, thank you.' She smiled and got up from the bale, put a hand on his sleeve and looked into his eyes. 'I'm quite fine now,' she repeated, the emphasis on the now, and squeezed his arm.

He returned her gaze, and Ella felt as if an understanding

had passed between them in that moment; from her side a message that said, yes, I am ready for whatever it is you want from me, I have loved before, but I am ready to love again, and from his, a commitment to love and protect her.

The picnic was perfect. As David had predicted, a breeze had picked up on the Downs, and they lay their rug out under a spreading tree. Arthur entertained them with stories of the prisoners of war he'd had helping on the farm and the problems the language barrier had caused at times. The funniest of which was when a German lad had mistaken Arthur's instruction to feed the chickens as an order to kill one of them to eat. He'd come in with the poor bird in one hand, still struggling, and a cleaver in the other.

'I didn't know what he was doing, and then I realised. I grabbed poor Bess from him and shooed him out the door. She was my best layer! After that, I tried to be clearer. He was a good lad though. Always worked hard and loved the animals. I was quite sad to see him go at the end of the war, to be honest.'

'What happened to him?'

'Sent home, as they all were, I suppose. He learned a bit of English while he was here and said he'd write, but he never did.'

'What about you, David – what did you do in the war, you've never talked about it?' asked Sheila.

'Oh, I was in the navy. Submarines.'

'How ghastly,' said Ella without thinking.

'Oh, it wasn't so bad really. Cramped, of course, but one made do. At least I was an officer so I had my own bed. Some of the chaps had to share a berth – one on duty, one off.'

'David's being modest as usual. He wasn't just in any submarine, he was a lieutenant aboard *HMS Ursula*, who made it through the war and sank quite a few ships and U-boats.'

'Where were you?' asked Ella.

'Oh, here and there; the North Sea to start with, then the Med.'

'Wasn't it awfully scary, being down there all the time?' asked Sheila.

'Do you know, it wasn't. I think we were all too busy to think about that, or too tired. We weren't underwater all the time either, of course. We did come up for air sometimes.'

Ella leant into him. 'I think you're very brave. I couldn't have done it.'

'And I couldn't have done what you did, saving all those lives, caring for our brave lads. Give me a U-boat to sink any day!'

'You don't mean that, surely,' said Ella.

David looked into the distance, as if remembering those underwater chases. 'No, I have to admit that I'm very glad it's all over and that I survived to tell the tale.' He smiled at her. 'I'd far rather be here.'

In the afternoon the breeze died down and the temperature rose. They made their way slowly down the hill, Arthur and Sheila in front, and David and Ella, arm in arm, following.

'What a lovely day,' said Ella.

'Perfect, I'd say.' David stopped and pulled her close, his eyebrows raised as if asking her permission.

Ella lifted her chin and looked into his eyes. Her heart gave a little flutter as he leant in to kiss her, and another as his lips brushed hers. She put her arms around him and returned his kisses, eager for more even before they had stopped.

The next day, Ella received a letter from Joan Nesbitt, née Malone, who had trained with them at St Thomas's and been across the corridor from them in the nurses' home.

'How did she know what had happened?' asked Ella, waving the letter at Sheila.

'I wrote and told her,' said Sheila, wiping down the table after their breakfast.

Ella stared at her. 'You did what? First you take my address book away so that I can't contact people, and then you're the one who decides when it's time to start being social again? It wasn't for you to tell people. I'd have told them when I was ready.' When I remembered them, she added to herself.

Sheila sat down, the cloth still in her hands. She bit her lip.

'What?' asked Ella.

Sheila took a deep breath and seemed to come to some sort of decision.

'Look. I'm sorry I went behind your back, but the fact is, Andrew and I felt that you were ready to branch out a bit, and it was time our friends knew what had happened and so I wrote to them. Joan wrote back immediately asking if she could visit. I thought there was no harm in it, to be honest. I mean, you're doing very well now.'

'And that gives you the right to organise my life? Have you always been so domineering?'

'Not at all,' said Sheila emphatically. 'I'm sorry I didn't check with you first. I thought you'd like the surprise. I was thinking of you, you know. You have good friends, Ella, people who love you very much. It's not fair to keep them out forever, is it? We all had such a time in London when you came home from the war, but we haven't seen much of each other since.'

Ella looked out the window at the blue sky, at the leaves of the chestnut tree gently rustling in the breeze. 'No, I suppose not. But I thought you said we hardly saw each other when I got back.'

Sheila waved a hand as if to say, 'you got it all wrong,' and said, 'I meant that I came down from the back of beyond for a few days and we partied like mad then. That one time, but it was several days. We were all so happy to see you again.'

'All right then. I'm sorry I snapped at you. It was just rather a shock. I've got used to our quiet life, but perhaps you're right. It's time to branch out a bit. I'll write back to Joan and invite her to visit, shall I?'

Sheila smiled. 'If you like,' she said. 'So I'm forgiven?'

'Of course. Am I?'

'Nothing to forgive, darling.'

Later that night, unable to sleep, Ella crept into the sitting room and took the third diary up to her bedroom. Shutting the door after herself quietly, she sat on her bed, holding the notebook in her hands, trying to calm her racing heart. She knew that she would read things she would rather not, and hoped she had the courage to face it.

*6th March, 1944*

*We've been called up! Maeve, Sheila, Joan and me. I can hardly believe it still. It took all my courage to ask Sister Cooper for permission to leave, rightly so, as it turned out. She was furious – she said I should have told her when I signed up at the beginning of the war. Well, I joined the reserves after Charles was killed, and I didn't tell anyone. I wanted to go immediately and get killed myself rather than live without him. Turns out I've had to wait another four years and now I don't want to die. Anyway, she said I was letting her and St Thomas's down, that I was doing important work for the war effort right where I was. I almost said I'd see if I could get out of it, but in the end, I thought of Sheila and the others going without me, and I held my ground. When Sister realised she couldn't go against the War Office, she gave in. She even wished me well and told me that I was a*

*good nurse and the QAs would be lucky to have me! Oh, and I've
always got a job on her ward if I want it. High praise indeed.
We are to report for duty at 0800 hours next Monday at Hatfield
House in Hertfordshire. Sounds like an elocution exercise! I hope it's
not unlucky to report on the 13th. I mustn't be superstitious. Of course
it'll be all right, it's only a day in the year, after all.*

Ella looked up and thought about wanting to die after
Charles's death. Yes, she remembered long days, dragging
herself through work and going back to the flat some nights
when it was still standing to drink herself to sleep. Months of
going through the motions of life, feeling disconnected.
Sometimes she saw herself as if from above, walking along a
street, or making a patient comfortable, saying the right words,
smiling the right smile, but not being in her body, not
experiencing the event. And there were the times when it felt so
tempting to step off the pavement in front of a bus, when only
thinking about what it would do to the poor driver stopped her.

She sighed and returned to the diary.

*Hatfield House, March '44
What an amazing place this is – a glimpse at how the rich live, even
though at the moment the house has been turned into a hospital and
the grounds are covered in tents, the grass between them rutted by car
tyres.
We don't know how long we'll be here exactly, but it'll be some weeks.
We have to do basic training and get kitted out. There will be lectures
and we're to be vaccinated against typhus, typhoid and smallpox. All
this was in a leaflet we were handed when we arrived. Also, we have
to learn how to put up and take down a tent hospital. I hope we have
some help!
We've been given rooms in the servants' quarters at the top of the
house – three narrow flights of stairs with no light to guide us at*

*night. We're two to a room, so Sheila and I are sharing again – we know each other's ways by now, so it's easy. Maeve and Joan are next door. The rooms are small and draughty, and the bathrooms are health hazards. The other girls are from hospitals all over England; it's odd being with so many unfamiliar faces again. I haven't been around so many new people since I started my training. I expect we'll all be great friends by the time we leave here.*

*The house itself has such grand rooms. The carpets have been removed and hospital beds replace the furniture, but there are priceless paintings by the old masters still on the walls, and beautifully painted ceilings above the busyness and misery below. I've never seen anything like it.*

Ella lay the book in her lap again and let the image of that ceiling come to her. She remembered looking up at it in awe, letting its beauty calm her when she was upset, inspire her when she was exhausted. She smiled as she remembered telling Sheila that it was that ceiling that got her through their training there.

And she remembered talks on France, the war, the injuries they might see, army etiquette. Lectures they dozed through in spite of the hard wooden seats. They were already nurses and thought they'd seen it all. Hadn't they worked in hospitals tending the wounded brought back from the various fronts? Weren't they even then looking after soldiers back from the war? Could anything be worse than seeing young men with limbs missing? Or burned and blinded? Or with spinal injuries which meant they'd never walk again?

It hadn't been the actual injuries that had upset Ella, but the way the men responded to them. Some were stoical, others resigned, but many were consumed with rage, resentful of the fact that their lives had been taken from them as surely as if they'd been killed on the battlefield. Many wished it were so, that they didn't have to face the pity or revulsion of the civilians at home; friends and family members who offered platitudes before turning away, horrified. Or worse, talked in bright voices about the future.

Ella shuddered at her memories of those young men. Men whose lives had been redefined, who gave up on their dreams, who no longer felt useful or relevant. She had felt impotent in the face of their pain — there was too little she could do to assuage it for them.

## 15

After a restless night, Ella awoke feeling tired and sore. She looked at the diary sitting innocently on her bedside table and frowned. She didn't have the energy for it today. What she'd read the day before had left her feeling bleak and angry. Or rather, not what she'd read, because that had been insipid and naïve, but rather the memories it had evoked. How could she have been so flippant in the face of so much pain? Had they all been like that, she wondered – was it some sort of collective denial?

She dragged herself out of bed and over to her dressing table. Her reflection showed a haggard face, with deep circles under the eyes and hair that needed a good cut. She decided to go into Hambleford and seek out a hairdresser. And while she was there, maybe David would take her out for lunch. Perhaps she should daub some make-up on first so he didn't get a fright.

David was delighted when she telephoned him. 'I'll take you to the Royal Oak for the best pub lunch in England, or so they claim.'

'Sounds lovely, although as long as it isn't Spam, I don't care whether it's the best or the worst. A burnt chop will do. Or bread, cheese and a bit of salad. Anything but Spam.'

'They'll do better than bread and cheese, I promise. See you at one.'

~

Sheila was making breakfast when Ella entered the kitchen.

'I thought I heard you talking just now,' she said, looking up from the eggy bread she was making with eggs from the hens Arthur had given them.

'I was talking to David. I'm going into Hambleford for lunch and a haircut. Want to come?'

'No, I won't cramp your style. And anyway, I need to do a few things here.'

'Oh? Like what?'

Sheila reddened. 'Oh, you know, this and that.'

'This and that?' Ella laughed. 'You've always been such a bad liar.'

'I'm not lying. I am doing this and that, some of it just happens to be at the farm, that's all.'

'Well, have a lovely day. I'm going to get the bus at ten from the village.' She fished a piece of eggy bread out of the frying pan with a fork and flipped it onto a plate.

'Mm, this is good. Long may those hens continue laying. Make sure you bring a bit of butter back from the farm, and maybe a side of beef!'

Sheila flicked a tea towel at her in response.

Becoming serious again, Ella asked her friend about their time at Hatfield House.

'What were we really like back then?'

'What do you mean?'

'I was reading my diary last night, and I seemed terribly

callow. There we were, getting ready to be sent to France, and I for one seemed to be treating it like a holiday camp.'

Sheila sucked in her bottom lip and thought for a while.

'No, I don't think we were callow. We were naïve, yes, but I think we all cared a great deal about the men in our care, and the soldiers we would be looking after in Europe. It's just that I don't think we could really imagine what it would be like. It was all very well talking about the bombs and the awful injuries we'd have to treat, but we couldn't imagine anything worse than we'd already seen. I couldn't, at least.' She reached for her cigarettes and lit one, tipping her head back and blowing the smoke up towards the ceiling.

'Was it awful?'

Sheila looked at her, her eyes narrowed. 'Yes, it was. Some of it. I'd have a stiff drink by your side when you read about it if I were you. Or let me sit with you and we can talk about it as you go.'

Ella's stomach sank. 'Thank you. I might take you up on that offer.' But really, she knew she wouldn't, that she would read in private and somehow manage the consequences. After all, she'd lived through it once, so it couldn't kill her.

She looked at the clock and gasped. 'I'd better run if I'm going to make the ten o'clock bus.'

'Take your time. It leaves at ten past these days – the timetable changed last week for some reason.'

Ella was just about to ask how she knew that, and then smiled. Of course Sheila knew. She was the sort of person who always knew everything.

'Have a lovely day – and don't forget that side of beef!' Ella ran out of the room with Sheila's laughter following her.

.   .   .

At one o'clock, with a new hairdo and make-up which the hairdresser had done for her (out of pity, Ella suspected), she walked towards the Royal Oak. She liked the town with its pretty market square at one end, the modest town hall, the clothes shops and grocers and hair salons. The lamp posts all sported baskets of flowers blooming in spite of the heat and the lack of rain. She was happy, and looking forward to seeing David.

And there he was, walking towards the pub from the other direction. He hadn't seen her yet, so she had time to study him in his a well-fitting suit, crisp white shirt, polished shoes. A young woman passed him and turned back for another look, and Ella felt proud that someone else would find him attractive too. He was tall and broad and carried himself well. She rushed the last few yards and smiled as he noticed her.

'David,' she said, and wanted to throw herself into his arms. Only the fact that they were in a public place and he had offices in town and may be recognised stopped her.

He seemed equally happy to see her, and less cautious as he took his hat off, swept her into an embrace and kissed her, right there in front of the pub.

'You look divine, I love the new hair,' he said, taking her hand and leading her into the bar.

They chatted over gin and tonics, looked at the menu, but Ella's mind wasn't on food. And she couldn't concentrate on what he was saying because she kept wondering what his hands would feel like as they caressed her body. He stopped talking and she had to shake her head to rid herself of the image of them naked together in bed and ask him to repeat what he'd said.

'Are you all right, Ella?'

She nodded, perhaps a little too vehemently. 'I'm fine.'

'You look a little peaky.'

'Not peaky, no.' She bit her lip, David watched her, a concerned frown creasing his forehead.

'David, we're both adults, and we can make our own decisions, so...' She had no idea how to carry on.

'Are you breaking up with me?' he asked.

Ella gasped. 'No – quite the opposite. I'm propositioning you!' She blushed.

David laughed and took her hand. 'Well, I'll be! Here I am, being the gentleman, and all along all you've wanted is my body.'

'Not all,' said Ella, 'I like your mind too. So?'

'Now?'

'Yes.'

'They have rooms here but...'

'Where then?'

'My house.'

They left and walked quickly along the high street and then turned off down a narrow lane. Minutes later, David stopped, took out a key, and opened the door of a tall stone house with a narrow front garden. He ushered her in, closed the door firmly behind them and took Ella in his arms.

'You're sure about this?'

'Absolutely. Now kiss me.' Her heart was pumping hard, and she could feel his, too, as they held each other. They kissed for a long time, and then he led her up to his bedroom and slowly they undressed each other standing in a shaft of sunlight from the open window. The net curtains blew gently in the breeze as David lay her gently on the bed. They caressed, following the contours of each other's body, learning the landscape, listening for the gasp of pleasure, the shudder of release.

'You know I've fallen in love with you, don't you?' said David as they lay together afterwards.

Ella lifted herself up onto one elbow and looked into his

eyes. 'And I you,' she said, and then lay down again. David played idly with her hair. Suddenly she was giggling.

'What's so funny?'

'I was just thinking how natural it feels to be here with you, but I feel naughty too, like a schoolgirl who's broken the rules.'

'You can break those silly old rules any time you like. Anyway, this is 1947 and the rules have changed since the war, don't you think? People are much more liberated these days.'

She snuggled in to him. 'I don't care if they aren't. I want to be here with you, that's all. Everyone else can think what they want.'

'Amen to that.'

A minute later he looked at his watch and apologised. 'I have clients this afternoon, I have to get back to work.'

'Of course,' said Ella.

'Quick sandwich before we go? After all, I did promise you lunch.'

'A sandwich sounds perfect.'


Ella sat on the bus on the way home with an enormous smile on her face. If anyone had asked her for loose change, as some returned soldiers did these days, she'd have emptied the contents of her purse into their laps. The sun seemed brighter than usual and the breeze through the windows caressed her skin lightly, just as David's fingers had not so long ago.

Sheila was out when she arrived home, and buoyed by the events of the day, she felt ready to tackle her diary again. She slipped her sandals off, got herself a glass of water and went upstairs to her room. Throwing the windows open wide to catch any available breeze, she sat on the bed and started reading.

. . .

*April '44*

*I'm so tired I could sleep for a week, not that the sadist who takes our drills would let me. I haven't even got the energy for the party tonight in the doctors' mess. We've been up every morning at half past five to run round the grounds not once, but twice in full kit: ugly, scratchy khakis and heavy, stiff boots. Then a cold shower before a meagre breakfast and a lecture or yet more jabs for this illness or that. Then it's time for elevenses – a cup of tea with no sugar, and on to roll call, which involves standing in front of the house come rain or shine, waiting for our names to be called, to which we have to respond, 'Here, Sir' and salute. Standing to attention for hours on end has to be one of the most exhausting exercises ever invented, and for what? Are we going to be snapping to attention all the time when we're nursing the boys in France? Of course not. It's all completely pointless. Yesterday, I got into trouble for not saluting an officer. I thought I was going to be court-martialled he got so up in arms about it. Honestly, I'm so confused about who we salute and who we don't. We're all lieutenants and there are some who don't warrant our stiff salutes, I just haven't worked out quite who and why.*

*After roll call we have to report to the wards to take over while the regular staff go on lunches and off duties. I wish I was one of them, not having to do all this stupid army stuff. Anyway, it's the best part of the day because we're doing what we're trained for and feel useful.*

*We get lunch at two thirty and then spend the afternoons either having self-defence lessons or learning how to put up the hospital tents. I can't imagine karate chopping some German spy who wanders behind our lines, but it may come in useful, I suppose – perhaps to keep frisky patients at bay.*

*As to the tents, well! Some pioneers help us, they're lovely lads, and in reality, they do most of the actual erecting of the tents, then we have to kit them out with operating tables, lights, beds (which we then have to make), all the things we will need including sterilising and sluicing equipment, trays of dressings, instruments, towels, drip stands, drugs and packets of blood (only pretend blood – water dyed red. We can't spare the real stuff), and all the other paraphernalia we need to do our jobs. We've also had to learn how to sterilise water in case there's no clean supply. And as soon as it's all up and ready, we have to take it all down and pack it away again. It takes days and it's too annoying.*

*I've just heard that tomorrow we're going to be allocated to the groups we'll work with in France. I hope I'm with Sheila, Maeve and Joan. Any of the other girls will do, too, except for Daffodil 'call me Daffy' Johnson. Daffy by name and Daffy by nature. She's a complete ninny and can't seem to hold an instruction in her head for more than two minutes at a time. She's always late, too, and gets into so much trouble. We set her watch forward without her knowing one night, and she still managed to be late for roll call.*

*Tomorrow we go to Austin Reed in London to be fitted for our dress uniforms. At least we'll be away from here for a few hours.*

*Anyway, time for bed. Sleep – heaven.*

Ella lay back and closed her eyes, smiling to herself. She did sound uppity in her diary, but she'd never liked taking orders that seemed unnecessary. The next day, when they got their allocations, she was relieved to discover that she and Sheila were allocated to the same hospital group along with eighteen others, including Daffy. Maeve and Joan were in another. All of them were going to France. They'd talked about it in the evening when the day's uniform fittings in London were over and they had a few minutes to relax in the mess with a whisky. Some were worried about the posting, now it was real, but Ella was glad that they knew where they were going, and wondered when they'd be off. She felt ready.

~

She heard the back door open and close.

'Ella, are you in? I'll bring you up a cup of tea,' she said.

'No, I'll come down,' said Ella. It was time they had a talk about things.

'Sheila,' said Ella as she entered the kitchen, 'you don't need to look after me anymore, you've done quite enough, and I'm feeling fine now.'

Sheila's face fell. 'So you want me to go?'

'Oh, good heavens, no! That's not what I meant at all. You can stay as long as you like, I love having you here. I only meant that I should be doing more of the cooking and cleaning. I haven't been pulling my weight. I can't believe I've let it go on for so long.'

'But I like looking after you.'

'There speaks Nurse Sheila!' Ella smiled. 'You've done a fine job. But now we're just two friends sharing a home.'

Sheila relaxed and smiled. 'I don't mind doing the housework – I find it soothing.'

'Well, I hate it, so I'd be very happy for you to do that and I'll take over all the cooking, so that's settled. Anyway, how was Arthur?'

'Very well. I went over to do some mending for him. His sister usually does it, apparently, but she's pregnant again and feeling sick as a dog, so I said I'd help out.' She pulled a package out of her bag. 'He gave me these as a thank you.'

'Stewing steak and kidneys – how wonderful!' said Ella.

'Yes, we can have a pie.'

'Isn't it funny how we get so excited about these things nowadays. I hope rationing ends soon and we can get back to eating normally. Not that we're doing too badly these days, of course.'

'How was your day – how was David?'

Ella felt the blush start at her throat and end at her hairline. 'He's fine,' she said.

Sheila looked at her and her eyes widened. 'Tell me all,' she said.

Ella waved a hand in the air. 'Oh, you know.'

'I think I do. Well, well. Is it love?'

Ella grinned, suddenly desperate to tell someone how she felt.

'Yes, it is. He's so warm and funny, such a gentleman. I had to seduce him. Oh, Sheila, I'm so happy.'

'You make a good couple, that's for sure. He's been in love with you since the day he met you, you just didn't see it.'

'Well, to be fair, I've had other things on my mind. But I see it now, and that's all that matters. Has Arthur said anything to you yet?'

'Not yet, but I feel it's coming.' Sheila grinned.

That night the friends had one sherry too many and danced in the sitting room to sounds from the big bands on the radio until they could dance no more.

Ella was too tired and squiffy to read more of her diary when she went to bed. Instead, she lay in her bed imagining David there with her and all the delightful things they would get up to. It took her a while to get to sleep.

Although her thoughts were of David as she drifted into sleep, her dreams were of the war; bodies left open and oozing after bombing raids, limbs torn off young soldiers and found hanging days later, in trees where they had been flung by the force of the blast, grisly reminders of the fighting, the ferocious battle for every inch of land.

She woke up sweating and went to the bathroom to run cold water over her hands and face.

She knew she wouldn't sleep again, so she put the light on and picked up her diary.

*May '44*

*We're on the move. We got our orders today. We are to live under canvas in some out-of-the-way place to prepare for France.*

*We were given our kit today too. Any romantic illusions of life in a tent were dashed a little more with every item on the list.*

*A tin trunk.*

*A bed roll (thin and lumpy).*

*Two blankets.*

*Small, flat pillow.*

*Canvas cot with folding legs.*

*A canvas wash bowl and stand (does canvas even hold water?).*

*A collapsible canvas bath (see above).*

*A canvas bucket (presumably for filling the leaky bath).*

*A Beatrice paraffin stove.*

*Lamp.*

*Device for hanging things from tent pole (looks like an implement of medieval torture).*

*All that, plus our spare uniforms and 'mess dress' have to fit in the trunk which we have to paint our names and hospital number on.*

*There won't be any room to take a nice dress or pair of shoes for when we're off duty, or hair rollers, make-up... we're going to look ghastly by the time we get to France.*

Ella cringed. Had she really thought it was going to be a holiday? She was disgusted at her former self; the flippancy, the superficiality, the prejudice. But then she wondered if, perhaps, they'd been led to believe that there would be time for frivolity, maybe to keep their spirits up, making them believe that life in the army would be the same as civilian life, just in a different location. From the little she remembered already, she was sure that hadn't been the reality.

## 16

Ella and David began to see more of each other over the next few weeks, and her burning need to know about her past was overtaken by her pleasure in the present.

They went to concerts in Southampton, the pictures in Hambleford, picnics on the Downs and dances wherever they were on. Sometimes they were joined by Sheila and Arthur, making a chatty foursome, but increasingly, Ella preferred the times when it was just her and David.

'I want to know how you haven't been snapped up before now,' she said one evening as they sat in the garden of the local pub enjoying the evening sun.

David smiled at her. 'I was waiting for you, of course.' He smiled at her over the rim of his pint glass.

Ella raised her eyebrows. 'So are you telling me that you could see into the future?'

He put his drink down and drew a hand through his hair. 'I suppose we should tell each other about our pasts. I'm surprised we haven't before now. I know you were married and lost your husband in the war, but that's all.'

Ella shifted in her seat. What had started as a throwaway

comment now felt ominous. David must have sensed her discomfort, because he took her hand. 'And if you don't want to talk about it, that's fine. I'll tell you about me.'

Ella swallowed and nodded her encouragement.

'I went to a boys' school, where the only woman we came into contact with was the headmaster's wife, and to be honest, we weren't even sure she was female. She had short hair and was built like a rugger player, thick-necked and steely-calved. During the holidays, we went to Scotland to my grandparents' house, on the windswept west coast, where no young girls in their right minds would venture for fear of having their hats blown into the sea and their hairdos spoilt. At least, that's what my sisters said.'

Ella laughed.

'Then, when I went to university, the few girls who were there were terrifying.'

'But you grew up with sisters, surely you were comfortable around women?'

'I was, but these weren't women, they were students, and all far more intelligent than me. I worked hard to prove myself, but even the thought of ever actually going near enough to any of them to ask them to a dance was enough to send me into paroxysms of fear. Yet somehow, any other girl didn't compare. We students were an elitist bunch.'

'So you really want me to believe that a man like you never took a girl out?'

'Oh, I took a few girls to dances, but never any more than that. Then I started work at a firm of solicitors in Southampton. One of the partners had a daughter, Ivy, who was beautiful and clever and in need of a young man to escort her to a hunt ball. Her father suggested me.'

'And?'

'I took her. Would you like another drink?' He nodded towards Ella's empty glass.

'Not until you've told me the rest of the story.'

David sighed. 'There isn't really that much to tell. We went about together for a while, but there was something about her that I couldn't put a finger on at the time, but now I see that she was quite disturbed. She would say the oddest things, and take silly risks, driving too fast on country roads, walking too close to cliff edges, that sort of thing. I thought she was testing me somehow – did I care enough to ask her to stop? Then sometimes she wouldn't talk to me for days on end, and then be all friendly again as if nothing had happened. I'm an uncomplicated sort of man, and I found her behaviour unsettling, so I ended it. I feel bad about that; I don't feel I treated her very well at the end, but I didn't know what to do. Unfortunately, her father then ended my employment. I think he was desperate to find her a husband, and once I'd taken myself out of the race, I had to go to make room for another unsuspecting contender. Anyway, how about that drink?'

Ella caught his hand as he stood up.

'Don't feel too bad, my darling. I'm sure she survived.'

'Oh, yes, she did that. She's married to a viscount now.'

'Well then,' said Ella. David smiled and went to get the drinks.

While he was gone, Ella thought about what he'd said. She felt sorry for the girl, Ivy, but glad that David hadn't fallen for her. Did that make her selfish? If it did, she didn't care. She and David were so happy together. She couldn't imagine him being unkind to anyone either, he probably said it out of guilt. He came back with a whisky for her and another pint for himself.

'So, after Ivy?' asked Ella.

'I became a submariner in His Majesty's navy and spent the war underwater with lots of smelly men. Washing facilities weren't too good on a sub, I'm afraid to say.'

'But you must have had shore leave?'

'Of course, and didn't we go mad then. You have no idea what it's like living in such tight conditions for weeks at a time. There was nowhere on the sub where we could actually reach both arms out at the same time. All we wanted to do when we got leave was stretch our cramped limbs and get as drunk as possible.'

'You make yourself sound completely depraved,' said Ella, taking his hand and stroking the soft hairs on the backs of his fingers.

'Not anymore.' He smiled.

'Oh, I should certainly hope you won't be on your best behaviour all the time.' Ella blushed. 'Shall we go?'

They tossed back their drinks and were strolling arm in arm towards Ella's house when a car came round the bend far too fast, swerved to avoid them, and came to a halt in the ditch by the side of the road, one rear wheel spinning. Ella ran over to see if the driver was all right.

He was pulling himself out by the time she got to him, and saying something, but he was so agitated that Ella couldn't make it out.

'Are you hurt?' she asked slowly and clearly.

'No, not me. I was on my way to the hospital to get help though – there's been an accident up the road, a few people need attention.'

In an instant, all Ella's training came back to her. She looked at the man and his car, stuck in the ditch, then turned to David.

'Can you take this man, Mr...?' She glanced at the stranger again.

'Ellis. Sam Ellis.'

'Mr Ellis to fetch Dr Myers from his hospital. It's the nearest one. I'll run home and telephone Arthur and ask him to take Sheila and me to the accident. Where is it, exactly?' She turned to Sam Ellis.

'About a mile past Chase Farm on the Hambleford Road.'

'Right,' said David. 'Let's go.'

They all ran the rest of the way to Ella's house, and she rushed in to get Sheila while David and Sam Ellis sped off in David's car.

Ella and Sheila gathered torches, cloths, the few first-aid items that were lying around the house, which amounted to three bandages and half a dozen sterile dressings, and filled a couple of old gin bottles with water. By the time they were ready, Arthur had arrived to take them to the site of the accident.

They were met with chaos when they got there. People were milling about aimlessly, getting in the way of a man in a dark suit who was attending to a woman on the verge whose legs were lying at awkward angles. Another man was howling as he rocked a child in his arms, and several women were sitting on the road, shaking. There was a bus on one side of the road, its front stove in by the tree it had crashed into, and a car on its side in the ditch opposite.

'Has anyone gone for the police?' asked Sheila in a loud voice.

One of the women said that a man had come along on a bike and they'd sent him off to see to it.

'Right,' said Ella. 'We're nurses, and we're going to help you all. Those of you who aren't hurt, can you just sit quietly, please? Thank you.'

Sheila had already knelt by the woman on the verge, so Ella looked over at the man with the child in his arms. She suddenly felt cold all over. Was this the place where she'd had her accident? She'd never asked exactly where she'd been found, she only knew it had been on the Hambleford Road. She shook her head and pulled her shoulders back. The man and his child needed help. Everything, and everyone else could wait.

'My name's Ella, what's yours?' she asked him.

'Alf Whitehead,' he sobbed. 'And this is Daisy, my little girl. I was bringing her home on the bus.'

'Well, Mr Whitehead, can I have a look at Daisy?'

He stopped rocking and relaxed his grip on his daughter so that Ella could examine her.

'That's better, Mr Whitehead. Now, can you hold this torch for me so that I can see properly? Thank you.'

There was a gash on Daisy's temple and cuts all over her face with glass shards embedded in them. One arm hung limply. Her breathing was laboured. Ella felt the girl's chest very gently. Broken ribs. She washed the cut on the little girl's forehead, but there was nothing she could do about the glass in the other cuts, and she couldn't do much for the dislocated shoulder either – she didn't dare bind it to those broken ribs.

'Is she... is she...?'

'It's important that you keep her very still. She's badly injured, but she'll live,' said Ella, praying she was right. She knew that in these situations, hope was one of the most important things.

'Oh, thank God,' said Mr Whitehead, and he started whispering to Daisy, telling her she was going to be all right, that the nice nurse would make her better.

Ella left them to see to the women sitting on the grassy bank. They were shaken, but the worst of their injuries was a sprained wrist. Ella bandaged it.

'Now, can you remember what happened?' she asked.

One of the women spoke up. 'We'd been shopping in Hambleford and had a spot of tea there before coming home. We were in the back of the bus. That man and his daughter were sitting right up the front. All of a sudden, that car came out of nowhere, driving really fast down the middle of the road. The bus driver braked hard, but there was nothing he could do. Is he all right?'

Ella looked around. She hadn't noticed a bus driver. Her stomach sank as she realised he must still be in the bus.

'I'll check now. Stay where you are, the police will want to talk to you.'

She ran over to the bus and peered in through the driver's side window. There he was, sitting in his seat, looking straight ahead through the shattered windscreen. He looked peaceful in spite of the fact that the bus's engine had crushed the lower half of his body. She searched for a pulse, but knew she would find none.

She heard sirens in the distance, and was glad the police were near.

Sheila joined her by the bus.

'How is she?' asked Ella, nodding towards the woman.

'She'll live. Nasty breaks though. I've done my best to immobilise them. She won't walk for a while. He's a bit bruised and sore, but otherwise fine.'

'Were they in the car?'

'Yes. He was driving. They're just back from their honeymoon.'

Ella shuddered. 'Well, I think they may be separated again, I'm afraid.'

Sheila frowned. 'What do you mean?'

'Bus driver's dead, and it sounds like it might have been your driver's fault.'

Even in the dying light, Ella saw Sheila blanch. 'Oh, how awful.'

They had no more time to talk as the police drove up and took charge. A few minutes later, Dr Myers also arrived with Rosie Fletcher in the ambulance. They spoke briefly to the sergeant and then approached Ella and Sheila.

'What can you tell us?' asked Dr Myers.

They were interrupted by a flash. The local reporter had

followed the police and was taking pictures and talking to people.

When he tried to ask Dr Myers a question, he waved him away.

'Not now, man, can't you see we're busy?' he said, and the reporter wandered away.

'Honestly, those newspapermen have no morals.'

Ella and Sheila agreed and then filled him in on the injuries sustained, and left them to it. Their part was over. Arthur, who had been sitting quietly with Mr Whitehead, took them home.

David was already there, making tea and looking for thermoses to put it in.

'That was thoughtful of you, but here we are,' said Ella as she flopped onto a kitchen chair. The others joined her and they recounted the events of the evening to David over strong, sweet tea.

'Where did you get the sugar from?' asked Sheila.

He tapped the side of his nose, and then immediately gave in to their demands that they be told.

'Well, if you must know, Dr Myers gave it to me. He said you might be in shock. I thought a drop of brandy in your tea would help, but he insisted that sugar worked better.'

'I'd like some brandy,' said Ella, and got up to get it from the sitting room. Returning with the bottle, she poured a good measure into each of their cups.

'Ah, that's better,' she said, taking a sip and sitting back with a sigh.

'Arthur, would you be able to pull Sam's car out of the ditch with the tractor?' asked David.

'Of course, I'll do it in the morning, it's too dark now. What a night. I only hope all those people are all right.'

Sheila and Ella glanced at each other.

'I'm sure they'll all be fine,' said Sheila. 'After all, they had two of the best nurses at St Thomas's attending to them.' They caught each other's hands and raised them into the air in a victory salute, laughing.

The next day, Dr Myers telephoned early to thank them for their quick and efficient response. All the patients were doing well and would recover from their injuries.

'It was all rather exciting, wasn't it?' said Sheila as she put the phone down.

'I don't know about exciting. Shocking, I think. But I must say I was amazed to find how much of my training came back to me, just like that.' She clicked her fingers together.

'Yes, once it's been drummed into you, it's there forever,' agreed Sheila.

Ella thought for a while.

'Do you know – I think I'd like to be a nurse again. I felt useful last night in a way that I haven't for ages. And it all came back to me. I knew exactly what to do.'

'I was thinking the same thing. But the reality is, it's not all like that. Maybe we just got off on the adrenaline. There's a lot of nursing that's drudgery.'

'Maybe, but I'm going to have a think about it.'

They were interrupted by a knock at the door. Ella got up to open it.

Arthur stood there with the morning newspaper folded in his hands.

'I've just pulled Mr Ellis's car out of the ditch, but I thought you might like to see this,' he said.

'Come in and have a cup of tea,' said Ella, taking the paper from him.

In the kitchen, she unfolded the paper and put it on the table. Emblazoned across the front page were Sheila and herself kneeling amongst the wounded. Ella hadn't even noticed the flash going off. The headline read, 'Local Nurses Save the Day'. The article underneath praised their quick reactions and efficient interventions. The reporter went so far as to say that they'd saved lives before the medical team arrived from the local hospital.

'Dr Myers won't be very happy that we've stolen his thunder,' said Sheila.

Ella, whose opinion of Dr Myers hadn't always been charitable, defended him. 'Actually, I don't think he'll mind. All he cares about is the welfare of his patients.'

Sheila raised her eyebrows and pursed her lips but didn't say anything.

'Perhaps we should go and see them?' said Ella.

Sheila shook her head. 'I think that really would be rubbing salt in the wound. I don't care what you say, I'm sure he would prefer to have got the credit for last night.'

'Perhaps you're right,' agreed Ella. 'I suppose it would look rather like we were expecting undying gratitude if we turned up anyway.'

The telephone rang.

'Hello, darling, have you seen the news today?'

'David! Yes, we were just talking about it. It's rather embarrassing being plastered across the front page.'

'Don't feel like that, you were marvellous. Both of you. Now I'm afraid I've got to go, I have a client waiting, but I just wanted to make sure you'd seen.'

They rang off and the telephone rang again immediately.

'Ella – you're famous,' said Andrew by way of greeting. 'You and Sheila are on page ten of *The Times*. "Off Duty Nurses Save Lives." I'm proud of you, old girl.'

Ella laughed. 'There can't be much else happening in the news if we get a mention,' she said.

Andrew asked all about the accident and Ella asked about the family, then they finished the call and she returned to the kitchen, still smiling. Sheila and Arthur pulled apart as she came in.

'Oh, don't bother about me,' she said. Sheila reddened and Arthur looked pointedly out of the window, shifting from one foot to the other and playing with the cap in his hands.

Later, Mr Whitehead knocked on the door with a large bag of home-grown vegetables.

'Thank you for saving Daisy's life,' he said as he handed it to Ella.

'I didn't do anything of the sort,' said Ella.

'Oh, but you did. Dr Myers said that if she'd been moved too much, her rib might have punctured her lung.'

'Well then, it just goes to show what a good nurse you are, keeping her so still. Well done.'

Mr Whitehead stood up taller and pulled his shoulders back.

'You really think so?'

'I certainly do,' said Ella.

He left soon after to go and see Daisy, having declined the offer of tea.

Ella rang Andrew again the next evening. She had a specific question for him, and after asking how he was, she got straight to the point.

'Do you know if I had motor insurance? Only I want to buy another car.'

She heard Andrew's sharp intake of breath. 'Are you sure?'

'Absolutely. I've decided to find a job, and I'll need some way of getting there.'

'A job? But why? You don't need the money if that's what you're worried about. Father left you quite well off, and then there's the money Charles left you, and the insurance from the flat, if it ever comes through.'

Ella clenched her jaw and gripped the telephone more tightly.

'It's not about money, no. It's about wanting to work. Now, did I have motor insurance?'

Andrew sighed. 'Yes, you did. I found the papers when I stayed after you came out of hospital and made the claim on your behalf. They're taking their time over it, but I'll chase them up. In the meantime, if you really have to buy another car, I can come down and help you choose one if you like.'

Ella smiled; it was difficult to stay annoyed at a man who wanted to help, even if she suspected it was only so she didn't choose anything too flashy.

'Thank you, Andrew, but you don't need to do that. I'll ask David to advise me.'

'So you're still seeing him then, how is he?'

She hadn't told Andrew much about her relationship with David, and didn't intend to go into it now, but it would have been unfair to say nothing.

'He's very well. We're seeing quite a bit of each other these days. You'll have to meet him next time you're down.'

'Speaking of which, Sophie and I were only talking about that last evening. How about we come at the end of the month?'

'Perfect. We'll look forward to it. And thank you.'

'Don't mention it. Just promise me you'll buy something sensible.'

Ella promised.

By the weekend she was the proud owner of an MG TC Midget in a rather sophisticated maroon. She drove David back to her house from the garage in Hambleford where she picked it up, and he was full of admiration for it.

Sheila heard the engine and came out to see the new beast.

'Well,' she said, 'it's very you.'

Ella realised that she hadn't even thought about the car she'd written off until then, when an image of something old, black and ugly made its way into her mind.

She laughed. 'The last one was big and heavy and probably chosen by Andrew to keep me safe. He'll die when he sees this beauty.' She stroked the steering wheel. 'Want to come for a spin?'

## 17

Ella and Sheila put the ration books into their handbags, tied their scarves under their chins and shut the door behind them. It was a windy day, the leaves were being stripped off the trees, whirling into the air before forming a restless carpet on the lawn. The late roses had taken a battering and were lying flattened along the sides of the path.

'I hate this,' said Ella. 'The poor roses don't deserve that after the heavenly scent they gave us all summer.'

Sheila didn't answer, she just buckled her coat more firmly around her waist and stepped into the wind, head down, clutching her bag in front of her with one hand and holding the neck of her coat closed with the other. Ella followed.

In the village there was a queue outside the butcher's. Word had got around of the delivery he'd had the night before, and tired of Spam, sausages and tripe, the local women were out in force to see what treats he had in store for them.

The war had been over for more than two years; no one could understand why they were still being rationed. The soldiers were home, the farmers were producing food, petrol wasn't rationed anymore, and the Jerries weren't blowing supply ships out of the water, so there was no problem getting food to where it was meant to be. There just wasn't enough of anything anymore. In spite of all those valiant young men and women who had lost their lives, there still wasn't enough. The women talked about it as they waited, the same conversation they'd had the day before and the day before that, all the days back to VE Day.

The door opened and the butcher stood there in his clean apron, hands on his hips. He smiled at the women gathered in front of his shop.

'The Chinese whispers must have been going round,' he said, and ushered the first customer through the door.

The first woman in the queue entered, the smell of fresh sawdust wafting out the door after her. All the women crowded in behind her, craning their necks to see what she got.

'A nice bit of brisket for you,' said the butcher, smiling.

Ella and Sheila stood in silence, holding their breath. Brisket. When was the last time they'd had that? Too long ago, that was for sure.

One by one, the women turned to leave the shop, clutching their meat to their chests, as if it was too precious to put in their shopping bags like the usual pound of sausages or yet another lump of offal. They caught each other's eyes on the way out, triumphant, as if they had won a prize, or had done something extraordinary to deserve the small bit of meat the butcher bestowed on them.

Ella and Sheila shuffled forward.

'Sorry, Mrs Dawson, all out,' said the butcher as the woman in front of them reached the counter. He looked genuinely upset.

'But what'll I give Kevin for his tea?' asked Mrs Dawson, her bottom lip trembling.

The whole village knew what Kevin was like, had seen the

bruises on Mrs Dawson's arms, the black eyes, swollen lips. When Sheila had first heard, she'd run home to Ella in a state, wanting to do something to help, but not knowing what.

'I don't know, Mrs Dawson, but I really am all out. The suppliers send what they have, and sometimes don't seem to count the number of shoppers I've got registered here. You know how it is these days.'

Ella stepped forward.

'Are you sure there's nothing left? You must have something – a chop, some liver, tripe? You can't go giving brisket and chops to some and nothing to others.'

The butcher shrugged his large shoulders.

'I've literally got nothing, not even for you two heroic nurses. It doesn't matter what I ask for, I just get what I'm sent. I'm sorry, ladies.'

Mrs Dawson's shoulders dropped as she turned to go.

Ella and Sheila left the shop with her, and stood on the pavement outside.

'Have you got anything at all at home, Joyce?' Sheila asked.

'Some veg, that's about it.' Joyce lifted her head, took a deep breath. 'I'll just have to make do, that's all. Thank you for asking, but I'd better be off,' she said and walked away.

Ella and Sheila stared after her, and then looked at each other.

'We've got to do something,' said Sheila.

'I agree,' said Ella, and turning towards home, they pulled their collars up and marched into the wind.

Back at the house they pulled all the tins out of the cupboard and put them on the kitchen table with the vegetables. Corned beef, sardines, peaches, condensed milk, Bovril, carrots, an onion, potatoes, cabbage, runner beans. There was flour in the larder, half of yesterday's loaf, porridge oats, some custard powder, a bit of honey in a jar. A pat of butter so small it was almost a memory. A pint of milk. Two eggs.

'Right, you do a pudding of some sort, I'll do a main,' said Ella, tying her apron on.

She gathered the onion, cabbage and corned beef. She sliced them all, poured a little lard into the frying pan and tossed them in. Joyce had three children, so she had to make it go as far as possible; she cracked an egg in, stirring furiously, and added some Bovril and water.

Meanwhile, Sheila had gone out to the garden and found a couple of fallen apples to add to the peaches. She stewed the apples with the honey and some ground cinnamon she found right at the back of the larder. She mixed butter, oats, and flour into a crumbly mess and tipped it on top of the fruit in a pie dish and placed it in the top of the oven.

Meanwhile, Ella was scrubbing potatoes, washing and slicing beans and carrots.

As the hash cooked, the kitchen filled with the aroma of hot fat and cheap meat. Ella wiped her brow, dreaming, not for the first time, of steak and new potatoes dripping in butter with a sprinkle of parsley, fresh peas and baby carrots. Or roast beef and Yorkshire pudding, thick gravy swamping the meat.

Sheila made custard with the last of the honey, the egg and half of their milk, poured it into a jug, tied a tea towel over the top with gardening twine.

'Everything ready?' she asked, looking at Ella arranging the hash on a serving plate. The vegetables were already in a bowl.

They put the dinner in a basket, covered it with a towel, pulled on their coats again, and headed into the village. The wind had dropped but the sky was glowering, threatening rain. Knocking on Joyce's door they looked around. There was hardly anyone about, the weather and lack of things to buy in the shops keeping them at home. They heard a child's voice from inside the house.

'Daddy, there's someone at the door.'

'Why you telling me? Go get your bloody mother.'

Sheila and Ella looked at each other, eyebrows raised.

A minute later, Joyce opened the door a crack, and then stood back and opened it wider, wiping her cheeks with a corner of her apron. A purple bruise was blossoming around her right eye.

Ella held the basket out in front of her. Joyce looked and her face brightened as she realised what it was.

'Who is it?' shouted Kevin from deep in the house.

'Only me, Sheila Marchmont,' Sheila called in response. 'I just popped in to ask Joyce if she had a darning mushroom, I can't seem to find mine, and I need to darn all my socks. How are you, Mr Dawson?'

Ella smiled and pushed the basket into Joyce's hands, and she and Sheila retreated.

'Thank you,' whispered Joyce after them.

'Darning mushroom?' said Ella as they walked away.

'It was the first thing that came into my head,' said Sheila. 'I notice you didn't say anything.'

'No, good on you and your darning mushroom.' She laughed.

'But we were too late,' said Sheila as they arrived home.

'For today, yes, but maybe a good meal will put him in a better mood for a day or two,' said Ella. She looked at the food that was left on the kitchen table. 'Sardines on toast?'

'Perfect,' said Sheila, rolling her eyes. 'Just what I've been dreaming of.'

'There's a nursing job going at the cottage hospital in Hambleford,' said Ella as they ate. 'I thought I might apply.'

Sheila put her toast down. 'Seriously? You don't think it would be too much?'

'Thank you for you unwavering support, dear friend,' said Ella. 'I think I'm ready.' She looked out the window into the darkening sky. 'I won't know if I am until I give it a try, anyway.'

'Of course you have my support,' said Sheila. 'You're a wonderful nurse. They'll be lucky to have you. And... after that accident last week, Dr Myers asked me if I'd be interested in a couple of days a week at his hospital if you were all right to be left. The matron wants to work fewer hours now she's a grandmother, and he thought I might suit the position.'

Ella stood and went round the table to hug her friend. 'That's marvellous news, Sheila, I hope you said yes.'

'I said I'd think about it. It would mean staying here, if you don't mind. I don't think I could afford to rent a place on a part-time salary.'

'Of course, you must stay here. Now, call Dr Myers and put him out of his misery, and I'll go and write a letter of application to the cottage hospital and pop it in the post in the morning.'

'I got it, I got the job!' said Ella when the letter came the day after her interview.

David picked her up and swung her around.

'Well done, my darling,' he said, and kissed her on the lips.

'Yes, congratulations,' said Arthur.

They'd come for dinner. David had found a bottle of champagne somewhere and Arthur had sent over a rabbit earlier, so it really would be a celebration. Ella had cooked up a storm, deciding against a roast, instead making 'lapin au vin', accompanied by every vegetable she could find. The aromas escaping the kitchen were mouth-watering.

Just as they made themselves comfortable in the sitting room with their sherry, Sheila arrived home from her second shift at Dr Myers' hospital.

She entered, pulling her headscarf off and shaking her hair out.

'I got the job!' said Ella.

Sheila pulled her into a hug. 'Of course you did. When do you start?'

'Next month.'

'Which ward will you be on?'

'I think it's such a small place I'll be doing a bit of everything, to be honest. It's not like Tommy's, you know.'

'Well, as long as you don't have to do too much time on Male Surgical,' said Sheila, and they both laughed.

'What's the joke?' asked David, raising an eyebrow.

'You tell him. I simply must change. Pour me a sherry, would you, I'll be down in a jiffy.'

While Sheila was changing, Ella told them the stories of their first bed baths as student nurses. When Sheila joined them, pink-cheeked and with her hair scraped back into a rather untidy bun, they were all laughing.

Over the delicious dinner, the men asked for more stories about their nursing days.

'Do you remember when we were waiting to go to France?' Sheila asked Ella.

Having read her journal, she had some memories, but wasn't sure which particular incident Sheila was alluding to. 'You tell the story,' she said, and sat back to listen.

David took her hand over the table; she'd told him that she sometimes found her memories unsettling. She squeezed his hand, reassuring him that she was all right.

'Well,' began Sheila, 'it was late May, 1944 when we were told to pack up all our gear and be ready to move out. You might think that that was a quick task. Throw a few things into a trunk, and off you go. But no! We had to pack up a whole hospital.' She looked around the table at the others, settling into her role as raconteur. 'We'd been practising the drill for weeks by then; every instrument had to be wrapped carefully in cloth, and those with moving parts had to be greased first. Then they all had to be sewn into hessian and packed in crates. The crates were then stamped with the number of the hospital, and the contents painted on the side. Then they were all loaded onto lorries. When we'd done all that, the tents had to be taken down and packed and stowed in the lorries too. Six lorries per hospital.'

Ella was wriggling in her seat. 'Yes, I remember it. It took us three days to dismantle the hospital and get it ready to go, and then we sat around twiddling our thumbs for another three or four days before we got the order to move out.'

'We were hardly twiddling our thumbs, you know. We had to do drills and training runs, roll calls and attend lectures on What to Expect. We hardly had time to think.'

'But it was exciting, wasn't it? We were actually going to be doing something useful, and soon. I remember lying awake at night, my heart thumping, just thinking about being in France.'

'It sounds exciting,' said David, smiling at her.

Sheila continued. 'We were ordered to be ready at 0600 hours on a Tuesday morning. We assembled in front of the house with our kit bags and trunks, and waited to be told what to do next. At about half past eight, we were told to go to the mess for breakfast, but no sooner had we got there than we were ordered out again — the hospital lorries had left and we were to follow in another. So no breakfast for us, not even a cup of tea.'

'Oh, yes, and there was such a rush for the best seats in the lorry,' said Ella. The doctors had cars, but no such luxury for us. We bundled into the back of the lorry and tried desperately to get the seats right at the back so we could see out.'

'Yes, and we got them too. Poor old Daffy was squashed right up at the front and said she never even glimpsed daylight for the whole trip. Anyway, we pulled out in convoy with the cars and caught up with the hospital lorries. The back of ours was open – it was one of those with tarpaulin over a frame at the back. It meant that people could see in, and there we were in our nurse's uniforms – we had to wear our dress uniforms for travel not the awful khakis – and every time we stopped, people would peer in, and when they saw us, they'd start cheering. Do you remember?'

'Yes! It was embarrassing at first, but after a while we waved back and even started chatting. It was heart-warming how well regarded we were. And we hadn't even done anything by then.'

'It was. And then you recognised where we were – not far from here, in fact, driving down the A3. You said we must be setting sail from Southampton, and of course, you were right, but instead of leaving that day, we stopped in the middle of nowhere and were ordered out.'

'It wasn't the middle of nowhere, it was the New Forest,' said Ella, laughing. 'Honestly, she was such a city girl back then,' she added, looking at David and Arthur.

'I might have been then, but my eyes have been opened now,' said Sheila, and she and Arthur shared a tender look. 'Anyway,' she continued, 'we were ordered to erect the hospital tents and be quick about it. I was furious, I can tell you. Three days to pack everything up, and then get it all out again and start all over.'

'But we didn't have to set up all the beds and instruments, did we?' Ella didn't remember that bit.

'Oh yes we did. Every last thermometer had to be unwrapped, checked and accounted for.'

'Seems like rather a waste of time,' said Arthur.

'It was, but I think they realised that they'd stuffed up, that we'd left Hatfield far too early and had to do something to keep us busy. Either that or it was the plan all along, just one final practice run.'

'We were there for quite a while, weren't we?' asked Ella.

'Just over two weeks. We finally left for France on 13th June, a full week after D-Day.'

Ella was growing agitated. The mention of D-Day had started her heart racing.

David stood. 'Enough of the past for now, I think it's time to toast the future.' He went to the kitchen and came back with the champagne and four fresh glasses.

He popped the cork, champagne spilled out over the lip of the bottle and Ella held out a glass to catch it. He poured out the fizz and handed it around.

'To Ella's new job, and Sheila's nearly new one. And good luck to all the patients you treat.'

Ella punched him gently on the arm. 'They'll be lucky to have us,' she said, and David put his arm round her and agreed.

'Thank you,' she whispered to him. 'Perfect timing.'

He squeezed her to him.

Joan arrived for the weekend without her husband, although he had been invited. Ella hadn't yet started at the cottage hospital, but Sheila was at work when she arrived.

'It's so good to see you, Ella,' said Joan as she got out of her car.

Ella was glad Sheila had shown her a picture of Joan taken at Hatfield House in her khakis, otherwise she wouldn't have known her from a bar of soap. She was tall and thin, her mousey hair pulled off her face into a severe bun which made her look older than her thirty or so years. But she had the most beautiful eyes Ella had ever seen. They were almost yellow with tiny flecks of green and gold.

'Lovely to see you, too, Joan. Here, let me help with your bag. How was your trip?'

'Frightful. I hate driving. What a gorgeous house you have.' She looked it over and then followed Ella into the sitting room.

'Tea?' asked Ella, gesturing to her guest to take a seat.

'Oh, I need something stronger after my drive. Have you got any Scotch?'

They sat with their drinks, Ella desperately racking her brain to think of things to say. Joan was not the chatterer that Sheila was, and she realised how unpractised she was at small talk.

'I'm sorry your husband couldn't come,' she said.

'I'm not,' said Joan brightly. 'He can be an awful bore. He's not one for a party, that's for sure. He lives for his work, and that's where he's happiest.'

Ella was rather taken aback. 'What does he do?'

'He's a university lecturer – mathematics.'

Ella gasped, and Joan laughed at her reaction.

'I know what you're thinking – how did I end up with someone like him? We met when I was posted to France. He was in the army and very dashing in his uniform. We were married within six weeks of meeting.'

'That was rather quick, wasn't it?'

'Yes, but it was war, surely you remember what it was like, "live for today", and all that. Although to be honest, I do sometimes ask myself the same question; but then, my father was a Presbyterian minister and married to his work and his parish, and Rex is married to his work and his university. They say women marry men like their fathers, don't they?'

'Oh, Joan, I'm so sorry.'

'Oh, don't be. You know the old saying, "you chose your bed

now lie in it". I'd say I'm managing better than my mother did —
I like my independence, whereas my mother perceived Father's
lack of attention as some sort of punishment and was never
happy. She felt she had to compete with God, and never had a
chance of winning. I just have to compete with maths. Anyway, I
really don't want to talk about it. How are you? I must say you
look in the peak of health.'

'I'm very well. Remembering more every day, thanks to
Sheila and my diaries. And seeing you has reminded me of
certain things already – like when we went to Brighton for the
day and you were sick on the way back in the train because
you'd eaten so much cake. You said it was the best you'd ever
had, and ate slice after slice.'

'Oh, don't remind me,' groaned Joan. 'We hadn't long been
training, had we? You must remember, I came from a household
where cake, or anything tempting, was treated with suspicion
bordering on paranoia. We weren't put on this earth to enjoy
ourselves, but to do God's work and stay away from the Devil's
temptations!'

Ella and Joan were laughing when Sheila arrived home and
joined them.

'What have I missed?' she asked.

'We were just reminiscing about our training days,' said
Joan, getting up to greet Sheila.

'You'll have to excuse me for a moment – I need to check on
dinner,' said Ella, and disappeared into the kitchen. She leant
against the table and took a few deep breaths. Something
troubled her about Joan, but she couldn't put her finger on what
it was. It was obvious that she was less accepting of the state of
her marriage than she was letting on, but that was only to be
expected – they hadn't seen each other for a while, so Joan was
hardly going to sob on her shoulder about it. But that wasn't it,
there was something else going on that Ella couldn't quite grasp.

Then she thought maybe she was being oversensitive, that she'd been keyed up about the visit, and needed to calm down a bit and stop thinking about everything too much. Joan was a friend,, they'd known each other a long time.

She took the stew out of the oven and gave it a stir. The rich meaty aroma made her hungry, but it needed to cook longer. That was the trouble with the meat they got these days, it was poor quality and took forever to become tender. She wished that Arthur and Sheila would hurry up and get married — she was sure her diet would improve even further when they did.

When she entered the sitting room, Sheila stopped mid-sentence and Joan became terribly interested in her cigarette lighter.

'Have I interrupted something?'

'No, not at all,' said Sheila too emphatically. Joan shook her head vigorously.

'Is dinner nearly ready? I'm starved,' said Sheila.

Ella was annoyed. What were they keeping from her? Had Sheila been giving Joan the health report? Telling her how hard it was to live with someone who had no memory? Making herself out to be a saint? No, that was unkind. Sheila had been marvellous, and patience itself. Ella told herself to stop being paranoid. Of course Joan wanted a progress report.

'Another half hour at least, I'm afraid. Another drink, Joan?'

An hour and several drinks later, they were all rather tipsy and Joan and Sheila were regaling Ella with stories of their escapades in London after the war, the week that Sheila had come down when Ella was demobbed. And the further down the Scotch bottle they got, the more outlandish the stories. Ella was tired just hearing about it all; where did she get all that energy? Sheila and Joan seemed to think it normal, going to parties and dancing with lots of men, or drinking so much that they didn't remember anything the next day.

Ella drank water with dinner, but Joan had brought a bottle of wine, and she and Sheila finished that off, although Joan seemed to drink most of it. By half past nine she was falling asleep on the sofa, and Ella suggested bed.

'Do you think she always drinks that much?' she asked when Sheila came down again having helped Joan upstairs.

'I have no idea, but she can certainly put it away, can't she? I don't think she's terribly happy with Rex, to be honest. Perhaps she just wants to let her hair down this weekend.'

The next day, Joan seemed perfectly fine. It was Ella who had a bit of a head, and she'd had the least to drink. They had a leisurely morning, filling the teapot regularly and chatting at the kitchen table. Ella wondered about David and Arthur coming for dinner; she'd assumed Rex would be there, and now thought that maybe she should tell them not to come, that having them there would rub salt in the wound if Sheila was right, and Joan was unhappy in her marriage. When Joan excused herself to go to the toilet, Ella put her dilemma to Sheila.

'I suppose you're right,' she said, not looking very happy.

Ella made the phone call. David understood and said he'd tell Arthur. Ella, hearing Joan start down the stairs, waited for her in the hall. As Joan reached the bottom step, Ella caught a whiff of gin. Without thinking she looked at her watch; eleven thirty. Joan raised her chin but said nothing and continued past her into the kitchen.

As Ella entered behind her, she raised her eyebrows at Sheila, who nodded very slightly. She'd smelled it too.

The day went downhill from then on. Ella didn't mean to judge, but she found it rather off-putting that Joan kept disappearing, and each time she returned she was a little less steady on her legs. She thought how unhappy she must be to have to drown her sorrows like that.

By late afternoon, Joan was slurring her words and hardly able to keep herself upright. Ella felt she had to say something.

'I can't help noticing that you're drinking rather a lot, Joan. Is everything all right?'

Joan turned to her, trying to focus on her face, but her eyes kept sliding off to the left and resting on her shoulder for a moment before being dragged back to her face, only to slide again.

'Let's go into the sitting room, shall we?' suggested Sheila.

They helped their friend onto the sofa and took chairs opposite her and waited. It didn't take long for Joan to start.

'Look at the two of you. You're so smug, aren't you, sitting there all prim and proper, judging me from your high horses.' She put her elbow on the arm of the sofa and tried to rest her chin in her hand, but missed and her head bounced off the armrest. She snapped to attention, her eyes glazed, and started again. This time, she managed to support her chin in her hand.

Ella watched, horrified. She'd never seen anyone so drunk, so obviously out of control.

'That's right, Mrs perfect bloody Elkington, you've got that sneer going well, haven't you? It's very convenient for you to have forgotten everything, isn't it? Wasn't so long ago that you had a few problems yourself, was it? And now you think you can judge others.'

Sheila gasped. 'Now, that's enough, Joan. Let's get you into bed.'

'What's she talking about, Sheila?' Ella's heart was thumping.

'She means your accident,' said Sheila, glaring at Joan.

'Oh, she won't tell you,' slurred Joan. 'Not your guardian angel there. She came to get you better, to make sure you didn't slip again. She wants you to believe that you were quite the socialite when you came home, doesn't she? That we all partied for days but the truth is–'

'That really is enough, Joan,' said Sheila firmly. She stood up and slapped her round the face. 'You need to sober up and apologise to Ella.'

Joan, hands to her face, swayed and made a sound like a cat mewling. She leant forward and drew her feet in as if she was going to get up, but they slipped away from her again and she fell back against the cushions.

'Joan,' said Ella, trying to sound calm, 'what was the truth you were going to tell me?'

Sheila made to stop her again, but Ella shut her up. 'Let Joan speak, please,' she said, giving Sheila a cold stare.

Joan sat up again, holding on to the end of the sofa. She spoke slowly, attempting to annunciate every word clearly.

'When you were demobbed you were a wreck, physically and emotionally. We could hardly get a word out of you. When we tried to help, you told us to bugger off. One by one you managed to send us away, and then you came down here and shut yourself off from the world.'

Ella turned to Sheila who had gone quite white and was biting her lip.

'Is this true?'

'Ella, you must–'

'Is this true?' repeated Ella.

'Yes.' Sheila deflated, sinking into the chair, her head dropping forward to her chest.

Ella got up and left the room. She was seething with rage. Sheila had been lying to her all this time, making her believe that she was quite the party girl, when, in fact, she'd been a recluse. And when she thought about it, that made more sense than anything Sheila had said; it was the reason she didn't know anyone in the village, that Arthur had said that they only knew she was there when she offered piano lessons. Something had happened in the war that had sent her off the rails, made her come home to lick her wounds. But the question she kept coming back to was why Sheila would lie about it.

She heard movement from the sitting room. Sheila was no doubt helping Joan to bed. Well, she could manage on her own. Ella sat in her room in the dark and let the tears fall. She felt betrayed by the person closest to her.

She'd never been able to abide liars. Other shortcomings she might overlook, but to her, lying was unforgivable. The incident that planted her belief was when Claudine Ferrers, a girl at her primary school had told her that her mother was dead and she lived with her father and an aunt. Ella's own mother had recently died, and so she felt a strong bond with Claudine, an unpopular girl with her untidy clothes and buck teeth. Ella had befriended her, invited her home several times, and one Saturday afternoon, had baked a cake to take to Claudine's family. She knocked on the door, and a tall woman with peroxide hair and too much make-up answered.

'Good afternoon,' said Ella. 'You must be Claudine's auntie. I'm so sorry about her mother. I brought you a cake.'

The woman looked down at her with a look on her face that Ella couldn't make out, and then she started laughing, holding her sides and rocking back and forth on her feet.

'I'm dead now, am I? Well, that's a new one.' She wiped her eyes and looked over her shoulder and called Claudine.

Ella's heart had found a new home somewhere near her feet; she felt embarrassed, angry and humiliated all at the same time. How could Claudine have lied to her like that, accepting her sympathy when she knew that Ella's own mother had died so recently. She saw Claudine coming along the hall smiling as if nothing had happened, dropped the cake, and ran home. She flung herself down on her bed and sobbed. Her father had found her later, her cheeks tear-streaked and eyes puffy. He held her hand, listened to her story, and reminded her of what her mother always said about liars.

'They are the ones who need help, for one lie leads to another and another until soon, they are at the centre of a web that they cannot get out of.'

'I can't forgive her, Daddy, I can't.'

'If you don't, it will hurt you more than it hurts her. You don't have to be her friend, but try to understand why she did what she did.'

'I think she wants to be my friend, but that's not how to make friends. I hate her.'

'No, it isn't, but perhaps she doesn't know any better way and that is why she is lonely.'

Ella thought about that. She could see the truth in her father's words, but she couldn't be friends with Claudine after that.

∼

Ella stayed in her room all the next morning, only coming downstairs to see Joan off.

'I'm so sorry I said those awful things,' she said as she stowed her bag in the boot of her car. 'You mustn't put any store in them. I was drunk, and I'm afraid I say stupid things when I've been drinking. My marriage is falling apart, you see, and I don't know what to do.'

Ella put her arms around her and held her for a moment. 'Stop drinking and start talking would be my advice to you, but it's your life, and who am I to tell you what to do. I seem to have made a mess of my own.'

Joan pulled away. 'I had a talk with Sheila this morning. I

know you're probably angry with her, but I believe she was doing what she thought was best. Please bear that in mind when you talk to her.'

Ella didn't answer, and Joan shrugged and got into the car.

'Drive safely, and good luck. Come again sometime,' said Ella. She didn't mean it. She'd seen enough of Joan for a while.

Ella watched until the car was out of sight and then went inside and grabbed her handbag and car keys.

'I'm going out,' she yelled into the house, having no idea where Sheila was. She had also seen enough of her for a while. She wasn't ready for the conversation that had to happen. She felt tender and bruised, sad and angry.

She drove along country lanes, the roof down, trying to blow away her anger. When she returned, Sheila was in the kitchen wanting to talk, her face twisted in apology, her hands knotting a tea towel.

Ella walked past her, poured herself a glass of water, resisted the temptation to throw it over Sheila, and went to her room.

After three days the atmosphere in the house was as toxic as mustard gas. Sheila skimmed around, keeping to her room as much as possible, darting out for food and drink when she thought Ella was out. But Ella didn't go out. She inhabited the house boldly, loudly, so that Sheila knew it was hers, that she was the hostess, the friend who had been wronged. Occasionally, she would go into the garden to breathe the fresh air and pick some flowers or gather some vegetables for her dinner. She would bang the door shut behind her so that Sheila knew that her chance had arrived; Ella didn't want her to starve to death, even if the idea of never seeing her again was attractive.

She knew she couldn't go on like that forever. She

telephoned Andrew to talk it over with him, and spoke to David about it, mentioning her anger and sadness to them both, but not her treatment of Sheila. There were some things they didn't need to know.

Andrew tried to soothe her, and David understood how hurt she was, but, in his lawyerly way, also understood Sheila's motivation. Ella listened, and was annoyed that he didn't take her side completely, but loved him all the more because even though he loved her, he was still fair and considered every angle.

It wasn't anything either of them said that made her seek Sheila out finally, but rather that she realised she hadn't mentioned her behaviour towards Sheila because she was so ashamed of it, of herself.

She opened and shut the back door as if she was going out but waited in the kitchen.

Sheila jumped when she saw her there, almost dropping the cup and plate she was carrying.

'We need to talk,' said Ella.

'Yes.' Sheila nodded, but didn't say more. Ella guessed she was gauging the mood before speaking, frightened of offending further.

'How could you?' asked Ella, her planned speech disappearing through the open window. The question contained all her hurt and all her anger, sapping her of energy.

Sheila couldn't look at her; instead she gazed at the plate in her hand as if reading off her answer.

'I thought it would help. I'm sorry, but I really did.'

Ella considered that. Had she needed that sort of help, and if so, why?

'Go on,' she said.

Sheila took a deep breath, still reading from the plate. 'When you came back, you were a mess. Popping pills all the time and drinking. You hardly said a word and when you did it was to be rather foul to all of us, quite unlike yourself. We knew you must have seen some awful things, and tried to get you to talk about it all, but you withdrew further and further away from us. No one could get through to you, and, as Joan said, you sent us all away, quick smart. I visited but you wouldn't let me in. Andrew and the family were the only people you'd see, and he sent us updates. You came down here and buried yourself away and all we could do was wait.'

Ella shifted from one foot to the other, searching her mind for memories or images to support what Sheila was telling her. There was nothing.

'So you decided to make up a past for me, is that it?'

'Something like that,' Sheila mumbled.

'What gave you the right? What on earth were you thinking? I'm having enough trouble remembering things, and you come along and play with my mind like that!' Ella thumped the table making cutlery bounce.

Sheila's head whipped up and she looked Ella square in the face at last.

'I thought I was helping,' she said.

'Do you have even the slightest idea what it's like to have to rely on people to help you piece the past back together again, the trust it takes, the anxiety I live with constantly that I'll never be the same again? And then you go and play games with my head like this? I thought you were my friend.'

Ella glared at her, but Sheila didn't look away.

'I did it because I love you, Ella. Because I didn't want you to have the pain of those memories. I thought if you believed you'd been all right when you came home, that when the memories of what happened in Europe came back to you, they might be easier to bear.'

'What other lies have you told me?'

'None, I swear. Just the ones about how jolly we all were

when you came home. I don't have to lie about anything else, because you were happy at other times. Or at least, if not happy, your feelings were understandable given what was going on.'

'Maybe my feelings were an understandable reaction to what happened in France, have you thought of that?' Ella shuddered. She didn't want to think about what might have made her react so badly.

'Of course I thought of that, but I also thought that your amnesia was like a gift; you'd been through all that once, and maybe you didn't need to go through it again.'

In that moment, Ella understood what Sheila had tried to do. She looked at her, opening and closing her mouth, but no words would come. She dropped into a chair and sat with her head in her hands. Sheila approached cautiously and put a hand on her shoulder. Ella took it and held it. Neither of them said anything as the clock ticked the minutes away.

Finally, Ella asked, 'What pills was I taking?'

Sheila didn't say anything.

'You owe me the truth,' said Ella.

'Benzedrine. You know, uppers. We all took it a bit when we were nursing overseas, it staved off the hunger pangs and gave us energy.'

They were quiet again. A bird sang outside the window and was answered by its mate.

'I see,' said Ella, lifting her head but not looking at Sheila.

She got up and left the room.

In the garden she sat on the browning grass. It hadn't rained since those awful thunderstorms in July, six weeks ago. The earth was parched, but Ella felt guilty watering it too often since they'd announced on the radio that there might be a water shortage. At the time she'd been annoyed — something else in their lives that would be rationed, but she'd soon accepted the idea. If the war had taught her nothing else, it had made her accommodating. She worried away at a hang nail till it bled and then wrapped her finger in her hanky, watching the blood soak through. She'd done worse to herself; she'd been a drug addict. The notion sat in her head like a rock in a barren landscape. She didn't doubt it was true, but she also couldn't build anything around it, no scenes of herself in the gutter swallowing pills by the handful, or gulping down tablets with the aid of bottles of meths. For that was how she saw drug addicts — debased relics with no self-regard. Had she been like that? Or was her addiction more genteel, her pills washed down with Scotch in a crystal tumbler, taken with toast and tea at breakfast?

She watched a line of ants climb up and over her leather sandal, keeping in formation, avoiding her skin. She was becoming uncomfortable sitting on the dried-out grass, the stalks stabbing her thighs and bottom, but she didn't want to move, didn't want to disturb the ants. She thought how lucky they were in their ordered little lives.

She wondered where they were off to with such determination and how they knew how to reach their destination, even when there was an obstacle in their path.

# 18

Ella woke early for her first day at the hospital. Dawn hadn't yet crept over the horizon and on up to light the lanes and fields of Hampshire. She lay feeling the beat of her heart and the weight of the sheet on her skin. Her neck was a little damp where it touched the pillow. It had been another warm night.

She got up and padded to the window, enjoying the texture of the carpet under her feet. Looking out, she saw stars in the sultry blackness and wished for a breeze, some clouds, rain. Anything but more of the same. The heat, she thought, could drive one mad.

She sighed and put the light on. Her new uniform lay on the chair like a pantomime costume; grey dress, white cuffs and apron, enormous veil, all starched to uncomfortable stiffness. Stockings, black shoes. She would put it on and become, once more, a nurse. Patients would trust and respect her, would accept her opinion, offer themselves and their bodies and their diseases up to her for treatment, their pained eyes following her every move, knowing that she had the power to make them better. Or at least, willing it to be so.

In the kitchen with tea and toast she wondered if she was up to it — the responsibility, the weight of disappointment when nothing could be done; her own as well as the patients'.

Pulling back her shoulders, she lifted her chin, and said, 'Nurse Elkington, you are St Thomas's trained, which means you are prepared for anything.' She laughed at her poor imitation of Sister Cooper and silently thanked her for her words. She had once believed them without question. Now she just hoped they were true.

Andrew rang to wish her luck and she heard Sophie, Laura and Billie in the background sending their best wishes too. Sheila came down as she was leaving.

'Good luck,' she said, looking Ella up and down. 'You look the part. How are you feeling?'

'Terrified,' admitted Ella.

By ten o'clock, she was drained. For the three hours she'd been there, she'd run around with bedpans, given injections, bathed several ungrateful women who would rather have washed themselves or not be bothered at all, and almost had a run-in with the doctor who commanded the place. He had been in Africa during the war and conducted himself as if he was still there, treating the nurses like coolies and the patients as inconveniences.

But she hadn't made any mistakes. The patients had had the correct medication at the appropriate times, there'd been no sloshing of body fluids out of bedpans, and she had bitten her tongue when she wanted to call the doctor a bully. So far so good.

What was troubling her more than anything, though, was that this wasn't what she remembered nursing to be like. She knew Sheila had thought civilian nursing dull after their experiences in the QA's, but this was beyond dull. She was a drudge. She was doing nothing that required her years of training and experience, except, perhaps, for the medicine rounds, but even they wouldn't tax a reasonably competent ten-year-old.

She had three hours off in the afternoon – another irritation she'd forgotten about, the split shift – and sought David out. Between clients, he took her for tea at a café on the high street and listened to her list of complaints.

'Give it a chance, Ella,' he said, taking her hand across the table. 'It's bound to be rather monotonous to begin with, but once you've shown them what a treasure you are, you'll be given more responsibility, more interesting jobs to do.'

Ella knew that may be true in a large teaching hospital, but not Hambleford Cottage Hospital. She smiled at him. He so wanted her to be happy.

'Perhaps,' she said. 'I think I'll have another sandwich,' she added, helping herself from the plate he'd ordered.

In the second half of September, when it had been dry for over two months, the heavens opened and overnight the countryside painted itself green again, and wild flowers bloomed in the hedgerows. Ella's mood lifted with the colour returning, even though after three weeks at the hospital, the work was as unstimulating as it had been on the first day. She hated the split shifts that didn't give her enough time to get home and do anything useful, but were too long to hang about in Hambleford. She'd talked to the Matron about changing things, but it hadn't gone well.

And then, one Tuesday morning, a young man was brought

in. He'd been in a motorcycle accident and had spent several hours in surgery. He was bandaged from head to foot, and Ella had to set up traction for him over his bed. He was quiet for a few hours, and then started murmuring. She went to him to find out what he needed, but he didn't open his eyes or his mouth. He didn't seem to know she was there. She took his hand, one of the few bits of him that wasn't injured, and spoke in a soothing voice.

'You're in a hospital, Michael. You've been in an accident, but you're going to be all right. Do you understand?'

There was no response. She sat a moment longer and then got up to attend to someone else. As she walked away, an ear-piercing yell split the antiseptic air.

She rushed back to his side. His eyes were wide, staring wildly about, his body uncannily still. Ella tried to calm him, aware of twenty pairs of eyes watching, waiting for her to return the ward to its healing calm. But there was no stopping the boy. He continued to scream and yell incoherently until Sister arrived with a morphine injection that silenced him, sending him off into dreamless sleep.

Ella made it to the solitude of the sluice room before her legs gave way and she sank to the floor, heart beating too fast, jaw clenched, and fists pressing into her eye sockets, trying to rub away the images that zoomed in to sharp focus and then blurred into fuzzy background to be replaced by another, more horrifying sight.

She was hyperventilating, sweat glistening on her brow when Sister found her.

'Whatever is the matter, Nurse?' she asked.

Ella couldn't speak through the veil of her fear.

Later, Ella tried to tell Sheila what had happened, but even then, words failed her.

'It was him screaming...'

'Who? Who was screaming?'

'The boy. All the boys. Screaming. Never stopping.'

Sheila brushed a stray strand of hair from Ella's forehead, let her hand rest for a brief moment on her cheek before reaching for the glass of brandy on the bedside table.

'Here, have a sip of this.'

Ella lifted her head and gulped greedily.

'Try and sleep now, Ella. I'll sit here until you drop off. It's rest you need. You're exhausted.'

Ella sank back into the pillows but she didn't let her eyes close; the boys might be hiding behind closed lids. But she knew it was time to know more about the war, about what she'd seen and done. And it would be better coming from Sheila than catching her unawares on the ward.

'Tell me about going to France,' she said, reaching for the glass again.

'I don't think it's a good idea right now, Ella. You're upset already.'

'That's why it's a good idea. I have to know. I can't let things surprise me at work like that again. Just tell me about getting there, our first glimpse of the war.'

Sheila looked at her, then crossed her legs and settled into her chair. She took a sip of her drink and lit a cigarette.

'Well, we were in the New Forest far too long. One day, Colonel somebody came along and told us all to make our wills. That got us all rather anxious. You said something about leaving everything to charity, and he said, "Doesn't matter who you leave it to, you won't be needing it if you're dead". He was such a cheery soul. Anyway, the soldiers went off days before us, but then the weather got really bad and we couldn't cross.

Turns out that that wasn't such a bad thing as even after the naval and aerial bombardments, it took longer to secure the area than the generals thought it would. The injured were evacuated rather than being treated there for the first few days.

'Eventually we got the word that we were moving out four days after the first boats left. Then we had to pull the hospital down and pack everything up, which took another two days, the lorries came and took us all to Southampton and we waited another day there. It was a dreadful crossing; we were all as sick as dogs, and when we got to Normandy we couldn't believe our eyes. All that training, those lectures about what to expect – they meant nothing. We were prepared for the wounded. What we weren't ready for was the desolation; the beach had been cleared, we were told, but it was a deserted battlefield.'

Ella felt suddenly too warm. 'I remember it – all those rolls of barbed wire pushed against the dunes.' She shuddered. There'd been metal prongs and wooden stakes heaped in great piles. Smashed-up amphibious vehicles were lying on their sides. The remains of concrete embattlements, scrap metal, tin hats and broken guns lay around. There was blood, rust-coloured, that had seeped into the sand, and tattered bits of khaki trapped under rocks and on the wire, hanging like spent flags.

'Yes, it was dreadful. And then we drove into the devastated towns. We'd seen bomb damage in London, but there, whole towns had been almost flattened. When we drove through, people would appear out of the rubble, waving British and American flags. God knows how they'd survived, and how they were living in the ruins, but they seemed happy to have been liberated from German occupation, and ran after the lorries offering us fruit and asking for cigarettes.'

Ella shifted in her bed remembering the taste of an apple

after the sourness of seasickness in her mouth. 'Those people had been through so much.'

'Yes,' said Sheila. 'And do you remember how the roads felt corrugated under the tyres from all the tank tracks? And the poplar trees standing like sentries in long avenues in the flat countryside?'

'And the white dust covering everything. And grimy children in torn clothes waved and ran after the trucks. We were treated like heroes, and yet we'd done nothing.' A tear slid down Ella's cheek.

'Ella?'

'I'm fine. Go on.' She wiped her face with her sleeve.

Sheila plumped her pillows for her and sat back down.

'We had to set the hospital up outside Bayeux, in an orchard. The pioneers did most of the work. They even dug us pits to put our tents in so that we avoided the shrapnel.'

'And they made us toilets,' said Ella, 'and put strips of hessian around them, held in place by metal posts.'

'That's right,' said Sheila. 'And they had no roof, so that in the mornings, if the planes flew low enough, they could see in. Those RAF boys could almost skim our heads!'

They laughed. It had seemed so infra dig at the time, but mattered so little really.

'I think that's enough for now,' said Ella, yawning. 'I might sleep.'

'I'll sit for a while and read, if that's all right with you?'

'I'd like that,' she said.

Ella's dreams were filled with apple trees and tents, planes flying low and bombs exploding. It wasn't until she started seeing the wounded being brought in with blood soaking into their clothes that she woke up. Sheila had gone, leaving the lamp on beside the bed. Its low light cast eerie shadows on the walls, and Ella examined them to turn her mind away from her dream. When, finally, she fell asleep again, she dreamed that David asked her to marry him.

She was still full of the dream when she saw him the next day. She'd been mulling it over, and had reached the conclusion that she didn't have to wait for him to ask. This was 1947 after all, and they'd fought a war to maintain their freedom. If a woman couldn't propose to a man now, well, they may as well go back to Queen Victoria's days. The world had changed, and people had to keep up. She would never admit to him that her reason for proposing now, rather than letting him take his time was because she wanted to have the security of having David beside her, of knowing that there was something good and pure in her life, before she felt able to confront the ghosts clamouring for her attention.

The rain hadn't yet let up (Ella was already thinking of the sun and the warmth with nostalgia), so they were having lunch at his house instead of the proposed picnic. David opened a bottle of beer and poured them each a glass.

'Here's to us,' he said, and clinked her glass.

It's now or never, thought Ella.

'I've been thinking,' she said, putting both hands on the table to steady them.

'Sounds ominous.' David raised his eyebrows.

'Be serious.' Her top lip felt tingly the way it always did when she had something important to say. She looked at him, those handsome brown eyes with the laughter lines beginning to form around them. 'Will you marry me?'

David's mouth dropped open and he stared at her for what seemed to Ella an unnecessarily long time.

'Aren't I meant to ask you?' he said eventually.

'I've asked you. So what'll it be?'

'Well, of course I want to marry you! It's just that I was planning a more romantic time and place. And I was going to present you with a ring and slip it onto your finger, and you were going to fall into my arms and swear to love me forever.'

'I will – love you forever, I mean, but as to the rest of it, we're too old for all that, aren't we? And anyway, it's the marriage, not the engagement or the wedding that matters.'

'Don't you want a big white affair with dozens of bridesmaids and flowers overflowing out of the church?'

Ella thought about it. Her fairy-tale wedding. Once it had seemed so important, but not now.

'I can do without. I just want to be married to you.'

'Oh, Ella,' he said, and kissed her.

At work, Ella kept a tight-fitting lid on her feelings. Each morning she conjured the worst scenario she could, of blood and gore, open wounds and screaming men, and when it didn't eventuate, she looked heavenward, although she wasn't thanking a god, but the stars above.

In that way she found she could cope with the worst the cottage hospital could throw at her, even the man in the motorcycle accident, Michael, who since that first morning, had calmed down, possibly due to the hefty doses of morphine he was receiving at regular intervals. The other patients were by and large a docile bunch. She spent her time mainly nursing the post operatives, and as she got to know them, her satisfaction with the job grew.

That's nursing, she thought, either you're rushed off your feet saving lives and don't get a chance to know any of the patients properly, or you have little to do and build relationships with the people in your care. It's a question of adjusting your expectations. Once she'd realised that, everything changed.

And because things were going so well at work, and with David, she felt that she was on solid ground and ready to read more about her time in France. So one evening when Sheila was out with Arthur, and David had gone to London for a few days, she took a glass of Scotch into the sitting room and sat down with the last diary. Flicking through the pages, she found herself in Bayeux.

She didn't need to read much to find herself there. The ground was throbbing from the shelling and her hands were over her ears. She didn't dare close her eyes; the need to see what was coming outweighed the desire to shut out her surroundings. The noise was unbearable — shelling, ack-ack guns firing, men shouting, engines screaming as they were pushed to their limits, planes taking off from the air base nearby, climbing fast.

It was raining and had been for some time, yet the air, instead of being cleansed was dense, heavy with dirt and dust which caught in her throat.

The pioneers had erected the tents, long lines of brown marquees for the wards, and further back, the sleeping and mess tents. The cookhouses were right at the back. Each ward had additional 'lean-tos', one to serve as the sluice room and the other to receive the meals from the cookhouse to await distribution. There was also a primus stove there for making tea and a small autoclave for sterilising equipment. The nurses snipped away wrappings and rubbed the grease from the instruments. They were open for business.

Ella changed her heavy boots for stiff new shoes and sloshed through the rain to the ward. The canvas floor was slick with mud and they hadn't even seen a patient, although all that was about to change. Sheila, Daffy and Ivy were already there, making up the beds, the fresh sheets whipping the air as they shook the folds out of them and let them float onto the mattresses. A blanket followed, the nurses using all their strength to tuck the ends so that the surface was as smooth as ice, and about as inviting.

Thirty beds in the ward, nineteen of them made up when the first casualties arrived. Daffy and Ivy disappeared to help in surgery, Sheila to prepare another ward, leaving Ella to face the horrors of the battle wounded on her own.

Her first patient had terrible burns over most of his body; his tank had been shelled and he'd been roasted inside. There were still fragments of clothing embedded in his skin. He smelled of sweat and fear, burnt flesh and urine. Parts of his uniform had been cut away for the surgeons to get at his broken limbs, but he hadn't been completely undressed, there hadn't been time. A label round one wrist gave his name and rank, the time he'd been given morphine, and the dose. Her first patient. Malcolm Brewer, Corporal.

Ella got the orderlies to put him into the bed closest to the curtained-off nurse's desk. He groaned as he was transferred, and then settled once again into his drugged sleep. She wondered if he'd been handsome; it was impossible to tell now. His face had been so badly burned it was just a weeping red oozy mess. His eyes were gone, melted away. One ear was missing. Ella took some deep breaths and wiped the tear away from the corner of her eye, then got to work, carefully removing the fabric from his flesh with tweezers, dropping it into a kidney dish where it lay in ever deepening layers.

She hadn't finished when another patient was brought in, and another, until the ward was half full of young men in various states of consciousness with a horrifying array of injuries. Ella didn't stop all day and most of the night, administering morphine and penicillin, giving out, then collecting bedpans, setting up drips and giving blood and fluids, feeding the one or two who could eat, reassuring, soothing, caring.

All this with the ground shaking from the bombs, and the ceaseless sound of machine guns in the background, but not far enough in the background. Every time a plane flew overhead Ella found herself waiting for the whizz of a bomb and sighed in relief every time she realised it had been an Allied plane and there would be no explosion.

At midnight, another nurse came to relive her so that she could have something to eat. In the mess tent, she tried to ease the tension in her muscles, but they were knotted so tight she couldn't release them, and she couldn't eat the fish or the stewed apples that were served. Within ten minutes she was back on the ward, tending to her patients, reassuring the men that they would live, that their war was over, that they could look forward to the rest of their lives, but she knew her words, for some, were hollow, that they would have preferred to die than live as they were now.

At dawn she crawled into her bed. Too tired to weep but with a knot in her throat that felt like the stopper to a well of tears. Nothing could have prepared her for this. She closed her eyes and saw Malcolm's burnt face and thanked the god she didn't believe in that he had died during the night without having regained consciousness, his lungs too badly smoke-damaged to allow him the breath of life.

Ella found herself letting the tears flow now that she hadn't had the time or the energy to allow back then. Sitting on her sofa in her comfortable house in Hampshire, she remembered those young men, repeating their names quietly to herself — the ones who had died and the ones who had lived to be evacuated home to try and pick up where life had left off before the war, before they were soldiers, before they saw death and felt fear, before they killed and in turn were destroyed.

She shivered in spite of the warm evening, and wished she could talk to David. She needed someone who hadn't been there with her, who knew his own horrors but would listen without interruption to hers. Someone who wouldn't always tell her that they had saved more than they'd lost. For what, she wanted to ask. For what?

And yet, she knew that they had made a difference, that for some, their care had not only saved their life, but given them hope. And no doubt some had settled back into their lives smoothly, taking up their old job, their evenings in the pub, their walks along familiar streets, their arms about familiar bodies.

She thought of Fred Miller who had lost his leg and with it his regard for himself as a man. He'd given up, but was now working and had been seen stepping out with a girl from the village. Perhaps there were more success stories.

She got up and stood by the open doors, letting the sound of leaves rustling in the soft wind calm her. Then pulling her cardigan around her shoulders, she dried her eyes and went to put the kettle on for Sheila's return.

The next few days were a chaos of activity. David returned from London full of stories and gifts; potted shrimp and pigeon pie from Fortnum and Mason, perfume from Harrods. Ella's hospital was full to bursting with polio patients and she was called in for extra shifts, only able to take one day off when Andrew and the family came for the weekend.

She hadn't wanted to put them off altogether. It was time

they met David, and Sheila would be able to entertain them when they arrived on Friday evening.

When she got in, the children were in their pyjamas waiting to say goodnight to her. Laura took one look at her uniform and declared that she would like to be a nurse when she grew up, then Sophie whisked them upstairs to bed while Andrew poured Ella a gin and Sheila checked the dinner.

On the Saturday, David arrived shortly after breakfast. Ella watched her brother weighing him up, asking him questions about his work, his family. She knew that he was only doing it because he loved her, and that later she and David would laugh about it, but still she wished he trusted her judgement.

On the Downs where they took a picnic lunch, David played with the children, giving them piggybacks and swinging them around by an arm and a leg like an aeroplane until he collapsed on the blanket next to Ella, the children still begging for more.

'You're good with them,' said Sophie. 'Do you want a family of your own?'

Such an innocent question, but suddenly the air was heavy with expectation, with breath held and hands frozen in the act of reaching for sandwiches.

David was the only one who seemed relaxed. He looked at Ella, and said, 'I do, as long as you do too.'

She smiled, and breaths were released, sandwiches seized, and the breeze started up again. Ella realised that they hadn't talked much about the future, only that they wanted to be together. Now the image seemed a little more focused, the composition a little fuller.

That night, at dinner, Andrew asked if they'd set a date for the wedding.

'Not yet,' said Ella.

David caught her hand. 'How do you feel about a winter wedding? I'd like it to be soon, but I know these things take time to organise, and although you said you didn't mind about a church wedding, I'd like one; I want to wait at the altar and watch you walk down the aisle, knowing you've chosen to spend your life with me. I can't think of anything that would make me more proud or happy.'

Ella leant her head against his shoulder. Until that moment she hadn't known how much she, too, wanted a church wedding, to get married in a white gown and have Laura and Billie as bridesmaid and page boy. 'I didn't realise you were such a romantic, but that sounds wonderful.'

Arthur cleared his throat and all eyes turned to him.

'While we're on the subject of weddings, I've asked Sheila to be my wife, and she's agreed to take me on.' He blushed deeply and looked at Sheila who was beaming.

Everyone talked at the same time, offering congratulations, and then toasts were made and Arthur slapped on the back and kissed on the cheek more times than he needed.

'You're a fine friend, keeping that from me,' said Ella later in the kitchen.

Sheila put down the tea towel she was wiping the plates with. 'He only asked this afternoon, and I had no idea he was going to announce it tonight. I was going to tell you first, but you were so caught up with the children before dinner.'

Ella smiled. 'It's all right. I'm so happy for you. But how are you going to get up to milk the cows every morning?'

Sheila grimaced. 'There are going to be certain challenges to being a farmer's wife, that's for sure, but I don't think I'll be expected to help with the milking!'

On Sunday at work, Ella was bolstered by memories of the night before while she cared for sick children and tried to soothe their frightened parents. There was no break to be had in the middle of the day, there were too many patients and too few nurses. One, Ginny, had a child of her own who'd been diagnosed with polio and had resigned from her job to look after him full time. Ella understood her decision, but she still needed another pair of hands.

'Nurse, nurse!'

Ella ran the length of the ward to Amory's bed.

'It's his breathing, Nurse, it's not right. Do something!'

Ella brushed past Mrs Gardener and felt for Amory's pulse. It was weak. His breathing was laboured, his face flushed.

'I'm going to get Doctor and we'll have to put Amory in an iron lung for a while. Please, sit here and talk to him while I get everything organised.'

'Will he be all right, Nurse?' Unshed tears made Mrs Gardener's eyes bright.

Ella was so tired of that question; how could she know whether he'd be one of the ones to pull through or one of the ones who died? But she couldn't strip Mrs Gardener of hope, that would be cruel.

'He's a strong boy, I'm sure he'll be all right. We'll do all that we can to see to it.' She squeezed Mrs Gardener's arm and bustled off to get Doctor Ruddock, wishing she had a magic healing potion.

# 19

These days, Ella found herself slipping into memories of the past whenever her focus wasn't demanded elsewhere. At first she'd fought it, but the memories wouldn't be stopped, so she'd finally accepted it.

One afternoon, she was thinking about the mobile hospital they'd set up in Bayeux. More and more Ella believed that one of the most important duties a nurse could perform in the absence of magic potions, was that of providing hope. They'd been in Bayeux five days, the wards were full and more men were being brought in from Caen every hour. Dakotas had been taking off, regularly flying those who could travel back to hospitals in England, but the reality was, there weren't enough men who were well enough to go.

Ella felt she'd never be clean. They were rationing water to two litres a day, and that was for washing clothes as well as bodies. The stench in the wards was indescribable; a mixture of blood, vomit and excrement, mixed with filthy, rotting uniforms and bodies that hadn't seen soap for weeks. Ella held her nose as she entered each time, and was always surprised at how quickly she got used to it once she was there, too busy to worry about air quality.

Several times, they'd been strafed by German planes in spite of the large red crosses painted on the roofs, and each time, the patients had yelled at the nurses to take cover as they lay in their beds unable to move, waiting, perhaps, for the bullet that would take them. When shells fell nearby and shrapnel pierced the canvas walls, the men covered their heads with pillows while the nurses lay under the beds until it was over. Then it was business as usual. One time, Ella had been clutching a full bedpan, and when she came out from under the bed, she carried on to the sluice room as if nothing had happened.

During ward rounds, the men lay to attention in their beds while overtired doctors examined their handiwork, admiring bone settings and stitching, and the lucky soldiers got their evacuation orders.

The burns patients were the worst off and stayed the longest. Ella hated having to change their Vaseline gauze dressings, knowing what agony it was. Morphine could only help to a point. Infection was never more than a breath away in spite of her high standards of hygiene. Ella waged war on germs as aggressively as the Allies waged war against the Germans, but even with the new miracle drug, penicillin, infections crept in and were almost impossible to treat once they'd taken hold.

'I'll just change your dressings, Jim,' said Ella one morning.

Jim Prentice had been on the ward since the first day, burns covering half his body. He bit his lips as Ella started carefully peeling away the gauze. The new skin was pink and raw, but the edges of the burns were putrefying and stank. Jim looked at her and held his nose.

'Is it bad, Nurse?' he asked.

She fixed a smile on her face. She didn't know what more to do. She'd sprinkled ground up Sulfa tablets straight onto the wounds and given him regular injections of penicillin. She was hoping that he might be taken to East Grinstead where there was a doctor doing wonderful work with burns patients, grafting new skin and even building new facial features.

'Not too bad, Jim. A bit infected where the new skin is growing, but we'll get you well.'

He released his nose and took her hand. 'You are telling me the truth, aren't you? I need to know the truth so I can prepare myself.'

Ella sucked in her bottom lip. 'Your burns are bad, and the infection isn't going as soon as I'd like, but it's not getting worse either. I'm putting you on the list for possible transfer in a day or two. Your war's over, Jim. You're going home.'

He looked up at the ceiling and sighed. 'Home,' he said, and closed his eyes.

Ella finished applying the new dressing and left him to his dream of home, knowing he'd be in hospital in England for quite some time.

Sheila bustled into the room, stirring up the air and making the pages of Ella's diary flutter. Ella sat up, pulled from her memory of Bayeux into the present. Sheila was holding a sketch pad and two magazines: *Harper's Bazaar* and *Vogue*.

'I've been trying to decide on a design for my wedding dress, and it's soul-destroying. I haven't got enough clothing coupons for what I want, but with my hips I need a full skirt.'

Ella looked at her friend with an appraising gaze. Sheila and her hips — she'd been hearing about them since the day they met. She smiled, as much at the memory as at the fact that she'd actually remembered something else. It seemed to her that the memories were coming back faster now, the gaps were filling in.

'Let me see what you've sketched.'

Sheila offered the pad. Her drawings were strong and bold, but the designs, with their full skirts tucked into a narrow waist and lacy bodices draping from the shoulder, or layer upon layer of taffeta and lace, were awful. Ella raised her eyebrows.

'What a shame you won't be able to do one of these,' she said, putting the sketchpad on the table.

'You don't like them.'

Ella thought about lying, but the thought of seeing Sheila walk down the aisle looking like a cross between a powder puff and a Little Bo Peep appalled her.

'No, I don't think they're you. What's in the magazines?'

Ella, whose wedding was actually sooner, hadn't had a chance to think about what she'd wear. She had always been less interested in clothes than most of her friends, but as they flicked through *Vogue*, she began to get an idea of what she'd like.

'Let's go up to London soon and get our dresses made there, shall we? Andrew can take us out for lunch, he'd love that.'

When Sheila left to see Arthur, Ella thought back to a wedding she'd seen in France. Bayeux boasted a beautiful cathedral, and the whole town had taken very little bombing, it had fallen to the Allies so quickly. On her first few hours off, when she'd been in France for about ten days, she took herself off for a walk. It was a Saturday afternoon, and the cobbled streets had been cleaned by the storm that had hit the week before and battered the surrounding area for three days. Windows sparkled in the sun and the buildings stood proud, as if they knew they'd been spared.

The bells were pealing, and Ella wandered through the

streets following the sound. It reminded her of the church bells at home, and she was momentarily homesick. Several children ran round a corner, almost straight into her, and pulled up short.

'Désolé, excusez-moi,' they chorused, and Ella smiled and said it was fine, she was still standing.

One of the older girls said, 'Anglaise?' and Ella nodded.

'Parlez-vous Francais?' the girl asked.

Ella held up a hand, the thumb and index finger an inch apart. 'Un peu,' she said.

'Bien. Je ne parle pas l'Anglais, mais je parle un peu l'allemande.'

'Vous habitez ici quand les Allemandes...?' She couldn't work out how to finish the sentence, but she didn't have to. The children were all nodding.

'Aimez-vous les Allemandes?' she asked.

'Non! Nous ne les aimez pas!' They almost shouted the 'pas'.

They all laughed, and the children ran off with an 'Au revoir, Anglaise,' much to Ella's relief, as her French had been stretched as far as it would go in that one short exchange. She hadn't told them that she spoke fluent German.

She turned towards the cathedral again, and found a café in the square to sit and have a glass of cassis.

A jeep drove up and three Canadian soldiers jumped out and sat at the next table. One of them leaned over and offered her a cigarette.

'I don't smoke, thank you,' she said.

'Why don't you join us?' he asked, pulling out a chair.

It would have seemed churlish not to, although Ella had been enjoying quietly watching the people who were out and about, shopping for the little that was available, strolling along, stopping to chat. It was such a normal scene after the chaos and busyness of the last week.

Fortunately for her, she'd hardly sat at their table when their attention was caught by a bride and groom exiting the cathedral opposite followed by their guests. They stopped in the square and a photographer gathered them into a tight group and held his camera up to his face.

Ella was surprised that there would be such a large wedding in the middle of a war, and wondered if they'd planned it a long time ago, or if it was a hurried affair, couples rushing to the altar now the Germans had gone. There certainly was an air of relief in the town, almost of gaiety. She shuddered. What must it have been like living under the Nazis?

There had been a lot of propaganda about them, but Ella had never been quite able to believe it all. Her father was German, after all, and he was a kind and loving man. He'd lived in England nearly all his life, attending university there, and changing his name from Wittgenstein to Whittington to prove his solidarity with the British, or perhaps to fit in better. Even after he was interned on the Isle of Man for some time during the First World War, he never said anything against Britain. He loved his adopted country with a passion, and always told Ella that although he knew that he was no spy, he understood the government's need to shut foreigners away just to be sure.

The one thing he loved and missed about the country of his birth, however, was the language, so Andrew and Ella had had lessons from an early age, and after their mother had died, they had a succession of German nannies. He enjoyed being able to communicate with his children in his native language, although only ever in private. Andrew and Ella had only used it when alone too, believing that it was somehow shameful to speak the language they enjoyed.

The wedding crowd started moving towards them, and as they passed, Ella thought how beautiful the bride looked in the intricately embroidered antique lace wedding dress that hugged her slender form and draped elegantly from the hips. It smelled strongly of mothballs.

She thought of that dress now, of walking down the aisle to stand next to David and become his wife wearing such simple elegance, such beautiful fabric. Something like that would be perfect. She just had to persuade Sheila out of a dress for her own wedding that used enough material to sink a ship and made her look ludicrous.

Her thoughts turned to the past again.

The Battle for Caen lasted two months, and for all that time, Ella's hospital was full. It wasn't until they'd been there almost three weeks, though, that they admitted German soldiers. Until then they'd been taken to the other British general hospital that had been set up in a convent down the road, but now, with so many wounded, they couldn't cope.

'I'm not treating them,' said Daffy when she was told they were coming. 'Those bastards are killing and wounding our boys without a care. I think we should leave them out for the crows.'

Ella, still not quite over her own shock at the prospect of having Germans in her beds, but surprised at Daffy's vehemence, said, 'What if our boys were hurt and needed help behind the lines – wouldn't you want them to get help from whoever was around? I shouldn't think the Germans particularly want to be here, but they don't have any choice, they're prisoners of war. And in the end, they're just men who need help.'

Daffy looked at her as if she was deranged. 'They're murderers, cold-blooded killers.'

'If you put it like that, so are our boys. At least, the Germans would say so.'

Daffy looked like she was considering Ella's statement, but as soon as she spoke, Ella realised that she was just thinking about how best to shut her up.

'Our boys are fighting because those bloody Jerries asked for it. They invaded Poland in the first place. Hitler is evil and so are his soldiers. I won't nurse any of them, and that's final.'

It was a battle Ella knew she wouldn't win, and also, in reality, one that wasn't hers. Daffy would be ordered to do her job by her superiors, or be sent home, possibly to be court-martialled. She shrugged and turned back to what she'd been doing, drawing up an injection.

They put the first few Germans in a side tent. The first one to be brought in had had both his legs amputated in theatre. When Ella saw him, she thought there must have been a mistake — he had soft, smooth skin and his mousy hair flopped over his forehead. He only looked about fourteen, far too young to be fighting.

As he started coming round from the anaesthetic, he called for his mother, turning his head from side to side as if searching for her, although his eyes were still closed.

At his bedside, Ella spoke softly to him.

'You are safe here, we will look after you.' And then she repeated it in German. 'Sie sind hier sicher. Wir kommen uns um Sie.'

He opened eyes filled with fear and pain, and looked into hers. She kept up a soothing prattle in German, telling him where he was, that she would look after him, that one day he would see his mother again. Eventually, he closed his eyes again and seemed to sleep.

Ella stood up, took a deep breath and straightened her apron.

The orderlies were bringing in more wounded. More Germans.

This time, they were old. Two men who were sixty if they were a day. One with wounds to the abdomen that had been hastily stitched and left uncovered, as was the way, and the other who appeared totally unhurt. Ella examined him and still could find no injury. She turned to the orderly who was having a quick cup of tea before returning to his post.

'What's the matter with this one?'

'Don't ask me, Sister. They found him in a heap next to his mate. He has no control of his muscles – can't stand up or sit up or anything. Bloody dead weight, I can tell you.'

Ella turned back to the man and looked at his label: Erwin Loder. That was all. No rank, no diagnosis. No drugs administered.

'Herr Loder, can you hear me?' Ella asked.

The man kept his eyes firmly closed.

She asked again in German. Still no response. Not even the telltale blink of an eye behind a closed lid.

'Nurse!'

She stood and tucked a stray hair back under her nurse's veil. 'Coming,' she said, and left the Germans in their tent and went into the main ward to attend to the others. They had quite a few Canadians in as well as the Tommies. She wondered what they'd think about sharing a ward with the enemy, and then she was too busy with the demands of her patients to give it more thought.

When Sheila came home from her evening with Arthur, Ella was still up.

'What did you think when the first Germans were brought in?' she asked without preamble.

Sheila took a moment, shucking her jacket and folding it

over the back of a chair. She lit a cigarette, blowing the smoke out through her nose and delicately picking a bit of tobacco from her tongue.

'I was shocked, I suppose. I don't think I liked the idea much, to be honest, but as soon as I saw them, their pain and fear and defeat, I came around. It was the defeat that was the worst to deal with, do you remember? They seemed diminished, hopeless.'

Ella thought for a moment.

'Yes, I do remember some of them being like that. But others were also very arrogant, as if it was an affront to be a prisoner and treated by the enemy.'

'Yes, there was that too. The SS were the worst. They were very belligerent. I remember one of them refused a blood transfusion because it might have come from a Jew, and then he tried to get all the Germans to refuse. Some did, others just wanted to survive, and by then, the fight was out of them. After a time, some of them got on quite well with our boys. Games of cards, sharing a few words, some had photographs of loved ones they showed around.'

'I don't remember much hostility – or am I just blocking it out?'

Sheila looked at her, her eyebrows raised and head tilted to one side.

'You don't remember the talk you gave to the ward before the first Jerries were brought in?'

'No. What did I say?'

'You came to me in high dudgeon. Daffy had just told you that she thought the Germans should be fed to the crows, and you said something had to be done. And before I could say anything, you marched back to the ward, stood right in the middle and called for everyone's attention.'

'Gosh, I must have looked impressive!'

'Oh, yes. Ears were tuned in, eyes were fixed, breath was stilled.'

'What did I say, exactly?'

Sheila stood up straighter, pulled her shoulders back and stared just over Ella's head. 'We are in a battle zone, and men on both sides are being wounded. We are about to admit German prisoners of war who need treatment. You may not like it, but you do have to accept it. They are men, like you, with wives, mothers, fathers, children. They are fighting for what they've been told is right, just as we are fighting for what we believe is right. I will have no continuation of the battle on my ward. Do you understand?'

'Golly – did I really say all that?'

'You did, and more that I forget now. By the end, everyone had the message!'

'And what happened to Daffy?'

'She had to do as she was told, but she avoided the Germans as much as she could, and wouldn't give them penicillin. She said that was only for our boys, and the Germans could have the Sulfa tablets. No one did anything about it, because she was running her own ward and at least she was giving them something, and it was reasonably effective. And I'm sure there were those higher up who agreed with her.'

Ella thought about what Sheila had said later that night when she couldn't sleep. She had a notion that she and Daffy had had a big argument at some stage — it must have been about her treatment of the Germans.

Later that week, she had lunch with David during her shift break. They were sitting in the garden of The Royal Exchange in

Hambleford, enjoying the autumn sun. Ella stretched her limbs and sighed.

'This is so nice. We're so lucky, aren't we, to have all this?'

'All what?'

'Oh, you know, gardens and English pubs and each other!'

David laughed and raised his glass. 'To gardens, pubs and us!'

Ella loved his laugh; the sound which started as a deep chortle that grew and then burst its way out of him, and the way his eyes creased, his mouth widened and he threw his head back. He was unselfconscious in his joy. She wanted to make love with him, felt the heat creeping up her thighs. As a distraction she asked him his opinion about what she and Sheila had been talking about. What would he have thought of nursing Germans?

He stared into his beer for a long time, until Ella wondered if he hadn't heard the question. She was just about to ask it again when he started talking.

'I'm not sure I could have done it. As submariners we were trained to hunt and destroy, to think of the enemy not as people, but as killers who wanted us dead. Who wanted to bring down everything we believed in, all that we held dear. I hated them.' He lifted his gaze to hers and let out a sigh.

Ella sucked in her lips. She hadn't expected to hear that from him. She thought of him as open and tolerant. She'd expected him to feel the same way as her, but why should he? He didn't have a German parent, he hadn't come face to face with Germans like she had, and have the chance to see that they were just the same as the British boys, the Canadians, the Poles, the Americans, the French. No, he'd been under the sea in a metal can playing cat and mouse with an unseen enemy. Of course he'd feel differently to her.

'And now, do you hate them still?'

'I don't know, Ella. I really don't. I try not to think about it too much. The war's over and Hitler was defeated. We can sit in pub gardens and enjoy a drink and each other's company in peace. That's what I fought for. That may be shallow of me, but it's how I feel.'

'It's not good enough, David. You can't write off a whole nation like that. Yes, you were scared and yes, you had to fight, but if you met a German now, what would you do?'

He looked away again as if searching the flower beds for an answer.

'I know that you want me to say I'd shake his hand and wish him well, and I probably would, but I'm not sure how sincere it would be. Old hurts linger for me. I had friends who were killed. Men who had families and a life ahead of them.'

'What about the German mothers who lost their boys? They cried too, the light went out of their lives the same way it did for so many people here. We were all doing what we had to, divided only by where we were born.' Ella drained her glass. She was upset at David's response. She wondered what other things they'd disagree over, important things that might drive a wedge between them.

He took her hand. She left it where it was, but none of her earlier feelings of lust were there. She took a deep breath. And then another.

'I've disappointed you,' said David.

'You've shocked me,' she said. 'I thought you were more forgiving.'

Many people shared David and Daffy's opinion. As Ella thought back to her time in Bayeux, she realised that she was in the minority in not hating the Germans for what they did. So many of the patients they saw were very young or really old. It seemed that all the men of fighting age in Germany were dead or elsewhere, and these boys and grandfathers had been conscripted as a last-ditch attempt to stop the inevitable. They didn't want to fight, they wanted to farm their land, put their feet by the fire at the end of a long day, just like many of the Allied soldiers did.

Friedrich, the young double amputee, was fifteen. He and the others conscripted at the same time as him were given two weeks' training before joining their companies. Ella had many long talks with him before he was transported to England as a prisoner of war. His two older brothers had been killed on the Eastern Front, his father had been called up at the same time as him, but they'd been separated and he didn't know what had happened to him. His mother was all alone looking after their small farm near Dresden, trying to stay alive. He feared for her safety, with the Russians coming from the East, and their brutal reputation preceding them. Not once did he complain about what had happened to him.

Before he went, he gave Ella a letter. 'Please get this to my mother if you can,' he said.

Ella put it in her pocket. 'I'll do my best,' she promised, and gave him a kiss on the forehead. 'Good luck, Friedrich.'

'Thank you, Ella. I'll remember you always.'

At the cottage hospital Ella had been busy with the polio patients all afternoon and had driven home in a light drizzle. It looked like the hot, dry weather was finally over. She couldn't stop thinking about what David had said. She was more troubled by it than she wanted to be. His reaction had made her realise how little she knew him, and yet, she wanted to spend the rest of her life with him. It seemed crazy.

There was also something nudging at her, a little burr caught in the fabric of her memories. She tried to catch hold of it, but it wouldn't be dislodged.

And she also couldn't stop thinking about Friedrich. She'd never heard from him again, nor had she expected to. She'd sent the letter to his mother, but had no idea if it got there, if she was alive even. And if he'd made it home, their farm was now tucked away in the Soviet sector and she didn't want to imagine what life there might be like.

So many people had come and gone, people who had touched her life in ways they'd never know.

# 20

After three weeks in Bayeux, the stream of patients slowed to a trickle and the staff could take a little time off. One afternoon, when Ella was alone on the ward preparing some of the men to be evacuated, Captain Jack Bailey, one of the surgeons, came to find her.

Ella finished what she was doing, even though she could feel the doctor's impatience. Well, he could wait, she thought, the patients were more important.

When she made her way over to him, wiping her hands on a damp cloth and straightening her uniform, he motioned for her to join him outside the tent.

'The Canadians are having a bit of a shindig in town this evening. I was wondering if you might like to come along?'

Ella hoped the surprise didn't show on her face. She'd been expecting a discussion about a patient. A dressing down about some aspect of her work would have been less of a shock than a request to go on a date. She looked at the captain. He was about thirty, she thought, but boyish-looking with his wide blue eyes and broad face. She hadn't had much to do with the doctors, busy as they all were in their own small worlds of theatre or ward. She'd seen Captain Bailey around Hatfield House, but even there, the doctors had been rather stand-offish and hadn't mixed much with the nurses or other staff. They'd had to turn up to lectures, but had always left immediately after they finished, and when the hospitals were being set up, they'd been notable by their absence, as if it was beneath them. Ella wasn't sure if she really wanted to start mixing with them now, but the idea of a dance was enticing.

Jack shifted from one foot to the other, and Ella realised that he needed an answer.

'All right,' she said. 'But I don't knock off until eight, so I can't be ready until nine at the earliest.'

'Excellent. I'll see if I can rustle up some transport for nine then. See you later.' He walked off, hands in his pockets, whistling. Ella laughed. A date in the middle of a war.

A plane flew low overhead, and she ducked instinctively, and looked up to see if it was one of theirs. She wondered if she'd ever hear a plane again without reacting like that.

~

At nine that night, she was ready in one of the two dresses she'd been able to squeeze into her trunk. As she slipped her feet into her shoes and felt the pinch of narrow toes, she almost wished she could wear her boots, which were nicely worn in and now felt as comfortable as a pair of slippers.

Captain Bailey had managed to hitch a ride for them in a transport lorry that was picking up provisions from town. They had to sit in the back on makeshift benches with the other officers who had wangled a ride and some time in town.

Vera, one of the theatre nurses, was there with Vincent Palmer, an anaesthetist, and Daffy was with Larry Jamison, another surgeon. Both of them were wearing their uniform, and

Ella remembered that civvies were not supposed to be worn except when on leave. No one said anything, however, although Vera cast an envious eye over her dress. Conversation was difficult as they rumbled along the road as the engine strained to get up the hill, and the tarpaulin covering them flapped in the wind. With all the jolting, Ella thought her back would never be the same again, and was glad when they reached the town and jumped down onto the road. Every house had a French flag flying, making the place look festive.

'This way,' said Jack, rather needlessly, since the lights from the windows of the building that had been requisitioned as an officers' club were practically blinding them, and the music drew them towards the large old house. Laughter and cigarette smoke drifted out through the door, and they made their way in. The room was crowded. There was a band on a low stage at one end of the room and couples were dancing energetically to the jazz tune they were playing. At the bar, men were standing three deep trying to get the attention of the barman, who was red-faced and sweaty. Ella looked for an empty table, but Daffy spotted one before her and steered her towards it.

It was hot and the music was loud, so they had to shout to be heard, and in the end, didn't bother. Jack held out his hand and led Ella onto the dance floor. He was a good dancer, sure of himself as he whirled her round, and she laughed as she spun, glad to be away from the work on the ward, the never-ending needs of the patients and the chaos of the war, if only for an evening.

At eleven, the lights dimmed and then came on again, and the catering corps brought in supper. Chicken and salad, apples and grapes, white bread and real butter. Ella wondered how they managed to get such good food when in the hospital mess they were eating tinned stew and vegetables.

'This is why we come,' said Jack in her ear. 'The Canadians

always do a good spread. I've heard the Americans' are even better.'

They stood in line, Ella hoping that it wasn't all gone by the time they got there, but there was plenty, and they returned to their table with plates piled high.

'I feel almost guilty,' she said. 'I feel I should take some back for my room-mate at least.' The band was taking a break, so they could talk in normal voices.

'She can come next time,' said Vincent. 'Since Caen fell, the Canadians are always throwing dances.'

As they ate, the doctors regaled them with stories about life in a tent operating theatre, and asked how it was going on the wards. There hadn't been much time for ward rounds and follow up, although that would change now that they were less busy, they promised.

The band started up again, playing slower tunes that invited couples to hold each other close and sway around the dance floor. Ella felt comfortable in Jack's arms, and lay her head against his chest, closing her eyes and losing herself in the rhythm of the music and his heartbeat. For half an hour, the war was a distant memory.

Before she and Sheila went up to London to see about their wedding dresses, Ella remembered that her mother's dress was in the wardrobe in the spare room. As she opened the door the smell of naphthalene and camphor escaped and she remembered again the bride in Bayeux, wondering what had happened to her. Then she took a step back, her hand over her mouth and nose, overwhelmed by the powerful odour. She waited a few moments before approaching the cupboard again, then she reached in and took the dress out. It was swathed in a sheet, and she carefully unwrapped it and held it against her. It was exquisite. A simple ecru silk shift with beautifully embroidered silk netting over it. It was exactly what she wanted. Taking her clothes off, she lifted the dress over her head and stood inspecting herself in the full-length mirror, head on one side, appraising her image.

The dress came to her mid-calf, but the netting was longer, making a short train behind her. Her mother may have been shorter than her, but she was also wider. Ella thought it would be easy enough for someone who knew what they were doing to adjust it for her. The veil was also silk netting on a simple headband with hand-sewn pearls. She smiled. Her parents wouldn't be there to see her getting married, but she would be wearing her mother's dress and veil, and Andrew would walk her down the aisle. It was the next-best thing to having them there.

After dinner, she showed Sheila the dress, who agreed that with a tuck here and there, it would be perfect.

'I can see you in something similar,' said Ella. 'And because I won't need them, you can have my clothing coupons to help towards your dress, although...' Ella hoped more coupons would amount to better quality fabric rather than more of the cheaper stuff and a wider skirt.

'You really don't like my ideas, do you?'

'I like simplicity and elegance rather than bold statement, I suppose.' Ella smiled. 'You have such a gorgeous figure you don't need frou-frou.'

Sheila smoothed her skirt over her thighs and turned to look over her shoulder at her bottom. 'You think so? I can't see it myself. I've always thought I had rather a large derriere.'

'Not at all. Anyway, all I ask is that you try on some things I suggest and then if you really don't like them, I won't say another word.'

'It's a deal, lady,' said Sheila in an American drawl.

They spent the rest of the evening planning their trip to London, the shops they'd go to, where they might eat. They'd decided to go up for the day during the week rather than stay the weekend, and Andrew had promised to take them out for lunch.

∾

Before they went, however, Ella had to talk to David. She didn't know how to broach the subject of his attitude to Germans, but she felt the air needed to be cleared. It wouldn't do to spend your life with someone brushing uncomfortable topics under the carpet.

Sitting in the pub one evening, she brought the conversation round to the topic.

'I don't want to talk about it, Ella. You have your opinion, and I have mine, and that's the end of it.'

Ella caught her breath.

'That is not the end of it. I am half German; our children will have German blood in them.'

'That's different; they'll be brought up here, with English values.' David's voice was terse, his jaw tense. Ella had never seen him like this before.

'This is important to me, David. Are you suggesting that we bring our children up not to question things, not to know their heritage?'

'They will be English,' he said, looking her in the eye.

Ella banged her drink down and got up from the table. People turned to look at her but she didn't care. She picked up her handbag and marched out of the bar without a backward glance.

Later, at home with a large brandy beside her, Ella wondered at her actions. She had been the one to want the discussion only to flounce out – yes, she had to admit that she had flounced – when it didn't go her way. Had she always been like that, as intolerant as she was accusing David of being? She looked at her watch and decided it wasn't too late to call Andrew.

'Hello, old thing. Everything all right?' he asked.

'Yes, I think so. I just have a question.'

'Ask away, I'll answer if I can.'

Ella paused a moment. 'I was wondering if I've always had a quick temper?' The tears gathered, and suddenly she found herself sobbing.

'Why, no.' Andrew sounded surprised. 'Ella, what is it, what's the matter?' Andrew's voice was full of concern.

She wiped her eyes, blew her nose and took some deep breaths.

'I've just walked out on David. He said he couldn't forgive the Germans for what they did and I took it personally and stormed off.'

Ella heard Andrew take a deep breath and let it out slowly. 'Oh, Ella. I expect most people in Britain haven't forgiven the Germans.'

'But I don't want to marry most people in Britain. I want to marry David.'

'Then talk to him. You love each other. I'm sure you'll work it out.'

'But what if we can't? What if I get angry again?'

'Do what Mother used to tell us to do; take some deep breaths, count to ten and pull the corners of your mouth into a smile. She always said it was impossible to remain angry with a smile on your face.'

Ella laughed in spite of herself. 'All right, I'll give it a go. Thank you.'

'Any time, Ella. Good luck.'

~

The polio epidemic was still keeping Ella busy at work, but in quiet moments on the ward, she continued to let her mind slip back to France and the very different nursing she'd done there.

A month after they arrived in Bayeux, they got the order to move on. The patients who hadn't yet been evacuated were sent to the other British hospital in the convent, and they spent three days packing up instruments, stripping beds and washing linen, stringing lines up between tents to dry all the bedding in between showers. It looked more like a gypsy camp than a hospital. As they packed their personal items, Sheila turned to Ella.

'I wonder where we're off to. I hear there's fighting up near the Belgian border. I suppose we can expect to be rushed off our feet wherever we are.' She sighed and sat on her trunk to close it. 'Well, Ella, wherever we're going, I'm glad you're here.'

Ella looked at her. 'What's the matter, Sheila?'

'Oh, nothing.' She shrugged. 'I suppose I just feel a bit tired, that's all. Too many dances these last few days, and not enough sleep.'

It was true, they had been out a lot. The Canadians had invited them again, and the RAF had had a do before they moved on, and the hospital up at the convent had had a send-off for them too, in a hall in Bayeux. And now they were all moving out and some of the friends they'd made they'd never see again, and there'd be new people to meet, new patients to treat, another move, and another, in a constant stream.

The next morning, they finished loading the lorries and waited for their transport. It had been raining on and off for the past two weeks, and Ella's spirits were low.

As they drove along the rutted road, she was horrified to see blackened tanks on the verges, the dead crews hanging half in and half out of the turrets and escape hatches. Ella covered her mouth and nose. She would have covered her eyes as well, but there was a ghoulish fascination in the scene; mile after mile of armoured cars, destroyed and left as reminders of the carnage. Dead cattle in the fields, the stench of decaying, maggot-filled bodies. And always the sound of shelling in the distance, the ack-ack guns firing away, planes flying overhead.

They stopped in Caen, the town where all the fighting had been for the past few weeks. There were hardly any buildings left intact and Ella was reminded of her night in the bomb shelter and her emergence into the devastation of London and her home. All these people were going through the same now, trying to save some of their treasures from the ruins, sleeping in tents, halls, the lucky ones staying with relatives and friends in other towns not yet bombed, or already bombed but with more to offer than this one.

They were ordered to set up the hospital.

'We've only bloody well come a few miles,' said Vera, stamping her cigarette into the mud. 'What was the point? Surely the ambulances could have brought the patients a few extra miles and saved us the bother of setting the whole place up again?'

No one answered her. They were probably all thinking the same, but orders were orders.

Jack approached and nodded to all the nurses.

'Off we go again, eh?'

Ella nodded. The doctors had become friendlier since the dances, and had taken to coming to the wards in the evening and having a cup of tea and a chat. They were all on first-name terms.

'Going to help get the tents up, Jack?' asked Sheila.

'That's what the pioneers are for, isn't it?'

'We have to help with our tents,' said Daffy. 'Many hands make light work, you know.'

Jack smiled and wandered off again.

'Bet he's gone to cadge a cup of tea from somewhere and sit with his feet up while we do all the work,' said Vera.

'Well, we'd better stop worrying about what he's doing and get on with what we've got to do,' said Ella.

'Oh, that's right, stand up for your boyfriend.'

Ella spun round. 'He is not my boyfriend, and I'm not standing up for anyone, I just think we should get a move on or we'll be sleeping in the open tonight, and I for one don't want to get rained on.'

Sheila caught her eye and smiled, and then they all stood open-mouthed as Jack returned with all the doctors and said, 'Point us in the direction of the erections. Tent erections, that is,' he added, blushing. 'We're here to help.'

Once again the pioneers dug trenches for the tents to go in to keep them below the line of shrapnel, and before dinner, all the accommodation tents were up and beds made. The cooks were in their tent kitchens producing a gourmet meal from tins, and as the light faded, the staff of the British General Hospital sat around on their trunks, chatting and smoking. They could smell fires off in the distance, and the horizon was obscured by smoke.

'I think we'll have to prepare for more burns patients in the next few days,' said Larry, and they all nodded.


Ella was rostered on to triage once they got the hospital up and running. It was her job to examine each man brought in and refer urgent cases to the medical team. Casualties were sorted as to the severity of their injuries, whatever their nationality.

The pioneers brought the stretchers in to her. Each of the wounded had a case envelope attached to a button on their battle dress with a note hastily written by the field dressing staff; gunshot wound R knee, complicated fracture L ankle, and so on. On their forehead, in indelible ink, was written the medication they'd been given, the time and the dose. Some went straight into surgery. Those who could wait she would clean up, dressing wounds, setting up IV drips and prepping for theatre. The men with no hope of survival were sent to the rather ironically named resuscitation tent to be kept as comfortable as possible until they died of their injuries.

At the end of her second day, Ella sat on her bed in the tent she shared with Sheila, feeling overwhelmed. All day, men had been brought in with the most horrific injuries; shattered, burnt, twisted bodies one after the other, until the resuscitation ward was full to overflowing, and she couldn't shut her ears to the pitiful sounds coming from it — young men pleading to live, calling for their loved ones, praying to God, screaming in pain, begging to die.

Sheila sat next to her, an arm around her shoulders.

'It's not your fault, Ella – none of us asked for this war, but if we weren't here, just think how much worse it would be for those boys. They'd be dying slowly on the battlefield, lying in dirt and mud on their own, with no comforting smile, no morphine to ease the pain. We may not be able to do much for them, but surely it's better than nothing. And look at all the others who go to surgery and get better.'

Ella wasn't to be comforted. 'Yes, and how many of them end up back on the front, sheltering from shells and bombs, staring down the barrels of the same guns, terrified that the next bullet has their name on it?'

Sheila sighed and shrugged. 'We're doing our best, Ella. We can do no more. Now, are you coming to the party? The RAF have invited us all to a dance. It'll take you mind off things, and I know you love a man in uniform!'

Ella looked at her friend, wondering how she could always be so positive, so unrelentingly gay. But she had to admit, too, that it was infectious, and, as Sheila always said, you can't save a life when you're off duty so you may as well party.

They caught a ride on a lorry and got to the dance late in the evening. In her uniform, Ella felt old and frumpy. She put a bit of lipstick on, took a deep breath, and entered the room. Heads turned, and several RAF men approached them with smiles and offers of drinks. Sheila turned to her and whispered, 'See you later,' and allowed herself to be swept off to the bar by a squadron leader. Ella smiled to herself; with men outnumbering women by forty to one, it wouldn't matter what she looked like as long as she didn't have a moustache and full beard.

The room was warm, the alcohol was plentiful, and she danced with several different men, hardly catching their names before being whisked off to dance with another. One, a flight lieutenant, reminded her a little of Charles, and she had to take some deep breaths so as not to run out of the room. She didn't know if she wanted to avoid him, or dance only with him, find out about his life, his loves, his dreams. In the end, they had one dance and she never saw him again. The war was like that — you spent an evening with people and never knew what happened to them after that. Ella thought there was both a sadness and an exhilaration in that; you could be whoever you wanted to be for that one evening, behave however you pleased, and never suffer the embarrassment of explaining yourself the day after. There were plenty of nurses who had a different man every night, or who got so drunk they had to be carried home. She wondered if she was too boring for any of that, too conservative. Although, if the flight lieutenant had asked, maybe she would have gone somewhere with him.

Ivy and Vera danced into her vision, laughing with their hands on the hips of the men in front of them. Ivy motioned to her to join them, and Ella put her drink down and joined the conga line.

In the morning she heated water on the primus stove to wash herself down with a facecloth before heading to the mess tent for breakfast and going back on duty. She didn't feel up to it, but she knew she had to keep going, that Sheila had been right, someone had to look after these boys.

That day, the injuries seemed less bad, and she had to send fewer men to the resuscitation tent. As she treated him, she had a chat with a Pole who spoke English as if he'd been born there.

'I have always loved everything about Britain,' he said, as she cut away his uniform so the surgeons could get to his wounds.

She smiled at him. 'Have you ever been there?' she asked.

'No, but I have seen pictures, and read books; Charles Dickens and Jane Austen.'

'You mustn't think that it's like that these days, things have changed a bit since they were alive.'

'Yes, but it is still a genteel society, I think, more so than Poland.'

Ella didn't know about that, but she didn't want to take away his fantasy.

'Perhaps, when the war is over, I will come to England and take you out for dinner,' he said.

'I'll look forward to it. I can show you the sights.'

She moved on to the next patient, and by the time she had a moment to stretch and look around again, the Pole had gone to the theatre.

A couple of days later, she had to go to Vera's ward to fetch some more dressings, and there he was, lying in bed, talking to Vera. Ella smiled and said hello.

'Nurse, here you are! I was just saying to Nurse Vera that you saved my life.'

Vera winked at her, and Ella laughed.

'I think the doctors did the life-saving, but you're very sweet.' She walked away with Vera to get the dressings.

'A lot of them flirt, but he must have a degree in it. He even asked Daffy to marry him!'

'Maybe it's all that's keeping him going,' said Ella. 'Keeping an eye on the future, bagging himself an English wife!'

Vera grinned. 'Sooner Daffy than me, that's for sure. He's not my type. I like the dark, brooding sort, not sunshine boy.'

'We'll have to see what we can find for you then, won't we? Are you coming to the pictures tonight? They're showing *Fanny by Gaslight* at the Canadian Club.'

'Wouldn't miss it for the world. I hear the Canadians are off soon. I'll miss their food.'

Ella stood up and stretched her back. The garden needed a lot of work and she'd started by deadheading the dahlias. It was early November, and because of the mild weather, the garden had produced bursts of colour until late October. The hollyhocks would have to be tied up too, and the hydrangeas pruned. She remembered her father at the house in Richmond, gardening at weekends, shirtsleeves rolled up, kneeling on a special pad, weeding, planting, talking to the young seedlings to make them grow. He'd had a man in to do the lawns once a fortnight in summer and less often in winter.

Ella smiled, turning her face up to the weak sun. She wasn't a keen gardener herself, only doing the bare minimum to keep the garden from overtaking the house — weeding, pruning, cutting back. But she had enjoyed the flowers all summer, and being able to sit out in the evenings and sip a gin and tonic before dinner. And Sheila had been a marvel with the vegetables.

She and David hadn't spoken since that evening at the restaurant the week before. She was still angry that the man she'd thought so open-minded was so intolerant on this issue. Could he truly love her if he really hated the Germans so deeply? Could he ignore her heritage? Even if he could, she couldn't.

But she missed him. Sheila had been tactful and not asked any questions, but Ella was sure she'd noticed something was wrong, and suspected that she and Arthur talked about it.

Her suspicions were confirmed the next evening when Sheila arrived home with Arthur and David and then promptly whisked Arthur off to the kitchen to help with dinner.

David looked awkward, holding his hat in his hands. Ella held her sherry glass tightly, angry to have been put in this position.

'I've tried to call you but–'

'I haven't been answering the telephone,' said Ella coolly.

'No.'

They stood in silence for a few moments, the fire crackling in the grate the only sound.

'I've missed you, Ella. More than you can know.'

Ella loosened the grip on her glass. She'd missed him too. Taking a deep breath, she counted to ten, pulled her lips into a smile, and said, 'Ich leiber dich.'

'And I love you, too. Oh, Ella, I've been thinking about what you said, that we were all doing what we thought was right, divided only by where we were born. If I'd been born in Berlin, I'd have been on a German U-boat stalking British subs, and I'd have been taught to hate the Tommies. It puts a different perspective on things, that's for sure.'

Ella moved away from the fireplace where she'd been standing.

'Come and sit with me,' she said.

They sat side by side on the sofa. Ella took David's hand.

'I'm sorry I walked out on you. I won't do that again. I'm sure we'll disagree about things in the future, and I may get angry – I seem to have a bit of a temper at times – but I'll be more grown up about it.'

David smiled. 'And I'll be more considered in my opinions. I don't want to fight with you.'

'Some things are worth fighting about, though, wouldn't you agree? I don't want you giving in to me just to keep me happy.'

'I won't do that, Ella. It's not in my nature to be passive, but you are very important to me, and perhaps we have both learned something from this.'

She smiled and leant in to kiss him. They both turned at a sound in the hall.

'You can come in now. I'm sure you've been listening, so you know all is forgiven,' called Ella, and Sheila entered carrying a tray of thinly sliced bread and shaved cheese, looking rather sheepish.

The next afternoon Ella was having a cup of tea in the kitchen and thinking that she and David needed to talk about where they'd live after they were married. She realised that she'd assumed he'd move in to her house, but maybe he was imagining her in his. They'd have to discuss it. She couldn't bear the idea of selling Bamford House, of clearing it of her possessions, her childhood. She was still coming across things – trinkets, books, pictures stuffed away in drawers – that reminded her of long ago. But it was more than that — just by living in the house she was reminded daily of little things; of Andrew tickling her until she begged for mercy, of her father sitting after dinner with his pipe, often unfilled, clamped between his teeth, as he listened to music on the gramophone; of the line of wellington boots outside the back door, her father's large ones, Andrew's in the middle, and her small ones in a neat row. If she moved, she'd lose the reminders of all those little, everyday events.

The telephone rang in the hall, and Ella brushed some imaginary dirt off her hands and went inside.

'Hello, Hambleford 462,' she said.

'Ella, is that you? It's Donald Richards here. I've been meaning to call you for ages.'

Ella leant against the hall table, holding the phone tight. The name seemed familiar, and the voice with its slight accent, but more troubling was the stabbing sensation in the centre of her chest, and the prickles of fear that spread out in every direction.

'Hello, Donald. How are you?'

She spoke quietly, trying to keep the tremor out of her voice.

'Very well, but I hear you've been in the wars.' He laughed at his own joke.

'I'm fine.'

'That's good. I was wondering if you needed anything. Your usual, you know.'

'My usual?'

'Yes. We could meet in Hambleford as we used to.'

Ella didn't know why, but she didn't want to see this Donald. 'I'm afraid I don't go out much these days, but thank you for asking.'

There was silence at the other end of the line, and then Donald said, 'I understand. Well, you have my telephone number, so if you do ever want anything... you know... just give me a ring.'

'Thank you. I will.'

When Sheila came in from shopping, she asked her about Donald Richards.

'Oh, yes, he's rung a few times in the last few months but never wanted to leave a message. In fact, he asked me not to say he'd called.'

Ella felt a chill in spite of the mild afternoon.

# 21

Ella had noted in her diary that August 1944 was a month of drizzle. Nothing would dry and the destruction all around them was getting everyone down. That and the exhausting work-hours and the constant dirt and stench, men fighting for their lives or giving up all hope.

They'd moved again, to a town near Falaise. The hospital was set up in the grounds of a chateau and the senior officers were billeted there. Not so the nurses, who were still in their tents, trying to keep dry. The nights were lit by tracer fire, and they worked accompanied by the constant sound of shells and the ground heaving around them. Increasingly, the Germans ignored the red crosses on the tent roofs and strafed them anyway. The nurses and patients would wear their tin hats and hope for the best. There wasn't much else they could do. One night, a staff nurse was hit and had to go to surgery. She woke in a bed next to the patients she'd been looking after.

Another night, a heavily pregnant civilian was brought in. Ivy had a little midwifery experience, so she stayed with the woman through her labour and helped deliver a healthy baby boy. All the nurses dropped in to see her when they could the next day, celebrating a new life for a change.

When she had time off, Ella noticed that there were more civilians about in the town, drifting back from wherever they'd gone to stay away from the Germans and the fighting. There were also signs on the verges declaring that they'd been cleared of mines. In a field behind the chateau was a vehicle graveyard, the wrecks stripped of every removable part. It was impossible to get away from the war.

Ella had been rostered on to theatre, and one night, after two days with hardly a break, she collapsed onto her bed. Sheila was already undressed, getting ready for sleep.

'This is ridiculous,' she said. 'I can't keep doing this. I'm so tired I could sleep for a week and then a bit more.'

'Me too,' agreed Ella. She paused and then pulled something out of her pocket. 'One of the patients gave me these,' she said, showing Sheila the bottle she held in her hand. 'He said they help keep you awake and alert, and make you less hungry too.'

'Benzedrine,' read Sheila. 'Yes, I've heard that lots of the troops take it.'

'He said it was in their ration packs, they're encouraged to take it to keep them going.'

'Well, anything that might help, I suppose.'

'Would you take it?' asked Ella.

'Me? Maybe. Yes, why not. I've only got four hours off now, so I might take one when I wake up and see if it helps. For now, I must get some sleep.' Sheila turned over and was soon breathing deeply.

Ella put the bottle on the table between their beds. Maybe she'd take one too.

∼

In theatre the next day, she felt clear-headed and alert. While Jack was closing after an amputation, she took the severed limb away to the incinerator and then started cleaning up the theatre for the next patient.

'You have a nice voice,' he said.

Ella hadn't even realised she was humming. She stopped abruptly, but he urged her to carry on.

'There's something different about you today,' he said, throwing the needle into a kidney dish and stripping off his surgical gloves. 'That's all, thank you,' he said to the orderlies and the staff nurse who'd also been assisting. 'Go and have a cup of tea before the next patient.' They looked at him gratefully and filed out. Jack looked back at Ella, eyebrows raised.

She didn't dare tell him that it was the Benzedrine. It made her feel fantastic, ready for anything.

'Anyone would think you were on drugs,' he said. 'That's what keeps me going, I have to say. Uppers to get going, and alcohol to slow me down. It's a terrible way to live, but there we are, we have to get by somehow, don't we?'

Ella looked at him, her mouth open and eyes wide. He seemed to think it was quite normal behaviour. Was she the idiot who hadn't realised that earlier? The one who had struggled on through tiredness that made her want to curl up in a spare bed on the ward and tell everyone to go to hell, exhaustion that made her vision blur and her mind play tricks on her? Just the other day she could have sworn that Sister Cooper marched onto the ward to inspect what she was doing. In fact, it had been Taffy, the Irish orderly, with a cup of tea for her.

'Is everyone using this stuff?' she asked.

'Everyone I know,' he said. 'I assumed we all were, although, seeing the difference in you today, I realise that you hadn't been. It's all right, you know, it's not addictive or anything.'

Ella smiled. Frankly, at that moment, she didn't care if it was; it made her feel alive again.

'If you ask at medical supplies they'll give you more,' he said as he left her to clean up.

In mid-September, they were once again on the move, this time towards Brussels. Ella no longer cursed the packing and unpacking of the hospital. It gave them all a short respite from the hard work of nursing.

They drove through flat countryside on straight tree-lined roads. Brussels was full of tall buildings and masses of flowers in formal flower beds. It almost looked as if the war had missed it entirely. The roads were wide and deserted. But in the narrow backstreets, away from the formal centre, they had joined a huge convoy of vehicles, tailing back for miles, and the going was slow. After Brussels, in every village they drove through the delighted shopkeepers would come and offer whatever they had, shouting with joy that they were free at last. Other people threw apples and grapes, so glad to see the back of the Germans. Men threw flowers when they saw there were women in the lorries, and blew kisses. Ella and her friends laughed and returned the kisses, until one time they stopped and were swarmed by locals wanting a real kiss from the 'preety ladies.'

Three hours after Brussels, but only about forty miles further on, they stopped. Ella and the others jumped out of the lorry, glad to stretch their legs and walk about a bit. She was hungry, thirsty and desperate for the toilet. Fortunately, the pioneers had got there the day before and dug the latrines.

After a cup of hot soup, they started putting up the sleeping tents, and after midnight, the hospital staff gathered for a drink and the medical superintendent, a gruff Scottish Lt Colonel called Niall McMurdo, gave them a briefing as to what to expect in the days ahead.

'There's fighting a few miles north of here. The Germans are retreating, but blowing all the bridges as they go. We, of course, are trying to stop them doing that. There are rather a lot of rivers between here and Germany, and we need to cross them with the least amount of delay. There will be many casualties, as always, so get some sleep tonight and start preparing at first light. Never forget the important job we do here, and the hope we provide for our soldiers.' He turned to the nurses who were sitting together to one side. 'Sometimes, a pretty face makes all the difference. Not that that's all you do, of course, but don't underestimate the fact that here you are women in a man's world, and some of these men haven't seen their wives or girlfriends, mothers or sisters for months. You remind them what they're fighting for.' He raised his glass in a toast, and they all drank.

'I think we do a darned sight more than just show a pretty face,' said Ivy under her breath.

'I should say we jolly well do. Let him try and run a ward, keep everything in order and get the right medication to the right person at the right time. First sign of someone wanting a bedpan and he'd be lost,' said Sheila.

'I think he's a sweetie,' said Daffy, and they all rolled their eyes.

The next day, they were getting the instruments unpacked when the first casualties came in, and for the next ten days, there was no time for anything else. On some days there were patients lined up on stretchers outside, waiting for a bed. Fortunately, the weather was dry and mild at last.

For the first time, they received quite a few Americans because of the operation around Nijmegen. Ella found one of them spitting on the floor.

'What do you think you're doing?' she asked. 'Do you need a spittoon?'

'No, ma'am,' he said, and turned away.

'Well, I must tell you, young man, that in our hospitals, we don't spit on the floor, unless you want to mop it, that is. We have enough work to do without extra, thank you very much.'

He shrugged but said nothing.

Ella left the ward that night in a rage. The Americans were so uncouth and so arrogant compared to the gentlemanly Canadians. Hadn't anyone taught them any manners? All afternoon they'd been demanding this and complaining about that, until she was ready to scream. At one point she was on the verge of telling them all that if they were well enough to complain about the care they were receiving, they were well enough to get back to the front.

She went to the mess tent and ordered a large Scotch.

'Bad day?' asked the barman, Corporal Harold Lightfoot, British Army Catering Corps.

'The worst. Bloody Yanks. They seem to think they're better than everyone else.'

'Aye, they do that,' agreed Harry, nodding as he wiped a glass. 'Trouble is, in some ways they are. We wouldn't be where we are today without them.'

Ella looked at him. 'That's treasonous talk, Harry.' She laughed. 'Anyway, I don't have to like them just because they're helping us. They're rude and ungrateful.'

'They have better food than us though. And if you need stockings or chocolate, I can get them for you through my contacts in the Rude Buggers Army. Pardon my French, lieutenant.' Ella smiled. Harry had been with the hospital since they arrived in France and the staff all knew him well. They often bought a few extras from him – he seemed to have contacts wherever they went.

'I could do with some stockings. And I'm sure Sheila would like some American cigarettes.'

'Consider it done, lieutenant. Come back tomorrow.'

'Where else would I go, Harry?'

'I hear the casualties are slowing down and the Americans are throwing a party in the next day or two. You know, keep up morale and all that.'

'Well, if the officers still standing are as rude as their wounded, I won't be staying long.' She was about to add that she'd go for the food, but thought Harry might be offended.

She had another drink and was joined by Jack, Vincent, Vera and Ivy who had come from theatre. Ella was glad to be in charge of a ward again. All this chopping and changing, one week in theatre, the next on triage, and then on the ward was tiresome, especially on top of the changes of location.

'I hear McMurdo's doing a round tomorrow,' said Jack. 'Wants to come and inspect us, see what we're up to.'

'Oh God,' said Ella. 'Something else to cram in to the day. And I've got a ward full of Americans. They have no idea how to behave. He'll go through the roof.'

'Well, it's not your fault they're uncouth. Anyway, he's not here to judge their behaviour but to raise our spirits.'

Ella snorted and her Scotch almost came down her nose.

'Don't make me laugh while I'm drinking,' she said. 'I can't see how a visit from the lord on high would raise our spirits at the moment. A good holiday might, but not a pep talk from McMurdo.'

They had another drink and then agreed that it was time to turn in. Wandering back to her tent, Ella cursed the Americans and McMurdo equally for giving her more work to do.

In the morning she announced to the patients that there was to be an inspection. She outlined the behaviour she expected from them and then took the staff off to one side.

'Nurse Atkins,' she said, 'I need you to talk to our boys and the Poles and tell them exactly what to do. Also, make sure the beds are neat, blankets tucked and pillowcase openings all facing away from the door. I'll see to the Americans myself.' She turned to the orderlies. 'Can you give the lockers a thorough going-over, and make sure all the wheels on all the beds and lockers are turned away from the door and lined up.'

They saluted her and went to get on with their task.

'If those Americans make trouble, I'll throttle them,' said Ella as she and Nurse Atkins turned to their task.

By the time they got word that Lt Col. McMurdo was on his way, all the 'up' patients were standing to attention beside their beds, and all those who couldn't get up were lying to attention under blankets pulled so tight they couldn't move. He stuck his head in, nodded to the patients, returned the staff salutes, and left. His batman popped his head in after he'd gone to apologise.

'He's running very late, sorry. But good work, keep it up.'

As soon as he'd gone there was a collective groan.

'All that for a head round the door and a nod,' said one man, trying unsuccessfully to untuck his blanket so he could breathe.

'Well, I still want my extra cigarettes – you promised, Sister,' said another.

Soon they were all clamouring for their bribes, and Ella was rushing around handing out Lucky Strikes like they were going out of fashion.

'What a joke,' she said to Sheila later. 'All that work for nothing.'

'Not for nothing, Ella. I hear we're going to be mentioned in dispatches for the outstanding work we're doing here.'

'Hmph,' said Ella. 'As if that'll make any difference. I'd rather have twenty more nurses here than a mention in a dispatch no one will ever read.'

Sheila lit a cigarette and nodded.

'Oh, I forgot – I asked Harry to get you some more American cigarettes. He should have them by now. Shall we go and get a drink?'

We did seem to drink a lot, thought Ella as she got up to get herself a glass of water and massage the blood back into her legs. She'd been sitting with them folded under her on the sofa, her favourite spot. She wondered what had happened to all the people she'd been thinking about; the doctors and nurses, orderlies and catering staff and all the others who had made for the smooth running of the hospital. Had they returned to Civvy Street and got on with their lives, putting the war and its horrors behind them? Had they had loved ones waiting for them, parents to celebrate their safe return, children to get to know all over again? She sighed; they had shared the intensity of the war, yet they knew little of each other's lives. Or perhaps it was because of the intensity that they had asked so much *of* each other and so little *about* each other, their days focused down onto the details of what was right in front of them, the lives they were saving and their own lives they were trying to preserve.

She stretched, drank her glass of water and dragged herself back to the present. There were two weddings to be planned and time was running on apace.

The day Ella and Sheila had set aside for their trip to London dawned clear and mild. They were up early and drove to the station for the 7.15 train from Hambleford. Ella was going to get her mother's dress altered. She knew where she wanted to go; her mother had always used a tailor in Soho for her dresses and alterations. Ella vaguely remembered having a special dress made there for something, but couldn't remember what. She was still shocked at the way London looked. There was little rebuilding going on because of a shortage of materials, and the city looked worn down, like a man who had lost his purpose. She felt like a stranger there too, no longer knowing her way around, but as they turned into Greek Street, her feet knew exactly where they were taking her.

Once she'd dropped her dress off they had the day to look for something suitable for Sheila. In Bond Street Ella saw just what she thought would suit her, but Sheila said no, she didn't like it. In Piccadilly, Sheila saw a dress she liked but Ella wouldn't enter the shop, saying that if Sheila wanted to get married looking like a pom-pom, she'd have to shop on her own. By lunchtime Sheila hadn't tried on a single dress, and they were both getting tired and grumpy.

Andrew revived them with champagne cocktails and lunch at the Ritz. He wanted all their news, and told them that Laura and Billie were very excited about the weddings – they were going to be in the bridal party for both. Since Sheila had no siblings or cousins she'd asked Laura and Billie to be her flower girl and page boy too, along with Arthur's nieces.

'Be careful, she'll want Laura to look like a nursery-rhyme character,' said Ella.

'Well, as long as it's not Humpty Dumpty, I don't think she'll care. All she wants is a pretty frock!' said Andrew.

Sheila laughed. 'It's very difficult choosing something when your best friend and self-appointed style critic won't agree with anything you like,' she said.

'Onward and upward, dear, we've got all afternoon.' Ella stood. 'We should go. Thanks so much for lunch, Andrew. It was lovely to see you. Give everyone kisses from us.'

By the time they caught the 6.05 train back to Hambleford,

Sheila had ordered a dress. It was white satin cut on the cross so it fell in soft swathes to the floor. As her wedding was in the spring, she'd chosen thin straps and a low back, but a jacket to go over it in case it was cold on the day. A long lace veil gave texture and a touch of antiquity to the outfit, a blend of old and new. Sheila was very pleased, and Ella thought it was perfect.

Ella slipped her shoes off and rubbed her feet. 'Shopping in London is more tiring than working on a ward all day. I'm exhausted.'

Sheila sat back and put her feet up on the seat opposite. 'I could do with a nice G and T myself.' She looked at Ella, her brow furrowed. 'You don't seem quite yourself, Ella. I haven't asked recently, we've both been so busy, but is it something you're reading in your diaries?'

Ella looked at the scenery flashing past them, England in all its late autumn glory, the leaves flaming in reds, bronze and gold, the fields already harvested and lying fallow for winter. 'I'm reading about our time in Belgium at the moment. McMurdo's just visited. I remember it as I read, and sort of fill in gaps as I go. But there are still bits I read and have no memory of at all. Tell me, did I have an affair with Jack Bailey?'

'Good old Jack! I haven't thought about him since France. No, you didn't, although I think he was very keen for a while. He married Vera, remember her?'

Ella gasped in surprise. 'She told me she was interested in dark brooding types, which is hardly Jack.'

'Well, maybe she was deliberately putting you off the scent. Apparently, she liked him from the first time she met him at Hatfield.'

'What a dark horse. Who else ended up as a couple?'

'Only one other; remember Daffy?'

Ella nodded.

'She married a Polish chap she met over there, a patient. Woitek something or other.'

Ella nearly jumped out of her seat. 'Woitek Dubanowski! I remember him. He read Dickens and Austen and thought he knew all about England. Are they happy?'

'I believe they are. I haven't really kept up with her, but I hear through the grapevine that she's expecting their first child soon.'

'Gosh,' was all Ella could say. She wondered how many other nurses had come home and married patients who were at rehabilitation hospitals in England.

'So, did you have a special someone out there, Sheila?'

Sheila blushed and searched in her bag for her cigarette lighter.

Ella waited patiently.

'Well, there was an RAF chap for a while, but then we were moved on. I saw him on leave in Brussels a few weeks later and we had a wonderful few days, but I think we both knew that we weren't meant for each other in the long run.'

'You're not sorry are you, now you've got Arthur?'

'Lord, no. Arthur is worth ten of Douglas.'

Ella ran a hand through her hair and down her neck, leaving it there as if massaging herself. 'And what about me, did I have anyone special?' She tried to sound casual.

'Strangely, no. You could have had any number of men, but you never seemed that interested. You'd go to dances and concerts with people and have a good time, but no one really got you hooked.'

'I sound like a maiden aunt.' Ella put on a glum face, and Sheila laughed.

'Not a bit of it. You were the life and soul of every party, and if you didn't think it was going well, you'd sit at the piano and churn out dance tunes for the rest of us. Men would line up to buy you drinks and lure you back onto the dance floor.'

Ella considered that for a moment. Was Sheila lying again, trying to make her believe she was popular and fun? She decided not to make a deal of it.

'To stop me playing, or because I was irresistible?'

'The latter, of course.'

'Oh, yes, I remember one time at an RAF do when the gramophone broke down and I played a terrible old upright piano that badly needed tuning.'

'We didn't care, as long as we could dance,' said Sheila. 'You saved the day.'

Back at Bamford House, Ella and Sheila got their long-awaited gin and tonic, and chatted into the night. And after Sheila had gone to bed, Ella stayed up, going over all they'd talked about. She felt rather guilty; it was true that in spite of all the terrible injuries the men sustained, the nurses and hospital staff had sometimes had fun.

In Belgium at the end of September, the steady stream of patients had reduced to a trickle, and they were getting as many evacuated as possible in preparation for another move. One afternoon, Sheila and Ella had time off together, and they'd gone into the local town with cigarettes and army-ration chocolate to swap for whatever they could get. They were used to being welcomed everywhere they went, and were surprised to discover that that wasn't the case here. They noticed also that a number of houses had swastikas painted on the doors. They found a café that was open and where the proprietor agreed to serve them, and in their schoolgirl French, they asked about them.

The café owner spoke perfect English, as so many Belgians seemed to, and told them that the town had had a lot of German collaborators, and that now, the townsfolk weren't letting them forget what they'd done.

'It is a town deeply divided. I do not know if it will ever heal.' He shrugged and wiped the counter fiercely. Ella and Sheila looked at each other, not knowing what to say. In the end, the owner filled the silence.

'We are not – how you say? – ungrateful for what the Allied soldiers have done. You have rid us of the German occupiers. But you have killed so many of our people too, and also destroyed our town and others like it. It will take many years to build again, and there are many who will not live to see it. That is why we do not welcome you. We want to get on with our lives without you.'

It was blunt, but Ella understood the sentiment. She'd been embarrassed often by the warmth of their welcome, the gifts people tried to press on them when they'd done nothing to deserve them. Perhaps this man was more honest.

When the hospital was almost empty, they were given five days' leave in Brussels. Ella wandered the cobbled streets, looking in the shops full of souvenirs and toys. Old women sat in doorways making lace. The streets were clean and wide, a world away from the alternate mud and dust of the hospital. But the best part of it all was the hotel. A double bed all to herself, a deep bath with as much hot water as she wanted, and a chef that hadn't heard of rationing. Ella would have been happy to stay forever.

Every evening there was a dance or a concert to go to, and the group of nurses from Ella's hospital met up to go together, often with others they'd met during the day; it seemed that all the hospitals were emptying, so a lot of the nurses had time off before the final push through Holland and into Germany.

They seemed to move more and more often after that. The hospital was always the same, but depending on the action in the area, the wounds might be different. At one time, there were lots of amputations from the mines the Germans had set as they retreated, another time, gunshot wounds were the main injury. Head wounds were always difficult to deal with, and the men stayed longer as they needed to be well stabilised before evacuation. There were still a fair few burns patients, and more and more often they saw men with battle fatigue who were quiet and passive during the day, but as soon as night fell and the shells starting falling nearby, they'd be cowering under their beds and screaming for everyone to take cover, or staring silently, tears wetting their cheeks.

Ella sat up straighter, suddenly uncomfortable. She felt the familiar fear creeping over her. Her heart was thumping, and she felt clammy all over. She was getting closer to the whimpering man; she'd managed to keep him at bay until now, and still didn't feel ready.

She got up and made herself a cup of tea. She needed to take her mind off everything she'd been thinking about for a while. She tried to concentrate on her book, *The Hollow*. Usually, she couldn't put an Agatha Christie mystery down, but tonight, her thoughts kept drawing her back to the war, and finally, to one scene in particular.

Christmas was approaching. The Germans had been pushed back to their own borders, and the hospital had been set up in Holland in the grounds of a monastery. The nurses were given a room each to sleep in, and the doctors were billeted with families in the town.

'I bet they're a darn sight warmer there than we are here,'

said Sheila after the first night in the cell. The walls and floors were stone, the beds low and hard under high, unglazed windows.

'The monks may be used to austerity and mortification of the flesh, but I'm not,' she went on.

'At least we're not too busy. Perhaps we could have a little sleep on the ward in a comfy bed,' said Ella, rubbing her hip that felt like it had been wedged between two rocks all night.

Sheila laughed. 'I'm just looking forward to warming up by the paraffin heater on the ward. I hope the boys were all right last night.'

'You think they might have frozen to death? There's quite a frost out there.' She pointed to the quadrangle around which the cells were clustered. The grass was tipped in white.

'No, I was wondering about the safety of the heaters in a tent, actually.'

'I expect we'd have heard if the hospital had burned down,' said Ella. 'Anyway, I'm off. I don't think the breakfast here will be up to much.'

Sheila agreed, and, pulling their greatcoats tightly around themselves, they started the trek down the hill to the mess tent. A cold wind gusted, and the low clouds threatened snow.

On the road from the monastery were burnt-out tanks, armoured personnel carriers that had been destroyed and stripped of anything reusable, shredded tyres, odd boots, tin hats, bits of clothing, bloodied and torn. Sheila and Ella walked past almost without noticing these days, inured to the savagery of war. All they wanted was to sit in front of a heater and have a hot cup of tea. Life had come down to keeping warm.

A few days before, someone had squeezed a piano into the corner of the ward, and when time permitted, Ella had played carols and cheery tunes to bring some festive charm.

Most of the battle fatigue patients were moved out as quickly as possible, evacuated back to England and a good rest, away from the noise, smell and sights of war. But there was one man, a young German, who hadn't spoken since he'd arrived, and who had an abdominal wound which had required surgery. During the day he lay without moving, whatever was done to him, but at night, he picked at his scar and every morning it was open and bloody again and he had to be taken back to surgery for stitching. They were treating the wound with Sulfa powder and he was on a penicillin drip to stop infection but he pulled that out, too, whenever he thought no one was looking.

'Ella, you speak some German, don't you?' asked Larry that day after he'd sewn Klaus's wound up again.

'Yes, some,' said Ella. She'd never admitted to anyone that she spoke it fluently.

'Would you mind having a chat with him then? Every time he rips himself open again, it's harder to stitch up again, and more likely he'll get an infection. Can you tell him that?'

'I have spoken to him several times already, but I'll try again. Maybe we should also try and understand why he's doing it.'

'I don't really care for all that psychiatric mumbo jumbo to be honest, but if you think it'll help, go ahead. Just as long as he understands and stops, that's the best thing.'

Ella nodded and made her way to the ward and Klaus's bed near the door. He was lying rigid, staring straight up at the ceiling.

Speaking softly in German, Ella said, 'Klaus, it's Ella. How are you?'

He didn't answer.

'I know you can hear me, so I'm going to talk, all right?'

Again, no response.

'So, you need to understand that every time you open your wound, you risk your health. We really want you to stop doing it so that we can help you get better.'

She didn't know how to go on. His silence was unnerving.

She didn't want to say anything to upset him, but she needed him to know that she was on his side.

She bit her lip and carried on, 'I understand that you must have seen some awful things; friends being killed beside you, you probably thought you would be next. And now here you are, in a hospital run by your enemies. But please know that we don't want any harm to come to you. We treat everyone here the same; you've all been through hell, and you deserve to get proper care.'

She stopped. She'd been looking at his hand on the blanket, but now moved her eyes to his face. A single tear slid from the corner of his eye.

The book fell from Ella's lap and she sat bolt upright, heart beating fast. She tried to slow her breathing, her racing heart. Perspiration stuck her hair to her forehead. She rubbed her hands together to stop them shaking. Klaus was the Whimpering Man, and nothing she could do would stop her remembering what had happened. She thought about waking Sheila so that at least she had someone with her, but decided against it. She would face this alone, whatever it was. She allowed her thoughts to return to Klaus.

She wiped his tear away gently and then took his hand.

'Where are you from, Klaus?'

'Hanover,' he said so quietly that Ella had to lean in to hear.

'How old are you?'

'Sixteen.'

Ella closed her eyes for a moment and shook her head. Just a boy.

She wondered how to go on. Would it upset him if she asked about his family, how he came to be fighting, what he was so afraid of?

'What did you like to do when you were a child?' she asked eventually.

Still staring at the ceiling, he whispered, 'Ride on my bike with my friends and play with my dog.'

'What was your dog's name?'

'Felix.'

'That's a nice name for a dog. Did you teach him tricks?'

He almost smiled. 'He could sit and beg and roll over.'

'Clever.'

Again, Ella paused, but she felt she was breaking through and couldn't stop now.

'Do you have brothers and sisters?'

His hand curled into a fist, and his face set again.

'I'm sorry. We don't need to talk about your family if you don't want to. Shall I tell you something about me?'

He didn't respond. Ella was vaguely aware of someone tinkling out a tune on the piano.

'Well, I bet you didn't know that I am half German. My father was born near Munich.'

He turned to her. 'Liar,' he said, and turned away again.

'How do you think I speak German? He taught me and my brother when we were little.'

Another tear fell. 'I had a brother.'

'What was his name?'

'Kurt.'

'Was he older or younger?'

'Younger.'

Ella dreaded what was coming next. Now that Klaus had started, he carried on, the tears flowing unchecked.

'He was fourteen. They came for us, told us we had to fight for the Fatherland. I told them that Kurt was too young, but they didn't listen. My mother tried to stop them from taking him, but they pulled him from her and kicked us out of the door at gunpoint. We had to do what we were told — we learned to shoot and throw grenades. They said that was enough, we didn't need to know more. We were cold and hungry all the time. The last thing my mother said to me was to look after Kurt and bring him home safe.' He shut his eyes tight, tears squeezing out and running through the down on his cheeks. 'We were sent to guard a bridge. It was our first assignment. Another company was setting charges to blow it up. The Americans didn't want it destroyed, so they came to stop it. We opened fire like we'd been told, and the Americans fired back. Kurt was hit. I put down my gun and ran over to him. One of our company ordered me back to my post but I didn't listen. Kurt's face had been blown off. His beautiful face was gone. I should have looked after him but I didn't, and then he was dead. So I stood up and shouted at the Americans to kill me too, but they had stopped shooting by then. The company setting charges on the bridge had run away.' He stopped talking and Ella once again wiped his face, stroked his hair off his forehead.

'It wasn't your fault, Klaus.'

He shook her hand away and turned on her, his face contorted in anger.

'How can you say that? You weren't there. I let my brother die.' He was yelling, and Nurse Atkins looked over. Ella waved a hand to let her know everything was all right and turned back to Klaus.

'I wasn't there, no, but there was nothing you could have

done to save your brother. You were told to fight and that's what you were doing.'

'And how do I tell my mother that, huh?' He spoke a little more quietly.

Suddenly Ella had an awful thought.

'Did you do this to yourself?' She indicated his wound.

He nodded. 'I couldn't go back to my mother uninjured when I had let Kurt die.'

'Oh God, Klaus, poor boy.' She wanted to hold him and take his pain away, but she knew it would be pointless.

'Your mother will be sad about Kurt, of course, but don't you think she'd be happy to have one of her sons home?'

He turned away again.

'Please, don't do this to yourself, it won't bring Kurt back.'

Ella had never heard a howl like it. Klaus threw his head back and let out a piteous cry that made her blood run cold.

Nurse Atkins approached again. 'Sorry, Sister, but the other patients are getting upset,' she whispered.

Ella nodded that she'd heard her, but kept her eyes on Klaus. He was quiet again, but Ella was aware that his hands were now both under the covers and there was movement. He was tearing at his wound.

She ripped the blanket off him and caught his hands, attempting to hold them down but he was too strong for her. She called for an orderly, and Bob arrived at her shoulder. Before she had a chance to tell him what was happening, he had gripped Klaus's arms and held them firm. Klaus started struggling, throwing himself from side to side trying to break free.

'I want to die, just let me die,' he repeated over and over.

Ella told Bob to let him go, but he kept hold of him.

'Let him go,' Ella shouted, and finally, he did. Klaus clutched the blanket to his chest, looking terrified.

Bob was panting from the exertion of holding him down. 'What do you want me to do, Sister? Shall I get something to strap him down?' He made a gesture of tying his wrists, and Klaus's eyes widened in horror. He ripped the drip out of his arm and scrabbled out of the far side of the bed. He ran, crouched over, blood seeping from his wound.

Ella ordered Bob to stay back, and went after him. He was in the corner near the entrance to the tent when she caught up to him. He fell to his knees and looked up at her, whimpering, his eyes wild and nostrils flaring.

Ella got down next to him. 'I'm not going to hurt you,' she said softly. 'I want to help you. Let me get you back into bed.' She reached a hand out to him and he reeled back.

'Do you need help, Sister?' asked Bob.

She rocked back on her heels and turned to tell Bob to get the bed ready.

Quicker than she could respond, Klaus got up and started running again.

He turned and yelled, 'You don't understand. You say you do, but you don't.'

As she followed him out of the ward, Ella saw the ambulance coming round the corner and Klaus still running, clutching his stomach. The driver stamped on the breaks, but not soon enough. The ambulance hit him with a dull, wet thud and Klaus's body was thrown into the air. He seemed to fly for a few moments, and then his body crumpled to the ground, splitting open, his guts spilling and his legs coming to rest at odd angles. The ambulance brakes screeched and it jolted to a stop. The driver leapt out, threw his cigarette away and said, 'I didn't see him, he came from nowhere, I didn't see him. Oh my God, I swear I didn't see him.'

Ella crouched down by Klaus, but there was nothing she could do. She doubled over and sobbed.

She didn't remember getting back to her tent, but Sheila handed her a cup of tea and poured a slug of brandy into it.

She knocked it back and held her cup out for more.

In Bamford House, she was trembling so much that she spilled the gin as she tried to pour herself a glass.

Stumbling up the stairs on legs that could hardly hold her up, she opened the door to Sheila's room and made it to her bed before collapsing.

'It was my fault. It was all my fault. I killed that boy. I wanted to help him but I made him run and he died.' She buried her head in the eiderdown and sobbed.

Sheila rubbed her back and made soothing sounds until Ella sat up.

'His mother didn't get either of her sons back,' she said, tears threatening to spill again.

'I'm sure you weren't to blame, Ella. It was war—'

Ella wiped her eyes. 'The bloody war,' she said, and crept away to her own room without another word.

In the morning, Ella sat at the kitchen table, hands around a cup of tea, and let the words tumble out of her. She described the scene to Sheila exactly as it had unfolded. Sheila listened in silence, never taking her eyes off Ella's face. When she'd finished talking, they sat quietly for a few moments, and then Sheila said, 'It's awful for you, Ella, to have lived with that all this time. But it wasn't your fault, how could it be? You were trying to help him, and you couldn't have known he'd run away, or that the ambulance would come just at that moment.'

Ella gave a hollow laugh. 'He told me I didn't understand, that I hadn't helped him. I failed him, Sheila, don't you see?'

'You tried, Ella. He was sad and angry about his brother, and ashamed of himself. You couldn't have done any more.'

Ella turned away and looked out the window at the clouds scudding across the sky.

'You were a mess after it, I remember. You wouldn't talk about what had happened. It was like you blamed yourself for all the death and misery – not just his. All you wanted to do was work and play the piano. There was one at the monastery and you sat there for hour after hour, playing and crying. No one could get through to you. That went on for days and days. Then we got the order to move on, only you didn't come with us. Turns out you'd volunteered to join a casualty clearing station in the north of Belgium, waiting to get into Germany. You hadn't told anyone, not even me. It was awfully strange without you, and you wouldn't tell me why you'd decided to leave the hospital, but it was as if with your decision someone had flicked a switch in your head. You were back to yourself again, even quite gay, the morning we left you there.'

Ella wondered what had happened. She remembered the piano in the monastery, of playing until she thought her hands would freeze, of the release it gave her. She played for Klaus and for all the young men they hadn't been able to save. And she played for herself, because she also needed saving.

In the days after her memory of Klaus, she talked little, and wrote much. Letters to Frau Hosler telling her about her son's courage, his love for his brother, and nothing of the senseless way he died. She had no idea if she'd find Frau Hosler, or if she'd send the letter if she did, but the writing was cathartic and the Whimpering Man, who had turned out to be a boy, left her dreams and became a sad memory rather than a looming threat. She tried to accept that his death wasn't her fault, that she could not have foreseen what would happen, but she still felt guilty. She wished she could have done more, assuaged his guilt, soothed his pain.

By the end of November there were fewer polio cases being admitted to the cottage hospital, but many still there, children with wasted limbs and wan smiles, parents with sadness etched into their features, grief for the bright future their children could no longer hope for. Ella came away each day feeling heavy with their disappointment. The only times she felt happy were when she was with David. He had agreed to move into her house after their wedding, and Sheila was going to live in his until she married Arthur. Their wedding was fast approaching, and they were busy with preparations.

## 22

The day before Ella's wedding in late December, friends started arriving at lunchtime. Joan was first, sober and single; her husband had moved out soon after she had visited at the end of summer. She looked more relaxed and had put on a bit of weight, which suited her. She made no mention of her previous visit, and neither did Ella — she gave Joan a hug and welcomed her.

Not long after Joan, Ivy and her husband Peter arrived, then Maeve and her husband Ron, and Ingrid and her Patrick. Vera, Nina and Edie came without their husbands, who all had to work. She still couldn't imagine Vera with the Jack Bailey of her memories, and was sad she wouldn't see them together. And much to Ella's dismay, Daffy was too close to giving birth to make it. She would have loved to meet Woitek again, to see him well and happy with his English wife.

'It's like a reunion of Nightingale House, isn't it?' said Joan when they were all there.

Ella looked at all her friends. They'd been close, she knew that from the pages of her journal, but those memories felt distant, as if they'd happened to other people. Having them there was like being amongst strangers, except they all knew her. She had been excited to see them all again, but now she wondered if she'd invited them just to fill her side of the church.

Sheila had prepared a simple lunch of cheese and pickle sandwiches, courtesy of Arthur.

As they ate, the men looked uncomfortable, not knowing each other that well, and the women kept up a steady stream of chatter, laughing at things they'd done, reminding Ella of scrapes they'd got into. Some sounded familiar, others she wondered if they were making up, or at least exaggerating. Surely she'd never done half of the things they said she had, she wouldn't have had time to work or study.

And through it all, she watched the interactions, the rivalries; Ivy obviously believed herself superior to Nina and Edie, but whether that was because she had a husband there and they didn't, or that she'd nursed in Europe and they hadn't, or some other petty reason, she didn't know.

Following Sheila into the kitchen she put down her tray of plates and glasses, and sighed, sinking into a chair.

'What's the matter?' asked Sheila.

Ella sighed again. 'I don't know. It's just that I don't really remember them that well. Were they always so competitive? I mean, did we ever all get on, or did we make the best of it because we were thrown together?'

Sheila thought for a moment.

'I suppose there is a bit of that. I haven't seen a lot of Nina or Edie since training days, but we write and keep up with each other's lives. You did too. You used to write more than me from France.'

Ella looked at her hands, clasped on the table in front of her. After a few moments, she said, 'I hate to admit it, but I'm not sure I like them that much. It feels as if we're drawn back into old roles we used to play and haven't grown or changed at all. Do you know what I mean?'

Sheila shifted her weight and leant against the sink. Ella watched, thinking she'd offended her in some way. It was entirely possible that Sheila loved all the women congregated in her sitting room and was about to give Ella a lecture on the finer points of each of them, or on tolerance and friendship.

Sheila sucked in her bottom lip.

'Come on, out with it – I've said something awful, haven't I?'

'No, Ella, not awful. But we have all changed, and I have to say, you more than the rest of us. When you came home from Germany–'

'Oh, yes, I know, you've told me before, I was different, wouldn't talk to you, sent you all away.'

'Well, yes, but it was more than that. It was as if all the things you'd seen, the horrors you'd encountered, had made you hate the world and everyone in it. You wouldn't look at anyone, let alone allow anyone near for a hug or a kiss. It was as if you couldn't trust anyone so you had to keep us all out. I think they're all chatting about the good times because nobody wants to remind you of what you were like. We wanted to help you, and we couldn't – you wouldn't let us.'

Ella still wondered what had happened to make her feel that way, and was cross with Sheila for bringing it up now, the day before her wedding. Couldn't she just have listened to her, told her she was being silly and to go back in and have some fun with her friends? Couldn't she have said that of course it was hard seeing everyone together after so long, and what with the wedding being the next day, perhaps it was a bit much and she'd feel different in the morning? Damn Sheila and her mistimed honesty! Now she felt she had to read the last part of her journal and find out what had changed her so.

'Anyway,' said Sheila, 'let's not let all this spoil your day.

Come back in and have some fun. We're all terribly fond of you, even if you're not sure about us.'

Ella frowned at her friend. 'You know I'm not talking about you, Sheila – what would I have done without you?' She held a hand out to her, and Sheila took it and gave it a squeeze.

'Come on then, put on your party face. They won't stay much longer, and tomorrow you'll be too busy to give them much time if you don't want to.'

Ella knew Sheila was trying to say the right thing, but she felt chastised, like she was being a spoilt child. She fixed a smile on her face, stood up, and said, 'I'm being silly. You're right, it's probably all the stress of the wedding. Let's go.'

When they'd all gone and she and Sheila had cleared up, Ella went to the bureau. She looked at her journals and the letters, and thought of all the memories they held, of all they'd been able to tell her about herself. She reached for the last diary but stopped herself. If her time in Germany was as traumatic as she suspected, traumatic enough to make her turn away from her friends, then the night before her wedding was probably not the time to read it. She closed the bureau, turned out the light, and made her way upstairs for the last time as Ella Elkington. She felt a shiver of excitement. And then a shiver of fear; there was something in her past that had threatened her happiness, had made her turn away from people who loved her. What if she felt the same when she remembered whatever it was? What if she felt she had to leave David and her life in Lower Worthy?

She shook her head and took deep breaths. She wouldn't let anything spoil her wedding day, nor her marriage.

The day of the wedding dawned clear and bright. Ella opened the curtains and took a deep breath. Her dress was hanging on the wardrobe door, the sun glinting on the tiny pearls sewn into the veil. She heard Sheila stirring in the room next door, and thought how odd it would be not to have her there after today. They had lived together comfortably, easily, and now she would have to get used to living with David, the man she loved, but in reality, knew less well than she knew Sheila, with whom she had lived and worked for years. What a strange thing, marriage is, she thought; you fall in love with someone, sign a piece of paper to say you'll stay together forever, through good times and bad, and yet in so many ways, there's still so much to know about each other. She didn't even know what David ate for breakfast, or whether he bathed in the morning or the evening, or both. Did he read the paper while he ate, or listen to the radio? All these things she would learn, and so much more. Would they annoy each other, or would their habits blend smoothly?

Her married life with Charles had been short and unusual in many ways. Because they couldn't live together from the start they'd had the opportunity to get to know each other slowly, to accommodate each other a habit at a time. She pulled the photograph of her and Charles at the registry office out of her bedside drawer and looked at it. It seemed a lifetime ago.

'Well, Charles, I think you and David would have liked each other if you'd met. I hope so, anyway. I love him in a different way to how I loved you; you pulled the carpet from under my feet and I fell head over heels in love with you. With David, the ground is firm, I have remained upright, but that feels good. I can see where we're heading, and there is nothing to make me giddy and lose my balance. I'll always love you, darling. Be happy for me.' She kissed him, and put the picture back in her drawer.

'Ella, are you up?' called Sheila. 'I've made tea and we need to get to the hairdresser in just under an hour. Andrew just called to say they're leaving now and will be here at lunchtime.'

Ella took her towel and rushed into the bathroom. Lying in the bath, steam rising, she assessed her body; pale, thin, lacking in shapely curves. Well, she thought, at least there'd be no surprises on the wedding night. She smiled, thinking of their love life. David was a sensitive lover, and they both enjoyed making love. At least that was something she knew about him, even if she didn't know if he had toast or porridge for breakfast!

'Ella, I hate to rush you, but we need to leave soon.'

'Coming,' called Ella as she stepped out of the bath.

Afterwards, the only thing that saddened Ella about her wedding day was that it was over so fast. Laura and Billie made perfect bridal attendants, taking their roles seriously and looking gorgeous. Billie in a dark suit with a bow tie in the same fabric as Laura's dress, a pale-pink silk that brought out the blush of colour in her cheeks. Her hair was in ringlets with a little crown of silk flowers. She'd almost cried with joy when Ella had presented it to her.

'I'm just like a princess,' she'd said, and hugged Ella round the waist.

But when she saw Ella in her dress, she stared at her open-mouthed.

'You look beautiful, Auntie Ella. Like a fairy queen.'

Sheila and Sophie went off to the church and Ella followed with Andrew, who was giving her away, and Laura and Billie. The children waved at everyone they passed on the road as if they were royalty, and Ella and Andrew laughed like excited children themselves.

The church had been decked out in gardenias and blood-red

roses that a friend of Arthur's grew in greenhouses and sold mainly to London florists. The scent was heavy on the crisp December air, and mixed with the smell of stone and polished wood of the church's interior. Ella took a deep breath.

'Ready?' asked Andrew.

'Absolutely,' said Ella, and took her first step down the aisle to the notes of Pachelbel's 'Canon in D', a long-time favourite of hers.

David turned to watch her and her heart gave a little leap and she felt a rush of love for him, and excitement for their future.

At the altar, she turned to hand her flowers to Laura, who was clutching her own so tightly the stems were breaking.

As she turned and stood next to him, David bent to whisper in her ear, 'You're the most beautiful woman I've ever seen. I'm so lucky to be marrying you.'

She grinned and wanted to kiss him, but the vicar started talking, and they turned to him and listened as he gave a sermon on the value of love and marriage, and then took them through their vows. Arthur stepped forward with the rings, a tear in his eye.

While they signed the register, a friend of David's played Paganini's 'Caprice No 24' on guitar, and Ella was spellbound. The acoustics in the small church were bright, the notes clear and sharp. She was almost sorry when it was finished and the organ took its turn to accompany the hymn they'd chosen, 'All Things Bright and Beautiful'.

As they left the church to the strains of Mendelssohn's 'Wedding March', David couldn't take his eyes off his new wife, and Ella felt a sense of love for the world and everyone in it. For the briefest moment she thought about what Sheila had said the day before, about her hating the world, and knew that even if it had been true at the time, it wasn't now. She beamed at all the guests, and stopped David halfway down the aisle to kiss him again, much to the delight of their friends.

After photographs outside the church, during which Ella got so cold she was sure her lips had gone blue, and her goosebumps would show in the pictures, she and David were driven to the pub where they were having the reception.

'Do we have to go?' Ella asked as they snuggled together in the back of the car. 'Couldn't we just sneak away, the two of us, somewhere cosy and toast each other in champagne?'

David smiled and kissed her. 'Plenty of time for that, my darling. But I want to show you off to all my friends, and you haven't really met my family yet; they'd never forgive us if we slipped away now.'

In the end, Ella was glad David had insisted she attend the reception. She liked his quiet, pipe-smoking father and his talkative, smiling mother. She even revised her opinion of her friends as she watched their lively enjoyment of her special day. And when David led her out in the bridal waltz, all eyes were on her, but she only had eyes for her husband.

# 23

'I'm so sorry, sweetheart. I'm spoiling our honeymoon. I just can't seem to shut out the memories.'

David took her hand. 'You're not spoiling anything, Ella. You couldn't. Being here with you is enough for me. I'm just so sorry I can't help, can't take the memories away.'

Ella smiled and stroked his cheek. 'Horrible as they are, I have to remember them if I'm to get all of myself back.'

'Do you want to talk to me about it all?'

Ella shook her head. 'I just wish I wasn't having such vivid recollections now, when all I really want to do is love you.' She kissed him on the lips, and then led him to their bedroom. They were staying in a hunting lodge on the shores of Loch Lomond that belonged to a wealthy friend of David's. It was the perfect honeymoon spot; miles from anywhere, and they were looked after by friendly but inconspicuous staff who fed them regularly and built roaring fires in all the rooms to keep them warm.

In the morning, after yet another night of dreams that dragged her back into her past, she told David she was going for a walk.

'Give me a minute and I'll be ready,' he said.

'No, my love, I need to go on my own. Sweep these memories out once and for all. I'll be back for lunch, I promise.' She smiled and tied her scarf under her chin, pulled her collar up and opened the door onto the cold January morning.

The scenery was beautiful — heathland in every direction and mountains in the distance. But it was also what had reminded her of her time in Germany so acutely.

In the casualty clearing station, Ella missed Sheila and the other staff from the hospital, but she'd had to get away, had to do something different with new people who didn't know about Klaus, and where she didn't get to know the patients. In a CCS, the work was all about dealing with emergencies and sending them back to the hospitals. Triage, a bit of surgery, and off they go. She wouldn't have to talk to any of them, get to know and like them. In fact, she wouldn't even know their names. And she'd be at the front, too busy to think.

She remembered the note she'd written to Sheila a few weeks after she'd left.

*I've been promoted to Captain, just imagine! We've got orders to move on, into Germany, thank the Lord. We've been sitting around in Belgium far too long in the last few weeks. The war is grinding to a halt; the Germans know they've lost, but they're putting on a show of bravado right to the end. There are skirmishes but no more real battles. The Nazis are pulling back into Germany from all fronts, leaving crops burning, animals slaughtered and roads mined in their wake. They certainly don't want to make it easy for us to follow them.*

*Later...*

*Well, apparently we're to go to a camp where the Germans say there is an outbreak of typhus that they're afraid will spread if something isn't done quickly. A special neutral zone has been set up around it so that we can go in safely.*

*It's not quite what I expected when I joined a CCS, but we probably won't be there very long.*

The night before they left, Ella was chatting to another nurse, Brigid.

'It'll be a change to treat disease rather than the terrible injuries we've had to deal with,' she said.

Brigid, a motherly older woman from Dublin, sighed. 'I just hope it isn't one of those death camps we've heard about – you know, like that place in Poland where they were killing all the Jews.'

Ella had heard about the place. In fact, it was rumoured that there was more than one, but she couldn't believe that the Germans would do a thing like that. Surely it was propaganda. She said as much to Brigid.

'I hope you're right,' she said, and carried on knitting. She was always knitting. Socks for soldiers, cardigans for her grown-up daughters, a matinee jacket for a friend's first granddaughter. Their conversations were punctuated by the clack of needles and Brigid's occasional muttered oath when she dropped a stitch or realised she'd forgotten to turn her row counter.

Driving to the camp was an alarming experience; the lorries had white flags attached to them in case some of the German soldiers didn't know that a neutral zone had been declared. And judging by the pot shots taken at them, some of them didn't, or didn't care. Several times they slowed, and Ella's heart started thudding as she wondered if this was the time they'd all be taken out and shot. But after a long and uncomfortable journey, they set up in a field close to the camp. It was flat country, but they were next to some woods and heathland. Some cherry trees were in blossom, but under their sweet smell was another, more powerful. A strange, acrid odour pervaded the whole area — rotten meat, woodsmoke and something else – perhaps animal dung. The air was heavy with it.

Setting up the clearing station didn't take nearly as long as the hospital, and they were almost done when a jeep arrived with a bigwig from 11th Light Field Ambulance. He jumped out of the vehicle and rushed into the CO's tent. After a few minutes, he left.

Lt Colonel Johnstone emerged not long after, ashen-faced, and called all the officers to a meeting.

'Seems we've been invited to hell,' he said. 'This place is a concentration camp with roughly sixty thousand people in it. According to Lt Col. Gonin, who went in this afternoon, there are piles of bodies lying around in various states of decomposition, and thousands of internees with typhus, dysentery, and God knows what else. The Nazis have been tossing bodies into mass graves, but there are more dying every moment and they just can't keep up. We go in tomorrow at 0800 hours. Prepare yourselves for the worst.'

Ella spent an uneasy night in the tent she shared with a young Irish nurse from Cork. Lt Col. Johnstone had said that the nurses weren't to go to the camp, that it would be too much for them. When she'd tried to argue that, surely, that's what they were there for, to look after the sick, he had looked at her sternly, unused to having his orders challenged, but his look had softened into one of compassion.

'I'm saving you from hell, Nurse. There's nothing you can do for the folk in there. We'll bring them out to you. Don't worry, you'll have a job to do, but I won't have women going into that death camp.'

He'd shuddered as he said that, and Ella hadn't argued further.

Walking through the Scottish heather on a cold winter's day, she saw only German scenery — barbed wire, muddy, rutted roads, a forest in the distance. Ella stopped for a moment, made herself look at what was actually in front of her. The loch was deep black, a few ripples disturbed its surface where fish rose to the surface and disappeared into the depths again. A light mist hung just above the ground, shrouding the path and making walking difficult. A hawk flew high overhead, and swooped suddenly, wings tight into its sides. Ella, trying desperately to keep herself in the present, was immediately cast back into the past, to the falling of bombs, the diving of planes. She pulled her collar up and walked on, heart pumping, though not from exertion.

After tea and dark bread with margarine and thinly spread jam, the nurses were told to scout round for somewhere to accommodate the internees. There was, they had been told by Lt Col. Gonin, a panzer training barracks about half a mile up the road, where a few thousand Russian and Polish internees were already being held. They were suffering from TB as well as starvation and numerous other ailments, but at least they didn't have typhus.

Brigid, Mary, Ella and the five other nurses of the CCS decided to go straight there. One of the cooks said he'd drive — he wanted to check out the stores at the barracks and requisition whatever they had.

Ella thought that she'd got used to the smell since they got there, but as they drove out of the paddock where they'd set up camp, she had to cover her nose and mouth and take shallow breaths. She noticed the others doing the same, pulling handkerchiefs out of their pockets and holding them over their faces. As they drove along the road it only got worse. Soon, they were driving beside a barbed wire fence. Ella asked the driver to stop. They may not be allowed to go in because of Lt Col. Johnstone's ill-placed sense of chivalry, or his fear that those of the weaker sex wouldn't be able to handle it, but they could still get an idea of what they were dealing with.

The eight nurses, trained in some of the best hospitals in the world and seasoned by their experiences in the war, climbed out of the lorry and peered through the fence.

There were huts and tents dotted about in filth. At first it looked like mud, but by the smell, Ella realised that it was human excrement. Skeletons sat staring into space or shuffled along aimlessly. One fell as they watched, and didn't move again. Another stepped over him and carried on.

To one side between two weathered wooden huts, Ella was horrified to see a mound of bodies. She gasped, her hand flew to her heart. She watched as a skeleton shambled up, pulled the coat off one of the corpses, put it on, and wandered off again, expressionless.

'Come on,' said Brigid, 'we don't need to see more of this, we need to get them out of there as quickly as possible.'

Ella turned away, the bile rising in her throat. It wasn't only the smell that was making her sick. She couldn't make sense of it; the Germans had asked them to come and treat an outbreak of typhus, but the people they'd just seen were dying of starvation. What was this place? What had been done to these people?

As they drove on, some of the nurses were crying but Ella sat rigid in the back of the lorry digging her fingernails into her palm.

The panzer barracks were enormous. Square after square of four-storey buildings built around spacious quadrangles. There was also a full-size theatre, officers' mess, cookhouses, stables, buildings to garage the tanks, cars and armoured vehicles. Off to one side there were large houses, presumably the married quarters and the training officers' accommodation. Most of the buildings had been hastily evacuated as part of the Neutrality Act, but there were still a fair few Wehrmacht soldiers about, strutting and swaggering as if they hadn't all but lost the war. Ella would have liked to get a broom and sweep them all out like the rubbish they were. Or hit them with it. She was surprised by her aggression, but didn't question it.

After some hours poking around, they decided which buildings they would take over and planned how they would start getting them ready for the typhus patients. On closer inspection, however, they realised that the departing Germans had sabotaged the water supply and hacked the toilets and hand basins off the walls in most of the buildings. They'd have to get the field hygiene station boys in, and enlist the help of the pioneers.

As they were driven back to their camp, Ella was making a list of things to do in her head, and it was already almost too long to remember.

Back at the CCS, they convened in the mess tent to hear what had happened in the Horror Camp, as everyone was already referring to it as.

Lt Col. Johnstone was visibly upset, unable to stop his hands from shaking as he reported on the day.

'The inmates have not been fed or given water for a week in anticipation of our arrival. There are, at a guess, ten thousand dead awaiting burial, and over forty thousand living, although many of them are more dead than alive. I would say that about three quarters of them have typhus, thousands have TB, all have dreadful skin conditions and dysentery, and approximately half are severely malnourished to the point of starvation. Today, all we could do was try and get water to them and basic food. Many of the survivors can't get up, let alone walk, so feeding is going to be a problem. There is a contingent of Hungarian guards who are lazy and tried to steal the food we were supplying for the internees. The SS who had stuck around are a sadistic bunch who seem to view their charges as subhuman. Over the coming days, they will all be assigned as a burial party. We need to separate the living from the dead as quickly as possible or we'll have more disease to contend with. Any questions?'

Ella put her hand up.

'Captain?'

'Yes, sir. I was wondering about priorities? Of course, getting a water supply and feeding underway are urgent, but can we get in to treat the typhus patients?'

'As I said earlier, there is little point in treating them in the camp; it's filthy, there's no space and the conditions are dire. We need to set up a place where we can properly wash and cleanse the internees and delouse them before taking them somewhere clean and bright. To that end, we have identified a stable block that will become a "human laundry", where we will do all that. Patients will then be transferred to your hospital in the panzer barracks for treatment so CCS priority is to get that set up. We'll call that Camp Two. We'll also need clothing and bedding, as much as possible from the houses around here. I've put in a requisition, but God knows when it'll all get here.'

There was more discussion of what needed to be done, but Ella lost concentration. There were muffled sobs coming from outside the tent. She crept out and found one of the young orderlies sitting against a tree, hugging his knees and rocking back and forth. When he saw Ella, he tried to get to his feet. She held up a hand.

'Don't get up on my account. I mean, at ease, Corporal. It's Robbie, isn't it?' She sat next to him.

'Yes, ma'am – sorry, Captain – Robbie Bryce.'

'Was it awful?' she asked.

He nodded, wiping his face on his sleeve. 'I've never seen anything like it, ma'am. Honestly, most of them in there are the living dead. Skin stretched over bones like parchment, dreadful sores all over them, nothing in their eyes, no hint of hope or life. But you know the worst thing?' He looked at Ella who shook her head.

'I can't imagine. Tell me,' she said, 'what was the worst?'

Robbie bit his lip to stem the tears. 'It was the silence. No one made any noise. None at all. They sat, they walked, they watched us, some of them even lifted their hands as if to wave, but not one of them made a sound.'

Ella tried to picture what it had been like, but even with their glimpse through the fence, she knew she couldn't imagine the real horrors he'd seen, and was suddenly grateful to Lt Col. Johnstone. She didn't need to witness such misery, nor the cruelty that had caused it.

Robbie took a shuddering breath and Ella looked at him again. He couldn't have been more than eighteen. Too young for war. Too young to witness such atrocity.

'I don't know if I can do it, ma'am. I don't think I can go in there again. I wanted to kill those SS men and women.'

Ella nodded. 'I can understand that, but Lt Col. Johnstone has other ideas for them – he's going to get them to face up to what they've done by burying the dead. Our boys will dig the graves, and the SS men and women will carry the dead by hand to be buried. And then, I suspect, they'll be arrested and, hopefully, pay for their barbaric deeds.'

'That's good.' Robbie smiled. 'Maybe I will go back, just to see those bastards – pardon ma'am – having to do that.'

Ella got up.

As Robbie got to his feet, he looked embarrassed, crushing his cap in both hands.

'It's all right. I'm not going to tell anyone about our conversation. But remember, it's only human to react like you did. Don't be ashamed.'

'Thank you, ma'am,' he said, and saluted.

When Ella got back to the hunting lodge David was pacing.

'It's almost three – I was just about to get up a search party.'

She took her scarf off, lifted her hair from her collar and shook it out.

David took her hand and led her into the lounge and sat her in a chair by the fire. He took a seat next to her and waited, her hand still resting in his.

Ella looked into the hearth and sighed.

'I was at the liberation of a camp in Germany. Belsen, it was called. Thousands had been killed and were left to rot. Thousands more were dying from starvation and disease. They hadn't been fed for a week before we arrived, and the guards were roaming around shooting people as we drove up. I don't know how anyone got through it, to be honest.'

David pulled her closer as she wept, the tears soaking his lapel.

He stroked her hair and said, 'I saw the newsreel. Richard Dimbleby reported from there. It was the most horrifying thing I'd ever seen; the images haunt me still. And you were there. Oh, my dearest, what can I say, what can I do?'

Ella shook her head against his shoulder and held on to him harder.

Later, over dinner, they tried talking of other matters — the places they'd visit in the next few days, the walks they'd do. David wanted to do some fishing.

'I want to catch some fish for your supper. Be a real man, feed you from the work of my own hands.'

Ella smiled. 'You are a real man. You don't need to do anything other than what you already do.'

David sighed and gave a thin smile. 'I wish I could ease your burden, that's all. When I see you caught up in ghastly memories it breaks my heart.'

Ella looked past him at a painting on the wall. It was a family portrait, the father sitting in the centre, stiff and formal, the mother standing behind him, her hand on his shoulder. She had a smile on her lips and gazed at the two children sitting demurely at their father's feet, the boy with his arm over the family dog.

'I want that,' she said, and David turned to see what she was talking about.

'You mean the picture?'

'Not the painting itself but what it depicts. A family, sure of themselves, happy. I need to remember my past so that nothing can catch me unawares. I saw enough men traumatised by war to believe that you have to face your past before you can conquer it. At least, I do. I don't want to be taking our children out and suddenly running for shelter because something's reminded me of bombs dropping. I don't want them to grow up with a mother who's anxious all the time. So I need to remember, and I need you to glue me together again when I fall apart, like you did this afternoon. Just by being you.' She reached for his hand and squeezed it.

'I'll always be here, Ella. And if it helps to talk, to tell me what you saw, what you had to do, don't stay silent.'

She smiled at him. 'I won't.'

After dinner, David took out his book and read by the fire, and Ella sat with a magazine on her lap but let her thoughts drift back to Germany.

The morning after her chat with Robbie, Ella left early with a group of pioneers, some of whom spoke a little German. They drove into the town of Bergen nearby and started knocking on doors.

'Guten Morgen,' said Ella at the first.

The short woman who had opened the door took one look at her uniform, shrieked and tried to close the door. Ella got her shoulder in and wedged it open, speaking fast, in German.

'I am with a British hospital. We are here to collect food, clothes and blankets for the inmates of the camp down the road.'

The woman's eyebrows rose towards her hairline. 'Camp?' she said.

Ella felt her anger rising. She still had the smell of death in her nostrils and couldn't believe that the people in town knew nothing of the camp less than two miles away from their houses.

She took a deep breath. 'Yes, the Nazi death camp. Bring out all your spare clothes and bedding. Now.'

The woman stared at her as if she was asking her to burn her house down and dance naked in the flames.

'Now,' repeated Ella.

An old man lumbered up the hall and stood behind the woman. 'Was ist es? Was möchte sie?'

'I am requisitioning clothing and bedding.'

He turned and walked back into the dark recesses of the house and banged a door shut.

Ella waited, still holding the door open. The woman shuffled from one foot to the other.

'I have nothing to spare,' she said.

'We'll see,' said Ella, and marched into the hall. She looked over her shoulder. 'Come on,' she called, and the two pioneers with her stepped over the threshold.

The woman remonstrated loudly, telling them that she and her father were poor, that they had nothing, but Ella remembered what she'd seen in the camp – these people were rich compared to the internees. In an upstairs bedroom she found a wardrobe full of men's clothing, and in another, women's.

'That belongs to my children. My Rolf and Beatte will need it when they come home.'

'Not as much as the camp survivors need it,' said Ella, and nodded to the pioneers who emptied the cupboards and stumbled downstairs under their loads. Ella looked in a chest on the landing and found sheets and blankets.

In every house, it was the same. Denial of any knowledge of the camp, and anger over the 'stealing' of their possessions. Ella was furious. She could barely restrain herself from shouting at the householders, accusing them of being Nazis and sanctioning the cruelty that was taking place just down the road. How could they not know? It was impossible.

Back at the CCS, the others had met with the same reception in other villages, but had collected a mound of clothes, shoes and bedding.

'We need more. Tomorrow, the pioneers can continue going door to door while we start scrubbing the walls, floors and stairs in Camp Two, and get some beds set up. If any orderlies can be spared they can help. How long do you think it will be before we get our first patients?'

'Could be any time,' said Brigid. 'The sooner they get people out of there the better.' She shuddered.

As it happened, it was a week before the first internees were transferred. A series of delays frustrated everyone, and saw more than five hundred people a day dying in the camp still. A decomposing baby was found in one of the water tanks, inmates still drinking out of it. Feeding was a massive problem, with the food too rich for the starving prisoners, and the guards stealing everything they could lay their hands on. Every day, hundreds of corpses were buried and always there were more. A hundred medical students arrived from London hospitals to help and were each assigned a hut in the camp. Their job was to feed the inmates, but first thing each morning they had to separate the living from those who had died during the night.

Ella saw the horror in the eyes of the men who had to go into the camp and listened to their progress. In the evenings the mess tent was full of shocking stories, the men recounting them to try and get them out of their heads so that they could go into the camp again the following day and face it all again.

'Bunks three high, three or four to a bunk, and the top ones shitting on the ones below because they're too weak to move. It's filthy. I can't describe it. These fuckin' Jerries treated those people worse than dogs.'

'If I had my way, we'd tip all them SS men into the graves and bury 'em alive,' said another.

'The women SS are the worst – they don't have any emotions. They look at what they've done and they don't give a hoot. In fact, I think they're proud of what they've done, all the people they've killed here.'

'Those poor sods in there are so desperate they even steal

from each other. It's like they don't believe they'll ever have enough of anything ever again.'

'Who can blame them, eh?'

'I found a corpse today, outside one of the huts in the men's camp, and it had been cut. I mean, the liver had been removed. Do you think...?'

'Surely not. You'd have to be really starving to do something like that.'

'They are really starving. They're *dying* of starvation.'

Ella got up to leave and everyone went quiet.

'Sorry, Nurse – didn't mean to upset you.'

'I'm fine. I just need to get some sleep. Goodnight.'

Walking back to her tent in the crisp moonlit night Ella wiped angrily at her tears. She hated the Germans, all of them. The SS for their cruelty and the villagers for their slack-jawed denial of wrongdoing. She was horrified at the idea that had her father not fallen in love with England, she might have been brought up in Germany. Would she have been any different to these villagers with their avowals of innocence, their hand-over-heart assertions that they knew nothing? The thought sickened her.

She went to find Dov Rosenberger, a corporal in the pioneer corps, who was bitter, often rather gloomy, but able to get hold of practically anything. She needed a pick-me-up. The price of getting anything from him was hearing his life story, which he told in an urgent voice, as if trying to press the words into the heart of the listener. He was a Jew who'd left Germany in 1930 when the Nazi party was on the rise and Jews were being blamed for everything from the loss of the First World War to the financial crisis. He'd wanted to fight, but 'enemy aliens' were only allowed to join the pioneers. Ella had often heard him offer to assassinate Hitler and rid the world of the 'despicable Jew-hater.'

She found him in the mess. Side-on to her, his profile was aristocratic; a long nose, arched eyebrow above a deeply set eye. He turned and smiled as she approached.

She turned to David whose chin was resting on his chest. His breathing was deep and regular, and Ella guessed he'd been asleep for a while. She took the book from his hands and laid it on the coffee table, then she lay down next to him, her head in his lap. He shifted slightly, let out a little sigh and opened his eyes.

'Did I fall asleep? What terrible company I am!'

Ella sat up. 'You looked so peaceful. I didn't mean to wake you, but I have a huge apology to make to you.'

David looked puzzled.

'I was angry at you for saying you hated the Germans. Well, this evening, I realised that I hated them too. The ones running Belsen were evil. They starved the inmates, then shot them for stripping a bit of bark off the few trees that were still standing to try and keep themselves alive. One day I was talking to a young woman who had just been brought into the hospital. She was a teacher from Holland and spoke very good English. I turned to get her some more soup, and when I looked back, she was dead. She'd died mid-sentence, her eyes staring at me in what felt like reproach. We had come too late and were offering too little.' David started to speak, but she held up a hand and carried on. She told him about her reception at the houses around Belsen and the denials she heard time and again that the locals knew anything about a camp on their doorstep.

'They must have known and they turned a blind eye. They allowed the cruelty, the barbarism. They were almost as guilty as the guards. And so unapologetic when I told them about it.'

David put his arm around her and tried to pull her close but she was too angry to be held and drew away from him.

David sat back, looked into the fire. 'I suppose they had to, though, didn't they? Deny it, I mean. They couldn't have lived with it if they'd admitted to themselves what was happening and done nothing.'

Ella got up and stood by the mantelpiece. She moved a candlestick and then put it back where it had been. 'Don't you defend them, David. They were all guilty.'

Ella looked away. She wanted to shout at David for being so reasonable. She took a deep breath and counted to ten before letting it out again. 'I'm so confused. I nursed German soldiers and they were just the same as ours – in pain, scared and a long way from home. But the SS and the civilians were awful.'

David went to the drinks table and poured two Scotches. Handing one to Ella, he said, 'It was war. You helped me to see that the information we were fed manipulated how we saw things, how we felt, even. Maybe they weren't bad people, just misinformed. The civilians, at least.'

Ella turned to him. 'One of the reasons I love you so much is that you are so reasonable. It's also one of the things about you that drives me round the twist!'

'And one of the things I love about you is that you get so passionate about things.'

Ella took David's glass from him and put it with hers on the table. 'I love you, Mr Ashton. You keep me sane and help me see the calm beyond the passion.'

## 24

---

Ella decided that for the rest of their honeymoon she wouldn't let her memories intrude. Every time she felt a scene from the past nudge at her consciousness she concentrated hard on whatever it was that she and David were doing at the time. They enjoyed a drive to Edinburgh and a look at the castle, several rather chilly walks and a visit to a whisky distillery where they tasted thirty-year-old single malt and decided never to drink anything else again.

When they got home to Hampshire and David parked his car next to hers in the drive, she felt a deep contentment; the honeymoon was over, but married life, normal life, started now.

Unfortunately, for Ella, that meant allowing the memories to surface again. She had reduced her hours at the hospital since she no longer had Sheila's help in the house, so each time she had a day off when David was at work, she'd get her diary out, sit on the sofa, and let her mind drift back to the war. And every evening, she would prepare dinner and bring herself firmly back to the present. At first she would tell David what she'd remembered, but his look of horror, his disappointment at being unable to make her feel better, soon silenced her. She kept her past to herself.

A full week after they'd arrived in Belsen, with five hundred people a day still dying from typhus, starvation, or the effects of eating army rations on an emaciated body, the first internees were moved out of the Horror Camp. German nurses from the panzer training barracks hospital had been ordered to work in the human laundry, stripping, washing, shaving and delousing the internees with DDT before they were given new clothes and taken in clean ambulances to Camp Two. These nurses were angry that they'd been ordered to work for the British, and had done their best to slow down the preparations. Ella had been called in to talk to them, to tell them what their countrymen had done, and to remind them that it was their duty to take care of the sick and needy whatever their race or religion. Many of them had listened, arms crossed over their chests, faces set in resignation or anger. None asked any questions, nor made any comment.

Ella watched the first internees as they arrived at the stable block for their scrub. Many were too sick to care what happened to them any longer, but some were more aware, and had seen the terrors of Auschwitz, and struggled against being stripped, fearing, no doubt, that they would be sent to the gas chamber. Ella had heard of the atrocities that had been uncovered there on the forces radio. The German nurses, until then having remained defiant and unhelpful, saw the human skeletons that were brought to them, and crumbled. Several cried when they saw the state of the internees, others got on with their job in a businesslike manner, but occasionally tried to talk to their charge in soft tones.

One woman started shrieking when she saw the electric razor.

'Nein! Please, no!' She did her feeble best to get away, wriggling in the nurse's arms. Ella went over to her and tried to soothe her.

'We just want to get rid of the lice that carry the fever,' she said.

The woman wouldn't be comforted, but any energy she had for protest soon disappeared. She started sobbing and pleading.

'My mother and sisters were shaved before they were sent to the gas. Don't kill me. Please don't kill me.'

Ella looked at her already short hair and ordered the German nurse to give her an extra dusting with the DDT and let her keep her hair.

Shaken, she left the German nurses to it, confident they were doing their job and not being unkind to the terrified inmates. She hurried to the hospital and joined her colleagues in admitting and settling their patients.

A week later, Ella was in her tent sucking on the little bit of Benzedrine-soaked cloth from an inhaler. It was a quicker way to get more of the drug into her system, and she needed it fast. She'd had little or no sleep in days, the demands of the patients were such that the orderlies couldn't cope without the nursing staff there all day and night. Dov had reintroduced her to the wonder drug that kept her going and fortunately he seemed to have an inexhaustible supply.

The patients were the most difficult Ella had ever had to look after. The sickest ones were the easy ones; at least they didn't roam around the hospital looking for food and whatever else they could steal. It was the others, the ambulant ones who were a nightmare.

At first, Ella and the other nurses had been sympathetic. Of course these people would want to have things of their own after all they'd been through. But after days in which they'd felt more like police than nurses, trying desperately to find and return items stolen from other patients and staff, their tolerance wore thin.

Ella left her tent and walked to the hospital. She needed to check on the drug supplies. The sun shone out of a clear sky, and she smiled at the inmates who were wandering about the grounds of the Panzer Training School which had become the new camp. Far too many patients were dying still, but at least it had slowed to a hundred or so a day, mostly from the after-effects of starvation. Or from overeating, their ravaged bodies unable to cope with the amount of food they crammed into them, their weakened stomachs and intestines rupturing and bleeding.

She arrived on the ward in the middle of a fight. The two male orderlies were holding several struggling patients apart with great difficulty.

'What is going on here?' she asked in English and then in German.

Another patient not involved in the fight told her that one of the patients had accused the other of stealing the bread he was saving under his pillow.

Ella sighed. She was fed up with the camp mentality of hoarding what you could. She felt guilty at her impatience, but enough was enough.

'Stop!' she bellowed at the men. It was enough to make them pause. She hastened over to them. The five patients involved were puffing from the exertion and the two being held were still straining against the orderlys' clutches.

'This will not do. There is plenty of food at every meal. I will not have hoarding on my ward.' She looked from one man to the next. 'Do you understand?'

She looked around for Henryk who spoke several languages. He was lying in his bed watching. She raised her eyebrows at him and beckoned him over. He had become her right-hand man in the last few days, translating for her from English to Polish, Hungarian, Italian and French. He covered most of the languages spoken by the patients. He shuffled over, a blanket round his shoulders, and spoke to the men, who eventually calmed down.

'And there will be a search after every meal from now on and any food found on the ward between meals will be confiscated.'

She turned on her heel and marched out, wondering how long the peace would last.

In the corridor she bumped into Dasha, a young Ukranian woman who was recovering from typhus. She'd been in Auschwitz but when the Russians were nearing, had been sent on foot with thousands of others to Belsen. Hundreds had died on the way, of cold and starvation, including her twin sister and her aunt; they'd survived the camp only to die on the road.

Ella looked at the number tattooed on her arm and shuddered, as she always did. But then she noticed her mouth.

'Are you wearing lipstick, Dasha?'

The girl smiled. 'Yes. From Harrods.'

Ella laughed. Harrods was the nickname of the clothing store where patients were sent to get a new outfit when they were well enough.

She made her way down there and found a hundred or more women 'shopping' for clothes, and clamouring for a lipstick.

Julia and Florence, the Red Cross volunteers in charge were having a hard time keeping up with the demand.

'Where on earth did it come from?' asked Ella.

'No idea,' said Florence. 'But it's popular, as you can see.'

Ella shook her head. 'There are a dozen things we need and have been requesting urgently, and we get lipstick.'

A while later, in the room where the medication was stored, she was recording the amount of penicillin they had left. That and Sulfa were the only drugs they had to treat the many infections the internees were suffering from, and they were running low. In spite of Col. Johnstone ordering more, they hadn't received any for days. She sighed, something that she did more and more these days in the face of the calamity that was her daily life, and locked the room as she left.

A few Benzedrine-fuelled days later, a British mobile general hospital arrived with two hundred staff, and equipment to treat hundreds more patients. Ella and the clearing station nurses got their first few hours off in almost three weeks.

'I don't know what to do with myself,' said Brigid as she and Ella walked back to their tents.

'I'm going to sleep until 1950,' said Ella. 'And woe betide anyone who tries to wake me before then.'

She lay on her cot and closed her eyes, listening to the steady drumming of rain on canvas, but sleep eluded her — she'd taken so much Benzedrine that her body couldn't relax enough to allow her to rest. She turned from side to side, cursing under her breath, and in the end gave up the idea of sleep and sloshed through the mud to the mess tent.

Brigid was there already.

'So much for sleeping for five years then,' she said when Ella joined her at the table.

'I have bags under my eyes big enough to pack my whole

wardrobe in. I feel so tired that my bones are aching, and I just can't drop off. It's so annoying.'

Brigid shrugged. 'Me neither. Too much going through my mind. I found that blooming Hungarian villain, Jozsef, going through the lockers on my ward earlier. I felt like taking him out and stringing him up. What is it with these people? Why steal from each other – they've all got the same. Exactly nothing. I could understand if they stole from us, but each other?'

Ella shook her head. 'They do steal from us. Madge found one of the men in the middle of swapping her cigarette lighter for an extra bowl of soup. And there's a thriving black market in blankets, tin cups, bits of uniform. The women in the sewing room are making clothes out of the bedding we give them. It's their mentality.'

'Nothing would surprise me about these people. I've had it up to here with them.' Brigid tapped her forehead with her index finger.

Ella sighed and agreed. She felt hopeless in the face of all the problems she had to deal with, and was worried that she would get to the point where all she could do was scream and shout. She had to work so hard sometimes to keep her temper in check. But did she believe that the internees were bad? She didn't know anymore, but they couldn't all be, surely. 'I'm not saying they were like that before, it must be life in the camps that's made them that way,' she said quietly.

Ella was surprised to hear herself defending them, when earlier she'd also wanted to knock heads together.

'I hate this place, to be honest,' said Brigid. 'Give me sick patients to look after and I'll work till I drop, but these people are all so ungrateful; "give me more food", "I need more clothes", "he took my drink", "she's wearing my top", And you'd think they're all royalty the way they swan around the place as soon as they're able. They should be made to work when they're better, earn their keep, that's what I say.'

Ella thought about it. Perhaps that wasn't such a bad idea. There were far too many people with too little to do. Many of the inmates were quite well now.

'We should talk to Col. Johnstone about it. There are plenty of jobs they could do and it might make them feel better, to be contributing again.'

The next day, once Ella had spoken to Col. Johnstone, she was in the storeroom swearing under her breath about the disappearing bed linen when she heard someone yelling. Imagining the worst, she stuck her head out the door. Jock, a Scottish orderly was dancing along the corridor and started shouting at the top of his voice. 'He's dead – Hitler's dead – only gone and shot himself in the head!'

Ella's heart skipped a beat. Could it be true? She ran to catch up with Jock and grabbed him by the arm.

'Is it true?'

'Aye, as true as you're standing in front of me. Just heard it on the forces radio.'

'Thank God,' said Ella. She almost sank to her knees, but then her training took over. She straightened her spine, lifted her chin and said, 'Jock – quieten down now. If you go hollering about this on the ward there'll be mayhem. We must tell everyone calmly. Go and gather the nursing staff for me, would you – we need to co-ordinate this.'

But it was too late. Suddenly the corridor filled with people, staff and patients, shouting, clapping, crying, yelling, laughing, dancing. Voices in a dozen languages raised in disbelief, gratitude, anger, surprise, relief. Ella was caught up in the tidal wave of humanity that swept out of the building into the quad. A young Polish man caught her round the waist and danced her past other couples swinging each other in tight circles, leaning back, laughing into the rain.

Patients were still dying in large numbers. The fighting carried on, the Germans more desperate and brutal the more obvious their loss became. Finally, on May 8th, the Germans surrendered and victory was declared throughout Europe. Celebrations lasted days, even the bed-bound patients managed to sit upright to cheer the end of the war and the beginning of the rest of their lives. No matter what those lives might hold, nor where they might be lived. They would see peace and prosperity after the nightmare of the last six years. The practicalities could wait until the partying was over.

The evening after peace was declared, one of Ella's patients called her over to her bedside.

'Hannah, what can I get you?' she asked.

'Just sit with me,' said Hannah in her broken English. 'My family – all are dead in Auschwitz. I die now, but I lived past the war.' She smiled, then winced. She'd been starved in Belsen and had had problems keeping food down since she'd been moved to Camp Two. She was no more than skin and bone.

Ella lifted her near weightless hand, averting her gaze from the number tattooed on her forearm, and took her pulse. It was weak and erratic. She considered getting a doctor, trying one last time to feed her, to keep her alive. And then she looked into Hannah's eyes and noticed the faraway look she recognised as death approaching. Ella took her shoes off, lay down next to her and held her until she felt that moment when life becomes death, the tiniest of sighs as her last breath escaped and Hannah's head rolled against her shoulder. And then she lay a little bit longer, wishing that it was she who had died.

$\sim$

On May 21st, five weeks after they'd arrived, four weeks since the first inmates had been moved out, and thirteen days after the end of the war, the staff and those internees who were able, were invited to witness the burning of the last hut in the death camp. Because of the typhus, the huts had been destroyed as they were emptied, but this was the last, and cause for celebration. A crowd gathered. There were journalists and film-makers, dignitaries and the top brass. At one end of the hut was a portrait of Hitler, at the other, a Nazi flag. As the flame thrower was wheeled into place, utter silence fell over the proceedings. Ella thought back to what Robbie had said about his first time in the camp; the unnatural silence. She shuddered. Beside her one of the Polish internees wept soundlessly. Ella took her hand and held it tight. A strange sensation started at the pit of her stomach and radiated through her limbs, into her heart and her throat, stabbed the back of her eyes and snaked its way to the top of her head. Her whole body felt as if it could fragment at any moment and she almost shook with the effort of holding herself together. So many people had suffered the unspeakable here — physical brutality that knew no bounds, loss of family, friends, hope. She found herself wishing that the SS guards and Hitler himself were in the hut that was about to be burned. In fact, she wished every German who had failed to stand against the Nazis and who in their silence had sanctioned the murder of so many innocent people could be burned in the hut. And with that thought she recognised the sensation in her body as the manifestation of impotent rage.

Brigadier Glyn Hughes stood on a makeshift stage with the other officers. He cleared his throat, and started to speak. Ella couldn't hear what he said, but she watched the effect his words had on the people assembled. Tears, anger and, more chillingly, the lack of emotion with which his words of (Ella presumed) victory over the Nazis and a brighter future, were met. It was as if having been terrified for their lives, some of the internees were terrified of expressing anything at all. When being Jewish, being disabled, being different in any way had been punishable by death, it wasn't safe to leak even the smallest amount of emotion. Ella felt the tension of a hundred people holding their breath.

And then twelve soldiers fired a gun salute and the flamethrower spat streams of fire at the hut. Hitler's portrait ignited and the murderer's face curled in on itself, twisted grotesquely, and was gone. Only then did a cheer go up.

Back in the mess at Camp Two, Ella slumped into a chair and stared at the wall. The ceremony had exhausted her, physically and emotionally. She folded her arms on the table and rested her head. Tears prickled behind her eyes and she had a lump in her throat.

'Overcome with it all?' asked Brigid as she took a seat and put her cup down.

Ella lifted her head to see the other woman smiling at her, and the tears started spilling down her cheeks.

Brigid pulled her chair closer and pulled her into her arms, drawing Ella's head onto her shoulder.

'There, there, missy. You let them tears flow now.' She patted her back in time with Ella's shuddering breaths, and kept up a low prattle in her soothing Irish lilt.

Eventually, Ella lifted her head and blew her nose.

'It was quite an emotional service, wasn't it?' said Brigid.

'It wasn't just that,' said Ella, wiping her eyes. 'Today is the fifth anniversary of my husband's death. He was on a hospital ship at Dunkirk. I can't believe it's been five years – sometimes it feels like yesterday, other times it feels a lifetime ago.'

'I'm so sorry.'

Ella shrugged. 'It's hardly your fault. It's this bloody war. We've all lost somebody, haven't we? Everyone is losing the people they love. Soon there'll be hardly anyone left and we'll all just go through life like sheep, clustering together for warmth, but not actually making any real human contact for fear that if we do, it'll sound the death knell for whoever it is we dared to get close to.' Another tear slid down her cheek and she wiped at it angrily. 'I've had enough, I really have.'

'Aye, you've been through a lot, and that's a fact. But it's finished now. Hitler's dead and the war here is over. Just the mopping up to do. All these displaced persons to make better and send home and then we can put our feet up for a while and then get on with life.'

'I can't imagine what that will be like, can you? Will the world ever be the same again?'

'Hopefully it'll be better – that's what we've been fighting for, isn't it? Now you go and get some sleep before you face your ward again. Here, take these.'

Ella took the sleeping tablets Brigid offered, thanked her and stumbled back to her tent. She took them with a slug of Scotch and was soon in a fitful sleep.

A week later, the first cabaret show was performed by the inmates for everyone at Camp Two. Ella was stunned at the talent. People who not long before had been at death's door sang their native songs, danced their folk dances, told jokes, did impressions of the staff. Henryk, her patient interpreter, did an impersonation of Ella telling off the inmates that had her squirming in her seat and which everyone else found hilarious.

'He's got you to a tee,' said Brigid, drying her eyes.

'Just wait till they do you – the grumpy nurse from hell, battling her way around the hospital, muttering oaths and putting curses on everyone.'

Brigid laughed harder. 'That'd be right.'

From then on, there was some sort of entertainment most night; sometimes a film, but often a live performance. The women in the sewing room made costumes out of practically nothing, rooms not being used for the hospital were plundered for furniture to turn into stage settings and props were found or made. Everyone who wanted to be busy found something to do, and the petty arguments and bickering almost stopped.

After one of the performances Ella was talking to one of the doctors.

'I can hardly believe they're the same people we pulled out of the death camp,' he said. 'And I can't think it's just the food and the penicillin that's made the difference. I honestly thought they'd been so dehumanised in that place that they'd never engage in life properly again, but now they're singing and dancing. And laughing for God's sake. Laughing!'

Ella nodded. 'You know what I think made the difference – to the women anyway? Lipstick.'

The doctor looked at her, eyebrows raised. 'Lipstick?'

'Yes. Those women didn't feel like women until it arrived. But when they put it on, they started caring about how they looked, didn't you notice? And the other thing was when they started putting on weight again and – well, they got their womanly shape back again, breasts and all, and their periods started.'

He reddened. Ella smiled to herself. These young doctors could still be so coy about discussing the human body with a woman, even a nurse. She had to admit to herself that she'd partly said it to get this very reaction. This one was a sweetie, and a well-known blusher.

'Well, I'd better pop into the ward before hitting the hay,' he said, and rushed off, leaving Ella laughing to herself.

'What's so funny?' asked a nurse who was helping an elderly patient back to her ward.

'Men,' said Ella, and took the patient's other arm.

Ella's light mood didn't last long. It was all very well joshing with the young doctors, but the everyday realities of the camp were no laughing matter. At the end of yet another sixteen-hour day, she collapsed on her bed physically exhausted but with her mind still racing along at a hundred miles an hour. Her thoughts were all over the place: a Dutch woman dying with her lipstick in her hand. A man punching another inmate in the stomach for asking if he could sit next to him. The staff barely able to keep order, dragging themselves through the wards as if they, too, were half dead from the long hours they were doing. Inmates still stealing anything that wasn't nailed down, and some things that were; she had found two men prising a sink off the wall in the bathroom.

The image that came back to her most, however, was of the incident that afternoon with one of the female inmates, Lydia.

'She gets more food than anyone else, and better bedding. You are a Jew-hater!' she had said, pointing to a woman on the other side of the room.

Ella felt the sting of her words. She worked so hard to be fair, to swallow her negative feelings about the ingratitude of some of her charges, their wheedling need, their disdain for others, their selfishness. Just the day before she had given the very woman now accusing her of injustice, an extra blanket, which she had immediately sold to someone else. Ella felt her blood rising.

'No one here is treated any better or worse than anyone else.' Her hands curled into fists.

Lydia had looked around the ward for support, and looked

several women in the eye before saying, 'Is that really true? We've all seen it with our own eyes, haven't we?' Again, she let her eyes roam the room, stopping to exchange glances with a number of other inmates. There was a mutter of support and Lydia turned to her again. 'See?' She waved her arms, encouraging the women to speak up, and the muttering became louder.

Ella stepped right up to Lydia and said in a clear, loud voice, 'I favour no person over another. Stop this now.'

Lydia smirked and turned once again to her audience. 'See, she threatens me because I speak the truth.'

And that's when it happened. Without thinking, Ella raised her hand and slapped her hard across the face. 'You are a troublemaker and a liar. Get out of my ward and don't come back.'

Lydia laughed in her face, but her supporters quietened to a whisper; they knew they couldn't afford to be banished, they needed a bed and food, the care they were given.

With one more look around, Lydia said, 'You are all cowards. These English are worse than the Germans because they pretend to help but they want the same – to kill us all.' Then she spat at Ella and marched out.

Silence fell over the ward. Ella stood, the spittle dribbling down her face. She wanted to cry. She wanted to shout. Instead, she stood and waited, she wasn't sure what for. Slowly, the women started talking again, going about their normal activities. No one said anything to her, but Ella knew this was their way of showing her they didn't really agree with Lydia, that they were not like her. Only then had Ella left. She had gone to the treatment room where she leant against the wall and shook and swore and cried. She had been wrong to strike Lydia, but the woman had got to her. She wasn't even sure if what the woman said was true – did she hate Jews? Did she have favourites?

Certainly, there were some inmates who were easier than others, did she unconsciously treat them differently? A kinder word, more time, a softer gaze? Would it not be normal to like some people more than others? If so, it would be unprofessional to show it, but she was only human. Was that a good enough defence? She felt so conflicted, so confused. She wanted to go home and never see any of these people again, not know what became of them. She no longer cared, and that frightened her.

She got up, rifled through her drawer and found some tablets. Hoping they were sleeping pills, she took three and lay back down on her army cot. Almost immediately her mind quietened and she was asleep within minutes.

The phone rang and brought Ella back to the present. She felt a twinge in her back as she got up to answer it. Too much sitting around, she thought, and she was determined to do more exercise in future. Maybe she should cycle to work.

'Hambleford 462,' she said into the receiver.

'Ella, Donald Richards here again.'

Ella's breath caught in her throat.

'Are you there?'

She was torn between slamming the phone down and letting this Donald speak. Perhaps he knew something about her that she needed to understand.

'Yes, I'm here,' she almost whispered. 'Who are you? How do we know each other?'

'We were in Germany together.'

Ella's heart started thudding. There was something about his voice. No, not his voice, his accent. And then all the blood drained from her face as she remembered.

'Dov?'

'The very same. Although I call myself Donald here. It was suggested that us German Jews living in England changed their names to fit in better.'

'Dov,' she repeated. She hadn't taken in what he'd said.

She sank into the chair by the phone and concentrated on breathing.

'I read in the paper that you got married. I just wanted to offer my congratulations,' said Donald.

Ella stared at the clock on the wall.

'Are you still there Ella?'

'Yes, quite. Listen, can we meet?'

'Of course. Shall I take you to lunch in Hambleford?'

'No, not Hambleford,' said Ella quickly. 'Southampton.' She didn't want anyone she knew seeing her with this man. This Dov.

They made an arrangement for the following week and rang off. Ella's heart was still thumping. She had a feeling that this man held something over her, and she needed to know what.

She entered the restaurant and searched the room for Donald Richards as he called himself now.

She saw him sitting by a window, smoking a cigarette. She'd never liked him, but as soon as she'd met him, she'd known she needed him. Taking a deep breath, she made her way towards the table. He stood when he saw her, and gave a curt bow.

'Ella, you're looking well,' he said as the waiter pulled out her chair.

She nodded. 'You too.' She wasn't sure how to continue. She'd been rehearsing what she wanted to say for days, but now that she was sitting here, the words failed her. Instead, they spoke awkwardly of life since the war. He asked about her new husband, but she didn't want to talk about David, didn't want her marriage tainted by this man knowing anything about it. Instead, she asked about him.

'I have been doing this and that. One day I will go back to live in Germany, but not yet. I want to be a rich man and make a triumphant return.' He gave a hollow laugh.

Ella cocked her head to one side. 'Triumphant – why?'

'You would not understand, not being a Jew, but for me it is important to show people that we will not be put down, that they cannot make us crawl, that we will not only survive, but thrive.' He spoke in a forceful tone, his mouth hard and his eyes gleaming with hatred.

Ella looked at him with a mixture of pity and revulsion. She had been as shocked and angered by the mass murder of the Jews as anyone, but his anger seemed unhealthy. She had no response for him.

He cleared his throat and sat back. 'I am sorry. I get carried away when I think about those things. Let us order our food and talk of more pleasant topics.'

Ella had no appetite, but ordered a salad. She wanted the meeting over; she wanted to be back in her house, safe in the knowledge that David would be home soon and they'd spend the evening together talking and reading, listening to the wireless, and that her life would carry on in its tracks smoothly, carrying her to old age with the man she loved. Sitting with Dov made her doubt all that. His pent-up energy, his bitterness about the war, his anger and hatred made her uneasy. She wanted to escape.

'I need you to answer a question for me,' said Ella as the waiter approached with her salad and Dov's fish.

He raised his eyebrows but said nothing.

When the waiter had gone, Ella said, 'Early last year, I was in an accident and when I regained consciousness I had no memory. I have spent my time since then piecing together my past.'

'I am very sorry to hear that.'

'I don't want your sympathy. I need information. I believe you can tell me something that I need to know.'

She rubbed her sweaty palms along her thighs and took a deep breath.

Dov looked at her, put his knife and fork down and lit a cigarette. As he exhaled, he said, 'Are you sure you want to know?'

## 25

---

Ella had cried herself into a deep sleep by the time David got home. He sat next to her on the sofa and stroked her hair. She woke with a start, but smiled when she saw her husband.

'How did it go today?' he asked. Ella had told him she was meeting Dov and that she wasn't looking forward to it. He'd offered to accompany her, but Ella knew she had to hear whatever it was Dov had to say on her own.

'Pour me a sherry and I'll tell you.' She sat up straight, trying to work out how to tell David what she'd discovered.

'Where do I start?' she said as he handed her the drink. 'I think I knew, or at least had started to suspect what he might tell me, but it was awful actually hearing it.' She stopped. He was her husband, and she loved and trusted him, but could she tell him everything? She had to. They must have no secrets.

David sipped his drink and waited. She appreciated the fact that he didn't rush her, didn't demand to be told, and yet, perhaps on this occasion it would have helped if he had. She bit her lip and wondered how he would take the news. Would he be shocked? Outraged? Sympathetic? Would he leave her? She took a deep breath.

'I was a drug addict.' She watched his face as she spoke, waiting for the outrage, the shock.

He put his drink down slowly, turned to her and took her hand in his.

'My darling girl, after all you went through, it would have been more of a surprise if you hadn't turned to something to help.'

Ella realised he hadn't fully understood.

'Donald Richards, or Dov as I knew him, was my supplier. He was a pioneer and with us in Germany. He used to get Benzedrine for us to keep us going.'

'We took it too, in the subs. It was in our rations; everyone took it to stay awake. That doesn't make you an addict.'

Ella shook her head in frustration. 'That's as may be, but I kept going. Dov kept supplying me with drugs when I got back to England. And not just Benzedrine.'

Now David did look shocked. 'So–'

'Towards the end I was taking drugs like they were going out of fashion, apparently.'

David started to say something else, but Ella needed to keep going now that she'd finally discovered what had happened.

'Please, hear me out, David, and then you can have your say.'

He nodded and sat back, his hand resting on her thigh.

'I came to hate Belsen and everyone there. The inmates hardly seemed human anymore. I felt sorry for them when they were ill, but as they got better, so many of them became nasty, complaining and manipulative.' She sighed and shook her head. 'I lost all compassion for what they'd been through, and then I felt guilty, because they had visited the gates of hell, and I should have had more sympathy. I hated myself in the end. I couldn't wait to get back to England, but when I did I hated

339

everyone here, too, because they hadn't been through what I had, and wouldn't understand.'

She smiled sadly and looked at David.

'I think that's why I was so angry with you for your attitude to Germans. I shared it. I hated them and what they'd done to everyone, but couldn't admit it to my half-German self.'

David opened his mouth to say something, but Ella carried on, gazing into the distance again.

'So, I came down here and hid away. Dov and I had kept in contact, and he rang me up one day to see how I was. I begged him to get me some Benzedrine, which he did. Once or twice he said he even got me something called marijuana which you put in cigarettes. I must have been desperate, because I don't smoke, as you know. I got to the point where I couldn't get out of bed without Bennies. By the end, he was also supplying me with morphine and Seconal to help me sleep.' She paused, remembering those days; the loneliness, the self-loathing, the inability to make sense of her life, or life in general. Nothing held any joy for her, she couldn't see a future.

She allowed herself a glance at David, who was looking at her with such love that her heart did a little flip.

'You can say something now, if you like,' she said.

He gathered her into his arms and held her tight.

'I can't imagine the horrors you saw at Belsen, and I can't imagine the horrors of being addicted to that awful stuff. All I know is, you're here, now, with me, and I'll look after you till the end of our days.'

Ella pulled away. 'I know you will, but I don't need you to look after me, I don't *want* you to look after me. I want you to be my best friend and my husband. I want you to trust that I am fine, and that I will turn to you if I'm not, but I don't want you feeling like you have to watch me all the time. I was damaged, but I'm not anymore.'

He smiled. 'No, you're not. And I won't be following your every move, but I'm here, Ella, whenever you need me.'

'I know, and that makes me so happy.'

There was one more thing Ella needed to do. One more niggling question she needed to have answered. She made an appointment to see Dr Myers.

David drove her there the next Saturday afternoon. It was almost a year to the day since the accident, but where last year the ground had been blanketed in snow, now it was carpeted with mauve-and-yellow crocuses opening their faces to the sun.

'Do you want me to come in with you, my love?' he asked.

'No, thank you, this is something I need to do on my own. I won't be long.'

'I'll take a walk in the garden then. Good luck.'

Ella walked up the front steps. A young nurse opened the door and told her that Dr Myers was waiting for her in his office. She walked along the wood-panelled corridor, glancing at the paintings on the wall without really seeing them, and knocked on the doctor's door.

He rose to meet her as she entered, taking her hand in both of his, and led her to a chair by the desk.

'Tea?'

Ella shook her head. 'No, thank you. I won't take up much of your time. I think you know why I've come.'

Dr Myers nodded and looked at her over his half-moon spectacles.

'You've remembered everything?'

'I believe so. I have faced some horrors, I can tell you. I was at the liberation of Belsen, did you know?'

The doctor raised his eyebrows.

'Yes,' Ella continued, 'it was awful and I still can't really talk about it, but I have made some sort of peace with myself over what happened there. I can't forgive Herr Hitler and the Nazis for what they did, of course, and I certainly will never forget, but I can live with my memories.'

'I'm very pleased to hear it.'

'Yes. I am also recently married.'

'Congratulations. He's a lucky man.'

'I believe I'm the lucky one.' She smoothed her skirt and folded her hands in her lap. She had one last thing to face; the letter. She took a deep breath.

'Dr Myers, you found a letter in my handbag that identified me. You and Matron then said you'd lost it. I suspect you did that for my sake, for which I thank you, but I'd like it back now.'

Dr Myers looked at her, eyes narrowed. 'You're sure?'

'Absolutely.'

He got up slowly, went to his filing cabinet and opened a drawer. He took out her case notes, and retrieved the envelope and gave it to her. It had been opened with a letter knife.

Ella took it. It was addressed to Andrew. Her hands trembled as she took it. She didn't want to read it here. She needed to be alone.

'Can I ask why you opened it? My driving licence was in the handbag as well, after all.'

Dr Myers cleared his throat, straightened his tie and sat down again.

'We needed to be sure that you were, indeed, the author of the letter and what relationship you were to the recipient.'

'Please don't lie to me, Doctor. You insult my intelligence, and yours.'

He looked abashed. 'All right, Mrs Elkington–'

'Ashton,' she said, and glanced at her wedding ring.

'Of course, so sorry, Mrs Ashton. I read your name and

address and thought it strange that I'd lived here since well before the war and never met you, or even heard of you. And then the accident itself made me wonder. You were found in a ditch on a straight stretch of a quiet road in the middle of nowhere on a cold, bright day with a strong smell of alcohol on your breath. In short, I wasn't at all convinced it was an accident.' He spoke in an even tone and looked her in the eye. 'And then your blood tests revealed high levels of certain drugs. We kept you sedated until we were sure you were over the worst of the withdrawal symptoms and your otherwise strong constitution did the rest.'

Ella nodded. 'That was clever of you, and once again, I am indebted to you for keeping the evidence from me. You must have been relieved when I woke up with no memory of the accident, or anything else.'

The doctor smiled. 'I must admit I was, but I always knew that you would remember eventually and that we would have this conversation. How do you feel now?'

Ella grinned. 'Not at all like I did when I wrote the letter, I can assure you.'

She stood, put it in her handbag and snapped it shut.

'Thank you, Dr Myers, for everything,' she said, and shook his hand.

She left his office, but didn't immediately leave the building. Instead, she slipped into an empty room and closed the door behind her. Sitting on the edge of the bed, she closed her eyes and allowed her mind to explore the days immediately before the crash. Andrew and Sophie's visits with the children had been her lifeline, even though she found it hard to act normally, and was frightened that they might discover her drug habit. But the idea of not seeing them was worse. The children reminded her that there was good in the world, that there was innocence and love. But after a while even they weren't enough. Forcing herself to put the card offering piano lessons in the newsagent's window had been her last-ditch attempt to anchor herself to the world. But as soon as she'd done it, she was terrified that someone might respond, that another person might get a glimpse of her life. For two days she'd sat, gnawing at her fingernails, unable to sleep without doubling the dose of barbiturates Dov had supplied her with. On the third day, she'd ran to the shop to take the note down.

A few days later, she'd written the letter. She was so calm. If anyone had actually seen her, they would have thought she was composing a letter to a friend. Now Ella knew that her outer calm belied inner turmoil. She had been desperate. Nothing in her life made sense anymore, nothing gave her joy and she couldn't see it changing. The numbing sleep of Seconal still didn't take away the nightmares of Klaus as he ran, screaming, away from her to his death, nor the images of the dead and dying at Belsen. She had written the letter as she downed several tumblers of whisky and a handful of tablets.

She took the letter out and opened it with trembling fingers. She remembered, more or less, what it said, but she had to read it before she could shut the door on that episode of her life. She had so much to look forward to now; the time for looking back was over.

*Darling Andrew,* she read.

*I am so sorry that you will have to deal with the aftermath of my decision, but you are the only one who can, and I know that with Sophie by your side, you will find the strength.*

*The fact is, I can't go on. The thought of living another day makes me feel sad, angry and exhausted. You mustn't blame yourself in any way. You have always been the best of brothers, the best of friends.*

*So, goodbye, my darling. Try to remember me with fondness.*

*Your Ella x*

Her heart was pounding against her ribs. She could hardly believe she'd felt so utterly wretched, but here was the proof. She remembered taking a handful of tablets, but then deciding that she didn't deserve the easy slipping away they would afford. She had always loved the thrill of speed so that was how she would die. She remembered getting into her car and pressing the accelerator to the floor, aiming for the tree.

Wiping a tear away, she felt sorry for the person she'd been back then, and grateful that she no longer felt that way. She stood, took a deep breath, tore the letter up and threw it in the bin.

In remembering the pieces of her life, she had found a way to live with all that had happened.

As she descended the front steps, David appeared from the rose garden. When Ella called his name, he turned and smiled.

THE END

# ACKNOWLEDGEMENTS

There may be one writer, but there is a team of people behind them, offering encouragement, tea, wine, a shoulder to cry on when nothing's going right and a kick up the behind when procrastination sets in. So...

A huge thank you to the members of my writers group who have taken critiquing to new heights and made the book better for it.

To my own beta readers who offered insights, and to Michael Cybulski and Sue Anderson at New Authors Collective and their team of eager readers who picked up on inconsistencies and offered suggestions – big thanks.

The team at Bloodhound Books is amazing. I couldn't hope for a more supportive and talented team to be working with.

To all the people who pick up this book and read it – thank you. I hope you enjoy it as much as I enjoyed writing it.

Lastly, to my friends who are always there when I need them. You're amazing.

And love and thanks, as always, to Neil, Holly, Connor and Tashi who keep me sane.

# A NOTE FROM THE PUBLISHER

**Thank you for reading this book.** If you enjoyed it please do consider leaving a review on Amazon to help others find it too.

**We hate typos.** All of our books have been rigorously edited and proofread, but sometimes mistakes do slip through. If you have spotted a typo, please do let us know and we can get it amended within hours.

info@bloodhoundbooks.com

Printed in Great Britain
by Amazon

38835727R00202